Grace by GREYHOUND

Elle Riorden

This book is fiction and should not be construed as an accurate historical account. All references to real persons, in name or deed, are unintentional.

Acknowledgements:
Cover Design: Original screen print by Linda Szabo, Soldier Woman Art Gallery
Song Lyrics: Superchick, Flogging Molly, Kelly Hunt

Grace
by
GREYHOUND

The Rainmaker

She never slows down.
She doesn't know why but she knows
that when she's all alone,
feels like its all coming down

She won't turn around
The shadows are long and she fears
if she cries that first tear,
the tears will not stop raining down

Only those who know the rain know Grace.
To know Grace is to stand naked against an insurmountable storm as from within the stillness of a single drop of rain. I know. I was there.

We stood together in the quiet dawn. A soft early morning rain pattered on the edge of the wide cedar deck overlooking her garden. I gazed across the lawn below at the vestiges of what once were well trimmed evergreens, lush peonies, vibrant tiger lilies and friendly carnations, bordered by a legion of loyal Hostas keeping her guard. I stood quietly for a very long time, safeguarding an image of the last vivid red blooms of geraniums nestled contentedly under the crimson blossoms of roses climbing on the trellis. Then I closed my eyes to lock it all away, secure in the recesses of my heart. A hint of lavender unleashed a flood of memories to tumble and cascade through my brain.

"Happy Birthday, Gram."

"Hmmm," she answered the way she always did when she was working through a thought. "What's my number?"

"Your number is eight-seven."

"What's yours?"

"My number is twenty-seven. I am the same age you were when my mother was born."

"Ahhh," she marveled. A gust of wind blew a strand of hair across my face. Her gentle fingers brushed it back. Darker clouds rolled in from the West. Autumn rain, crisp and refreshing always brought the promise of change.

"Are you ready, Gram?"

She answered the way she always did. "Where's your car? Let's go! No one will even know we're gone."

I chuckled. She could make me smile even when I was sad. The clouds tumbled low, mounding and curling one above the other in layers as we turned and walked away for the last time. I drove through residential areas, through downtown metro, through the park leading to the falls. The road divided to follow the river. I parked at a guardrail and walked a narrow path to the edge of a familiar steep embankment overlooking murky rapids below. I had come to these falls many times. Perhaps I hoped the raging current below would somehow wash away the confusion and make sense of the questions churning in my head. I searched the depths of the poppling, tumbling whitewater. I closed my eyes and willed the sound of the rushing force to flood my cavernous spirit with answers. There were only images bobbing up and down in the foam, disappearing, then bubbling up again.

"Let's go," she urged.

As I turned away from the rocky bank, the echo of the waterfall became the sound of a distant memory.

I drove slowly through the empty morning streets. Then I turned into a quiet back lot. My aunt Maire said that she never cried. I knew that feeling. There was a hurt so deep I couldn't reach it. I sighed and lifted a single black travel bag from the trunk of my car and dropped it to the gravel, tugging it behind me as I walked across the drive, it's two small glider wheels clumsily bumping and jiggling as if dragged its feet on purpose. My grandmother was not reluctant.

"Where are we going?" she pressed.

The bus parked beside the door belched out a pungent odor of diesel. I passed through a wood door into a square room. A long Cosco table bore a sign to serve as notice that travelers should MOVE THIS WAY SINGLE FILE. The clerk, a woman younger than me sat at the end of the table typing, her long nails efficiently popping up and down against the keys. The printer on her left spit out a long stream of tickets. Without looking up, she counted the cash I handed her. With her other hand she ripped off a series of tickets, inspecting each one carefully. "Well, it's not O'Hare," I whispered, looking around.

"Here is your itinerary. Chicago, Rapid City, Billings, Coeur d'Alene, Spokane to..." she paused and fanned out the folds the length of the paper. She looked up, finally. The jeweled stud in her nose and the ring in her lip glinted in the fluorescent light. I wasn't much older than she, but I felt ancient. "That's three days." I stared blankly at the band tattooed around her finger.

"Thank you." I scanned the room. The walls were lined with a complexity of faces. I wondered what dreams, what secrets each heart here locked away in its own vault. I realized I was staring. I quickly removed my jacket and tucked it into my bag. I pulled a gray Hoodie from the bag and slipped my arms through the sleeves and clipped my hair back. I looked around. 'Better,' I thought.

I was exactly where I belonged. This was a journey I needed to make in solitude. So I shuffled in a nondescript, motley procession to board a waiting bus. The October wind blew stronger. The patter of rain turned to a steady shower. Sadness engulfed me.

"You can do it," my grandmother reassured me. "Just put one foot in front of the other. Take one step at a time." A hollow looking woman with salt and pepper hair brushed past me. I watched her scurry up the steps and disappear into the bus, the tail of her blue flannel shirt flapping behind her. "Come on," my grandmother urged. "Take the step." The toe of my shoe rose to the first step, then the second, then the third. I faced two rows of seats, many of which were already occupied by expressionless travelers. Halfway down the aisle a vacant seat offered solitude and ample legroom. I slid in next to the window, pulled the hood of my sweatshirt close around my face, popped a tiny white ipod speaker into my ear and closed my eyes. The bus lurched forward, careened around a corner and settled into a rhythmic sway. Voices around me melded into quiet chatter, interrupted occasionally by the high pitch of a baby's cry or resonance of throaty laughter. I leaned my head to rest against the rim of the large metal window frame. The clouds turned charcoal gray. I pulled a fleece wrap out of the bag tucked under my legs, wrapping it around my shoulders and up under my chin next to my cheek. Huddled safe behind my own private waterfall, alone against my own inner storm, I stared, not seeing, mesmerized by the steady pounding of rain streaming seamlessly down the windowpane. My grandmother nestled close to me. "Are you going to rest now?"

A man across the aisle watched silently. His brown weathered face defied age. His wide-brimmed Stetson was the color of buffalo fur. A silver lizard secured a narrow leather belt at the base of the crown. Tucked into the belt was a single eagle feather. The feather draped across the brim just over his left shoulder. A turquoise ring on his finger gleamed under the amber dome light of the bus. The braided leather chain around his neck secured an intricately beaded medicine wheel of brightly colored porcupine quills.

"We live in conflicting times," he murmured without looking directly at me. I nodded, shifting my gaze. He fixed his focus somewhere down the dim aisle toward the front of the bus. "The events of this year are testimony to that. Banks and major industries are in financial crisis; thousands of homeowners are laid off from their jobs and foreclosed from their homes and the first black presidential nominee has rallied the nation by offering radical changes to the economic landscape." I tried to shut him out. I had my own thoughts. This past year every preconceived notion of who I was, where I was going and how capable I might be to face the storms looming on the horizon was challenged. "You are troubled," he said quietly in a deep steady voice. I turned to meet his gaze. "I am Yoki Two Eagle." He extended his hand. "It is said that the way we respond to crisis and change in many ways determines how we will live the rest of our lives." I stared at him. His gaze left mine to search beyond me. "Our people look upon storms as part of the natural flow of life. It is at these times that we grow stronger and learn to see more clearly with newfound wisdom. We see the best and the worst in our own nature." He paused and looked back to me, no doubt to ascertain if I was open to the conversation. He decided my silence was invitation to continue. "Finding a balance comes from walking the strong path of mindfulness, keeping our footing by being interconnected with all things. In times of conflict it is good to test all things and to hold fast only to that which is good."

"Finding that balance is the purpose of my journey," I answered, slowly. "Stop," I told myself. "Don't let this stranger pull you in."

"It is the purpose of everyone's journey," he said.

I turned back to the window. "Is that what you've been trying to teach me, Gram?"

"Of course," she answered.

"Of course," I whispered. Her words filled the air around me. "Of course."

As I watched the rain flow down my window, thoughts ran through my head like the currents in the river. I was raised in the shelter of my grandmother's love. She was my rock. She taught me the three things she knew best: faith, hope and patient love. Whenever I felt sad, lost or confused, like now, she would tell me a story. Her stories took me to that place in her heart where her spirit lived. I closed my eyes to the rocking of the bus as those stories replayed in my mind.

Each October, under a bright harvest moon, my grandmother celebrated her birthday by offering a prayer of thanksgiving for her many blessings, for the gift of strength and for the peace of enduring faith. Then she would ask for more. She prayed that God's angels would always be near, keeping her from evil and her children from harm. Then, with the passing of October came winter. Winters are long on the prairie. Blinding blizzards and subzero temperatures bring death when the river turns to ice. My grandmother's spirit saw her through many winters. Her Danish ancestors endowed her with a gentle spirit, easy smile and the determination to keep going, despite all odds. She was bright and friendly. She lived her faith and walked in spirituality and love.

My grandfather Jack was Irish. His grandparents journeyed to the prairie with a promise from the U.S. Government of a good life on fertile soil. Natural grassland was turned up into huge clods as row after row of prairie was plowed into long furrows. The prairie farmers did not know then that every turn of the plow was creating a disaster which had not been seen before. They thought the rain would follow the plow. They were wrong.

My grandmother's father, Ben, made a living for his family from the gifts of the land and the river. He carried blocks of ice cut from the frozen river to cool the bottles of milk he delivered from horse-drawn buggy door to door. Her mother, Ida, washed and scalded each empty bottle to refill and chill. She was raised and nurtured in a traditional family. My grandmother's grandmother, Jennie Sondergaard, lived with them in the big farmhouse. She crafted exquisite wardrobes with delicate ruffles and intricate stitches for each change of season and whim of fashion. There were dainty crinoline collars and warm woolen lapels. There were gored skirts and silk blouses with flowing ties. My grandmother spent every day with her grandmother. The foundation of who she became was formed in that bond. She was carefree. She never knew hunger. She never knew loneliness. She never knew ridicule. She never knew fear. The prairie was her playground.

My grandmother shared a bed with her grandmother. They snuggled together throughout the frigid winter nights. Every night, her grandmother, Jennie, removed her false teeth and put them into a glass of water. One night, as Jennie climbed into bed, she placed the glass of water with the soaking teeth on the windowsill. The next morning, she rose with the dawn, as usual. Grace peeked out from under the warm quilt and watched in wonder as her grandmother scraped her fingernail across the frost-covered window. Then Jennie reached for the glass. The teeth had frozen solid. My grandmother stared at her grandmother as her grandmother stared at the teeth. The two of them laughed so hard it brought tears to their eyes. I loved that story because it embodied all the love and trust that my grandmother taught me.

The faint whirring sound of the bus engine rocked my brain in rhythm to the spattering of rain on the window. Soon I was lulled into the first sleep I would have in over a week. The ache in my heart loosened its grip as the lumbering, lurching bus carried us farther and farther away from the spiritual gutter of Blackwater Manor and the degraded existence my grandmother had been forced to endure.

I slept, but not soundly. My body shifted and moved in an attempt to find some comfort despite the cramped leg space and unforgiving molded seat backs. I drifted in and out of dreams. Somewhere in the space between consciousness and unconsciousness, a faint vision danced. What was that music? Was it a jig? Where was it coming from? I peered back through the space between the seats. The hollow looking woman who boarded ahead of me met my gaze with a stare. I shivered and looked away. Far in the back three energetic toddlers tumbled playfully. Their young mother controlled them as best she could without waking the infant in her arms. A young man sprawled across from her, his leg barricading the aisle, music blasting from his earphones. Directly behind them the narrow metal door of the bathroom unlatched, gaped open, then swung back and latched again. One of the toddlers, dressed in bright pink leggings and a pink sweater over a pink patterned dress, ducked under the young man's leg. He scowled. The little girl slowly made her way forward, grabbing onto armrests for balance. She looked back at her mother and then up at me. I pulled a chocolate chip snack bar out of my bag. Her eyes twinkled and she paused for a moment. She took the bar and ran back to her seat. The mother nodded and smiled. The other two toddlers scrambled from the seat, ignoring her grasp. I pulled out two more treats. I held one up for her. She shook her head and smiled. They scurried back and settled in. The bus pulled into a station. The driver barked out orders for those departing. Others waited at the curb to board. The young mother nudged the toe of the young man's sneaker. He shuffled to his feet and grabbed a couple of bags from the overhead compartment. She rose and herded her little family up the aisle, past my seat to the exit. The little girl paused next to me. "Move along, Grace," the mother scolded.

"Grace," I whispered.

"That's my name!" my grandmother exclaimed. I stared at the child, eyes shining, clinging to the hem of her mother's jacket. As they waited below on the sidewalk for the driver to unload a stroller and another large bag, the little girl stared up at us with a smile. They turned and disappeared down the street as the driver swung the door closed and took the wheel. Grace, the grandmother, was ending her journey. Grace, the child, was beginning hers.

"Remember this time and cherish it," Grace reflected. "Don't take your eyes off those babies. If you do, when you look back, you won't recognize them. I know they won't recognize you. Listen to your mother and say your prayers. OK?" My heart ached. My grandmother's childhood was a happy time but it was over much too soon. My childhood was not a happy time but it was blessed. God gave me Grace.

Yoki interrupted my thoughts. "Life is hard," he said. "It takes our time, our effort, our good intentions, our noble ideas, our dreams and our sacrifices and then it demands more. We need the rainmaker."

I turned to him. "The rainmaker?"

"The spirit of the rainmaker brings a change for renewal," he answered. He studied me, as if he were looking for something beyond what he saw. I nodded blankly and turned back to reflections of Grace.

The rains stopped in Grace's life the summer of her eleventh year. The plowed furrows turned to dust. Blowing dirt created black blizzards. There was no summer rain. There was no crop. There was no money. There was no winter snow. There was no sun. There was only dirt. Grace, not yet seventeen, found work as a governess in town in exchange for a place to stay while she finished high school. She worked hard and the young couple that hired her enjoyed having her there. She was an energetic, joyful young woman. She tended babies, cleaned house and cooked meals.

She first saw Jack in the butcher shop. She occasionally noticed him walking in the street, dressed in crisply pressed pants and tight black sweater, his hat cocked always just a bit forward over one eye. Grace's sister, Una, noticed him as well. She told Grace she expected him to be at the Saturday night dance. Grace dressed in her best sweater and pencil-thin skirt. She curled her hair with a hot iron, rouged her cheeks and glossed her lips. The babies were fed and put to bed and she walked alone to the dance, her step brisk and light, wondering what wonderful things might happen. The man she had set her mind to meet stood across the bright gas-lit room at the edge of the dance floor surrounded by a circle of smiling friends. Determined, she walked directly to him and said, "Hello, I'm Grace."

He smiled and reached for her hand. "I'm Thomas. Everyone calls me Jack."

"Why Jack?" She blushed.

He winked. "Thomas John. Jack is easier." The others laughed and the chatter continued. Una smiled coyly, but did not introduce her sister into the group. Chagrined, Grace left.

"You should have asked her to dance," Jack's brothers chided. "She's the one we told you about." He shrugged, dismissing them. He stayed with the group, swinging to the music late into the night.

Like Grace, Una worked for a family in exchange for a room in town. Una was younger than Grace and more outgoing. She laughed easily at Jack's jokes and applauded his antics as he walked her home. The next morning the Annan farmhouse bustled with chatter as it did every Sunday after Mass. Una swept dramatically through the kitchen. "Guess who danced with me last night? Thomas John Riorden!" She twirled past the stove, reaching for a coffee cup. "He's very sweet." She tossed back thick curls from her face. Her mother's frown followed her. "What?" Una countered, humming and spinning around the kitchen, her eyes wide with feigned innocence. Grace, flushed with anger, threw down a towel, turned on her heel and stalked from the kitchen, slamming the door behind her. Ida Annan stood facing Una, fists on hips in reproach. Una brushed her cheek with a kiss. "I know, Mother. I know." Una loved her fun but she loved her sister more. She knew what she must do. It was not likely that Grace would entertain an apology, so instead, on the train-ride back to town, Una rehearsed what she would say to Jack. 'I won't be the one you ask out. I'm leaving for college and I won't come back. This small town is boring me to distraction. He would protest. 'You have a home here.' She would say. 'You have a job here. Ask my sister Grace.' 'Yes,' Una thought. 'I'll see him this Wednesday at the meat market and I'll tell him.'

Next Sunday, throughout the long Mass, Grace and Una sat solemnly, shoulder to shoulder in the pew, next to their parents and younger brothers and sisters. Grace stared stoically straight ahead when Jack walked past in the communion processional. After Mass on the drive out of town and down the long country lane to the farm, she was tightlipped and pensive. Back in the farmhouse kitchen, the sweet aroma of pies, pungent spices of ham baking and sausage frying and the aroma of fresh brewed coffee stimulated conversation, but Grace did not join in. Then the phone rang. Grace's father answered.

"Who is it?" Grace's mother asked impatiently.

"Jack Riorden."

"Well, who does he want?" Ida asked.

Grace's father laid the receiver on the table and crossed the room to take his chair at the head of the table. He laid his napkin on his knee and looked up. "You, Grace. He wants you."

Ben Annan disliked Jack. He never said why. Grace's mother liked him because Grace liked him. The dog, an imposing Great Dane, seemed to agree with Ben. Whenever Jack came to the farm, which was every Sunday, the dog growled at the car door. Jack harbored many fears, but what he feared most was embarrassment. How could he get past the dog, up the long, pristine sidewalk to the front door of the farmhouse without being chased and possibly bitten? This Goddamn dog would not humiliate him. He stood at the meat counter of the butcher shop, pondering the problem. He kneaded the ground meat and molded it into a round mound. A shiny black Model A rolled past. His eyes followed it down the street, scanning the horizon as hatred for the dog welled inside him. His fist slammed against the counter. Meat splattered everywhere. He looked down at the mess. His eyes widened. "That's it!" he exclaimed under his breath.

That evening Jack met the dog's loud barking and challenging growl with a pound of fresh-ground beef. He flashed a cagey smile as Grace exclaimed, "Oh, you are clever. I'm surprised you didn't think of that before!" Grace's dad found the dog dead the next morning. Despite Ben's objections, Grace married Jack in the fall.

"Life takes all our effort, our sweat, our noble ideas, our dreams and sacrifices and then it gives us obstacles and disappointments," Yoki interjected. "Has life been that for you?"

"I wasn't thinking so much of my life," I replied. I was thinking of my grandmother's."

"Oh." He leaned in attentively. "Is your grandmother still with you?"

"Yes, she is," I answered, repositioning my earphones. I closed my eyes and retreated.

Jack's father, Fergus Riorden, took a risk and borrowed $5,000 to put in one more crop. The crop failed and the bank foreclosed. Jack's mother, Nora, moved her children to the well-heeled Cathedral district to stay with family and attend a private Catholic high school. Jack's brother, Sean, dropped out of school to help his father redeem the farm. Sean worked alongside his father from early morning light to sunset. At sunset Fergus climbed onto the buckboard, reigns flying, to disappear into the night.

Grace's parents, Ben and Ida Annan, lived conservatively, but well. Their home had gas lamps, running water and an indoor toilet. Grace expected life to be good. Jack expected life to be easy.

The Second World War brought food rationing. Grace took care to put each red and blue token of change from every purchase into the little pockets of her ration book, snapping it tightly closed. One morning she asked for a bag of sugar for baking. The store clerk smiled and said, "I wouldn't think you would need any more sugar in your house. You two sweethearts seem to have more than enough!" Grace blushed and hurried home, giggling. This was the life she dreamed. She soon learned, however, that life can be a series of tough times and tough issues that sabotage our dreams.

Jack was often late to work. The butcher shop doors did not open some days until midmorning. Customers complained. Grace, determined to preserve the values she had been taught, the image she was born to portray, had Jack's breakfast waiting, his shirt pressed and his pants creased when he woke. Then she strolled with him through town to the butcher shop, pushing Crystal Ann in the pram as Mary Caye toddled beside her.

Acer was born. With the family of five crowded into the small apartment, the children were always underfoot. Jack rose later each day. Ida noticed that the house was becoming unkempt. Grace looked exhausted. When Ida voiced her concern, Grace pointed out to her mother that there was always steak on the table.

Sean had a plan. A farm stood vacant next to the home place. Sean lent Jack the money. A farm would be a good place to raise children. They could get a dog. Jack moved his family into the farmhouse. There were no lights, no running water. The toilet was an outhouse. Grace hid her disappointment. Jack and Sean put in the first crop. Grace hauled water and lit lamps. She carried buckets of corncobs to burn for heat and cooking, making the small, old empty house as warm and inviting as her imagination and meager furnishings would allow. She spent spring days outside with the children playing under her feet while she nurtured a wild rose bush into bloom. She planted her mother's tiger lilies. Jack was energetic and obedient when Sean worked beside him. When Sean drove away, however, Jack erupted in tirades of discontent. The work was too hard. This crop would never feed them. He should have never left town. He could never farm on his own. He had no help. He had only one son.

Sean unloaded dairy cows. Grace was thrilled. She remembered long afternoons riding with her father in his milk truck, chatting with friendly neighbors. Jack, however, lapsed back into his pattern of sleeping later and later into the day. Grace knew that dairy cows needed to be milked. She replaced her disappointment with determination. Early one morning, she gathered her young brood of three and admonishing them to not make a sound as they scurried out to the milk shed. Settling the milk bucket between her knees, she began a rhythmic motion with her fingers. The milk streamed into the bucket. The heat from the cow's belly was warm as she leaned her head against its flank. Mary Caye, Crystal Ann and Acer played in the straw beneath her stool. As she finished milking each cow, she dumped the bucket of milk into the large stainless steel can standing nearby. When all the cows were milked, she pushed open the large wooden gate and turned them back to the pasture. Then she turned back to the milk can. She knew she would have to empty it into the cooled tank in the next room. She was seven months pregnant. With a concerted burst of energy, she rolled the can from the milking room to the storage room, over the heavy wooden sill, crashing it onto the stone floor. She caught and steadied it. "Help me, God!" she prayed. The children scrambled to her side, their little hands pressed firmly on the bottom of the can. "No. Stand back now," she warned them. "Shoo." She gave a mighty heave. The can lifted. She felt something inside her tearing away and groaned. "Oh, my God!" she exclaimed, but she could not let go of the can. If she did, it would land on one of the children. "Oh, my God. She whispered again."

Suddenly two strong arms encircled her. Brawny hands grasped the handles of the can and a stern voice said, "Let go." Sean held the can effortlessly while she ducked under his arm and scuttled the children out of the way. He dumped the can of milk into the cooler and closed the lid. His jaw clenched. His eyes flamed, but his voice was soft. He turned to the three children. "Go get your father."

"Jack's not here," Grace began. She thought she might say he had gone to the field early to inspect the crop.

Sean stopped her with one hand to her shoulder. He turned again to the children. "Get your father out of bed!" Grace knew that Jack would not forgive her for allowing him to get caught sleeping, but she could not argue with Sean.

The children raced to the house and timidly shook Jack awake, then skittered out of his way as he jumped from the bed. He dressed quickly and was seated at the kitchen table when Sean walked into the kitchen. Sean shot him a dark, withering stare, which softened when he saw Grace, steadying herself against the kitchen sink. Humiliated, Jack shuffled a stack of papers. She would pay for this.

Another month passed. Sean worked at Jack's side as Grace cooked and carried meals to the men in the field while harvesting her own crop of green beans, tomatoes, potatoes and beets. Flies, drawn by the sweet smell of corn cut from the cob, swarmed. Grace, now eight months pregnant, escaped from the closeness of the kitchen to stand in the breeze and hang wash on the line. A twinge of pain gripped her. The pain was different this time. It seemed to want to split her in half. Waves of pain overtook her. She inched her way along the clothesline to the side of the house, to the kitchen door. Her skull throbbed. She stumbled into the kitchen and collapsed. She couldn't bother Jack now. She would wait. It would pass. She braced herself. The pain shot through her like lightening. She groaned, despite her will to be silent.

Mary Caye gaped from the doorway. Her mother slumped across the table, the phone cord dangling from her hand. A pool of dark liquid formed on the floor. Mary Caye ran screaming into the yard, hands waving wildly. "Daddy! Daddy! Mama's dying! Come quick! Mama's dying!"

Sean burst through the door first and took charge immediately. Jack stood back, aghast at the sight. Sean scooped her up and cradled her into the waiting car. He slid behind the wheel and motioned for Jack. "Get in!" Less than an hour later a child was born. The baby was tiny and frail. Grace did not have the strength to hold her.

A round-faced nun lifted the pink bundle. "What is the baby's name?"

Grace breathed a fervent prayer. "Hail, Mary, full of Grace. The Lord is with thee." Then she drifted away.

"Maire," the nun exclaimed.

"Another girl," Jack muttered.

Yoki's burly brown hand reached across the aisle of the bus and patted my arm. "Strength can come from facing the storms of life, from knowing loss, from feeling sadness or heartache, from falling into the depths of grief." I nodded in recognition. He continued. "Storms are a fact of life on the prairie. Sometimes they come up suddenly and surprise us. Other times we can see them forming. Then they hit us and we ride out the force and veracity as best we can."

"Yes," I heard Grace say. "We know something about storms."

Until this past year, I didn't really know my Aunt Maire. Until this past year, my Aunt Maire didn't really know Grace. The storm of the past year had torn each of us from our foundations and tossed us together, dropping us in a place we could not have imagined.

Years passed and the family grew. Quin was born. Grace faced each day with its own unique set of experiences and circumstances. Every new dawn gave her an opportunity to grow and add to the depth of character and increase her abilities. Every experience and every child was a gift. She saw value in every person who entered her life, whether they brought friendship or adversity. There were times, however, when she longed for the life she knew before Jack, a life of gas lamps and lace tablecloths, crinoline collars and dainty pumps.

Sean maintained constant vigil, circling the farm, appearing without warning. The children learned instinctively to fly to the bedroom at the sight of Sean's car turning into the drive. Grace no longer made excuses. No need. Sean knew. He sipped freshly brewed coffee and nibbled on a warm cinnamon roll or cookie just out of the oven as the children stood at his chair, touching his arm and listening to his stories. He called each child by name as he pulled dollar bills from his khaki western-style pants. Then he stood by the window to wait for Jack.

Faith was born. Dierdre arrived the year after that. Aiden followed. Sean bought land and a farmhouse. Sean and Jack dug a foundation and moved the farmhouse next to the family's home. One of the houses pulsed with life. The other stood quiet in dark repose. Sean and Jack tore down the adjacent walls. The two buildings gaped nakedly; prairie sky stood above, prairie wind whipped between. Tarps hung for walls.

Ralph was born. Crystal Ann and Acer mixed, scooped and poured concrete into the foundation from a single wheelbarrow and mixer. Maire and Quin hauled lumber and steadied boards while Jack pounded and sawed. Grace looked on in pride, snapping pictures from Jack's Brownie camera. Her husband was now a carpenter. Ward, Bric and Seth were born three years in succession. Each year found the house in a new stage of disarray. The children ascended to the second story on wooden ladders and slept under the stars.

Jack brought home a load of baby chicks. "There is no chicken coop," Grace argued. Jack caged the baby chicks in one of the open rooms. He rigged warming lights and the children hauled hay to bed them. Aiden called them 'peepers'. Liam and Riley were born.

On Saturday night Grace and Jack drove the big Chevy into town to the U & I Family Grocery. Grace handed a grocery list to Maire. Grace never left the passenger seat of the big Chevy. Jack didn't allow it. Grace knew Maire would get exactly what was written on her list and no more.

Maire pushed the cart through the aisles while Acer and Quin found each item on the list and dropped it in. Maire held an envelope of coupons while she checked each item off the list, making sure the exact right thing was there. Quin pushed the cart into line at the checkout counter. She knew the woman standing behind the counter in the green apron would ring each item, check each coupon and ring up the total. She knew the woman would open a large spiral notebook marked *CREDIT ACCOUNTS* by the register and write the amount. Then the man in the green apron would carry the bags to the car. Except this time was different. The woman behind the counter reached for the book, but she didn't write the total on the page. She planted her hands squarely on the counter and looked down into Maire's face. Her words stung like a slap. "Go out and tell your Dad there's no more credit."

Maire stared at Acer and Quin, thinking, 'OK, which one of us is going to tell him?' She turned to the clerk and said, "Thank you." She knew her mother would want her to be gracious. They walked to the Chevy in silence. Maire spoke the words through her mother's car door window. Grace's eyes grew dark. She stared straight ahead as tears welled up. She blinked hard. For the first time in her life, she felt shame. Maire, Quin and Acer piled into the back seat and Jack backed the car away from the curb. No one spoke on the long drive home. Jack parked the car in front of the house, got out and slammed the door. Grace walked into the house. Maire and Quin followed.

"Where's Dad going?" Maire asked.

"To the barn," was all her mother said. "Don't go near the barn."

"Where's Acer?"

"He went with Dad. Don't go near the barn."

Mary Caye took a potato casserole from the oven. Crystal Ann sliced bread. Maire set plates on the table. Quin opened a book. Faith and the younger children busied themselves with toys and games. Grace reached for the wall phone and dialed a number. She had something to trade. After the phone call, she walked straight out the door. With the sun setting behind her, she waved her arm and circled the hens. Maire ran ahead of her, eager to help. One by one, Grace caught the chickens, swiftly rung their necks, cut off their heads, scalded, singed, plucked and dunked them into a vat of ice water. Then she took a large knife and scraped it down across a sharpening stone. With swift, efficient strokes, she filleted each chicken and carefully positioned the pieces in a plastic bag, securing each bag with a twist-tie. She nestled the bags onto a large cookie sheet, which she placed in the refrigerator to cool. She worked methodically, skillfully, and tirelessly into the night.

The next morning Maire matched her step for step as she walked determinedly to the garden. "Pull up the carrots." Grace pointed to the long rows. "I'll get the tomatoes. I don't want them bruised." Maire tried to keep up, not lingering to play in the dirt, sensing the importance of the mission. She carried bundles of carrots to the house, dunked them into tubs of ice water and lightly scrubbed them clean. Grace placed them in clusters of six into plastic bags and tied the twist-tie, laying the bags, one on top of the other into a roasting pan. Grace washed each tomato, patted it dry and nested it into a large round mixing bowl lined with a towel. Grace decided she could spare a couple dozen eggs. She washed and dried each one and placed it gently in a mixing bowl nestled into a layer of towels. She loaded the big Chevy with the produce and Jack again drove them into town.

Grace cradled the Pyrex mixing bowl of bright red tomatoes as she walked staunchly and purposefully through the doors. Jack waited stone-faced behind the steering wheel for Grace to reappear, load her arms again with produce and march back into the store. Then grocery clerks, aprons flapping, followed her back to the car, loaded bags of groceries into the back of the Chevy and waved as Jack drove away. Grace had her groceries. Grace had her victory. Grace would not be shamed again. She had a standing order for dozens of chickens, dozens of eggs and all the tomatoes she could spare. The sale of chickens, eggs and vegetables would buy food for the table and materials for the house. Grace prayed for strength and she found it within the power of her own spirit.

Lyssa was born. Jack joined the two houses with an atrium. Grace finally had a proper and secure home. Grace used every resource open to her to furnish it. She collected green stamps and redeemed Betty Crocker box tops with a vengeance, trading them for appliances, dishes, rugs and household goods. A year later Grace gave birth to Ursula. Grace made up her mind that her youngest children would have the life she knew her children should have.

I remember only fleeting images of my mother, Faith. I know that Grace and Faith were more than mother and daughter. They were kindred spirits. Grace once told me, "Faith possessed hopes and fears and hidden wishes. She braved the unknown to discover what was beyond the threshold of fear. When you do cross that threshold and fly free of fear, you will see, as I did, as your mother did, that life is not what you imagined it to be." I always wondered at those words, coming from a woman who obeyed her husband's every command, gave her life over to her children and never left her prairie home.

One bright spring morning Faith rose early to help Grace iron cassocks and press white cotton shirts for Mass. Maire was already polishing shoes, lining them against the wall on newspaper. Her father's words echoed in her head, 'I want to see myself in that shine!'

Delicious scents of cinnamon rolls fresh from the oven, ham baking for Sunday dinner and fresh-brewed coffee mingled with Jack's Old Spice, Grace's Argo Spray Starch and a bunch of fresh lilacs from the bush outside the dining room window. It was Dierdre's confirmation day. Mary Caye, Crystal Ann, Acer, Quin, Maire, Faith and Dierdre piled into the hump-backed green Plymouth that Jack bought Mary Caye when she graduated from high school. Mary Caye sat behind the wheel. Dierdre, squeezed against the shift stick in the middle of the front seat, held a beautifully wrapped statuette of the Blessed Virgin. Crystal Ann got in on the passenger side. Maire climbed into the back seat behind Mary Caye. Faith slid in next to Maire. Acer stood beside the car.

Mary Caye counted her passengers. "Where's Quin?"

"He's still in the house," Acer replied dryly.

"Why?" Mary Caye opened her car door to step out. "He's serving mass in thirty minutes."

Jack suddenly appeared and yanked the door open. His broad stubby hand reached across Maire, grabbed Faith's collar, pulling her onto the gravel drive. "Get out! Help your mother." He pushed Quin into the car. Quin crawled over Maire and into the middle where Faith had been. Jack slammed the door and waved for Mary Caye to drive. Not wanting to be late for the service, she shifted into gear and sped away.

As the Plymouth sped out of sight, Faith took charge, arranging the younger children in the back of the family station wagon, entreating them not to squirm and get wrinkled. Then she stood by the car door and waited. Jack took his time. He selected a shirt, then changed his mind. He didn't like the tie. He searched for a handkerchief and went back for a cough drop. Grace reminded him of the time. "Let them wait!" he barked. "They're not so important that they can't wait for us." They did not wait. The altar boys lit candles. The organist started a hymn. The bishop stood ready to lead the processional.

Blaze maples and tulip poplars lined the highway in full foliage as the green Plymouth sped east on a two-lane highway, up and over a tall hill and down toward the railroad tracks at the edge of town. Crystal Ann practiced a hymn. Acer watched the road. Quin replayed the scene at the house. Dierdre smoothed the freshly pressed white lace on her confirmation dress. A shelter belt up ahead blocked the full view of the tracks. Mary Caye peered through the trees. The railroad crossing lights were quiet. The guard arm was upright. She counted the miles and the minutes. They were late.

Suddenly Maire screamed! "Train!" She didn't see it, but she shuddered under its dark power. The gigantic hooked nose of a freight train shot headlong through the trees. Time froze. Six souls converged in blinding terror. The bright morning sky flashed with brilliant stars. A legion of angels descended. Then Hell unleashed it's fury. Acer lunged across the seat, grabbed the steering wheel and cranked it hard. Mary Caye slammed her leg down, heel to brake-pedal, clutch to floor. The humpbacked Plymouth lurched sixty-degrees to the right. It's freshly polished hood smashed headlong into the cement pedestal under the crossing arm. The crossing arm, still upright, smashed into the windshield just as Crystal Ann crashed through, landing on the hood. Steel rails skimmed past Mary Caye's head, lifeless against the shattered window. An earsplitting shriek of steel against steel pierced the quiet countryside. Then abruptly there was silence.

Mary Caye, trapped behind the steering wheel, watched helplessly as Crystal Ann lay unconscious across the crumpled hood of the car. Blood trickled from Dierdre's face, imbedded in the dashboard. "Dierdre? Dierdre? Can you hear me?" Dierdre drifted from consciousness as blood streamed down the white lace of her dress. "We have to say the rosary. Now, Dierdre. It's time to say the rosary." Dierdre made a gurgling sound. "It's your turn," Mary Caye insisted. "You have to say the next mystery. It's your turn. Can you hear me? You have to!"

Sirens wailed through town. Jack's brother, Grigor, ran from the church. Sean and the paramedics were already there. Mary Caye, Crystal Ann and Dierdre lay on stretchers. Chunks of glass and blood and crumpled steel covered the road. Quin crouched in the ditch. The ashtray protruding from the back of the front seat cut his face open and broke his nose. His shirt was soaked. Acer stumbled toward him and fell. Maire found them there and cradled Quin's head as he choked on gushing blood.

The long family station wagon piled two-high with children in the back seat sped east, slowed to a crawl, then inched to stop. A line of cars stretched ahead. A train sat idle on the tracks. Jack exploded. "Now we have to wait for the train! We're late! Goddamn it! Now we're late! We'll never make it in time!" He turned his fury on Grace, shaking his stubby fist in her face. "You and your children!" She stared straight ahead. He turned to glare at the children, piled two deep. "Shut up back there!" They knew better than to make a sound. He turned on Grace again. "You can never be on time! You are nothing but a burden! I should have divorced you long ago so you could run back to Chauncey!"

"Now, Jack, It'll be all right," Grace answered quietly. Jack pounded his fists on the steering wheel. He peered wildly, first through the windshield and then out through the side window trying in vain to see ahead. He jammed the shift into reverse and the long paneled station wagon jerked backward. The car behind inched back. "I'm going around," he growled. Then he stopped short. His hands went limp on the steering wheel.

Sean walked slowly towards them, his face drained of color. "You'd better come with me," he said gravely. Jack stared, terrified. Grace knew what that meant. She flung open her car door, stumbled onto the grassy slope of the ditch, caught her footing and ran headlong down the middle of the highway ahead of them both. She stumbled and fell to her knees, horrified at the sight. Her children lay crumpled and strewn, like weeds from the mower. Paramedics bent over Dierdre, limp on a gurney. The white lace and ribbons Grace had starched and pressed just hours before were matted in blood. Grace threw herself over her child and wailed inconsolably. Grace knew how to deal with the hard facts of disappointment, sadness, fear and grief. She had been denying her feelings for years, but she would not lie down for this. This moment was between Grace and her God. She had prayed every day of her life, believing in the promise that her children would be safe. Now she demanded that God make good that promise. Grace had God's favor. The prayer she prayed every minute of every day of her life at that moment was answered.

Dierdre observed the scene in detached wonder as the angels suspended her in time and place. She heard their clear melodious tones. She drifted toward their waiting arms. Then she heard her mother's anguished sobs. She saw her own body, bloody and broken.

"You must go back now," the angels directed.

The only passenger in the big Plymouth that seemed to survive the accident unscathed was the crystal statuette. A paramedic retrieved it and returned it to Mary Caye in her hospital room. Mary Caye's broken leg was cast. It would heal. The glass was removed from Crystal Ann's face. The scars would heal. Quin's broken nose was set and stitched. It would heal. The Bishop confirmed Dierdre as a disciple of the Catholic Church, the same time blessing her with the Last Rites as she lay still and motionless. Grace knew in her heart her daugher would live. She would heal.

Grace knelt alone in the hospital chapel. Looking back on the gruesome events of the day, only one thing was clear. From that moment on, survival would be her victory because she knew then, that with prayer, it was possible. Knowing that, she had nothing more to fear.

Grace prayed the rosary daily, on her knees, in the living room, at the seat of her favorite chair. Jack, not to be outdone, joined her, assuming the role of the priest, leading each mystery with a lilting voice, stopping suddenly to growl a reproach to one or more of the children, or worse yet, to chastise Grace for not teaching them to recite the rosary properly. His angry outbursts reached new heights with each session. Faith cringed every time she heard his voice calling the family together to pray. "God, please don't let him single me out," She begged. "Please, God, get this over with!"

A legal battle raged with the railroad. The railroad settled. Jack deposited the money in the bank the day the check arrived. Sean said, "No. It's not going to go that way. That money is not yours. These children will go to college." Jack argued. Sean said he would pay for the college himself, if that's the way it had to be, but it would be the last time he did anything for his brother ever again, if that's the way it had to be. Jack gave in. He rarely defied Sean. Mary Caye and Crystal Ann left for college in the fall. Acer would be next, then Maire. Sean was firm in this. "The others will get on that school bus and get to school! Things are going to be different!"

Grace learned that facing the storms of life begins with knowing they will come. She hoped and prayed daily that there would be fewer and fewer of them to plague her, but she knew she would face whatever came. She knew she would stand strong in the storm. She knew that facing the force and the darkness of fear would not be easy. It never had been. She knew when the storm blew hard, her faith would be there to steady her.

Prairie people say they can see storms coming at them from miles away, knowing there is nothing to be done to stop the destruction. Grace knew this to be true. One sweltering hot day the air grew heavy as dark clouds whirled overhead. Grace raced across the wide gravel circular drive between the farmhouse and the cattle yards. "Yoo-hoo!" she called, frantically waving a dishtowel. Every child knew that her "Yoo-hoo" demanded immediate action. Jack pulled the station wagon close to the house. "Get in!" he ordered as the tip of a twister tail dropped through the clouds.

"No!" Grace objected, looking frantically toward the cellar.

"Get in or I'll leave you here!" he roared above the howling wind. She obeyed and the car spun around and out the drive. County roads sprayed billows of gravel dust as elm and oak and cottonwoods whizzed by. The sky went suddenly dark as the car sped on, Grace clinging to the dash board, Jack peering through the front windshield at the looming storm, the children cramped and huddled together in the back seat, bracing their hands against the windows, the ceiling and the seat. The ominous gray and black cloud ceiling broke into jagged white tips and the funnel spun, churning up billows of earth ahead of them. The wind whipped the car, pelting it with hail. Sharp lightening pierced the ground, followed by an earsplitting thunderclap. Terrified, the children watched, helpless, as the angry twister turned in its path and headed straight toward them. Branches crashed into the windshield and stuck in the wipers. The car sped forward through the countryside. Then Jack slowed, turned sharply down a country lane and pulled up to a farmhouse. Jack jumped out, covered his head with one hand and tugged at a cellar door with the other. Grace gathered her children close to her, clinging to the babies, rushing them to underground safety. She huddled her family close on the dirt floor as the wind howled, hail beat against the cellar door and the earth shook. Jack groped along the wall for a lantern. He lifted the glass and lit the wick. Peaches! The cellar was neatly lined with wooden shelves, every shelf stacked with Ball Dome glass canning jars filled with tomatoes, green beans, meats and peaches! Jack picked up a jar, twisted the lid, stuck his finger and his thumb deep into the opening and pulled out a plump slice of juicy peach. He popped it into his mouth and winked. He grinned and twisted opened the lid of another jar, then another. He looked around for something to scoop with. There was nothing he could see, so he just passed around the jars. The glow of the lantern glinted in Jack's silly, toothy grin as he smacked his lips with the delicious mischief of stolen peaches. The storm raged above them as Jack lifted a small harmonica to his lips and piped out a jig. The children bravely tapped their toes and nodded obediently to the beat until suddenly, as abruptly as it started, the storm was over. Jack drove home slowly, so as not to miss a glimpse of any of the sensational destruction along the way.

Grace's sister, Blair and her husband Samuel had taken refuge in town. After the storm, they returned to their farm to assess the damage. The cellar door gaped wide open. Someone had been there. Several jars of Blair's prized peaches were opened and devoured! As days and months passed, Blair recounted the tale many times, each time adding a new embellishment. To hear the story, listeners were certain Blair and Samuel were lucky to have escaped with their lives from the double jeopardy of the killer storm and the killers in the storm shelter. Grace and Jack heard several versions of this story that year and for years to follow. Every time Blair retold the tale, Grace frowned in that all-too familiar signature look that said, "Just don't say anything. It'll blow over." The children knew that meant they were sworn to secrecy, probably for life. Grace's children lived by one unbreakable code; a promise made to their mother may never be broken. Her children knew that their mother would forgive them, but her God would not.

Seated in my cramped space on the bus, my thoughts turned faster than the wheels carrying us through the night. I shifted my weight and leaned forward, peering out my side window. Tops of pine trees flew past. It occurred to me that the more the landscape changed, the more it appeared to remain the same.

One day while Grace was ringing out clothes, she discovered that the diamond from her wedding ring was missing. She searched frantically through the water and the clothes. She patted down every inch of the tile floor. She retraced her steps throughout the house and to the clothesline and back. There was no diamond. She concealed the loss as long as she could, turning the silver band, hoping no one would notice. Then Mary Caye announced that she would be married and proudly displayed her own diamond ring. Grace's sister, Jacelyn remarked, "Jack should replace Grace's diamond. He's got a brand new tractor. He's got a brand new car. Grace should have a new ring. Can't Jack afford a ring?" Jacelyn taunted her relentlessly. "You can't go on wearing that bare piece of silver on your finger."

Grace just smiled. "Yes, and I've got all these kids. Maybe I'm not married. Maybe I can just leave!" Mary Caye offered to buy her a less expensive stone to put into the ring. Grace said, "No, Jack will replace it."

A pot-load of bawling red-faced heifers arrived. "You'll have to build fences," Sean announced.

"We have nothing to feed them," Jack argued.

"That's what the silage is for," Sean countered. The children watched and listened. "You kids have a new job, now," he said. He lay his hand on Jack's shoulder. "There are cattle feeders from Iowa and Nebraska to Colorado, Kansas and Missouri. Find them. Sell these calves and I'll send more."

The roar of the engine braking along the gravel road and the growl of the gears downshifting to make the narrow turn up the long driveway soon became the only constant in their lives. Adolescence and high school seemed unreal compared to the lucrative enterprise. The strong, willing children divided the chores and planned for the next load. Jack stood at the fence, barking orders that none needed to hear. They knew what needed to be done, but he needed to prove to himself that no child knew more than he did. His damn children would not be taking credit for what he built. By God he would not be disrespected! With increasing unpredictability, he flew into fits and rages. The children, exhausted from managing the workload as well as from dodging his unrelenting mood swings, learned, as Grace had, to stay out of his way and above all else, hide their achievements.

Grace believed that the onslaughts of stress, grief and danger that she faced in her life made her stronger. It never occurred to her that she might be knocked down. She told herself that these storms could not last forever. It may have seemed to those who observed Grace that she was a fool or a victim or self-destructive. Grace knew that each new barrage awakened in her a spark of defiance. Grace knew that she did not need to be as powerful as the storm. She only needed to be strong enough to stand. She may have stood shaking in fear. She may have stood shaking her fists. It didn't matter to Grace what others thought. As long as she stood with faith, she would be strong enough.

Every day with Jack was a torrential storm. Grace taught her children not to speak until they first determined his mood. She taught them to hide their emotions and their opinions until they first assessed his disposition. Living with Jack was like standing unprotected in the eye of a twister. It may blow up debris and then jump right over or it may burst through, ravaging whatever stands in its path. Yet, the sound of his voice when he sang, the high-spirited tunes he played on the harmonica, the lingering scent of Old Spice on his face, the brogue in his voice when he spun his stories was intoxicating. He played the harmonica like a piper pipes a jig. To be sure, Jack was a charming will o' the wisp, a leprechaun with a pot of gold, a lilting voice, a twinkling eye and a quick step. Jack was also dangerously, carelessly, recklessly unpredictable.

One summer afternoon after an exhausting day of mowing hay, lifting and hoisting small square bales from the field to the hayrack and stacking them neatly into sturdy layers, the children rode a stack of hay bales as tall as the house along a dirt road from the field to the farmyards. They unloaded the bales and stacked them along the fence line by the barn. Jack called to them from the cab of the John Deere tractor. "Get on. I'll give you a ride to the house." Happy for a breeze on a sweltering day, they piled onto the empty flatbed. The big tractor, with the wide rack in tow, rounded the circular drive in front of the farmhouse. Jack turned in his seat to look back at them and grinned a toothy grin. The breeze cooled the faces of the children after an exhausting day in the sweltering sun, but the children wanted to jump off. They could not. The tractor circled the drive again, this time faster. Grace heard the squeals. Jack again passed by the house without stopping. The tractor took another loop at high speed. Now the children were wide-eyed terrified.

"Stop!" Quin called to his father.

Aiden cried out, "We have to jump!"

"No," Faith called back. "He's going too fast! Hang on."

Grace ran from the house waving a dishtowel. She stood squarely in front of the tractor, but Jack didn't stop. She jumped back, narrowly escaping the front tire as it skimmed past. Again the tractor circled the yard. The hayrack bounced, only two of the wheels making contact on the gravel. With every turn the grip of gravity pulled the children closer to edge. The circle tightened and the speed increased. The wagon bounced higher and tilted. Faith gripped the slats of the rack. "Find something to hang on to!" she called. Quin, Maire, Dierdre and Aiden gripped the side rails. Faith pulled Ursula to her chest and wrapped Lyssa's arms around her neck. She grabbed Riley's belt and pulled him to her. "Don't let go! Don't let go, no matter what happens!" she screamed. "Where's Liam?" She grabbed his wrist. "Hang on! Don't let go!" she shouted. The rack careened, flinging the helpless bodies to the gravel below. She tucked her body, pulling the four children into her. A tire whizzed by, skimming the top of her head. The tractor skidded to a stop in a spray of gravel.

The older children scrambled to their feet, nursing scraped and bruised legs and arms. Grace stood over Faith, crying, shuddering, arms outstretched. Faith gingerly loosened her grip, unwrapping each of the babies, one by one from around her neck. Grace carefully checked each child for injuries as, clucking and hovering and crying and hugging, she ushered her entire little brood into the house for comfort. It was over. Jack drove the tractor away, hayrack bumping and rocking along behind.

Faith stood alone, brushing the gravel from her jeans. 'I am invisible,' she thought and wondered if ever there would be a time in her life when she would be able to cry. A jig played in her head. There, smirking mischievously in the blinding rays of the setting sun reflecting across the gleaming green hood of the John Deere tractor was the toothy specter of a leprechaun. Now would not be that time.

Tires crunched on gravel. Sean stepped out of his pickup and strode silently through the front door into the kitchen, scanning the faces in the ominously quiet room. He seated himself at the kitchen table, where Grace calmly placed a cup of coffee and a plate of cookies. Then Jack breezed through the door.

"Here's a riddle for you, Sean. You remember the riddles that Pa used to tell?" His voice ricocheted off the ceiling and around the room. "You stand beside a shimmering pool, deep as the deepest depths of Hell. Beckoning to you is a pot of gold glimmering in the swell."

"Leave it," Sean ordered gravely. "That is a riddle you never want to solve."

Jack taunted him. "Within the depths are seven stones. Each has a riddle all it's own. Solve a riddle and a stone will appear to lead you to the treasure there."

"Jack!" Sean growled.

"My children are smart," Jack sneered, "but not smart enough to solve the riddle of the leprechaun!"

Those who were pulled into Jack's game were not always sure what winning meant. Was it being happy? Was it being successful? Was it the thrill of putting others at risk? Was it the affirmation that after the dust settled, others may be face down on the gravel, but he was still standing? One thing was clear. For Jack to win, everyone must lose.

Time passed and the children grew. The big yellow school bus continued to stop at the house each morning to carry them to school. They did not all get on the bus. During spring planting and fall harvest and winter when the snow needed to be cleared and cattle fed, some stayed at home. The school principal telephoned. Grace offered excuses. Furious, Jack warned him. "Get over it, by God, or I'll take them all out of school!" Then he turned on Grace. "Why do you tell everyone our business? It's nobody's God damned business how we run our lives. You would like to take them all into town, leaving me here to run this place myself! Well, go then! Take your precious children to town and get out!" She did not fear him. Ever since the gruesome day her family was snatched from the jaws of the oncoming train, she feared nothing.

When Grace and Jack started out, there were many others that faced the same hard times. They learned to live one day at a time. Each day was a step toward that time when they could look back with pride and tell their story. They were young. They thought strength meant going faster, harder and longer. Jack solved a problem by overwhelming it or wearing it down. He attacked a problem only after studying its various parts. He turned it over and over, deciding how the game must be played in order for him to win. The game sustained him. Grace solved a problem by giving it over to faith, trust and love. Faith sustained her. Trust released her from the grip of fear. Love released her from the pain of loneliness.

Vietnam brought a foreboding more fierce than any Grace had ever known. Acer boarded a plane, dressed in military uniform. Grace darted to the television whenever a news item aired. She walked the walk of desperation to the mailbox every day for any word that her son was still alive. Months passed.

One Sunday morning Mrs. McMullen stopped her after Mass. On the farm, Grace was isolated from neighbors and community, but at Sunday Mass all things came into balance. Mrs. McMullen clung to Grace. "I know your son, Acer is there. Maybe you could ask him to look after my boy?" Grace squeezed her friend's hand.

"Of course I will do that. Don't worry. I will pray every day for you and for your son." Then she leaned in close to Mrs. McMullen. "And please, pray for me." The next day Grace met the mail carrier at the mailbox. "Dear Acer," she had written. "Mrs. McMullen's son, Mike is coming to Vietnam. Please look after him and make sure he comes home safely with you." Years later, at Jack's funeral, Acer and Mike McMullen laughed at the absurdity of that letter. What her son did not realize is that from the moment Grace wrote the words, she stood taller, stronger in faith and more powerful in spirit. She had mailed the letter to her son, but she had sealed a pact with God. He would send his angels. Her son would be safe. She knew it.

The farm and the cattle operation flourished. The children grew into determined achievers, having learned from their mother how to get along and having learned from their father how to win. Narcissistic children of narcissistic parents, the offspring of Grace and Jack Riorden began to choose sides in their own dark game.

The younger children graduated from high school and talked of college. "No," Jack said firmly. But each determined child produced scholarships and grants and, one by one, each boarded the bus for college. Those that remained were forced from obscurity into Jack's radar.

One freezing January Jack summoned Faith to follow him to the open silage pit. Faith wasn't one of his sons, but she was strong and she would do. She scaled the bunker and stood on the mound. Jack and Faith each struggled to maintain footing on the snow-covered surface, digging and scraping at the ice-packed silage. The calves bellowed below. Jack, impatient and cold, raised the pitchfork over his head and jabbed the tines straight down with all his might. The ice-packed heap did not give. He stiffened. Faith followed his stare. The tines of the pitchfork had pierced the top of her leather work boot, straight through to the mound beneath.

"Take it out!" Faith ordered.

"What?"

"Take the pitchfork out!"

With a mighty yank, he pulled the pitchfork up and away. Blood oozed from the top of her shoe. She limped to the side of the bunker, gingerly hoisted herself over the side and dropped to the ground. Pain shot up her leg and through her body as she trudged through the ice and snow to the house. Jack stared at the bloody trail. Then he turned to the bellowing calves below. "Girls!" he muttered.

Chester was a furry pup when Seth first brought him home in a cardboard box and presented him auspiciously to Ursula, the youngest, then in grade school. Chester followed Ursula through the house and darted between her fast moving feet as she dribbled across the basketball court. A cross between a Newfoundland and a Lab, he grew as quickly as Ursula. Ursula grew into a graceful, intelligent athlete. Chester grew into a monster of a dog the size of a small calf. He bounded toward cars pulling into the drive, his wooly, curly head and imposing round eyes nearly filling the car window as his huge paws rested on the door. He chased squirrels across the yard, scurrying and leaping ahead. He would grab one gingerly by its neck, shake it in his large jaws and toss it into the air, catching it, tossing it again and catching it again until the squirrel was reeling. Then he would suddenly release it and step back to watch. Was he laughing?

Jack hated Chester. Maybe he feared his strength. Maybe he resented Chester's imposing nature. Maybe he was jealous because the dog was loved. When Ursula left for college, she left Chester behind. He bounded behind Jack as he strolled across the yards, Chester's long strides nearly overtaking Jack's short ones. He jumped effortlessly through the weeds, following the big John Deere tractor, nipping playfully at the tires speeding through the tall grass. One day while Jack was mowing with the sickle mower, he turned the tractor in a sudden wide sweeping circle, catching Chester's leg as he romped in the weeds. Chester's painful yelp echoed through the grove of trees to the house. Grace heard and knew what that must mean. She ran to meet Jack as he led Chester, limping and bleeding. "Serves him right," Jack snarled.

Grace made a nest of old quilts in the garage. She bandaged his leg and set a plate of food and a bowl of water next to him, answering his whimpers with her own soothing voice. "There, now. It'll be all right. Take a bite. Take a sip. It will make you feel better." His huge silent pain-filled eyes fixed steadily, trustingly on her knowing kind ones as she stroked his head, wrapping and rewrapping wide bandages she formed from torn cotton towels.

"Leave Him!" Jack growled.

"I'm sorry," Grace whispered.

"Women and dogs!" Jack muttered. "They are underfoot and in the way." Later when Grace looked in on Chester he was gone. Jack insisted that he must have run away. Grace knew then that everyone in Jack's world was expendable.

Jack became increasingly anxious. He was afraid of being alone on the farm. He was afraid of the winters. He was afraid of storms. He was afraid of being stranded in the snow. He phoned neighbors for assurance that someone would be ready to plow out the drive at a moment's notice. He lamented that he was alone, all alone. He threatened to "walk away from the whole thing," saying, "I can always sell it. By God, It's mine, and I can sure as hell sell it." Throughout it all, Grace remained gracious and refined in her approach to the community, to her husband and to her children. There was one man, however, who was never well received. Dachs Raben, a neighboring farmer began a weekly routine of visiting the Riordens.

One Saturday morning, when he knocked at the door, Grace lead him to the kitchen. She offered him a seat and brought a cup of coffee and a cookie. "No, thank you," he said abruptly. "I just came to tell you that I am ready to buy your land whenever you are ready to sell."

Jack smiled and shook his head. "No, no. It's not for sale."

Dachs was not deterred. "You might as well sell now while you can enjoy the money. You know I'll own it one way or the other." Grace put down the coffee pot and moved the plate of cookies out of his reach. Dachs was insistent. "You know it's too much for you, now. You know you'll never turn it over to your sons. Sell it to me now. I'll give you a good price."

Grace never interfered with Jack's business. This time, however, she stood up and pointed her finger squarely in his face. "Over my dead body!" She was shocked by her own boldness but did not back away. Dachs was shocked by her anger but did not apologize. Jack was shocked by her strength but did not say so. Dachs backed to the door and left as abruptly as he came.

"Jack," Grace offered quietly, "why don't we just rent a place in town for the winter? We can come back in the spring."

The more Jack thought of it, the more he liked this idea. The more he liked it, the more it became his own. He was renewed with a burst of activity. His desk became a hub of negotiations. Jack poured all of his charm into the endeavor. Realtors scrambled to find temporary housing, preferably the Cathedral district. He may have hinted at selling his land, but he never would. Farm ground was in demand and he would have his pick of the finest farmers around to cash rent. But then he had a better idea.

Jack offered to make Bric a full partner in the operation. Bric proposed the plan to his bride, Doreen. She agreed, but only if Bric would finish college. The game was on. Doreen spent untold sleepless nights at the farm, waiting patiently to drive Bric home after he had plowed, planted and cultivated throughout the night. Then he would rush to class. A relentless sleep-deprived cycle of work and classes ensued. Autumn brought the harvest. The crop exceeded any crop before it. Bric approached his father to make good their deal.

"I never promised you that!" Jack dismissed him with a forceful wave of his hand. "This farm is mine. It was your decision to help me. That was your business. That was your choice." Whatever fury was unleashed from Bric's spirit during that drive home remains with Bric but when he arrived, he was calm and determined.

"We're not going to farm," he declared quietly.

"We're not going to farm?" Doreen was incredulous.

"I'm going to medical school. I'll show him. Who needs him?"

Doreen was dumfounded. "We didn't discuss this!" She stopped, bewildered, to take it all in. "I thought I married a farmer!" A new thought presented itself. "How will we pay for that? What'll we do for money?"

"I promise, you, Doreen. I will make this right."

The following winter Jack approached Riley, the youngest son. Riley was kind and loving like his mother. Jack offered him the same deal as he had offered Bric. Like Bric, Riley agreed, attending classes by day and farming by night. When the crop was harvested Riley also approached his father to make good their deal. Jack declared a second time that he had promised no such thing and dismissed him as he had dismissed his brother. Riley, like Bric before him, left the farm. He never did speak an unkind word of his father, but he never did return.

The third winter brought Jack's seventh son. Seth was a banker, pragmatic, savvy and insightful. He was skeptical. He saw an opportunity but he knew it needed to be handled carefully. Seth was engaged to a young woman, a professional in her own right. Seth and Kristin both knew the value of the Riorden enterprise. Seth proposed that he borrow the money to buy equipment and enhance the land. In return, he and his father would be full partners. Seth approached his father with a contract. Jack scoffed at that, refusing to sign, instead appealing to his son on a personal level. "You owe it to me," Jack said. "You owe it to me for all I've done for you."

The crop flourished under Seth's agrarian skill. Seth and Kristin were welcomed into the small farming community, but religion soon became a point of contention. Grace and Jack insisted that Kristin join the Catholic church before they marry. It was never clear whether Grace or Jack lead that charge, because Jack would end every argument with, "Honor your mother. It's what she wants."

Kristin proposed a solution. "Everyone warns us that your Dad will cheat you out of this crop the same way he cheated Bric and Riley. We have hundreds of thousands invested in this venture. That's all right. I agreed to this. If we lose it, we lose it. We will come back from that. That's not important. So here's my offer to you. If your Dad screws you, if he cheats you like he cheated your brothers, you will join my church and become a part of my family. We will live a decent life apart from this craziness." Seth knew this was a clear and simple solution to both issues. The answer would be in Jack's hands.

Autumn brought abundant harvest. The wedding was simple and elegant. The priest and the minister both gave blessings. The complacent lull was short-lived, however. Soon the call came from Seth's uncle, Gordon.

"Seth, I'm at the elevator. You'd better get down here. Your dad is selling the grain."

There was only one rule to Jack's game: the one who wins, wins. When Jack's brother, Grigor died, Jack called on Acer, now an attorney, to contest Grigor's will. Jack claimed he was with his brother during those final days and he had a holographic will, a handwritten note. Handwriting analysis challenged the validity of the signature. Frantic, emotional testimony and angry threats from Grigor's spouse ensued. The judge ruled that Jack should have a share of his brother's estate. It was whispered that Jack bullied his brother during his last days of illness into writing the note. Some said that Jack wrote it. Grace remained quiet on the subject. She would get her house in town.

Jack hired a prominent builder in the area and then locked himself in his office hour after hour, day after day reconstructing the builder's blueprints. Grace basked in Jack's triumph. Who could imagine that the butcher she married would take her from a shack on a farm to an estate in town? Grace staked off a plot of land for her garden. She planted rows of tomatoes, green beans, cucumbers and onions. She added roses to the landscaping and transplanted her mother's tiger lilies from the farm. Grace thought that her mother would have been proud.

Jack soon grew restless in the new home. His sons didn't come to visit as often as they had. They didn't jump when he called. The house was old news. He needed a shed. He stood overlooking Grace's garden from his office window. He would have the best shed in the neighborhood.

Backhoes tore into Grace's garden. Tires dug deep ruts into her pristine lawn. With gulping thrusts, hydraulic forks ripped the green plants from the ground, dumping them into a truck bed on the street. Grace looked on, heartbroken. She realized that even this latest conquest would not be enough to satisfy her husband. Perhaps nothing would. The Lincoln and Forever rose bushes, her mother's daisies and tiger lilies and the promise of fresh tomatoes in the spring were gone. A shed the size of a small cabin stood in their place. Locked inside the shed was an oversized John Deere lawn tractor. Jack often rode it across the yard in sweeping circles. Grandchildren sat in his lap and waved as their parents snapped pictures. Lyssa defiantly ordered a load of dirt for a flower garden in front of the house. Jack sent the truck away. "Grace has had enough of gardens," he scolded.

Just before Thanksgiving, Jack decided to install a remote door opener in the shed. Jack ordered Grace to stand under the heavy door to hold it open and in position while he fastened the unit. She stood obediently in the cold rain, ignoring the ache in her arms and legs while he located tools and studied the directions. He took his time. She didn't complain. Then something happened. A spring broke or he let go or the cable recoiled. The door dropped. She crashed to the cement, crumpled under its weight.

Lying flat on her back in the emergency room, the pain she felt from the injury was magnified by the pain of hearing her husband telling physicians, nurses and technicians how clumsy and silly she was to have gotten pinned under a garage door. They wagged their heads at her foolishness and agreed she was lucky to be alive. Her foot was broken in several places. Her arch was crushed. She knew Jack would use her injury as an example of how useless she was to him. His sons, he would say, were good help.

I reeled from my thoughts, searching the faces of my new friends on the bus to get my bearings. 'We all wear the mask of illusion,' I thought. 'We appear strong, hiding what is fragile; we appear brave, hiding what we fear; we appear resolved, hiding what we doubt.'

My cell phone blinked. I flipped it open. It was Maire. "You should get here in time for dinner on Thursday. We'll eat out. Do you want a tour of the town? What? You're breaking up. I'm losing you." Her voice drifted into static, while my thoughts drifted to another time, another phone call.

When Grace called upon her children for support, it was usually at Jack's bidding. One particular day Grace phoned Maire to ask her to lunch. Maire arrived at the house to find Grace packing sandwiches, cookies, a Mason jar of water and a thermos of coffee.

"Are we going on a picnic?"

"We are going to the farm to plant trees. Will you come with us?" Maire knew that was not a question. The pickup bed was piled high with small seedlings. There was a posthole digger and a jug of Miracle Grow wedged next to the end gate.

Driving past farmland along the two-lane country road, Jack tilted his head backwards toward Maire. "Seth says I'm going to Hell."

"What?" That was not what she expected.

"Seth says unless I'm born again, I'm going to Hell. What does that mean, born again? Do I have to crawl back into my mother's stomach and be pushed out again?"

Maire couldn't tell if he was joking or serious or just trying to get a rise out of her. "No, that's not what born again means at all."

Grace turned in her seat. "Are you talking about the Catholic Church or some other church?"

Maire stifled a laugh. It struck her as comical that her mother should be so animated, but then, Maire reasoned, they were talking about the one subject on which Grace was truly passionate."

"I'm talking about the bible."

"You tell me something, then." Grace shook her finger at Maire. "Does this have anything to do with the Pentecostal Church?"

Maire lowered her head and bit her lip, grinning. "Well, that's where I got saved," she answered.

"I thought so!" Grace retracted her finger but not her emphasis. "That's Dachs Raben!"

This time Maire did laugh out loud. "What?"

"He threatens to take our land from us every time he sees us. I told him it would be over my dead body!"

"Oh!" Maire understood. "My money's on you, Mom." She knew her mother probably would go to her grave defending her land.

Jack parked in front of the farmhouse. "Do you want this house?"

She didn't expect that from him, either. "What? No. Why?"

"I hired a lawyer about a will. Not Acer. I hired someone else. Do you want the house?"

"No. Don't do that. I can't afford the taxes. Surely someone else would put it to better use."

"I asked every one of my kids. They all say they would sell it in a New York minute!"

"Oh."

"What do you think of that? They don't even care about the Thomas J. Riorden name. No one appreciates it."

"Hmmm."

"You're in the will."

"Well, Dad, there's nothing I need. Why don't you and Mom just spend it and enjoy it?" She had another thought. "Give it to Elle."

"Elle?" he roared. "No! She's a bastard."

Grace jumped. "Jack!"

"No." He waved Grace away. "I've put you in the will, Maire, along with my other children, but not Elle!"

"OK, OK."

"You don't need a house?"

"No, I'm doing fine."

"You don't need a car?"

"No, I'm good."

"How are you going to take care of yourself?"

"Don't worry. God takes care of me."

Jack laughed. "God is dead."

"Jack!" Grace flashed, horrified.

He laughed again. "Didn't they tell you? He died two thousand years ago."

"My God is alive, Dad. He helps me all the time," Maire answered as she unloaded the trees and the posthole digger. She set to work, digging holes, filling them with Miracle Gro and water and tamping them down. Jack stood at the end of the row, marking a straight line.

When they finally reached the end of the row, Jack said, "Hop up into the truck and sweep out the back." Maire crawled into the truck. Two scrawny, dried up seedlings lay discarded in the truck bed. Maire held up the shriveled roots.

"Do you want to plant these?"

"No," Grace murmured reluctantly. "We'll just throw those away."

Maire smiled down to her. "I think you want to plant them."

Jack peered over the side. "Grace, I told you not to bring those along! Those trees are dead!" He grabbed one. "Don't you see this? There's no dirt on it." He shook the little plant by its roots. Maire cringed at the doleful expression on her mother's face. She did not want to see one more thing in her mother's life destroyed by indifference and arrogance. She was going to plant the damn trees.

"Dad," Maire interrupted, "I'm going to show you something about God. I'm going to share with you a little secret. Do you want to know a secret?"

"Yea," he answered and dropped the plant.

Maire winked at her mother and jumped down from pickup bed. "Here are two holes that we dug here. I'm going to plant these trees and show you that the word of God will make them grow."

"Ha!" Jack scorned.

"OK, you do that," Grace said.

Maire filled each of the two holes with Miracle Gro and water and carefully spread the roots and filled the hole with dirt. As she tamped down the dirt she said, "The scripture we are going to pray is 'Behold, I make all things new.' Now you've got to agree."

"Sure, I agree," Jack sneered.

"Amen," Grace whispered reverently.

Maire continued. "You asked me this afternoon, Dad, how a person gets born again. It's a simple prayer. You believe that Christ died for your sins and will forgive you and you ask him to be your personal Lord and Savior to help you live your life and to live in your heart. Do you believe?"

"Yes," Grace answered.

"Naaa," Jack jeered.

"Dad, You have to agree or it's not going to work."

"OK," Jack allowed.

"Amen, then," Maire continued. "Behold all things will be new. These trees will grow strong, healthy and tall. One for you, Mom and one for you, Dad."

"I have one more project," Jack declared on the ride home. I need you to dig a hole in the front yard so I can pour a foundation.

"Isn't this a job for one of your sons?" Maire protested.

"I asked them," Jack answered. "They just laugh. They won't come."

"Why not hire it done?"

"It's too expensive." He growled at her. "If you won't help, Mom and I will do it."

"Right," she thought.

Maire returned to Scanlon Circle, where she dug for three days in the intense summer heat. Grace hovered with a dishtowel, swatting gnats that swarmed over the sweat on Maire's back. "Get away. Let her work," Jack growled.

Finally, Maire reached a depth that pleased him. The three of them stood together, staring into the hole. "What are you going to doing with this?" she asked.

"I'm having a guy from the monument company bring a granite block and set it in."

"Dad, it'll look like a gravesite."

"I just want them to know that this is what I did," Jack insisted. "Then no one will forget Jack Riorden."

She looked at him, amused. "What makes you think they'll forget you?"

"They will! When I die, I'll leave everything to Grace. They'll steal it from her and sell it, probably to Dachs Raben!" It was the ultimate threat. He smirked with satisfaction as Grace's eyes darkened. "I'll put this monument here and everybody will know that I built it."

"Why don't you put your name on it then?"

"Because I can't. All the city will allow is the number. I would if I could. Believe me."

Two days later, Maire got another call.

"We need to dig holes in the back," Jack declared.

"I thought the hole in the front was the last project." Maire argued, but she knew if she didn't go to help, he'd have Grace digging in the dirt.

As she walked across the wide lawn behind the house, she saw twenty-five flags, each marking a spot where she should dig. She went to work digging the holes and pouring the concrete for the support posts. She worked for hours before Jack finally emerged. "Now we need to put in the poles." He pointed to twenty-five wrought iron panels, each with pineapple shaped iron ornaments welded onto the top.

"This will be endless," Maire thought as she lugged a heavy wrought iron support post across the yard and tipped it in to a concrete hole. Grace joined them and took hold of one end of a wrought iron panel. Jack tugged as best he could on the other end, but dropped it suddenly to the ground. The panel jolted and spun Maire back. Jack snarled, "Maire, you step back and let Mom hold it." Then he thundered, "Grace, you hold that and don't you drop it!"

Maire regained her footing. "No. I'm not letting go." Jack shoved the panel, twisting and jerking it violently. Grace stumbled back. "We should go in," Maire warned. We shouldn't be outside in this heat."

"We're finishing!" Jack barked back. "I want my sons to see what I built when they visit this weekend."

"You built?" Maire muttered. She worked for hours, lugging the panels into place, while Jack and Grace looked on. She finished just as the sun set.

Back in the house, Grace moved slowly, warming a bowl of soup for supper. "You wanted me to style your hair tonight," Maire reminded her.

"It's too late!" Jack barked. "Let it go."

"No, I'm fine," Grace sighed. "I really want my hair done before company comes."

"No!" Jack snarled. "I said let it go. You just go home!"

Maire rose early the next morning, thinking she should drive over and wash and style Grace's hair before Jack awoke. It was seven-thirty. He wouldn't be awake before nine-thirty or ten. She thought she should call, but didn't want to wake him. Before she got out the door, her phone rang. "Can you come over and do my hair?" Grace whispered.

"Sure," Maire answered heading to her car. "Right now?"

"Right now."

I looked up from my thoughts of Grace and Jack and Maire to see a young woman board the bus. She was young, well-dressed, introspective. She nodded and passed by to the seat behind me, just across the aisle. She stored her bags under her feet and then adjusted her position, trying to find a way to get comfortable.

"Why isn't she talking to us?" Grace whispered. "Does she think we're invisible?" I reached over the aisle and extended my hand.

"Hi. I'm Elle."

She smiled back. "I'm Sonja."

"Are you traveling a long way?"

"Not far, Washington." She instinctively rubbed her finger over the wedding band on her hand. "It's my first anniversary."

"Congratulations."

"Thanks. I'm kind of nervous."

"You don't like to travel?"

"It's not that." She smiled self-consciously. "Where are you headed?"

"Oregon. I'm taking my grandmother there. She's never been this far."

She nodded and looked around. "Where is she?" I touched the palm of my hand over my heart. Her eyes softened. "Oh."

She turned back to her book and I turned my gaze back to the window.

"Is that better, Gram?" I asked.

"I like this part of the journey," Grace mused. "Not like before."

"Not like before." I echoed.

Grace and Jack celebrated their wedding anniversary in a banquet room at the Sheraton, just beyond the waterfall. Grace's sister, Blair, who, over sixty years before stood with Grace as her maid of honor, sat at Grace's right. Grace and Jack proudly displayed matching wedding bands, which they designed themselves. The identical rings each featured a center stone of sapphire with a diamond encrusted band. Grace had faithfully worn the silver ring with the missing stone, firm in her belief that Jack would buy her a diamond. This ring proved Jack's love; that their life together was good.

Autumn turned to winter. Although Jack's anger was becoming the axis of their lives, Grace focused all her emotional and physical strength on encouraging him to be happy. Grace phoned with another invitation. "Will you spend Christmas Eve with us?" She whispered.

"You'll be alone?" I asked, surprised. "Where is everyone?"

"I don't know," she replied quietly. "I suppose the children and their families all have other plans."

Grace stood at my elbow while together we prepared traditional oyster stew and cranberry Jell-O salad. I set the table with a Christmas tablecloth and napkins and sprigs of holly and Grace's special Christmas plates, the ones with red cardinals on the rim. We peeled and cut apples and spread them into the pie crust. The scent of cinnamon filled the room as the pie baked in the oven. Grace dressed in a bright Christmas sweater and her best pearls. Jack dressed in a gray cardigan and tie. I served them as they savored the meal and sipped on sparkling apple juice.

I was finishing graduate school but we didn't discuss that. Grace didn't know the questions to ask and Jack was determined not to acknowledge a woman in business. Anytime the subject came up, his singular comment was always that I would never make as much money as a doctor or a lawyer. So we chatted about the neighbors and Christmases past.

"I have to go soon," I apologized. I cleared the dinner plates and set the apple pie on the table.

"Where will you go?" Grace reached across the table to squeeze my hand.

"I have a date."

Grace's smile wrinkled her nose and dimpled her cheeks. Jack scowled. I cut the pie into slices, placing each piece on a dessert plate in front of each of them, kissed them both and left them to enjoy the rest of their evening.

An hour down the Interstate my cell phone rang. It was Quin's wife, Cheyla. Grace was hurt. She had been rushed to the hospital. I spun the car into the meridian and raced against time as I sped back through the night. When I arrived at the hospital, the family was huddled in the waiting room, exchanging conjectures and explanations. Quin's daughter, Chloe, said she stopped by the house with a Christmas gift. She knocked on the door but there was no answer, so she walked through the kitchen entrance. Her grandparents lay unconscious on the kitchen floor. Grace lay flat on her face. Jack sprawled on top of her. A nurse interrupted Chloe's story to announce that Grace was out of surgery. The group dispersed. Quin offered to take Jack home. I headed to intensive care.

I sat at Grace's side, holding her hand and stroking her cheek. She stirred and cried out, "Mother! Mother, where are you?" I leaned in close. She looked at me through glazed eyes and smiled. The door opened and a nurse in green scrubs stood in the doorway.

"You'll have to leave."

I looked up. "What?"

"You'll have to leave. Visiting time is over."

His brusque indifference sent the intensity of hot steel through my veins. It occurred to me that it was time someone stood by this woman. "Did you think I was a visitor?" I glared at him, not moving. He returned the stare, then nodded and backed out of the room. The door closed softly behind him.

The next two weeks blurred into sleepless nights of bedside vigil. Jack's sons drove him to the farm, took him to lunch and dinner and sat with him at the house while he rested. The brief moments he spent at Grace's side were filled with tension. If she were sleeping, he shook or poked her until she woke. He chastised her relentlessly for being awkward, clumsy and now, the most damning of all, invalid.

Dr. Ahsan and Grace had a long history. He had replaced both of her hips. Grace spoke to him as an old friend. "I told you, no pain! You saw to that. Thank you for everything, Doctor."

He held an image to the light. "This is your leg, Grace. Do you see this?" She leaned in and looked closely. "This is the only bone that is your own. The rest I built for you." He reached out and touched her hand. "You must be careful not to fall again." Grace straightened in her chair.

"I did not fall."

Jack interrupted. "Grace, you know you did. You went to the freezer to get ice cream for the pie and you slipped and fell."

She turned to face him squarely. "Jack, you know and I know I didn't fall!" Grace spoke in code and trusted Dr. Ahsan to understand what she couldn't say. Jack spoke with authority and trusted Dr. Ahsan to leave a silly woman to her husband. Dr. Ahsan dismissed it all. This wasn't his area. Grace's words rang in my ears. "I didn't fall."

Grace knew that life would not be easy. She knew that to keep going she must keep hope alive. She leaned on her faith for shelter from the storm and the lifting of her burden. Grace had nurtured four physicians, five medical professionals, two attorneys, and four entrepreneurs. She had over one hundred grandchildren and great grandchildren. There was no reason for her to doubt that she would be cared for the way she had cared for her family. Grace deserved peace. She deserved respect. She had something to offer. She was worth knowing. Grace prayed that she would outshine her husband's darkness. I prayed that she would outlive it.

The big bus cabin grew quiet. Yoki read his book. Sonja dozed, lounging across two seats behind me, her toes sticking out into the aisle. I pressed the tiny earphones back into my ears. Rhythm and sound pulsed through me.

"Do you love it?" Grace tapped her fingers to the spirited beat.

"You're a super chick, Grace," I whispered.

"Oh, you," she giggled.

So stand in the rain
Stand your ground
Stand up when it's all crashing down
You stand through the pain
You won't drown
And one day, what's lost can be found
You stand in the rain

The Turtle's Back

Everybody needs to belong somewhere
Life can feel so alone without someone who cares
and when life becomes something just to get through
That's when I'm glad that I belong to you

I roused from a deep sleep to voices overhead. Broad shoulders loomed over me and arms reached across me. Startled, I shook myself awake. Narrow eyes squinted down at me from behind wide rimmed glasses.

"Now you woke her. I told you to be careful."

"What is going on?" Passengers leaned over me, staring at something below my window. I slid across the seat and scanned the shoulder of the highway, the grassy ridge at the lip of the ditch and the sharp drop to the river below. "I don't see anything. What is it?"

"There!" The sleeve of the man's weathered mountain jacket brushed against my face. Annoyed, I pushed him back. There at the river's edge was a procession of turtles. The bus increased speed and the crush of passengers quickly shifted, faces pressed against the windows at the back of the bus. The man took the seat next to me. "I'm fascinated with them. They are among the oldest living creatures on earth. They will be alive long after we are gone. I was at JFK when diamondbacks closed the runway there." He turned to include the others. "I'm researching along the river. Turtle populations are the fastest response to climate change of any other species. Young and old alike are changing their habits."

Yoki leaned in. "They are adapting their behavior to survive."

"Yes, but I wonder what the limit is to their ability to adapt."

Yoki nodded. "In this world, the slower you move, the faster you die. But the turtle knows better than any creature how to defy death. Listen, can you hear the coyotes? Turtles annoy the hell out of coyotes." Laughter rippled through the bus.

An Asian woman with sleek, dark hair and ancient eyes perched on the arm of her seat facing us. The driver scowled back at us from the overhead mirror. She lowered her voice as her eyes moved from one to the other as she spoke.

"During a time of hardship and famine a grand-mother and granddaughter were rejected by their families as too much a burden. The old woman's family voted under a dark moon to abandon the two and for-age ahead into the forest where they would gather and bake soi. In hunger and haste, they dismantled their tents and loaded all they owned onto the backs of oxen and rumbled away, trampling the dry grass beneath them, leaving the old woman and her granddaughter alone with nothing. The woman despaired, but starvation and exposure were not the most imminent danger. The commotion woke a sleeping serpent. The ground swelled as the serpent's mighty body slithered toward them. They clung to each other, trembling in terror, but to their amazement, the serpent lowered its tail, hoisted them onto it's back, and carried them to a cliff over the ocean. At the edge of the cliff the woman held her granddaughter's hand tightly and together they jumped."

"Oh!" Sonja exclaimed.

Ancient Eyes smiled. "The two did not drown, for their souls were strong. They immediately transformed into a shark and a turtle. As the serpent slithered along the coastline toward the forest and scent of baking soi, the woman and her granddaughter were swept away by the current. Soon they arrived on the shores of a village where they transformed back into their human form and were welcomed, fed and offered a home by the village natives. Unable to stay on land, the grandmother gave the villagers a song to sing from the rocks and promised that when they sang to her, she and her granddaughter would come."

"I have heard of this legend," Sonja said. "Is it truth or fiction?"

"The difference between truth and fiction," Ancient Eyes smiled, "is that fiction has to be logical."

"So which is it?" Sonja pressed.

Ancient Eyes pulled her shawl close to her. "The truth is that to this day, the turtle and the shark swim together. The logic is simple wisdom; one should be careful not to wake the serpent." She winked and returned to her seat.

Yoki joined in from across the aisle. "Before the earth was here, all was water. Far above the clouds lived a powerful chief. His pregnant wife craved the delicacies of the bark of a root of the great tree in the middle of the spirit world. It was a tree with four large roots, stretching out to each of the four sacred directions, and bearing many kinds of fruits and flowers. One night she dreamed that the great tree was uprooted. The woman woke to find the dream fulfilled. When she leaned through the hole left by the uprooted tree, she lost her balance and fell. The birds transported her on their wings, and the great sea turtle received her on his back. There she planted the handful of roots and plants that fell with her from the spirit world." Sonja moved forward in her seat. Ancient Eyes peered out from behind her shawl. Yoki continued. "The spirit woman bore twin sons. The right-handed twin created beautiful hills, lakes, blossoms and gentle creatures. The left-handed brother created jagged cliffs, thorns and predators. The right-handed twin was truthful, reasonable, goodhearted and straightforward. The left-handed brother lied, fought, rebelled and made selfish choices. Consumed with envy, he killed his brother and threw his body over the edge of the earth. Furious, the spirit woman rebuked him. In a fit of jealous rage, he cut off her head and threw it into the sky. Then he threw her body into the ocean." Sonja gasped. "Now the spirit woman falls and rises eternally, joining heaven and earth through cycles of time while the turtle balances on its back the outcome of the never-ending, ever-shifting war between spirit and ego." He smiled. "She is revered."

"Well, that's good," Grace concluded.

"Yes," Sonja agreed. "That's good."

Grace was raised in a culture that had a limited view of women's prospects. Her accomplishments were not her own. Her home and her possessions were secure only as long as her husband allowed it. Jack told her that every day. Still, her faith endured. She traveled a journey that took her from wealth to subsistence and back to wealth through sixteen births, three hip replacements and a variety of broken bones. Still, Grace's faith endured. Grace knew that recognition would never come to her, but she relished in the prospect of success for her daughters and their daughters.

Grace knew that throughout her journey her decisions determined her direction and her direction determined her destiny. When Jack's health failed, those decisions put her squarely in the path of a violent battle between spirit and ego. She faced the challenge as she always had. She prayed. Then she did one more thing. She wrote me a letter. The letter said simply, 'Come home.' I didn't know it at the time but opening that letter put me at an intersection in my own journey that would change not only my life but hers and Maire's as well.

Near death, Jack was airlifted to University Hospital. Now he lay recovering in a hospital bed at St. Christopher's. His personal nurse stood over him. "Are you still mad at me?" He glared back at her. "Well, then, you'll be happy to know I'm going on vacation. I'm off to Ireland. You won't have to deal with me for a while." She smiled kindly. "What would you like me to bring back?" He eyed her suspiciously.

"A rosary," Grace offered.

"A rosary!" the nurse echoed. "Perfect! Do you know why?" He softened his glare. "It's Ireland! Will you try to behave while I'm gone if I promise to bring you a rosary, blessed from Ireland?" He nodded.

After she left the room, he scowled and looked away. "I'm not staying here. I will not die here in this hospital or in a damned nursing home!"

I stood in the doorway, feeling the ache in my grandmother's heart as she sat silently, attentively in a straight-backed chair next to his bed. "Do you want to go home?" I knew I would pay a high price for those words.

"Yes, let's go home," Grace echoed.

His eyes darted quickly to me. Then he looked at Grace. "How?"

"We'll just leave," she said. "If you want to go home, we'll go."

"You can't take care of me. Look at you! You can't do anything. You're no good to me! How can I go home?"

"I've taken care of you for over sixty years. I can take care of you now," Grace protested.

"I'll stay with you both," I answered. What was I saying? I had just graduated. I had volunteered for a history making presidential campaign. MBAs all over the country were out of work. I should have been concentrating on my future. "It's a perfect solution," I offered. "I'll stay with you while I job hunt." I saw two images of myself. One stood tall, beckoning them to rise from their despair and follow. The other tried with all her might to stuff the first one down. What was I doing?

Grace brightened. "Yes, let's go home." She patted his hand. "You'll feel better there. You'll see. Let's go home."

He reached for the phone, pushing the IV out of the way. "What's Quin's pager number?" He punched in the numbers, scowled, paused to think and dialed a second number. "Not there? Have him call me." He dialed again. "Duracare? I need a hospital bed, oxygen and transportation."

By nightfall, he was home. The bed they had shared their entire married life was shoved against the wall to make way for the new furnishings. Jack barked orders and wielded the portable phone like a sword. Now there was a new game. He told everyone Grace was the invalid and this business was all for her benefit. Grace quietly acquiesced, drifting from room to room, unpacking hospital bags and writing grocery and pharmacy lists. They were home. Disaster was averted, at least for the time being.

"How will you do this on your own?" Quin challenged. "How will you find a job, maintain your life and do this too?" My heart sank. Grace had taught me that we are all responsible for our own choices. I knew this one would change my life forever.

Every moment of every day sucked me deeper into the Riorden vortex. Jack woke angry and stayed angry most of every day, bullying Grace, calling her useless, throwing things at her and barking at her until she jumped. She couldn't jump far. Her femur, broken in the Christmas mishap had healed, but she was confined to a power chair. He was more mobile than she, but refused to take care of himself or her. I couldn't leave them alone. I hired personal assistants for each of them. One by one, Jack dismissed them or they refused to return. I hired more.

I planned another anniversary party. Grace's brother, Colin, was there. Parkinson's Disease had sapped the strength from his muscles but not his spirit. Like Grace, his faith endured. He stood at the back of the room with another distinguished white haired man. I didn't recognize him. "Elle, this is my good friend, Chauncey," he said. "We've been friends since high school." I stared, speechless. So this was Chauncey.

"You're Grace's granddaughter," he said. "I've heard many good things about you. You're grandmother is fortunate to have you." He held my hand in a warm exchange. I was captivated. He looked toward the table. "Grace seems happy. I'm pleased to see that." I was speechless. All I could do was smile. So he did exist. I always thought he was just one of my grandfather's curses.

Colin stepped in to rescue me. He handed me a little book. "Your grandmother knows this prayer. Make it your own. Add to it. When God hears you speak it, power will be unleashed." I opened it. The lines were underscored and highlighted.

"This is yours. I can't take your copy."

He dismissed my objection. "Read it. Use it. Pass it on. Pray with your grandmother. Claim your power."

Colin and Grace shared long sweet phone conversations about life and children and growing up together, and their enduring bond of faith. Jack talked over her or coughed loudly or turned the television to peak volume. He took the phone, turning the conversation to his own illness, his own pain. He always finished with a joke, to which Colin obligingly laughed. Then he hung up the phone, imitating Colin's hand tremors.

Colin's daughter phoned early one morning. "Dad wants to speak to Aunt Grace."

I leaned down to wake her. Jack threw back the covers. I gave the phone to Grace and guided her chair to another room. Jack ordered me to help him. He screamed at me for disrespecting him and threatened to get even. I closed the bedroom door. This was a moment for Grace.

The morning of Colin's funeral brought renewed fury from Jack. "You go ahead!" he screamed. "Selfish! You don't care about me! You'll be glad when I'm gone!"

"Now, Jack," Grace coaxed.

"Just call them. Tell them you're not going." He held the phone in his hand, blue veins standing out against his white, tissue-like skin. I marveled at the contrast between his fragile health and the fearsome countenance he exuded.

"No, Jack. He is my brother. I am going."

Quin entered with Dierdre close behind. She lifted Grace's hat from the table and handed her a mirror and her bag. Quin helped her from the wheel chair to the passengers seat while Dierdre planted herself firmly in the driver's seat. I watched from the kitchen as they drove away. Disgusted, Jack retreated to the bedroom. The day grew quiet. Each time I looked in on him he was sleeping. Late in the afternoon I heard him in the hallway.

"Grandpa, I can help you," I called, moving to him.

He shuffled into his office. "Take these numbers and double check them for me," he barked, handing me a ledger and several large envelopes. Taxes are due." Then he locked the door behind him.

When he finally emerged, over an hour later, his cane wobbled precariously. "Wait, Grandpa! I'll help you," I called.

"Get away from me," he bellowed. "I don't need any help. Get away!" The teakettle whistled. I turned to move it off the burner and he went down hard against the wall and then to the floor, yelping in pain.

I rushed to him, supporting his head, looking for sign of injuries. "Don't move. Stay still. I'll help you up."

"Get away from me!" He slapped feebly with his free hand, the other pinned under him. "I don't want you! I never wanted you here! I want my sons!"

"Grandpa, Quin's at the funeral. Bric's on call at the hospital. Liam is out of town. Seth is thirty minutes away! Let me help you!"

"Get away! Don't touch me! Call Seth!" He slapped me again, then his hand dropped to the carpet, lifeless. I brought pillows to cushion his head and back and left him crouched on the hallway floor while I scrambled for the phone to dial for help.

When Grace returned from the funeral, Jack detailed in anger and anguish, the series of events that occurred because she left him alone. He was abandoned and he fell.

"He was not alone," I assured her. "I was here. He just fell."

"I was alone!" he screamed. "She was not here! You wait! This family will abandon you, too!"

"Now, Jack," she attempted.

"Don't 'now, Jack' me! They'll abandon you too and then..." He paused, trying to think of the most dire thing he could say. "They'll sell everything to Dachs Raben!"

"Jack, you know that's not true."

"I am the only one stopping them!" He waved his hands at a mental vista of all they owned. "When I'm gone, they will sell it all! Then you will be sorry!"

His voice boomed the warning throughout the night. She ignored him, pretending to sleep. He waved a shaky fist and disavowed her love. "You're just waiting for me to die so Chauncey can come back!"

During these midnight outbursts I hurried upstairs to stand in their bedroom doorway. "Is there anything you need? Maybe some tea to help you sleep?"

"Get out! Get out of here!" He screamed through the darkness. "Take your grandmother with you! Both of you! Get out! I am not your prisoner!"

The wedding of Dierdre's daugher, Caireann, was fast approaching. The morning of the bridal shower, Jack was obstinate, petulant and sullen. He was angry to be left behind. "I forbid you to go!" he screamed from his chair at the table. "Ouch!" He doubled in pain.

Grace was firm in her resolve, just as she was the morning of Colin's funeral. She was going. Her hair was styled. She wore her melon-colored Chanel jacket with the ruffled neck and sleeves. Her crescent jeweled mother's pin with the birthstones of her sixteen children sparkled on the lapel. She positioned her hat and turned away from the mirror. Jack sat in the kitchen in the chair in which he allowed no one else to sit. She spritzed her wrists with Estee Lauder Beautiful and approached him with a cheery kiss. He turned his face and pushed her away.

"This shower is just for the girls, Jack." Grace soothed his shirtsleeve and patted his hand.

"No," he argued. "I need you here."

"The party is just across town, Jack. I'll call from there."

Dierdre stood at the door. Dierdre's husband, Derek, sauntered to the table. "I'll sit with you, Jack. The Cubs are playing the Twins today. It should be a great game."

"Your personal assistant, Guy, will be here soon," Grace added. "You should have everything you need until we get back."

"I will not be here when you get back!" Jack warned.

Dierdre wheeled Grace to the door, chattering and giggling in high-pitched joviality. I followed.

An hour later the shower was in full swing. Caireann wore a mock wedding veil made of ribbons. Sisters of the Riorden guild shifted and moved about the room in orchestrated gaiety. My cell phone beeped. It was Guy. "I can't wake Jack!"

I stepped through a sea of wrapping paper. "Call 911! We're on the way."

Bric's wife, Doreen stood suddenly at my side. "What's wrong?"

"Guy can't wake Grandpa."

"I'll drive." Doreen grabbed the keys from the counter. Grace watched me, motionless.

I walked back to her and leaned close. "Grandpa's not waking up. We'll go there now." She gripped my sleeve. "You'll be right behind me." She nodded solemnly without speaking a word.

Guy met me at the door. I rushed into the bedroom. Doreen stayed on the sidewalk, cell phone to her ear. Guy leaned over my shoulder as I leaned over my grandfather. His face was drained of color. "Grandpa?" I stroked his cheek. His skin was cold and gray. His eyes were closed. He wasn't breathing. There was no pulse. "I think he's gone." I held his hands in mine. "Grandpa." I stared at his hands. "Where is his ring?" Guy followed my eyes. His wedding ring was on his left hand but the massive gold and onyx ring he always wore on his right hand was missing. Guy looked faint.

"Where's Derek?" I asked, remembering he should be there.

"He left. He said he had shopping to do and errands to run."

"Really? Derek?" Derek was a steadfast Twins fan. He would never leave his invalid father-in-law or the Twins and the Cubs, mid-game. "He hates to shop." Bric pulled up to the curb. The paramedics unloaded their gear. The spoke briefly, then they came through the front door as Dierdre wheeled Grace through the back door.

"Jack!" Grace cried out in anguish. "Where's Jack? Where is he?"

Bric and the paramedics brushed past. "We can't go in right now," I said to her. "We need to stay here."

Family members gathered in the kitchen. Down the hallway, the bedroom door gaped open. The medical team worked feverishly over Jack's body. An arm reached out and swung the door closed. I knew I wouldn't be able to keep Grace in the kitchen much longer. Finally Bric and the EMTs emerged from the bedroom with Jack strapped to the gurney. Grace sped her power chair to the front foyer. Bric stepped out in front. "Would you like to say a word to him?" Grace inched her chair forward. She laid her hand softly on his chest and gazed at his lifeless face through the oxygen mask. Bric nodded and the attendants lifted the gurney over the threshold and wheeled him out the door. I stood beside her as she watched them go. Then I went back down the hallway to close the bedroom door.

A pool of blood soaked into the carpet in the middle of the room. Why the violent attempt at reviving him? His eyes were closed when I got there. Who closed them? Why did Derek leave? Who else was there? Family members roamed from room to room. The clamor of cell phone conversations merged with the clamor of questions in my head. Who took his ring? How did he die?

I drove Grace to the hospital emergency entrance. Quin approached, announcing solemnly that Jack was gone. She sat stunned and speechless as her children paraded slowly past him on the gurney. Acer sat staunchly at his head.

When we arrived back at the house, I slipped down the hallway to the bedroom. The door was open. The carpet was spotless. The hospital bed was gone. Who could have done that? They were all at the hospital. I turned to find Grace staring up at me, exhausted and in shock. I lead her into the bedroom, settled her into her bed and lay next to her as she cried herself to sleep. I dozed off. Then I sat straight up. The house was silent. Where did they all go?

The next morning was eerily quiet. Still stunned, Grace stared beyond the kitchen window at the gray morning sky. She didn't speak for a very long time. Then she suddenly turned. "I want to see him now." She looked back out the window. "Let's just go. No one is here. They won't even know we're gone."

"All right," I answered. "We'll go."

"Good," she said, flipping the switch on her power chair. She wheeled to the bedroom where she reached for his favorite suit, hanging in the closet next to hers. She touched her cheek to the sleeve of the blue shirt she ironed for him every Sunday before Mass. She opened a bureau drawer and handed me a silk striped tie. She reached into a bottom drawer and pulled out a plastic bag with shoe polish and a small oily rag. Then we sat together at the table, polishing his shoes just as she had done every Saturday night for over sixty years. This time would be the last. I heard my grandfather's voice. 'I want to see myself in that shine!'

Grace stood over her husband at the funeral home, gazing upon his face. She smoothed his hair back from his forehead and combed the fine white strands with the little black comb she had taken from his bathroom and stashed safely in her purse before we left the house. I stood far against the back wall behind her, close enough to catch her, should her knees buckle, but far enough away to allow her this moment with her beloved and her memories. Her solitude was soon interrupted.

"Dierdre is outside," the director whispered. "She's demanding to see her father."

"Later," I said. "Tell her she will have to wait. This moment is for Grace." I heard voices outside the door. I heard Dierdre storm out. I heard the tires of her car spraying gravel in the drive as she sped away. I knew I would not be forgiven. She was entitled to be with her father and I was no one.

Within minutes, Dierdre had mobilized the Riorden guild hotline. The sisters of the Riorden guild wielded unyielding authority and power over their spouses and by extension, the family. Grace once told a daughter-in-law that although Jack was the head of the family, she was the neck, and she could turn that head any way she wanted. Of course, Grace was speaking the truth. She had learned to balance Jack's egocentric obstinacy by faith, patience and sheer determination. Grace spoke of survival. Guild translation was that manipulation by feigned submission wielded control. Dierdre announced that there were instructions for the funeral. She produced tablet pages written in Jack's own hand, issuing commands underscored sometimes two and three times. *NINE PAUL BEARERS. NOT SIX. NINE. ALL MY SONS.* The sons were directed to remain standing throughout the funeral. They were forbidden to leave the casket at any time until it was at the grave. Altar boys were named. Readings were stipulated. Songs and soloists were assigned. Two funeral homes and two locations were contracted. Priests were named. Finally, his last order read, *NO ONE SHALL CHANGE THESE INSTRUCTIONS FOR ANY REASON!* I wondered how Dierdre was able to work so closely with her father without being seen by either Grace or me.

Grace would not remember Jack's death. She would not remember the long days of grief leading up to the funeral. She would not remember the memorials or the rosaries. She would not recall the sea of flowers or the endless procession of faces pressed up against hers. Grace would not remember that she was made to sit through the ordeal twice, in two separate communities, standing sadly, lovingly at the casket not once but twice, bidding her beloved mate farewell. Grace was invisible and alone. Jack was their chief. Now he was gone and the great family tree was uprooted. As they peered into the massive black hole, the vortex pulled them in and they plummeted. They were about to land on their mother's back.

Grace might easily have asked why her life was so difficult, but I never heard her complain. Her children, on the other hand, had much to say. Mary Caye remembered no electricity in the house. Crystal Ann remembered hauling water from the cistern. Dierdre and Lyssa described baking rolls and buns every day with desserts, cakes, cream puffs, doughnuts in great variety by scratch. Ursula remembered secondhand clothes collected from women in town. Ralph recalled overshoes filled with paper and coats tied with twine. Bric and Seth remembered chores in freezing or sweltering temperatures. Liam and Riley remembered pot loads of cattle, countless fence holes dug and fence posts pounded. Quin described building milk stations and milking cows each day at dawn and again at sunset. Ward talked of cutting hay along the railroad. Acer remembered pouring cement for the house and barn. Grace did not join in. She knew that winning often meant losing, standing meant risking a fall and ownership meant coveting more. This was her reality, but it was not her truth. Her truth rose from her spirit. She listened to her children and she knew their stories did not include her.

During one of the two rosaries for Jack at one of the two funeral homes, Mike McMullen touched Acer's elbow. "Do you remember me?" He grinned. Acer's eyes widened. He turned to the others. "We were Americal Division, the meat grinder."

Acer looked around the group. "We were just green farm boys, straight from the field, dropped smack in the middle of Hell."

Mike broke in. "When I was sent to forward fire base, Acer met me at the chopper." The two men stood gazing at each other but seeing a far distant time in a far distant place.

"So how did you two find each other?" Quin asked.

"Oh, that's a great story," Acer laughed. "I was deep in country, drenched from the monsoons and thinking I would never get out of there alive when I get a letter from Mom." He looked at Mike and they both laughed. "Dear Acer, the letter said. Mrs. McMillan's son, Mike, is coming to Vietnam. Please take care of him and bring him home safe. Love, Mom." Acer threw his head back laughed at the absurdity. The group joined in with quiet chuckles.

Acer's wife, Delilah, came forward. "I think that's the first time I have ever heard you speak of Vietnam. I have never heard your stories."

"There's nothing to tell," Acer shot back. "Life is war." The subject was closed. Acer left the group to greet a family coming through the door.

The next morning a cavalcade circled the drive of St. Jacob's Church as bells chimed. Grieving family members passed through the doors, one by one asserting his or her own presence. Acer and Maire stood together by the coffin. Acer hung his head and sobbed. "Talk to him, Ace," Maire offered. "Say what you want to say to him. Say it now."

Acer bent over his father. "I did everything you asked," he said. His voice broke.

The group gathered around the coffin. Acer took his place by his mother. Grace looked around the room and beckoned to me. I came forward and she whispered, "Stay by me." Then she was engulfed in a swirl of black suits and whisked away.

Liam's task was to read a scripture. I found him seated in a dark anteroom, staring into space. "Is it time?"

The priest spoke in honor of a man, who although he had never traveled more than three hundred miles in any direction from where he was born, controlled sixteen lives across the country and two continents. Then it was over. The priest handed me Jack's wedding band. I placed the ring on Grace's finger. She leaned forward and kissed my cheek.

"Thank you, Sweetheart," she whispered.

The procession exited the church. Grace gripped my hand. "I'm right here, Gram. I'm right here."

Bric and Seth stood by the curb next to the Suburban. There was no room for me.

The morning was a typical overcast March morning, with the promise of spring in the midst of a late snow shower. Soft flakes swirled through the crisp air. Lingering snow banks fringed dirty patches of ice as the caravan of Escalades, Navigators, Excursions, EXs, X5s and assorted hybrids crept south on a long stretch of county highway. At a point where two county roads met, an officer stood in salute. Maire gazed out the windshield of her Ford Focus. There was the farm. Memories flooded back. Two trees towered over the roof of the farmhouse. "My God!" she exclaimed. "I knew they would make it!"

The motorcade slowed and the hearse pulled to a stop near an enclosed tent. The red Explorer broke ranks and pulled ahead, front and center. It backed into a space near the hearse. Bric and Seth, collars up, soft woolen scarves snug about their throats, their dark curls tousled by gusts of morning wind, circled around back and swung the door open. Aiden and Ralph took hold of Grace's power chair, lifting their mother easily and effortlessly. The four set the chair firmly on the cold ground where Ward, Riley and Liam joined them. Slowly Grace crossed the frozen grass, her makeup impeccable, her jewelry refined, her face framed by the wide brim of a velvet hat. A soft net covered her eyes. A single small feather, ironically whimsical in the face of grief, flicked in the wind from the rim of her hat. I watched her closely. She stared blindly. She appeared dazed, detached, drained. She looked drugged. I scanned the crowd. She was eerily alone in the middle of a cold, forbidding circle.

The priest offered a eulogy and prayers. I saw an image of my grandfather's fist inches from my grandmother's face. The priest intoned a litany. The crowd responded. I heard her hushed voice through the dark night warning him that I was approaching from the lower level. I protected her from him while she protected him from me. My heart ached.

Aunt Maire stood at my side. What Maire knew of me she summarily dismissed. What she knew of my mother she didn't say. Now she stood beside me. On cue, flowers and handfuls of dirt from a bucket labeled *DIRT FROM THE FARM* were thrown onto and around the casket. The family cluster disbanded and the caravan snaked slowly back to the church.

Maire steered into a parking place just ahead of me. I sat with my hands resting on the steering wheel as family members walked past me, greeting each other in jovial familiarity. Maire stood watching me. As I stepped out of the car, voices quieted and backs turned. The sound of my boots crunching on the frozen gravel echoed through the courtyard.

Maire curled her arm around my waist. "They grope in darkness with no light. He makes them stagger like drunkards. John 12 tells us that Jesus has come into the world as a light, so that no one who believes should stay in darkness." I heard but couldn't focus. "Jesus told them. Walk while you have the light, before darkness overtakes you. The man who walks in the dark does not know where he is going." She paused in the doorway. "Speaking of light and dark, why is it they all look like Ford Agency models? Ah, I see." She pointed to a professional photographer working the room. She froze. "Oh, oh!"

I looked up to see an imposing figure lurching headlong at us. It was my uncle Aiden. He was just one angry man, but his fury unleashed a legion of fiery demons that filled the air and sucked the oxygen out of the room. Those demons were familiar to me. Wherever the Riordens went, they were there. I stumbled backward. "Never step back." Maire's hand held its position on the small of my back. "Look with soft eyes at your enemy. See the place where tides and seasons and all places of the earth become one. That is the center of the soul." We were a morbid trio. I stood nearly five foot seven in heels. She stood less than five feet in her sensible Mary Janes. He towered over both of us, his nostrils flaring, his strong shoulders rigid and tense.

Then as swift as a light breeze, as light as a morning shadow, my mother passed in front of me. She moved without sound to stand squarely in front of Aiden. She smelled of agarwood incense. Her hair fell in unruly waves to her shoulders. Her trench coat hung loosely about her tall, slender frame. She raised one gloved hand to his barrel chest. The other raised gently to his fist, clenched in rage. She stayed his fury with unyielding calm. Time stood still.

He suddenly shook himself free of her spell. "He's controlling me from the grave!" he wailed. Then he stalked away.

She turned to me. Her eyes were the endless blue of a summer sky. I breathed her in. "Mom!" She glided from the church hall into the brisk air. I quickly followed. Cold March sleet stung my face.

"I can't stay," she said.

"No, please. Stay with me."

"This is as much as I can do, now." She sighed, backing away. I wanted desperately to memorize every inch of her. "There is something you will need in that house."

"The house? You were there?"

She winked. "I was there." She looked over my shoulder. I turned to follow her eyes. Acer and Quin were approaching. When I looked back, she was gone. A man was watching me from the curb, one hand resting easily on the roof of his BMW, the other on the steering wheel. 'I know you,' I thought. He nodded in recognition.

"Who is that guy?" Maire asked. "He asked me to give this to you." She handed me a note.

"Maire, my mother was here."

She put her arm around my shoulder. "Your mother was fearless." Her eyes followed the BMW disappearing down the street. "That is uncharacteristic. Every Riorden fears something. It's why they do what they do." She turned to face me. "The important thing is that you know she was here. Someday, all will be clear. All this darkness will end."

"Maire," I shuddered. What if there is no light at the end? What if the tunnel is all there is?"

She shifted her attention, changing focus as easily as she changed her shoes as she stared at Quin and Acer. Crystal Ann, Dierdre, Ralph, Bric, Seth and Lyssa joined them. "There it is," Maire stated emphatically. "They're planning Mom's death." I shuddered as Aiden joined them. "Don't worry about him," Maire said. "His tirade had nothing to do with you."

"Huh?"

"He was just trying to dump his negative energy." She sized me up. "You look like a good dumping ground."

"I'm surprised a religious zealot like yourself would be interested in metaphysics."

"Hey!" she protested. "It's in the bible. Look it up!" She lit a cigarette and stared at the band of siblings. "What's more blinding than the break of dawn? What is the pleasure that yields no pain? What rights nothing that is wrong? What consumes what it abstains? What measures a man's girth but only on earth? What exalts as often as it shames? What fury wears the mask of mirth while letting go to lay its claim?"

"What is that?" I asked, disconcerted.

"It's a riddle with seven clues. Dad said we were too stupid to figure it out." She shrugged. "I never did, but I have a feeling that the answer would tell us what Acer is up to." She headed across the parking lot. "Let's get out of here. I could use some real coffee."

In the days and weeks that followed, Grace slept through most of every day. Grief enjoyed its stay. Jack was gone and with him went all she knew of herself. She cried out to him in the night. He spoke to her in a voice only she could hear. "All right, all right, I will," she whispered. "Don't worry. It will be all right. I'll be there soon." I held her hand when she reached out in her sleep. I stroked her temples when she woke, suddenly alone. Every morning I opened the curtains to show her the bright, beautiful day outside her window, praying she would see it.

Then the phone rang. One of my professors walked through Big Box on Good Friday, headed for the plumbing section. He turned to his wife, clutched his chest and crumpled to the floor. As he lay dying in the aisle of Big Box between the tile and the fixtures, his wife tried in vain to find someone to assist her in a store that covers a quarter acre and asks you to serve yourself. He was an easy man to love. The world was a better place while he was in it. Suddenly he was gone.

I entered a cold stone building, passing through a long white corridor into a crowded gathering. "I am the mother-in-law," a woman said, extending her hand. "You were a friend? A coworker? A student? I'm sorry for your loss. You must have been close." I wondered at her ability to reach beyond her own grief to comfort strangers.

My uncle Seth stood at my side. He shook my hand. He looked embarrassed. His wife, Kristin, joined us. "Seth, I'm ready to leave," she ordered.

"I'm just here for Kristin," he shrugged, and quickly followed her out of the room.

"Odd," I thought. "Why so distant?" A chill ran through my body. The room spun around me. Trembling, I quickly retraced my steps down the white corridor, down the white side stairs into the night. There was my car, across the lot. "You can make it," I told myself. "There is the door. Here are the keys." I found the wheel. I found the seat. I sat, shaking, gripping the wheel. It felt like the universe was crashing in waves, splitting heaven's doors wide open, sucking in souls. Images flew through my brain, slicing at my heart. There was Grace's brother Colin, Grandpa Jack, my professor and friend, a young physician from the community who suddenly died in his sleep, someone in the news found in a field, a well-known politician. "Not my Gram!" I gripped the steering wheel and stared through the windshield to the gray sky. "God, You cannot have my grandmother. Not yet!"

The braking of the bus interrupted my thoughts. The driver swung the doors open to board passengers. A strikingly beautiful Native American woman stepped on. Her silken hair shone with a blue luster. She stopped next to my seat. "May I sit here?"

"Sure." I slid my leg off the aisle seat.

"I'm Tiffany." She bent over to arrange her bags under her feet.

"I'm Elle."

She turned deep hazel brown eyes to me and then looked away, folding her hands in her lap. Then she looked at me again. "Running away or running to?"

"Excuse me?"

"Everyone I know is either running away or running to. Which are you?"

"Neither. Maybe both." I smiled. "That's a very good question."

"I know. I ask myself that question every day now." She unzipped the wallet in her lap and pulled out a small photo.

"She's gorgeous," I said. "Her spirit seems to be speaking."

"Mmmm," she nodded. "She has a lot to say." She cradled the photo reverently. "Not long ago, my husband died suddenly, unexpectedly." She traced the face in the photo, lost in thought. "It was suicide. I was devastated. When I buried him, I buried myself in grief. One day I opened my eyes I saw her staring back at me." I searched the soulful eyes of the little girl there. "I decided that I had better come to life. I had someone else to take care of."

"You must be very brave."

"Yes," she answered, glancing at me and then back at the photo. "Some days I carry her. Some days she carries me."

"Where is she now?" I asked.

"Right here." She held the photo to her chest. "I am that little girl. She is the reason I must survive. I must take care of her."

Yoki reached across the aisle and laid his weathered hand on her sleeve. "There is a kind of love that makes us want to be better than we are." She moved to the seat beside him. I reached for my earphones.

'Inner child,' I thought. Did I have one?

One morning a Cardinal appeared on the sill outside Grace's bedroom window. "Look!" she exclaimed. "Do you see?" The bird appeared every day, scratching on the sill. She watched, mesmerized. When it disappeared, she sat quietly, searching the snow-packed rooftops, willing it to return. "Is it there in the branches? No. That's not it. That's a finch. Do you see it yet? There it goes. Quick! Help me." She pushed the toggle on the power chair and sped ahead of me, catching the doorsill and chipping off a sliver of oak in her hurry to follow the bird to its next perch. She circled the wide living room, peering through the length of windows. She wheeled around and sped past me, through the foyer into the kitchen. There she stopped abruptly. "Shhhhh! There it is." The red bird perched outside the kitchen windows, just beyond the table. There was the reason the bird perched there. The Cardinal had a mate. They had built a nest in the rose trellis. We pushed aside the kitchen curtains and moved the table toward the window. "Quick! Get the camera. Are the batteries charged?" I dashed around the room as she sat poised and still, willing the bird to stay. We giggled excitedly like schoolgirls, watching and waiting and clicking and capturing every movement of the little miracle that brought such unexpected joy to my grandmother's heart.

Grace woke each morning a little earlier, to sit at the breakfast table and wait to catch a glimpse of the new little family. Whenever her own sad family telephoned, she quickly changed the subject to events of the day in the life of the red bird. The red bird sang a song that only she heard; a song that drew her over the threshold from the kitchen to the garage and from the garage to her front step. From the front step, she moved to the bird feeder. She filled the bird feeder every day and returned to the window to wait. The red bird's song had lifted my grandmother from the desolate dark crevice into which she had slipped and had set her back on her path.

News came that Grace's granddaughter Abigale, three or four months pregnant, lost the child. Grace was sympathetic but there were eggs in the nest. Grace was guarding her spirit as closely as the Cardinal was guarding that nest.

"Do you think you might like to write a note to Abigail?" I asked.

"Yes, I must do that. The eggs are hatching. Look at their little beaks. Where's the mother? Oh, there she is in the grass. She's getting a bit of food."

Easter was just weeks away. Every Saturday morning Star Mart's flower delivery truck stopped in front of the house. Ward had placed a standing order for a bright, cheery bouquet of flowers to be delivered every Saturday morning. Grace raced her chair to the door to meet the familiar face of the delivery driver. She reached out and nestled the flowers in her lap, smiling broadly. It occurred to me that Grace met most people with a smile.

Liam's wife, Elise, stood in the foyer admiring the blooms Grace proudly displayed. "Wow! Why didn't I think of that? I missed that opportunity entirely. Now I'll have to think of something else!" Grace held her hand and they giggled together.

Riley called daily. He described the Texas heat and the bumper to bumper traffic. He laughed out loud at her stories of squirrels playing on the rooftops. Riley ended each call with the cheerful reminder. "Be sure to get your hugs today. Everybody needs at least twelve hugs a day. I love you, Mom."

"I love you so much," Grace answered.

"I love you more," Riley responded.

"Oh, you!" Grace giggled.

March rolled into April. Soon it would be Easter. We ventured into Talbots to buy a suit. Grace ran her fingers across the fabrics, deliberating over the right

colors and the right accessories. We strolled through
the mall to Macy's where Maire and Grace scrutinized
jewelry and pondered lip colors. The two of them
tried hat after hat until they found one with just the
right brim. "My husband won't be with me," Grace
told the attentive sales associates. "He died this year.
He always bought me an Easter suit," she added wistfully. "We always picked it out together."

On the first Saturday morning in April, the familiar sound of a motor purred in the back yard. Grace
propelled her power chair into motion. She stopped
at the bay windows overlooking the deck and the
yard below. She waited patiently until the handsome young man riding the mower glanced up. She
waved and knocked on the window. He waved back
and grinned. She swiveled the power chair in a half
circle and headed toward the door. "Hurry, hurry.
He's coming this way. Hand me that plate of cookies
and that banana." Down the ramp she sped, the plate
of cookies and the banana in her lap, past the Cadillac and Ford 4x4 and out through the open overhead
garage door to meet him on the step.

"Slow down, Gram!" I called. "He'll wait."

Liam stepped sideways to dodge the wheels of the
power chair. "Watch out. That thing will run over
small children," he laughed. He engulfed her in his
warm embrace, kissing her. "Here I am, your faithful
gardener. Happy Mother's Day, Mom."

"What? It's not Mother's Day!" She shook her
head in feigned surprise.

"Every day is Mother's Day, Mom," he replied
with a kiss.

She laughed out loud and kissed him again, holding his hand tightly in hers. "Oh, you!" Then she paused, her face wrinkling into curious concern. "I don't think I have any money. How can I pay you?"

"Mom, Dad always handed me a dollar when I mowed for him. You can give me...hmmm." He paused, smiling into her face until at last she couldn't resist and smiled back. "You can give me a hug and a cookie."

"And a banana!" She threw her hands up and laughed. One of Grace's greatest strengths was her ability to laugh. I watched the two of them, basking in the warmth of this private moment. 'If God were keeping a balance sheet,' I thought, 'this snapshot would clearly measure this son's worth.'

Maire came on Good Friday to wash and style her hair, bringing a bottle of Estee Lauder's Beautiful, and a glittering bracelet. Saturday morning was bright and clear. Maire suggested we go to Royal Court to brunch. Grace glanced at the clock.

"What's wrong?"

"Star Mart hasn't brought my flowers yet."

"Oh," Maire laughed. "We'll wait, then. We've got all the time in the world."

"That's right," Grace smiled and adjusted her hat in the mirror.

Royal Court was packed but our table was ready. The waiter removed a chair and we rolled Grace's chair up to the edge. Maire placed several brightly ribboned packages on the table. Grace giggled with anticipation as she carefully unwrapped each one. Maire held up a bag tied at the handles with a bright ribbon. Grace reached in and pulled out a wooden plaque and began to read. "Jesus Christ Is Lord and Savior."

Maire leaned across the table. "Your God is God, Mom."

Grace smiled. "I know." Maire laughed.

A woman stopped at the table. She was elegant in a light silk jacket over a tunic dress. Her hat was wrapped in silk and organza. Her nails were manicured. Her hands were soft and supple.

"I love your hat," she said, smiling broadly.

Grace looked up and beamed. "Yours is lovely, too."

"People don't appreciate hats anymore."

"That's true," Grace answered shyly. This was Grace's first social contact. She had no idea what to say next.

"I'm Grace." The woman leaned forward. "My friends call me Gracie."

"Oh, my goodness!" Grace reached for her hand. "My name is Grace."

Gracie reached down and grasped Grace's hand gently. "How delightful! We have the same name!" She laughed. "I love your suit. What a beautiful ring. Are you going to Easter Vigil? We are."

"Are you Catholic?" Grace asked, no longer shy. "So am I. Are you from around here?" The two women chatted and laughed like close friends. Both were named Grace. Both had large families. Both were Catholic. Each had recently lost her husband. Both modeled stylish hats and stunning diamonds on manicured hands, poised in elegant old-world demeanor. Two strangers with similar joyful souls leading parallel lives in very separate universes had found each other. One was bold, victorious, gregarious. One was shy, lonely, timid.

"My family is waiting for me," Gracie said wistfully. "I must leave now, but I would like to give you something."

"Give me something? Why?"

"This is a special day." Gracie reached into her bag and handed her a glistening emerald green rosary.

"Oh! For me?" Grace turned it over and over in her fingers. She handed it back to Gracie. "I can't take your rosary."

Gracie took Grace's hand in her own and closed her fingers around the rosary. "It's from Ireland. I had it blessed there. Please keep it and pray for me. She glanced at the table behind her. Pray for my son."

"Your son?" Grace looked around. "Is he sick?"

Gracie pointed to the table toward the back of the room. "That's my son and his wife and child." A young woman and man and infant were seated at the back table. The young man struggled to stay steady in his seat.

"Was he in an accident?" Maire asked.

Gracie's eyes filled with tears. "This world so easily discards its wounded."

Grace squeezed the rosary and reached for Gracie. Gracie bent down and kissed her cheek. "I'll pray for you every night," Grace whispered."

"And for my son?" Gracie entreated.

"And for your son," Grace assured her.

"I know you will." Gracie stood back, clasped her hands and smiled. "It's like looking into a mirror."

Gracie maneuvered her son's wheelchair around the tables toward the exit. Then she stopped. "We have devoted our lives to caring for others, Grace. It's important now to find our own voices. Take care of yourself." She waved and disappeared out the door.

Grace looked down at the rosary in her hand. "I have a rosary from Ireland. It's just like Jack's." She reached across the table and whispered, wide-eyed. "And I have a new friend." She smiled, her eyes twinkling. Then she whispered, "She's a black woman! What would Jack have said to that?" She tucked the rosary carefully inside her tiny bejeweled bag. "She's Catholic." She looked up in wonder. "Do you think she's Irish?" Maire stifled a laugh. I felt a weight begin to lift. I allowed myself to take a breath.

Easter was bright and joyful. Grace hovered in the kitchen as her daughters prepared the Easter meal. She inspected the dining room as her granddaughters set the table with care. Grace's granddaughter, Breanne brought her mother-in-law, Kaaren, to the house after Mass. Kaaren, diagnosed with Alzheimer's, had a soft, sweet smile. Grace attended to her that morning as if she were Ms. Cardinal attending the nest. She fussed over Kaaren and took her to the private viewing spot at the window. New life. How magnificent.

On Mother's Day, Grace hosted a garden party. The grandchildren planted flowers around the yard and hung baskets on the deck. Grace chose a wide straw hat for the occasion. "Sprinkle the water in first," Grace instructed. "The water has to be in the bottom of the hole. No, wait. Mix in the Miracle Gro. Now tamp the dirt down. Make a little ditch around the plant. Water it again." Each child followed her instructions obediently, hugging and laughing and standing back to hear her praise. "Good. Very good!

That's right. That's good." Crystal Ann arrived with Grace's sister, Jacelyn. Grace looked up at them and squinted, tilting her head comically. "When did you two start wearing hats like me?"

With June came thoughts of Father's Day. "What can we do to honor Jack?" Grace asked.

"How about a movie?" I suggested. "You and I could make a movie with all your family pictures and Grandpa's favorite music. Would you like that?"

She beamed. "We can give one to each family," she exclaimed. She sat patiently, day after day, at the kitchen table, sorting photos. She waited at my elbow, watching in amazement as the images came to life on the screen. She took each photo from the scanner, backed her power chair out of the small office, turned it deftly around in the hallway and sped back through the kitchen to put it right back into the album. She was meticulous and tireless in her efforts. This movie was the story of her life. She poured all her energy into it. She chose the music carefully. She liked Guy Lombardo, but she knew Jack would like Bing Crosby or the Rovers. She tapped her fingers lightly and waved her hands to the beat as images danced across the screen. "Is this really mine to give?"

"Absolutely, Gram."

"They will love this!" she announced. "When can we give it to them?"

"Soon. You sign the cards and we'll mail them out for Fathers' Day."

"Then get me a tablet. I have to practice signing my name." The days passed quickly. She had peered through the darkness and fallen. The Cardinal caught and lifted her. She was finding a balance between the dark of the past and the light of hope.

The movie was finished. "Now," I said, "we have to burn the DVD."

"Burn it? No, don't burn it. It's good! We didn't make a mistake!"

I laughed. "It's OK. I'm not going to destroy it. When I say burn, I copy the movie to a disc. It's just what it's called."

"Oh." She thought about that, then shrugged and smiled. "OK, then."

Grace popped the DVD into the player before breakfast and let it run up to the place where the last two songs started to play. When she heard the last two songs she knew the funeral scene was next. "That's too sad," she said. "We won't watch that. Let's go back to the beginning." As each frame passed on the screen, she recited the names of children and grandchildren, occasionally stopping to exclaim, "There's Jack. Look, how he's always smiling. He was such a happy man. There was never a cross word between us."

Lyssa sent her The Golden Girls and I Love Lucy, but the only video she watched was her own. The week before Father's Day, she signed cards to each of her children and grandchildren. Corner Drug had a corner post office where she could easily roll in and park while we personally addressed each small bubble-wrapped package containing the movie and waited in line. When it was our turn at the counter, she looked up from her wheelchair. "I'm sending Father's Day movies."

"Oh?" The clerk began weighing and stamping each package.

"I made this movie." Grace stretched forward and placed her small hand on the counter above her.

"Oh, really?" The clerk leaned over the counter and looked down to where she sat in her chair. "You must be very talented. I don't even know how to use a computer." Grace beamed. The clerk stacked up the pile of packages. "You must have a big family." Grace straightened proudly.

"I had sixteen children."

"Oh, my! The clerk smiled at her. "I think it is they who should be giving you a present."

In the days that followed Grace waited by the phone and watched the mail for a response from her children. Liam's wife, Elise, phoned to say that she and her daughter, Lauren, had spent the entire evening watching it completely through, from beginning to end. "It was wonderful!" Elise declared. Grace was pleased to hear it. Another week passed.

"Why isn't anyone else calling?" She opened her red phone book and began dialing to ask her children if they had watched her movie.

"It's just too sad, Mama. I just can't," Mary Caye replied.

"That's strange." She said as she hung up the phone. "If I can watch it, why can't she?"

Meanwhile, Grace's sister, Blair, moved into a nursing home. Now she was becoming increasingly agitated and angry. "I want to see Blair." Grace announced.

"It's an hour drive," I cautioned.

She dismissed that with a tilt of her chin and a toss of her hair. "I have a comfortable car and a good driver." She smiled. "It'll be fine."

The nursing home stood bright and visible, nestled into a bank of trees. Grace held a freshly frosted cake protectively in her lap as we rolled past residents in wheel chairs in the corridor and residents seated at tables. Blair sat at a table by the window with their sister, Jacelyn. Grace proudly displayed the cake with the frothy pink boiled frosting as she rolled up next to Blair's chair and leaned over to kiss her. Blair brushed her away.

"What's wrong with your hair?"

Grace pulled back, hurt and surprised.

"Hello, Blair," I said, positioning Grace's chair at the table.

"What an effort you made to be here, Elle," Blair said, glaring at Grace.

"The effort was all Gram's," I offered. "She baked this angel food cake just for you and look, it's her special boiled frosting."

Blair turned on Grace. "You should comb your hair. Didn't you bring a comb? You used to be careful about your grooming."

Grace's sister, Jacelyn turned away to the next table to chat with someone there.

"I'm going to my room," Blair announced.

"We'd better leave, then," Grace responded sadly. "Don't you want a piece of your cake, Blair?" I quickly cut into the cake's perfectly frosted peaks and scooped a curl of ice cream on each dish. Grace tapped Blair's dish with her fork. "Try a bite. It's very good. You'll like it. Try a little bite."

Blair pushed her hand away and snapped, "No. I don't want cake."

Grace leaned forward and gave her a kiss and a light pat on her hand. "I love you, Blair."

"Your son was here," Blair blurted out. "I spent a week in the geriatric psych ward because of him! As if this place isn't bad enough!"

"My son?" Grace repeated incredulous. "Which son?"

"Acer! I suppose he smells money!"

"Oh, no!" Grace shook her head earnestly.

"Oh, yes!" interrupted Blair. "You watch! He'll do the same thing to you!"

Grace gripped my sleeve. I pulled her wheelchair back and away from the table, wheeling down the corridor and through the front doors, back into the sunlight. I transferred her into the car and drove away.

"What was that about?" she sighed. "Why was Jacelyn there? What's going on?" She checked her appearance in the mirror and straightened her hat. "What's wrong with my hair?"

"Nothing, Gram. It's perfect. Forget them. There's a Dairy Queen. Want to stop?"

She brightened. "We should have kept the cake."

June turned to July. "The house is quiet," Grace complained. "Let's go out. Let's do something."

"OK. What shall we do?"

"I don't know." She shrugged.

"Well, then, let's drive through the neighborhood and see what we see." She smiled at the idea of a new adventure. I backed out the drive and we drove slowly through the residential area. Down the street to the left, was a staged tea party. A large tapestry hung in the open garage doorway. An oversized ornamental rug lay in the drive. Two women sat at a table, chatting and laughing. I parked the car and walked around to Grace's side. The two women walked over to meet her.

"I'm Grace Riorden." Grace held out her hand.

"Oh, my goodness," one of them exclaimed. "We walk past your house every morning. How do you keep your roses so beautiful?"

"You have to water them early in the morning," Grace answered shyly. "Roses and tomatoes like a drink every morning." I stood back. Grace had lived here for years and had never met these two.

I paid for the table and tea set. "I have no way to get these to her house. Do you suppose someone might help me with that?"

"My husband will bring it," one of them offered.

"Really?"

"For Grace? No question."

Then the second woman joined us. "We're done for the day. Take these pink goblets. Here, take this pitcher and this cookie jar. They'll make a perfect set."

Grace was radiant as we drove back to the house, her soft hands guarding her treasures. In the kitchen, she unwrapped and carefully polished each of the goblets and the cookie jar. Then she waited patiently at the kitchen table by the window, watching the street. Within the hour, a pickup pulled into the drive. She powered her chair down the ramp to meet them. The two men laughed as they jumped down from the truck to hug her as if they were her own sons. Grace was easy to like. People were drawn to her. How could they have known that she was finally doing things other women had taken for granted their entire lives?

"Where do you want your table?"

"In here. Right in here." She turned the chair around and sped back up the ramp, through the kitchen and into the sunroom. "Here. Right here." She stopped before the bay windows overlooking the deck, dressed in glorious blooming colors.

Maire arrived with a large shopping bag. "Ma, you said you wanted something to do with your time. I thought you might like to paint."

"Paint?"

"Yes, it's easy. Look." She took out a large case full of brushes and colors in little tins and unfolded an easel. Maire looked around the room. "We need a place to set up." Then she saw the table in the sunroom. "Where did that come from?" Grace smiled and drove her chair ahead.

"I bought it," she beamed.

"Good shopping, Ma!" Maire positioned the easel by the window to capture the light. "Try it."

Grace hesitated and shook her head. "I don't know how."

"Oh, nobody knows how. It just happens." She handed her a brush. "Load up that brush with your favorite color." Grace looked up at Maire and back down at the brush. She touched the brush tip to the bright orange tin. Then she pushed it, twirled it and lifted it up onto the paper on the easel. She swirled it into a circle and back into the paint and again circled it onto the paper. "You made an orange." Maire clapped her hands. Grace smiled. "You can paint whenever you like, every day if you like. We'll frame your pictures. This will be your studio, your very own private sanctuary."

Caireann's wedding was 30 days away. The house bustled with activity. Dresses had to be fitted, food had to be ordered, flowers and cake had to be tasted, landscaping had to be done. Wedding pictures, which would be taken in the back yard and from the upper deck, had to be staged. An entourage of bridesmaids, cousins, classmates and family filled the house past midnight and on into morning. Grace was exhausted. Dierdre was relentless. "No one ever slept in the Riorden house", she exclaimed.

I scheduled water therapy at St. Christopher's Wellness Center. She sat on the steps of the hot tub with her sore knee in the swirling foam, marveling at the 'big, fat women' that stepped over the side and slipped into the bubbles stark naked. "I guess you can wear any kind of suit in here," she scoffed, crinkling her nose. She floated in my arms on a long slender floating device that everyone called the noodle. "I don't like noodles! Too fattening!" She brushed it away and laughed. She renamed it the floater and steadied herself as she peddled in the water. Her therapist, Jalen, sang softly into her ear as they rounded the pool and counted down her exercises. She massaged her neck and listened patiently to Grace's stories. "I'm going to swim and I'm going to dance at this wedding," she declared resolutely.

Bric hired a contractor to install grab bars in Grace's bathroom. The installation of grab bars turned into an order for custom-made cabinets and a drive-in shower. Negotiations between Bric and Doreen and the contractor over choices of colors and fixtures and tile amplified the wedding chaos. Large plastic sheets covered the doorway between Grace's bedroom and her bathroom. Her toiletries were moved to a bathroom on the opposite side of the house in the laundry room, which was down a long hallway, past the living room and the office, across the large kitchen, around the corner and through the sunroom. Getting across the house and slowly inching her power chair past the narrowly set washer and dryer to the small toilet space was a chore that was not often well executed. There were times when she called to me through the door to bring her clean underwear. Lyssa saw the soiled underwear in the laundry room and threw out all Grace's soft, lacy underpants, filling her drawers with heavy paper Depends. I found Grace in tears in her bathroom, tearing the heavy paper garments to shreds. "Look what she has left me to wear. Look! I won't wear these ugly things. No one asked me! I've never worn these in my life!" She threw a Depends to the floor. "I won't wear these!"

"OK, Gram." I grabbed a trash bag. "Let's get rid of them!" We cleared out the drawers and carried the bags to the garage. Grace gave a mighty heave and a big black bag sailed across the drive to land next to the garbage bin. Then she sniffed in disdain, turned her chair around and waited by the car.

Once inside the fragrant isles of Macy's, I summoned a sales clerk who fussed and tucked and whispered and giggled as Grace carefully selected new underwear to refill her lingerie drawers. Revitalized, we returned to Scanlon Circle.

Doreen stood waiting in Grace's bedroom next to a commode. "I won't have it," Grace scolded. "It's there in plain sight of everyone, including those workers finishing the bathroom! I am not an invalid!"

Doreen was unmoved. "I had two aunts that used ones just like this."

The next Saturday Bric and Lyssa arrived together in a show of unity. Lyssa announced they would drive her to the doctor for an examination to determine the cause of her incontinence.

"I am not incontinent!" Grace shouted. "You've taken away my bathroom!"

Lyssa rebuked her. "Mom, what's wrong with you? This house has many bathrooms!"

Grace shot her a withering look. "They are either too small for my chair, in the laundry room, under construction or downstairs. Don't speak to me like that. And I will not have a male doctor probing me. I will not go."

"Mom, you've had sixteen children," Bric scoffed. "You've never before complained about a male doctor."

"You be quiet." She glared at him. "That was different. I'm not going."

"You don't have to go to a male doctor, Gram," I said. "There are plenty of fine female doctors in the city."

Bric grabbed my elbow, pulling me aside. "Stay out of this," he seethed. "You do not understand the politics of medicine."

"This is your mother!" I spit back at him. "She is fragile. She is grieving. You've got her home torn up from one end to the other. Are you trying to push her over the edge?" He glared at me. Lyssa crossed the room and put the power chair in motion, leading Grace out the door and to the car. I stood at the kitchen window shaking with anger. Who were these people? I darted to the lower level and grabbed my running shoes from the closet. My mother's words came back to me. 'There is something you will need in that house.' I walked from room to room. What was it?

As I loped through the quiet streets, my mother's image flashed before me. She looked like me, or rather I looked like her. 'If she was fearless,' I wondered, 'why had she bolted when she saw Acer and Quin? The man in the BMW seemed protective. He left me a note. There was so much going on, I didn't even read it. Where did I put it?' I remembered Aiden's tirade. 'Why was he so angry? Why did he come at me?' I saw Grandpa Jack's face. 'How did he die?' There was so much I didn't know, but there was one thing I did know. When the Riordens buried the truth, it stayed buried. An hour later I was back at the house but Bric and Lyssa had not returned.

I dialed Bric's cell. Lyssa answered. "Gram has water therapy in fifteen minutes. Are you on your way back?"

"She's not going to water therapy today. We're taking her to lunch."

"Water therapy is the one thing Gram enjoys without pain. Don't take that away from her."

They returned late in the afternoon. Lyssa parked Grace's power chair in the middle of the kitchen and left without a word. I transferred her to a soft leather recliner in the sunroom, lit the fireplace and sat next to her.

"Bric stood there while a man put his hand up inside me," she sobbed. "It felt like a knife! I couldn't make him stop!" I held her tight and rocked her gently in my arms. She looked up at me. "We didn't even go to lunch!"

"Where did you go?"

"We met Crystal Ann instead."

"Shall I make a sandwich?" She was already asleep in my arms. I wrapped her in a soft shawl and held her close as contractors, electricians and plumbers passed by the sunroom in silence, displaying the respect and courtesy her children would not.

"Don't worry, Gram," I whispered. "It will never happen again."

There were now fifteen days to the wedding. Grace and I shopped for a suit. Grace chose a lavender Ralph Lauren silk jacket with matching shell and white silk pants. She bought a lavender hat with lavender and white ribbons and shoes of soft pink leather. We stopped at the bead shop. The owner patiently strung pearls and listened to Grace's stories of weddings past and weddings to come. Grace left the store wearing the pearls. She announced that she would definitely come back and make gifts for her granddaughters. A new world was opening before her of social conversation and shop attendants that called her by name and new achievements, a world of strangers kinder to her than her own children.

Maire stopped by early Friday morning to wash and style her hair. When she was settled under the dryer, I touched Maire's elbow and led her to the sunroom. The little drop-leaf art table was pushed back against the wall next to the fireplace. The four petit point chairs were piled on top of the table. The easel and the paints were stacked into the rungs of the chairs.

Front and center in the sunroom was a large leather couch, positioned in front of the large television.

"Hey! What's going on here?" Maire was instantly in motion. She pushed the couch back to the windows and brought the table and chairs back to the window. She set the easel back into place by the window and placed the paints and paper back onto the table.

"Come back tomorrow morning and Lyssa will have this all pushed back against the wall again," I said.

"Why?"

"Who's going to stop her? This is a flop place for her children now to play video games and stay out of her way. When Grandpa died, this ceased to be Gram's house."

Caireann asked that we make a video for her wedding reception. Each morning and after lunch before her nap, Grace drove her power chair into the office to sit at my side, laughing at the songs and the clips. "Wasn't Jack wonderful? He was always smiling."

Seven days before the wedding Dierdre arrived to edit the video. Caireann protested. "No, Mom, it's done. We don't want to change a thing. Gram made this." Dierdre stomped out of the house, fuming.

Lyssa arrived with shopping bags, hanging sparkling outfits by the hanger hooks from the tops of doorways. The sitting room looked like a showroom. She announced that Grace would wear one. "Never mind that outfit you bought," she proclaimed. "You are the queen. You should be the center of attention." She rummaged in the back of the closet and pulled out heavy black leather lace-up shoes. The family descended. Wedding mania set in. The deck filled with flowers. The tent stood in place. Each remaining task, strategically executed, brought a higher level of tension to the house.

Finally, sometime during the afternoon before the wedding, just hours before the rehearsal luau, the disc jockey arrived to pick up the video. I pushed the button to eject it. There was no disc. I questioned everyone in the house. Lyssa's youngest daughter, Brianne, clicked off the blow dryer and replied, "Mom and Aunt Dierdre took it to edit and make copies."

"Why would they do that?"

Lyssa's eldest daughter, Abbey, skillfully wielding a curling iron, responded. "Aunt Dierdre is giving them as gifts."

Dierdre arrived, handing a copy of the video to the DJ. Undeterred, I followed her. "Why would you do that? It was Gram's gift to Caireann. Why didn't you ask me to make copies for you?"

She spun around in contempt. "This has nothing to do with you."

Lyssa arrived. She took Grace into the bedroom and locked the door. When they emerged, Grace was wearing the silk lavender. They quickly ushered her to the car and drove away. Bewildered, I stayed behind. They returned with Grace and the rest of the family about midnight in a gust of giddy laughter. Raucous chatter continued for hours. At 2:00 a.m. I asked Dierdre to move the party to the lower level so Grace could sleep. Dierdre jumped to her feet and defiantly ordered everyone to clear out.

"Dierdre," I reasoned, "I didn't ask you to leave. I only asked you to take the conversation downstairs."

But Dierdre didn't answer. Within minutes she had ushered everyone out and the house was again eerily quiet.

The next morning Lyssa arrived to again whisk Grace into the bedroom and lock the door. Grace reemerged looking regal in a sparkly jacket, black silk skirt and of course, wearing the heavy black leather lace-up shoes. This time, Grace refused to leave the house without me. Lyssa paced angrily while she waited for me to join them for a silent drive to the church. Dierdre, perky and stern, escorted Grace majestically to the front pew, clasping her mother close in an iron grip.

At the reception, while the video played on a giant screen, Liam asked that Grace be recognized for creating the video. Grace beamed. Dierdre glared.

The music began. Acer wheeled his mother to the back of the hall to a circle of chairs where the Monsignor and her tuxedoed sons held court while she looked sadly out across the crowd. I found her there.

"Would you like to join me on the dance floor, Gram?"

Acer gripped the side arm of her wheelchair. "No. She'll stay with us."

I leaned down to whisper in her ear. "Are you sure?"

"Yes," she answered. "Never mind. It's all right." She knew she was stuck. She knew she would not dance that night.

The days following the wedding should have been a respite for Grace. Instead, curiously, her children did not leave. Acer and his wife, Delilah, stayed at the house. The kitchen echoed with breezy chatter from breakfast past lunch. Grace asked her son if he watched Jack's video. He said, no. He was busy with a trial and the girls, of course, occupied his time. Grace said, "Well, then, let's watch it now."

Grace, sat in her power chair while the video played. Just before the final songs Acer glanced at his watch and began to fidget. He stood up. "Would you like to go out to supper?"

"Not yet," Grace did not move from her place, remote in hand. The funeral scenes played out on the screen before them. "Look, there. There I am, in the middle, alone." Grace paused the picture to view herself in the silent open space.

"How about Blackwater Manor," Acer asked.

"Blackwater Manor?" Grace clicked off the remote. "That's assisted living."

"That's where your sister Jacelyn is staying. Wouldn't you like to have dinner with her?"

"No, Acer. She can come to dinner with us at Royal Court. I'm not going there."

"It's like a hotel, more like a lodge. There's water therapy there."

She looked up at him suspiciously. "No, Acer. I don't want to go there."

We ate at Royal Court, her favorite restaurant. Grace complimented the waiters as they passed by the table. Acer didn't eat. He frequently left the table to speak on his cell phone. When we arrived home, there was a caravan of cars lining Scanlon Circle. "What are they all still doing here?" she exclaimed.

"They just want to be with you a while longer," Acer answered lightly. Her children, however, did not join her. Instead, they huddled outside in closed discussions.

"It's late," Grace announced. "I'm going to bed." I sat by her side while she recited the rosary, drifting into sleep. Each time she drifted off, one or more of her children burst in, offering an elaborate good night message, unconcerned that they were waking her from a peaceful rest. It occurred to me that they appeared to be putting on a show for their own benefit.

Finally, only Bric lingered in the hallway. He moved in close to me and grabbed my elbow, hissing into my face. "Everyone here knows what you are doing."

"What does that mean?" I pulled back. "What do you think I'm doing?"

"It is inappropriate for two women to sleep in the same bedroom."

"What in God's name are you suggesting?"

"Leave our mother alone!"

I stared at him as he seethed and stuttered and flamed out of the room, putting two fingers to his eyes and then pointing them back at me. I sat frozen for a very long time. "Who were these people?"

I rose the next morning and looked in on Grace. She was still sleeping. I found Lyssa at the kitchen table redistributing Grace's meds. She did not speak. She wrote deliberately, with precision, on a yellow note pad. I poured a cup of coffee and sat across from her at the table. "You wrote fifteen milligrams of Aricept. She's not getting that." She pulled the tablet away from me. Teeth clenched, jaw rigid, she continued to write. "Gram hasn't been tested for Alzheimer's. She doesn't have a prescription for Aricept."

She put down her pen and glared. "I am a nurse. Bric is a doctor. We know what we're doing." She went back to writing feverishly, determinedly.

I watched as she dropped two five milligram tablets into the morning section of the med box and one more into the night section. "Lyssa, fifteen milligrams a day could be dangerous." I reached for the med box. She slammed down the pen, snatching the box from my hand, tilting her chin and squaring her shoulders to glare arrogantly, defiantly back at me.

"You don't know what you are talking about. You have no business here. Get out!" I couldn't grasp her words, her actions were astoundingly unexpected. The only sound I clearly discerned was the rumble of distant ominous thunder. She bristled with rage. The air cracked with an explosion of instant heat. Then she lurched at me, screaming. "You do not belong here. She is my mother! She is my mother! She is my mother!"

I stepped forward, stunned, my face squarely in hers. "Then please try to remember that. Without a prescription, five milligrams is risky enough." The heat of her glare followed me as I moved away and down the hall to check on Grace.

"What were you girls arguing about? I could hear you all the way down the hall."

"Nothing, Gram." I reconsidered. I had always been honest with Grace. "I want Lyssa to be careful with your meds."

"Yes," she replied, alert to the issue. "You and I always counted out Jack's pills carefully. We never made a mistake."

Lyssa was at the bedroom door. "Why don't you get up? We thought we would take you to brunch."

"Who is we?" Grace questioned.

"Not Elle. Just Crystal Ann and I. And not brunch, really. Just coffee. You may want to eat first."

Grace was suspicious. "All right. I'll be out in a minute. You wait out there, Lyssa."

"No. I'll help you get dressed." Lyssa pushed past me, closing the door in my face, locking me out. I stood next to the door and waited. The lock eventually turned again and they emerged. Grace was dressed in a new soft suede jacket Lyssa had bought for her to wear, complete with another glittery shell and black pants. Lyssa pinned the crescent mother's pin with the diamond crown and all the birthstones of her children to the lapel of her jacket.

Grace stopped the power chair in the doorway of the kitchen. "Elle should come with us."

"She's not invited," Lyssa said firmly. "Just us." She flashed a cold, emotionless smile. "We want to spend private time with our mother." She gave Grace a strong squeeze.

Lyssa directed Grace's power chair to the garage door and then left her there to wait while she backed the Cadillac into the drive. Grace turned and whispered determinedly, "I'm not going to Blackwater Manor."

"Then tell them no," I whispered back. "I cannot go with you this morning, but I know you are strong. Just tell them no. You are their mother! This is your life! You raised these people. Tell them what you want."

"What's going on?" she pleaded.

I watched Lyssa hurrying back to the garage door, seething with anger. "I don't know, Gram. I don't know. I love you. Be strong. I'll be right here when you get home."

The morning passed and they did not return. I occupied my time by scheduling job interviews and returning phone calls to search committees. The presidential campaign was heating up and I was missing out on the opportunity of a lifetime. Then I heard the door open. Bric's "Hello!" echoed through the house.

"I'm in the office," I answered back. He appeared in the doorway with Lyssa close behind.

"Where's Gram?" I asked.

"She's napping at our house. She'll spend the day there."

"Oh?" I leaned back in the chair. They both looked guardedly resolute. Lyssa folded her arms defiantly.

"We want to talk to you," Bric said.

"OK"

"Privately."

"Privately? We're the only ones here." I shrugged. "OK. Give me a minute. I have to send this email first."

"Now!" He shoved my chair away from the computer, pushing the keyboard aside. His aggression startled me.

"I'll talk with you. Just not right now. I'm sending an email."

He reached for the arm of my chair and spun it around. "Get out of Dad's chair!" he snarled, both hands firmly on the armrests.

"What on earth?" I kept my voice low, my eyes even. I centered my energy. I was not going to back down. "Are you intimidated because I sit in Grandpa's chair?"

"It is you who should be intimidated!" he exploded. "It's Dad's office! Dad's chair! You have no right to sit in it. Get out!" Lyssa stood rigid, arms crossed, blocking the doorway. This was nuts. "We want you out of this house!" Bric repeated.

"What is wrong with you?"

"It's time for you to leave. You should leave!"

"What is your problem? You didn't object to my being here when Grandpa needed help. You all said you were grateful that I was here. What is different now?"

Bric's tone changed. "I have a very generous offer for you." He held a set of keys, dangling from the key ring was a bright yellow laminated letter J.

"What the hell is this?"

"Not here." He glanced around. "We need to go to neutral ground."

"Neutral ground?" I reached around him to the keyboard. "I have to send this email."

"You will listen to me! You will listen to me now!" Bric stood solidly between me and the desk."

"Fine. Let's go." I grabbed the strap of my bag and brushed Lyssa out of the way. I walked through the kitchen and garage, down the drive to my car. Bric rushed past me. He barred my car door with the side of his body. "You're going with us, but not in your car."

"No. I'll meet you if you like, but I'm not going with you." I had a flash image of them dropping me at some out of the way place, and returning to the house to change the locks while I was gone.

"You will do as I say!" Bric growled into my face, holding my car door shut with a bear claw grip. I turned back to the house. He jumped in front of me as I reached the garage door, wedging me against the sill, pulling back on my arm. The inner heat that forewarns anger beyond reason rose in me from my toes to the tip of my head. I threw a left block. He ducked back.

"Get away from this house, or I'll call the police!" I flared.

"Call the police! Hah!" His hand gripped the door.

"This is my home." Every muscle in my body was poised for recoil.

"This is not your home!" His voice resonated across the cul-de-sac. Hearing the echo, he looked around, probably remembering that his peers lived in the neighborhood.

"The motor vehicle bureau, the IRS, and the US Post Office all believe and will verify that this is where I live."

"This is Dad's house!" he hissed, but he knew he couldn't argue the facts. He spun around, and with Lyssa close at his side, retreated and drove away. I walked through the house, checking the locks on every door. My temples throbbed. I felt sick. The entire family was in town, yet except for Lyssa standing guard, the house was empty throughout Bric's entire tirade. The room spun wildly. I dropped to the floor, stunned. I was ambushed.

The next morning Grace pulled back the kitchen curtains and stared out the window. "What are those voices?" Ralph and Lyssa chatted cheerily while they trimmed the flower beds. "Why don't they go home?

Where have they all been staying? Not here." We watched them, bustling across the yard, laughing too loudly, it seemed. Acer pulled into the drive. He entered the kitchen and gave Grace a cheery kiss. He ignored me. "Tell them not to go into these flowers under the window," Grace insisted. "The baby birds might still be in there. Don't touch the roses." Acer complied and went outside to give the instructions. Ralph waved back at her. She peered through the kitchen window. Acer came back and led her out the garage door and down the ramp to supervise. "Not there. Don't pull those out," she pointed and shook her head. They pretended to pull the flowers anyway. "No. Not that one." They laughed back at her. She picked up the hose and threatened to spray them. They scurried around her chair. They were mischievous children, reliving another time. I watched from the kitchen window. It occurred to me that Grace had always been and still was the only one in this large family of hers that was based in reality.

Acer came back into the house and waved me into the office. "It's time for me to tell you what is going on." I stood, gazing at the four walls of Grandpa Jack's inner sanctum. "Sit here in Dad's chair." Acer motioned toward the very chair that had the day before enflamed Bric.

"I'm good right here." I stood next to the door.

"Bric and Lyssa were wrong yesterday. They handled that badly. So I will tell you now that we believe that it is time that Grace move to Blackwater Manor."

"Why?" I asked in amazement. I glanced at a larger than life photo of Grace at eighteen. "She is just now coming back to life. Why lock her up now?"

"We're not locking her up. It's a wonderful place. Her sister, Jacelyn is there. She will have water therapy."

"She has water therapy now. She should be able to live her life here. She deserves that."

"There's no one to care for her."

"I'm here. She's healthy. She just needs help transferring from her chair. Grandpa was near death, but no one pushed him out. She loves her home. There's plenty of money. The farm is in a trust. This house is hers, free and clear. What is the point in depriving her of that?" The words came tumbling out. He did not interrupt. The more relevant question in my mind remained unspoken. "What do you people want?"

He frowned, then quickly changed his tone. "Don't be judgmental," he cajoled. "Just come with me to take a tour. What can it hurt? Don't be stubborn."

I locked eyes with him, but in my head I reasoned with myself. I knew a job offer could take me away from her. Winter was approaching. I felt it's chill. "I'll go with you," I said finally. "We'll look at it. We'll consider it as a possible temporary reserve option, should she need it."

We arrived at Blackwater Manor, a wide expanse of stone and tile hallways with side foyers and private dining areas. "Look," Acer pointed to an old-fashioned dining room with lace tablecloth. "Mom can eat in here just like she did on the farm." One big difference, I thought, this was not her dining room, and the residents wandering slowly past were not her family.

"It's just like home," Ralph offered as he joined us. Acer lied. It was not an impromptu tour. A woman accompanying Ralph introduced herself as Blackwater Manor's Chief Executive Officer.

"We'll start our tour here. Are you one of the family staying in the West wing?" I knew at once from their expressions that this was information Acer and Ralph would rather I not have. "We have just two resident apartments available. They go quickly. So you'll want to decide soon, before these are gone." I couldn't grasp what she was saying. The entire family was staying here? Ralph quickly changed the subject. He launched into a list of questions that would prompt the CEO to convince me that this would be the lovely, caring environment advertised on the website. There was everything she could possibly need, including a pharmacy, shops, a beauty salon, a library, formal dining, call assistance, water therapy.

Acer rose to his feet. "Let's see the pool. Our mother loves water therapy."

We entered a glassed in area where a small narrow two-lane pool was joined by another smaller hot-tub. "Is this where water therapy takes place?" I asked.

"Well, we exercise here, in groups, of course," she answered. "We don't have individual therapy. Everyone goes at his or her own pace. If someone can't keep up with the group, we move them into a slower group."

I dipped my toe into the water. "It's cold. Gram won't use this pool. The water is cold."

"Oh, I assure you, it's in compliance," she responded.

"It's in compliance," Acer repeated, stooping to tip his fingers into the pool. "It does seem a bit cool."

"Well, I'll have it checked," she offered. "I'm sure it's in compliance."

"She won't use that pool," I said. "She has a private therapist now and a warm pool." Ralph scowled. "I'm just saying that she won't use it, Ralph."

The CEO led us back to the front entrance. Acer and Ralph wanted to speak to her privately, but she cut them off. "Will you be staying here as well?" she asked. "I know it is the intent of the family to decide before you all go back to your homes, so we'll make room for you if you wish. You can just get a feel for it, that way. Of course there's the matter of Jacelyn's referral fee. We'll write her a check when Grace is admitted."

Acer thanked her and the three of us made our way across the parking lot to the car. When we arrived at the house, Grace was napping. Acer drove off in his suburban to run an errand. Ralph disappeared into the lower level to pack. I went back to finish my work in the office. A light on the office phone flashed. Nothing was private in Jack's house. He monitored everything, including the phones. I depressed the blinking button. Ralph's voice came through the speaker.

"I know your feelings for her, Seth, but you're not here. You don't hear what she's saying. She and Mom have a bond. We need to get her out of this house. Mom is fickle and easily swayed. She'll forget about her when she's gone. We're running out of time. Say she's abusive. Say she's unstable. Just get her out."

"Saying it doesn't make it true," Seth interrupted.

"It does in our family. She needs to be gone. Stat!" My head and heart ached. I didn't want to hear any more.

"I understand," Seth answered back. Do what you have to do. Just leave me out of it."

Stunned, I clicked the speaker off. These people were not my family. Who were they? What did they want? What could they possibly hope to gain from this? What did Seth mean when he said they were running out of time? They were dark strangers controlled by a dark spirit. I stood in the office, staring at the anniversary photo of Jack and Grace trying to see beyond the polished pose. Ralph stood in the doorway. I turned to face him. It was like looking into a deep hole. I had to be careful not to fall through. I was holding on to Grace, but there was no one holding on to me.

"Why do you want me out? What is going on that I don't know? Why do you see me as a threat?"

Ralph's glance shot to the phone on the desk. "That was a private conversation. You were listening?"

"What is going on? Why do you want me gone?"

Ralph began to shake, his eyes tearing. "I love you. I want you to trust me. I will until the day I die be grateful for all you did for Dad, for Dad and Mom, I mean."

"I'm trying to believe that." I responded sadly, biting down hard on my lip. "Why is everyone so angry? What is so urgent?" I tried to see beyond the person to the soul. All I saw was darkness. My eyes were drawn to something he was holding. It was a set of keys with a single yellow laminated letter J.

Ralph continued. "We all want this to stop. We want all the confusion, all the chaos to end."

"What confusion and chaos?" I asked.

"We have done Dad's bidding all our lives, without even a thank you. Now he's gone and we want to be done with it. We just want to get on with our lives."

"Gram's still here."

"Mom's just a pawn. It's time for us to take care of ourselves. We want our lives back."

"That is why you want me out? That is why you want me out 'stat'?"

Hearing his own words thrown back at him, Ralph turned defensive. "You need to go. You need to be gone." I stared at him, speechless. Lyssa appeared behind him, arms folded. Dierdre appeared resolutely behind her. What the hell? Were they hiding in the woodwork? Acer towered over them. Dierdre, Lyssa and Ralph withdrew.

"I'm sorry it has come to this." He squared his shoulders. "Let's negotiate. What will it take for you to give us your support?"

"Support for what?"

"Mom needs to be in Blackwater Manor."

"She will never go."

"She will go if you are not here. What will it take to make it worth your while to leave?"

"What are you talking about?"

"I am, we are prepared to offer you money." He watched my face closely. "You tell me how much. Dad would want that."

"Grandpa would want that?" I couldn't imagine any circumstance in which my grandfather would have wanted that. "I don't want Gram's money. Gram won't leave."

"Then what is the answer? You're the MBA." His tone was sardonic. "You're the planner. It's what you're trained to do. Give me a plan."

"You can't sell the house while she's alive. It's stipulated in the will. So it's not one or the other. You'll have to maintain the house even if she did move to Blackwater Manor. So, if it is truly your intent to provide for her best interest, then pay for the apartment. Let it remain empty until she needs it, or until someone else in the family needs a place to stay. She could offer that instead of a hotel." He smiled wryly.

"She will only agree to that if you talk her into it. Will you do that?"

"I will speak to her, but you must agree to allow her to live peacefully in her home until she decides. It must be her choice. Agreed?"

"Agreed."

The next morning I told Grace what Acer proposed. She would have an apartment in case she ever needed it. If she allowed this, it would greatly relieve her children of their collective concern for her well-being and there would be no more talk of Blackwater Manor. "All right," she said finally. "You write it. Get some note cards and write exactly what I say."

Grace's children arrived, crowding into the large kitchen, filling it with chatter and shrill laughter. I took Maire's arm and motioned her aside. "I need to ask a favor."

"Sure, what is it?" She was barely listening. Her eyes followed her brothers, gathering in a tight circle.

"If I needed to, could I stay with you for a while?" I surprised myself with my own timidity.

Her eyes narrowed. "You are young," she tossed back without hesitation. "You have every advantage. You have an education. You have money. You have good credit. Get your own place." My heart went numb as she moved away into the family mix.

Grace read each of her conditions as her children huddled in front of her. Condition one was if she allowed the apartment to be reserved, no one would again ask her to move. She would decide when and if she ever wanted to do that. Condition two was that no one would speak of the matter outside the family. There would be no more emails or secret meetings regarding an apartment at Blackwater Manor. She hated the thought that her private life would become impersonal gossip. Condition three was that her children must agree to cease and desist their attempt to manage her life. The confusion and secrets must stop. She paused and looked firmly at each of them. "This house is mine. It will remain mine until I die. It will not be sold. There's enough money. You don't need it."

Lyssa spoke first. "Can I email just the immediate family? They will want to know."

Grace looked at her squarely, sternly. "No. You be quiet."

Then it was Ralph's turn. "Shouldn't Aunt Jacey be told? She's your sister. After all, she is expecting you to join her at Blackwater Manor." Grace shot him the look that can only come from an exasperated mother to a determined child.

"Jacelyn is in on this too? What does she get out of this? A referral fee?" Her children were beginning to understand that she was a stronger woman than they realized.

Bric stood up. "Mom, may I have those cards?"

"No. I will keep them."

"I just want to read them for myself."

"No." She held the cards firmly in her hands. Grace's children gathered their things and left the house, piling into their cars, vans and SUVs. She followed them to the front door and waved from her chair as each pulled away from the drive. Bric stood back. Unnoticed, he reached for the index cards and dropped them into his jacket pocket.

The next day Grace and I returned to water therapy. She loved the mobility it gave her. In the water she walked from one edge of the pool to another. "Let's race!" she called, propelling herself ahead of me. When we returned, she lay on her bed to nap. I sat with her until she dozed off, peacefully. "I love you, Gram," I whispered.

Liam met me at the top of the stairs leading to the lower level. "Please forgive me," he started, then he stopped. He searched my eyes and continued on. "I'm here to help you move." I stared, stunned. A moving truck was parked outside the patio doors at the lower level. Workers bustled from room to room, loading the truck. Clothes on hangers hung out of boxes. Drawers lay empty on the floor.

Angela, Grace's personal assistant, stood behind us, peering into the room. "Bric just fired me."

"Is he still here?" Liam asked quickly.

"No, he's gone." Her voice drifted off as she observed the disorder. "Can I help?"

"I'll pay you," I offered.

She pursed her lips. "I don't think so. I think you will let me help you as a friend." She dropped her bag and took charge of the clothes, directing the movers.

Liam pulled me aside. "You cannot stay here. You are not safe."

"What are you saying? How could I possibly be in danger?"

"You cannot protect her any longer. She cannot protect you."

I stared at him in disbelief. "What are you talking about?"

"She will have her own issues to deal with. Look around. Is anything else yours? Don't leave anything behind. Lyssa will have a cleaning crew here in an hour."

"What do you mean her own issues? What is going on? They kick me out, fire her personal assistant and clean out her house? She's right upstairs!" The room spun wildly. I doubled over. He caught me. "I can't breathe."

"It's stressful," he said.

I walked through the patio doors, out into the night as Liam locked the door behind me. I stood on the lawn under a starless night as the movers pulled away, headed for a storage area. "Why are they doing this?"

"Because they can."

Images and words swirled through the night like a dark tempest. I drove, without direction, away from a home that was not mine, from a mother who was not mine, on a course that was not mine. Finally, exhausted and reeling with confusion and pain, I pulled off the Interstate to pass slowly through quiet elm and cottonwood-lined streets.

Cheery flowers bloomed in the flower box at the entrance of a brick building. A neon light flickered in the window. I walked through the heavy glass and oak door into a smoky dim interior. Faces looked up and then looked away. A couple at the bar abruptly ceased conversation to fix absent stares in my direction. A waitress bustled from behind the bar to peer into my face. "Wow!" she exclaimed. "You must be Faith's daughter." I nodded. She stood for a moment staring, then motioned toward the muscular man with the unruly flop of hair locked in a heated argument with another man at the back of the bar. "You're looking for Ronan."

Ronan turned deep green eyes in my direction. He circled around the bar, ducking as the other man hurled a bottle at his head. It splattered against the brick wall.

I scanned the room. My mother was here? "Your note said I would be welcome anytime." He nodded and tossed his apron to the waitress, slipping his arm around my waist to steer me back outside.

"This is not over!" the man roared from the end of the bar.

Ronan motioned for me to follow as he drove through town to a small bungalow. The kitchen was immaculate. It smelled of fresh baked bread and roasted beef. He lit a Marlboro and opened a beer.

"You don't want to know why I'm here?" I asked.

"I can guess." He waved his hand toward a room through the hallway. "It's nothin' fancy," he said. "It's a bachelor's house, you know. You can stay as long as you like. The bedroom's all yours. You'll like it." He settled into the leather chair and flipped the recliner back. "I'll stay right here tonight." I dropped my bag on the bed, smoothing my hand over an exquisitely stitched quilt. Had my mother run her fingers across the same stitches? "Will you have a drink?" he called through the door.

"No, I don't think so."

"Fine. You're all right, then?"

"No, I don't think I am," I whispered. The tremor inside my head gave way to tidal wave. I knew somewhere beyond the thoughts crashing against my skull, there was quiet. I curled my body around the soft edges of my bag and waited for the silence to find me. I knew, despite my dread for whatever was to follow, I was safe in this place. A narrow slip of light reflected hues from the next room. Ronan lounged in his chair, puffing on a cigarette, sipping a beer, staring at the television screen. "What are you watching?" I called through the darkness.

"The History Channel," he answered absently.

The voice of Howard Hunt drifted into the room. "He is the darkness reaching out for the darkness. Eventually it's either going to be you or him."

Then it was Henry Kissinger. "Power is the ultimate aphrodisiac."

Then Nixon's voice boomed through the air. "Goddamit! I am not a crook!"

Although I had no reason to imagine it then, there, but for God's Grace, would one day soon go my uncle Acer.

As the memory of that night replayed in my head, I looked around the bus cabin at the faces of Yoki, Sonja, Tiffany, Ancient Eyes and the researcher. 'I see total strangers more clearly than my own family,' I thought. Suddenly the riddle flashed through my mind. I reached for my cell phone.

"Do you know what time it is?" Maire yawned.

"Oh, no. I'm sorry. I lost track of time."

"Are you all right?"

"I think I've just solved the first clue."

"Clue? What clue? What are you talking about?"

"The riddle. Grandpa Jack's riddle. What's more blinding than the break of dawn? I know the answer."

Her voice became stern. "Stop it. Sean told us when we were kids to leave it alone. Solving that riddle will take you to Hell. Forget the riddle."

"OK. Sorry. Sorry I woke you." I flipped my phone shut and stared out at the starless sky.

The researcher leaned over the aisle and smiled mischievously. "What riddle?"

when everything I was is lost
I have forgot but you have not
when I am lost you have not lost me
you have not lost me

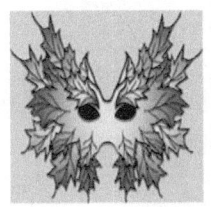

Poor Fen and The Will O' The Wisp

If I ever leave this world alive
I'll thank ya for the things you did in my life
I'll come back down and sit beside your feet tonight
Where ever I am you'll always be
More than just a memory
If I ever leave this world alive

The big bus rumbled west past pine trees, buttes, prairie fens, glacial mountains, narrow passes and glistening rivers and lakes. "What fools we are not to realize the power of the gentle touch of Grace," I mused.

"You're smarter than that," she whispered.

"That's because I've been listening to you, Grace."

My phone beeped. It was Maire. "Where are you now?"

"Just coming across Wyoming into Montana."

"How's the weather?"

"We've driven out of the rain. Now there's a spitting snow shower. How is it there?"

"I can't understand you. There's no reception in that God forsaken wilderness you're going through." The phone transmission garbled, then disconnected.

"No kidding," I thought.

The bus stopped for a passenger pickup. A young woman bounded up the aisle and stuffed her bags into the overhead, draping her colorfully tattooed well-toned arms across the seat in front of her as she continued a conversation with a man who boarded just behind her. She exuded energy. He was introspective. They were similarly dressed in jeans and leather vests with Harley logos. "So, I don't know." Her voice was like a warm breeze. "Sure, the baby is still tiny, but she'll be much happier with my mother."

He settled against the window, turning his face back toward her. "Well, of course I miss my kids, too, but we've gotta go where the work is. Scrap metal isn't moving. If I don't work this out, I can add my marriage to the list of casualties in this wreck of an economy." She rested her chin on the back of his headrest. They chatted easily across the seat, sharing similar dramas of divorce, custody battles, getting laid off and looking for jobs. She was on her way to the iron mountain mining district in Montana. He had been on the reservation making deals for scrapped cars. It had been a rough year for both of them. Once they rode Harleys. Now they rode the bus. The economy may have gone off course, but their journey continued.

"What are they talking about?" Grace used that tone whenever she didn't understand or approve. "She looks like a boy. Is that a boy?" I chuckled. It occurred to me, eavesdropping on their stories, that this bus ride was much more than just another trip on a tedious journey. The struggle to carry on, despite oppressive adversity makes the story worth telling.

The bus rolled into a Cenex station and stopped again. Three college girls dressed as Bridezilla, Cat Woman and Elvira boarded, the lights from their cell phones glowing in the dim cabin as they huddled together, texting and giggling.

"I completely forgot that this is Halloween," the tattooed ironworker exclaimed. "I need to find a costume!" Her eyes twinkled as she gazed mischievously at the three.

"Maybe you could go as a tattoo," the scrap metal collector offered with a smirk.

"Ha. Ha." She leaned across the seat back to slap his arm. "And you can be Scrap Man!" The bus steered away from the detour route to the interstate, lumbering past storefronts decorated in flaming orange pumpkins.

Elvira leaned into the aisle to take us all in. "Someone tell a Halloween story!"

"Yes!" Bridezilla's eyelashes sparkled as she stabbed the air with the stem of a black rose. "Something scary!" The bus driver glared back at us through the rear view mirror.

The researcher grinned mischievously at me. "Well?"

"All right," I began. "I'll tell you the tale of a schemer who was trapped in his own game." The researcher settled back in his seat. Cat Woman's whiskers danced in anticipation. I continued. "Jack was known throughout the land as a deceiver and a manipulator who plundered unsuspecting travelers.

As word of Jack's tricks spread far and wide, the Devil resolved to seek him out and test him. One evening when the moon was high and yellow, with the crisp chill of autumn in the air, Jack wandered through the night on his usual path. It was there that he stumbled across the Devil, standing bent and crooked in the road. 'I know you, Devil,' Jack called out. 'No doubt you have come to take me away with you. Won't you share a drink with me before we go?' The Devil joined him with the glint of a gnarled smirk and the two drank late into the night. Just before the sun broke through the misty dawn, Jack rose to go, but the bartender stopped him. Someone had to pay. The Devil refused, of course. He was there at Jack's invitation. Jack claimed he had no money, but he offered the Devil a compromise. 'Transform yourself into a silver coin,' he suggested, 'and I will use that coin to pay the tab. Then when the bartender is asleep you can change back into your true form.' The Devil laughed at Jack's guile and agreed, transforming himself into a silver coin. Jack plunged the coin into his pocket, next to a crucifix. Bound by the cross, the Devil could not transform back to his original state. Jack danced in merriment. He had tricked the Devil Himself. The Devil was furious, demanding to be set free. Jack knew he could not carry the Devil in his pocket indefinitely so he offered another deal. He promised to free the Devil but only if the Devil promised not to trouble him for ten years. The Devil bitterly agreed. Jack tossed the coin high into the air and the Devil vanished. Ten years passed. Then one night Jack again stood in that very same spot facing the Devil. 'I know why you're here,' Jack called out. The Devil glared menacingly. 'Here is my field,' Jack exclaimed, waving toward acres of trees. 'If you help me harvest my brightest fruit, I will go willingly.' The two stood sizing each other up in the middle of the winding dirt road. Jack didn't dare move until the Devil flashed his grin and nodded. The Devil scuttled up a tree trunk and slithered through the branches, plucking the ripest, most delicious fruit from the highest limbs. He scanned the road below. Jack was nowhere to be seen. Quickly he moved to slide down the trunk but he could not. Jack leapt onto the road and erupted in wild laughter. 'Ah hah! I have carved a cross on the base of the tree! You are trapped again!' The Devil leered at Jack from the shadows. 'Say Devil,' Jack called, bursting with the pride of victory. 'I will release you, as I promised, but now you must agree that I have won and upon my death you will not claim my soul!' The Devil flashed a sardonic grin. The deal was done and the Devil again vanished. Jack lived out the rest of his life confident that his place in Heaven was assured, but when Jack died, St. Peter stopped him at Heaven's gates. 'No, no, Jack!' Peter declared. 'There's no place for your wicked soul here!" Bewildered, Jack found himself right back on his usual path, facing the Devil. 'Jack,' the Devil declared, 'You are destined to wander forever between light and darkness.' Jack shuddered. 'However,' the Devil added, 'I have enjoyed this game, so although I cannot take you with me, I leave you with this single ember from Hell's fire to light your way.' Jack protested. 'Surely you will not be defeated?' The Devil smirked. 'Very well. Here is one last contest. You stand at the edge of a shimmering pool deeper than the deepest well. Fathoms below you sits a pot of gold shimmering in the swell. There are seven stone steps that will lead you but none will appear without solving a clue. When you reach the bottom at the mouth of the cave, the prize will come to you.' Having said this, the Devil vanished. 'The game continues,' Jack declared smugly. The October wind blew strong and the ember began to fade. 'I will solve the Devil's riddle,' Jack declared, 'but first I must ward off the growing darkness.' Then Jack hollowed out a turnip and nestled the spark of Hellfire safely inside. Ever since that day, Jack wanders between the planes of good and evil, a will o' the wisp, searching in the darkness for the clues that will set him free. Travelers across time claim to see the ghostly glow of Jack's lantern. Most who cross paths with the cunning specter are tricked out of their lives and out of their souls. Be warned, especially on Halloween, when the fog that separates the dead from the living lifts and Jack wanders from his usual path. Carve out a pumpkin and place a candle inside. The glow reminds Jack of his fate, and deters him from continuing his mischief."

Bridezilla shivered. Cat Woman, and Elvira receded into the depths of the dark cabin, whispering over text messages. The tattooed iron worker settled back into her seat. The scrap metal worker pulled his cap over his eyes and rested his chin on his chest. The researcher winked, clicked on his reading light and buried himself in his notebook. Sonja flipped open her laptop. Ancient Eyes pulled a ball of yarn from her bag and began to knit. A lone deer grazed in the moonlight on a far slope as Yoki gazed into the darkness and the prairie sped by.

Grace knew that whatever her strengths, she could not prevent the storms that loomed on her horizon or the obstacles those storms would toss in her path. She could not dispel the dark shadows that would be cast there, challenging her sense of self, her enthusiasm for living and her strength to go on. Grace's journey, beset with Jack's mischief, followed a sinister course. She could see the storm coming across the prairie. Jack told her this would happen, then he set it in motion.

Shortly after I arrived in his town, Ronan stood with me outside a large Victorian house. Columns surrounded the wide porch at the top of wide welcoming steps. As Ronan turned the key, a horn honked in the street. The same man who threw the bottle at him in the bar waved an angry fist and drove on.

"Who was that?" I asked, watching the pickup speed away.

"Just a neighbor. It's a border dispute. Nothing for you to worry about." He ushered me inside. "You'll be more comfortable here." He winked. "We don't want people to talk. Sure, you're welcome to stay as long as you like. You'll be safe here."

I walked through the large living room, the kitchen and the stairs to an open landing above. "You still haven't asked me why I'm here."

"No matter. You'll tell me when you're ready."

Quiet night descended on the little town as I sprawled across the bed, bathed in silver ribbons of light streaming through the blinds. I thought I smelled a hint of agarwood incense. Suddenly there in the distance, across the lawn was the flash of a light. There it was again. I rose up on my elbow, peering to following the glow. A shadow came closer and crossed under the streetlight. It was Ronan, walking the perimeter of the yard. A comforting peace washed over me. So this is what a hero looks like, I thought.

Early morning brought sunlight streaming across the bedroom. I woke slowly from a long peaceful sleep. The leaves of the cottonwood trees outside the window gently rustled in the breeze. My cell phone beeped. I leaned over the side of the bed and scooped it out of my bag. It was Grace's familiar voice on the phone.

"Where did you go? Where are you? Did they chase you away?"

"No, Gram. No. They can't get rid of me."

"Good. Will you come to water therapy with me?"

"Yes, of course. Don't worry. I'll be there."

"Where are you?"

"Not far." An hour later, I arrived at Scanlon Circle. She met me at the door, but she had changed her mind. She wasn't feeling well.

"I'm not sick, really." She was looking for the words to describe what she felt. "It feels like what Jack described." Whenever Jack would become agitated, his physician suggested a Lorazepam, or something like it, to calm him. He called it a sleeping pill. He did sleep soundly. The next day, however, and for days to follow, he would sit with his head on the kitchen table, dazed and barely able to keep his eyes open. I inspected Grace's med box. There were the familiar pills and there were new ones. I dialed her physician's answering machine. His nurse called me back. She said that Bric had prescribed Aricept and something else for anxiety. I asked if Grace had been anxious. She said she didn't know. I asked if Grace had been tested for Alzheimer's. She said, no, but Bric had noticed symptoms. I remembered the argument with Lyssa. I asked the nurse what dose was advisable. She said that with just five milligrams she should not experience uncomfortable symptoms. I asked what symptoms were expected.

"Possible incontinence, nausea, dizziness, agitation," she responded. I looked again at Grace's med box.

"The morning containers have ten milligrams each. There is another five milligram pill in the evening container."

"No. No, that's too much," she answered quickly. "She's not been diagnosed. It's dangerous to start someone out with that much. No. She could have a seizure or stop breathing. She should have only five milligrams. No more." Then she added, "Talk to Bric. He's filling her meds these days."

"Is it appropriate or even ethical for a physician to prescribe for his mother?"

"Talk to Bric."

I recalled the conversation with Ralph. "Mom's just a pawn."

"Gram, this small pill is called Aricept," I explained. "You should examine your own pills every morning and every night. There should be only one of these at night, and none in the morning. There may also be a sedative in here. I can't tell. Ask Bric to tell you what he is giving you. Can you remember that?"

"Of course," she snapped. "I don't have a problem with my memory. I have a problem with my children! You and I examined Jack's pills before he took them. He said not to trust anyone."

"That's right, Gram. You do that. Look at your meds before you take them." I sat with her as she drifted to sleep. "I love you, Gram."

My cell phone was beeping. It was Maire. "Mom needs to get out of the house. I'm worried about her. That house is evil and I'm not just talking about the help!"

"How about the apple orchard? We can go there for lunch."

Grace waited in her power chair by the window. She wore a red suede jacket and a straw hat with a colorfully striped brim. Maire stood in front of her with open arms. "You are always dressed for the occasion, Ma."

Grace tapped the brim of her hat. "I just picked out what I think I'll have fun in. My favorite."

"What do you want to do today, Ma?"

She thought for another minute. "Pleasure." The word rolled off her tongue like a wish.

The country orchard sprawled before us. Grace read from the sign in the drive. "There are over thirteen varieties of apple trees here and seven acres of pumpkins." She spanned the view to take it all in. "Really!"

Maire jumped out with the portable wheel chair. "Let's go to the gift shop." Behind us a small train filled with children drove by. Ponies grazed near the pumpkin patch. The delicious scent of freshly baked apple pie met us at the door. Crisp apples were piled high in lathe baskets around the room. Cooled bins of bright red and yellow apples lined the walls. "Would you like a slice of fresh pie?" Maire pointed to a glass case.

"Look there!" Grace motioned toward the back of the room where apples rolled down a chute onto a conveyor belt. A man in a bright apron sorted them, examining each one as it passed. "I used to do that," Grace called over the whirring sound of the conveyor motor, her hair lifting lightly in the breeze from the open door behind him.

He waved. "Do you want to help me?"

"Oh, my, no," she laughed. Then she added with a look of scrutiny. "Make sure they're polished clean. Don't let any with worms go by."

He reached into the basket by his side. "Here's a Red Delicious and a Freyburg, hand-picked just for you." Grace grinned and cradled the apples in her sweater as we rolled past a group of children seated in a circle around a storyteller. She reached out as we passed to touch the hand of one of the children.

Back at the front counter, we ordered warm cider with a cinnamon stick from a waitress in a bright red apron with a white apple stenciled on the front. Maire brought a jar of deep crimson jam to the table. "Would you like this with your toast tomorrow morning? I wonder if it's difficult to make apple butter."

"Who cares? We can buy it here," Grace laughed.

Maire brought three plates of pie. "It smells heavenly," Grace exclaimed. "The pies we made! Every Saturday!" She took a bite. "This pie is almost as good as mine."

The next morning a brilliant sun rose across the sky as I drove east from Ronan's little town to escort Grace to Mass at St. Jacob's. I dialed her number.

"Hello," a voice answered.

"May I speak with Grace?"

"Who is this?" the voice demanded.

"Who is this?" I shot back.

"Grace is sleeping." The words were brief, the tone impersonal. She was a stranger in a long line of strangers from the agency Bric hired. They came and went with each shift change. Some introduced themselves. Others didn't bother. They were demeaning and dismissive, not always responding to her call. She asked them their names. "I told you already," would often come the impatient reply.

"You should wake Grace," I said. "She won't want to be late for Mass." She was silent so I asked again, "May I know who is speaking?"

"I'm not allowed to wake her," she answered and abruptly hung up.

I stared at my phone. I stared at the road, stretching ahead of me. Then I hit redial.

"Hello."

"This is Elle Riorden. I'd like to speak to my grandmother."

"I'm not allowed to wake her," she snapped and hung up again.

"Oh no, you did not just hang up again!" I muttered, redialing.

This time Grace answered, sleepily. She became instantly alert at the sound of my voice. "Oh, my goodness, Elle. What time is it?"

"Gram, you have plenty of time but you might like to get up and have breakfast."

"I told them to wake me. They never do. They don't listen to a thing I say!" She was angry. I could tell she was moving about.

"Gram, wait for the girl to help you. OK? Tell the girl to help you."

I could hear her calling to the aide, "Yoo-hoo!" Minutes passed. Finally I heard another voice in the room.

"What do you want, Grace?"

"I want to get up! I want to go to Mass! I told you last night!"

"Gram? Gram?" I waited for her to come back to the phone. I heard voices arguing on the other end of the line. Then Grace was back.

"She won't listen to a word I say."

"Remember, Gram, they work for you. Tell them what you want."

"They don't listen to me. They say they work for Bric."

"It's your money, Gram. You are their boss. Fire them if you don't like the way they treat you. Grandpa Jack did." This got her attention.

"That's right. Jack didn't stand for this. Neither will I."

When I arrived, I found Grace in her newly remodeled bathroom, carefully applying her makeup.

"You know, I used to be able to do this without even looking in the mirror." She reached for her perfume and gave her wrists a light spritz. "All the women asked how I did that without even a smudge." She giggled and wrinkled her nose as she turned her chair around and reached out her arms to me. "I missed you so much!" I stood aside to let her drive past. "Watch your toes, my barefoot girl!" She looked down and laughed up at me. "Where are your shoes?" She reached up and I leaned into her as she kissed me softly. The sweet scent of her filled my senses.

"There is the Grace of God," I whispered, as she sped away down the hall. I reached absently to flip the light switch. I stopped cold. It was wet. I stepped back to take another look. Water stains trailed from the light switch on the wall down to the woodwork along the tiled floor. There were more stains from the light sockets. I reached down to touch the woodwork. The wood was damp.

I found Grace in the kitchen, showing the aide how to cook her egg. I reached for a spiral notebook on the kitchen table and unclipped the pen from the front cover. The aide rushed from the stove to snatch it from my hand.

"That's private. We document everything."

I took the notebook back. "Then you won't mind my writing a note in it for Bric."

She grabbed the notebook from my hand a second time. "Only agency staff is allowed to write in it."

"Then you will want to document that there is water coming out of the electrical outlets in Grace's bathroom." I watched her reaction. There was none. "Have you noticed?" She stared at me. I couldn't tell from her expression if she was aware, surprised, or shutting me out. It was time to go. I made a mental note to follow up.

The aide buckled Grace into the passenger seat. I climbed into the back seat. I studied her reflection in the rear view mirror. She stared back at me. "We won't be phoning the grandchildren on their birthdays anymore. We are not comfortable making phone calls for her.

I patted Grace's shoulder. "How do you feel about that, Gram?"

Grace glared at her. "Birthdays have always been important. Just get my red address book. I'll call them myself."

We arrived at St. Jacob's Church. The aide helped her from the car and wheeled her chair up the long ramp. Grace's sister, Cara and her husband, Gordon waved from across the church. Grace beamed. I positioned the wheelchair next to the angular pew. The aide sat next to Grace. I walked around Grace's wheelchair, motioning the aide to slide over. She didn't move.

"I'm not allowed to leave her side," she declared firmly.

I pushed in next to Grace. She slid over to avoid my sitting on her lap. Liam joined us, giving Grace a warm kiss. His two sons did likewise, bear-hugging her as I slid to the left, making room for them to sit next to her. Then Quin slid in. I slid farther to the left, pushing the disgruntled aide farther to the end of the pew.

After Mass, Liam rose and unlocked the brakes on the wheelchair. "Where would you like to eat, Mom?"

"There is food at the house," the aide blurted. "I am instructed to feed Grace there." Liam took hold of the back handles of the wheel chair and pushed Grace toward the exit. "She doesn't need to go out," the aide objected.

Quin stood at the car, while Grace lowered herself into the front seat. "Where do you want to eat?" he asked.

"Royal Court," Grace answered immediately.

"Royal Court it is," Liam declared. It was a short drive across town. The aide furiously typed text messages while Liam and Quin and the younger grandchildren helped Grace from the car and pushed her wheelchair inside. Then Bric arrived.

Grace looked at him squarely. "Where do you go to Mass?" Bric chuckled and moved around the table to stand by the chair at the end. "Sit!" Grace ordered.

He sat, reluctantly, then looked across the table at me. "Where do you live now?" he smirked.

"There's water running out of the electrical plates in Gram's bathroom," I countered evenly. "Your contractor needs to open that wall back up."

Grace shot a dark glance at him, then at me. I rose, kissed her on her cheek and whispered, "I'll call you, Gram."

"Where are you going?"

"I'll call you tonight, Gram."

I did call. I called every morning to be sure she was awake, reminding her to enjoy the day. "Get outside and visit your plants. Are there tomatoes on the vine yet? I thought I saw tomatoes out back."

"Where? I didn't see one."

"Look outside in the garden. They're there. We'll go look together."

"Where are you?"

"I'm just a phone call away, Gram. You have my number. It's right in the front of your red address book."

"I try to call you, but the girls won't help me."

"Then I'll call you, Gram, every morning, every evening. I'm right here. I won't leave you."

"You better not. You're the only one I trust."

"Maire will be there Friday to wash and style your hair."

I phoned every evening to close the day with a prayer. Whenever she said she wanted to go to water therapy, I was there, but I was not the only one. Bric and Doreen began to show up unexpectedly. When they did, I excused myself to sit in the sauna. "Bric has a sauna in his house," she announced proudly. I knew that Grace was torn between her beloved children and her beloved granddaughter.

One morning just before water therapy the letter carrier stopped. He was a long time friend. He had appealed to the Postmaster General that, neighborhood covenants aside, Grace needed to have her mail delivered to her door. He got approval and proudly delivered the mail to her each day, listening to her news and sharing her stories. Grace and I stood outside, watering the roses. He motioned me aside, not wanting Grace to hear. "Grace's mail has been rerouted."

"What?"

"Her power of attorney signed a document. The mail is rerouted to his address. She'll only receive junk mail."

"There is no power of attorney."

He took a deep breath. "I've said too much. Call the Postmaster General."

"She gave no one her power of attorney. Do you know who signed the request?"

"I know."

"Tell me."

"I've said too much. It's a family thing. I'm only telling you because I hate to see this happen. You need to take it from here."

"What does the document say?"

"The document says that Grace is incompetent to handle her own affairs."

"Who signed this?"

"I think you know," he answered sadly. "Call the Postmaster General. Please don't use my name. I've said too much. Good luck." He took Grace's hand and chatted for several minutes. She brought a plate of cookies from the kitchen and he took one. After he left, Grace drove her power chair close to me where I stood waiting for her on the sidewalk.

"Why did they chase you away?" She was now accustomed to speaking in the presence of the aide. She had no choice. She had been stripped of her privacy.

I changed the subject. "Would you like to go to water therapy?"

"Just us?"

"Yes, just us." The aide scowled and reached for the phone. "I'll go in and get your purse and hat." I walked through the foyer and through the living room, headed toward the hallway to Grace's bedroom. I stopped. There was an odor of gas coming from the fireplace. I got on my hands and knees and peered under the fireplace grate. The pilot light had gone out.

The aide had gotten Grace settled into the passenger seat and was walking around the front of the Cadillac. "You need to call Bric and tell him there is gas leaking from the fireplace." She didn't respond. "Do you hear me? This is dangerous." Refusing to acknowledge me, she planted herself in the driver's seat and backed the car away from the house and into the street.

Minutes later, Grace was floating in warm, soothing therapy water. "Don't get my hair wet," she cautioned as I rested her head on my shoulder.

A white-haired gentleman waded towards us and stood looking down into her face. "Well, Grace, I didn't recognize you without your hat."

Grace looked up at him and immediately grabbed my arm to right herself and find her footing. "Well, Monsignor," she said, "I didn't recognize you without your pants!" Her face turned from pink to crimson as she realized what she said. He threw his head back and roared with laughter. She laughed, too. Grace was a new woman, free to express her own thoughts, surprised at her own amusement, at least for the time being.

Back at the house familiar feelings of emptiness took over as Grace drove slowly from room to room. "It's so quiet without you here, without you and Jack, without the children."

"Let's check your email," I suggested, searching for a diversion, a way to return her to her earlier humor. "Are your helpers checking your email with you every day?" Grace shook her head. The aide stood motionless, not responding. "Odd," I thought. Grace followed me into the office. The aide followed Grace. "Show your helper your computer skills." I looked over her shoulder as Grace moved the mouse. An error message popped up. I dialed the cable company. The technician asked for identification. Grace rattled it off proudly without hesitation. He came back on the line.

"That was disconnected."

"Who disconnected her cable?"

"Bric Riorden. He signed as power of attorney for Grace." Grace's eyes turned black. The aide stood in the doorway, expressionless.

"Why didn't anyone tell me?" Grace asked.

"Indeed," I answered. I looked up at the aide. "Give Grace some privacy."

She hesitated. "I'll just be outside the door."

"Whatever!" I tossed back. "Why don't you call Bric and report the gas leak?"

"What? What are you girls talking about? What gas leak?"

"There's water leaking down the wall in your new bathroom. The pilot light's gone out. Maybe the carpenters hit a line when they were working."

"I noticed the water on the wall last week but no one listens to me," Grace scolded.

The aide spun around and reached for the phone in her pocket. She frantically punched the keys as I closed the office door behind her and turned the lock. I heard her brushing against the door, turning the knob. I sat silently, waiting for Grace to speak.

"Why did they chase you away?" she asked sadly.

"Because you trust me. I tell you the truth." Her round, sad eyes studied mine. "Because I support you. Because I want you to be happy and strong."

"I am getting stronger, aren't I?"

"Yes. Remember, Gram, you're their mother. Tell them what you want."

"I'll call Acer," she declared resolutely as she cradled the phone and dialed. Delilah answered, chatting for a half hour and then promising to tell Acer to call.

Days passed, but Acer did not call Grace. Instead, he phoned me. "You need to stay away from her," he growled. "We offered to pay you. You agreed to stay away from her. You're upsetting her."

"I told you then and I'm telling you now. I don't want Gram's money. I'm worried about her. She is being given drugs she doesn't want for an illness that hasn't been diagnosed. She's deprived of her mail. She is disconnected from television and email and you think I am causing her to be agitated?"

"It's obvious how hostile you are."

"This is not a game, you miscreant! This is your mother! This is her life! Why are you doing this?"

"You are out of step. If you can't buy into the plan, then stay out of my way."

"Out of step? What are we, soldiers? What plan?"

"Stay away from her!"

"You cannot keep me from Grace."

In the days to follow, hot August winds shook the tree-lined cul-de-sac. Sudden surges of energy burst through the house. The lights flickered and dimmed, refusing to light when switched on, then blazing without warning when switched off. A parade of electricians set up elaborate surveillance cams. Switches and dimmers worked fine until the electricians left, then flickered relentlessly. The solar light in the back yard burned ghostly amber. The last electrician to tackle the problem shook his head and threw up his arms in confusion as Bric turned to Doreen. "I think its Dad!"

Doreen rolled her eyes. "Bric thinks Jack is haunting the house."

Bric hesitated at the threshold and then rushed headlong inside. "I need some of your records, Mom. He hurried past her to the office. She put the power chair into motion and followed him.

"Stop! I'm responsible for those records. Don't get them mixed up. Dad kept very good records. I know where everything is."

The lights in the office suddenly went out. Bric found the switch and flipped it repeatedly. Nothing happened. He stood back, staring around the dark room. Then slowly, the bulb began to grow from dim to bright.

"It's freezing in here!" Bric zipped up his jacket and wiped perspiration from his face. The light flickered again and went out. Bric quickly rummaged through the drawers. He grabbed an armful of binders and brushed past Grace.

She sped after him. "Where are you going with those?"

"I need these," he muttered as he bolted through the kitchen, into the open air. "I can't find the taxes. Did Acer take Dad's will? I'll be back." He spun out of the drive and sped away. Doreen stared after him.

Suddenly a thunderous gushing sound filled the air. An explosion of water shot two stories high onto the roof, tumbling back down from the roof against the windows of the sunroom and the dining room, drowning the deck. Doreen frantically dialed Bric's cell phone. "He won't come back!" She threw up her arms, jumped into her car and sped away.

I dialed Liam. He arrived in minutes. Plumbers followed with a street crew, lights flashing. They worked quickly and efficiently as I stood with Liam at the base of a magnificent rainbow spanning the breadth of the enormous spray. The cleanup crew arrived to assess the damage. I opened the door overlooking the flooded deck. "There is no reason for that line to have erupted," the technician was saying. "We replaced the casing and the gasket but the gasket wasn't cracked."

"Maybe Bric is right," mused Liam as he leaned down to kiss Grace's cheek. "Maybe Dad is here."

Grace looked up at her son with conviction. "Of course he's here. He's always been here."

In that case, Liam smiled, "I hope he thinks I did a good job mowing the lawn."

Grace chuckled. "Oh, you!"

I turned to Grace. "Let's get out of here."

"Yes," she replied. "Let's just go." Minutes later the Cadillac idled under the canopy of the Wellness Center. The aide wheeled Grace to the front desk while I found a parking space. I entered the doors to the lobby just as Grace proudly presented her membership card. The woman at the counter took the card and swiped it. Then she paused, puzzled, handed the card back to Grace, smiled apologetically and waved for me to join her at the far end of the counter.

"I'm sorry; your grandmother's membership is on hold."

Grace watched us closely, listening. "Go on to the dressing room, Gram," I called. "I'll meet you there." Then I turned back to the clerk. "Why didn't you call me?"

"I understand her son, Bric is handling payment of her bills, now."

"Did you call him?"

"We did call, several times last month and several times this month."

"And?"

"And he does not return our calls." She looked helpless to know what else to say.

"It's all right," I assured her. "I'll take care of it. Add the next couple of months as well. That will take her through Thanksgiving. She may not want to go out after the first snow falls. In the meantime, this is my cell number. I am confident you will call me before disturbing my grandmother with any other embarrassing issues?"

I floated on the warm water, watching Grace happily exercising with the therapist, telling the same stories she had told many times before. A woman bobbed next to me. "We just loved Jack," she interjected. "He was so much fun! He always made such a fuss! I miss seeing him here. Are you one of her helpers? I know the whole family. The sons are doctors. I know them all well. It's a big family. I know every one of them. Their family is something of a legend. I never did get to know her very well, but I sure do miss Jack. So charming! His sons are just as charming as their father."

On the way home, Grace pointed to Star Mart as we passed. "I need some things. We're out of bananas." She hesitated, "Although, I don't know how I'll pay for them."

"What are you talking about, Gram? Where's your check card? Where are your check blanks?"

"Gone. Bric took them. There's nothing left in the office."

"Do you have any cash?"

"No."

I was in a hurry, but I remembered the stories I had heard of Grace never being allowed to shop for her own groceries. I was determined to find everything she needed. Grace wasn't worried. She knew I wouldn't let her down. When we arrived back at the house, Bric and Doreen and Quin were waiting in the kitchen. "How did they get in?" Grace asked. I piled the bags on the kitchen floor. Bric and Quin stood against the sink, exchanging jokes about women shopping. I was too angry to speak. Grace cut them off. "There was no money for water therapy and there was no money for groceries. You took my check card and my check blanks and I want them back."

"We'll get the rest of the things you need," Doreen shot back dismissively.

"Elle bought what I needed. There were no groceries in the house."

Bric cut her off. "We'll take care of it."

Grace turned to me and whispered sadly, "How quickly it all goes. In a blink of an eye, my family is replaced by strangers. The children I knew are gone."

"Don't worry, Gram. I'm not leaving."

"I'm counting on it," she said.

I kissed her cheek and left, promising to call. Less than an hour later she called me.

"Elle, I need you to call Gordon. He wants to speak with you."

I hung up and dialed the number. "Gordon? It's Grace's granddaughter, Elle. Gram asked me to call."

"Elle, I telephoned Grace to tell her the sad news that her sister Blair had died. Blair had an episode, apparently a reaction to a new drug, but it wasn't caught and she died shortly thereafter."

"Oh, my God!"

"Blair appointed me executor of her estate, and I remain so, despite Acer applying for a reappointment."

"What? Why would my Uncle Acer think he should be executor?"

"Grace should have received the disbursement of will by now. We were surprised not to see your mother at the funeral," he added, "but given her ill health of late,"

"She didn't know," I replied. "No one told me. Wait! What ill health?"

"Your Uncle Bric tells us that she's not well."

"My grandmother is well enough," I retorted. "I think it is her family that is failing!" He didn't respond to that. I wondered if I could I trust him. "My grandmother's mail has been rerouted to Bric."

"How can that be?" he questioned. "She's a capable woman!"

"Exactly," I answered. "Gordon, I need you to do something for my grandmother."

"Sure. Anything."

"I need you to take that letter of disbursement to Gram at her home."

"Of course, but I don't understand. If her mail is going to her sons, they should have given it to her by now. Why don't they want her to receive her own mail?"

I took a deep breath. "They have declared her incompetent."

"No!"

"I have the document from the Postmaster. Bric signed as her agent, although, as far as I know, she did not grant him power of attorney."

"I will pay a visit to Grace myself. I will personally explain these documents to her."

"You are a good man, Gordon."

"I'm not going to get in trouble with Bric am I?" I listened for humor in his voice, but I heard none.

"Probably. Do you care?"

"Well, I have a very good attorney." This time he did laugh.

"Right."

Streaks of lightening flashed in the distance. Thunder rumbled overhead and lightning bolts streaked from sky to ground. Bright crimson leaves whipped into a frenzy as rain blew sideways onto the drive in front of Grace's house. Grace begged off water therapy, saying it was cold outside and she didn't want to get her hair wet. She had other things to do. Crystal Ann brought a load of pumpkins. Lyssa brought tall sheaths of cornstalks from the farm. Despite the rain, Dierdre bundled her up to view a homecoming parade. Dierdre insisted the street patrol escort Grace to a restricted VIP viewing area. Grace said she was tired, but Dierdre ignored her reluctance, saying that no one ever sleeps in the Riorden family. Then after they had all gone, Grace phoned. "There's going to be a party. It's my birthday next week."

"I know! So, tell me about the party."

"It's supposed to be a surprise," she whispered. "A certain someone isn't supposed to know." I wondered if she were referring to herself or to me. "It's going to be huge! It's going to be even grander than Jack's ninetieth birthday party."

"Really! How exciting."

"All the children will be there." Then I heard Quin's voice in the background.

"Delivery boy!" There was muffled laughter.

"Quin asked me if I needed anything, and I said I was out of Pepsi, and here he is." I heard her put the phone down. "Oh, what else is in that bag?" Then she was back on. "I always ask him where the bill is and he always says that Bill wasn't at the store!" I heard Quin laughing. "You don't have a cap. You have to have a cap to have a bill!"

"Gram, you have company. I'll call you later."

"Yes, you do that. Aren't my children wonderful? They take such good care of me. There is nothing that I need now. They will take care of it all."

I hung up. "No more!" I walked for hours in the misty autumn fog. The moon was a glowing hazy orb. I looked for Ronan's light. "Where are you? I need you to ward off the darkness."

Early the next morning I sat in a front booth of the friendly family-style Perkins restaurant, home of caramel apple and fresh pumpkin pie. I watched Maire's small, lithe figure in black jeans and denim jacket strode through the crowded parking lot toward me. Her auburn hair was cropped short and freshly styled into a sleek, metro look. She eyed me, assessing the damage. "You look great! Love the hair. I'm not sure I like my new look. I'm going back today." She looked at me again. "It's good you are out of that house."

Maire divided her time between a confectioner's kiosk in the mall and Macy's. She sold sweet chocolate morsels in small, expensive, beautifully wrapped portions. She reached across the table, pushing a cellophane-wrapped bundle toward me. "How's Ma?"

"She's looking better, but a bit fragile." I took a bite of soft fudge.

"I hear that she's been to see Bric's new digs. Did you see the signage?" She chuckled and lit a cigarette. "I'm surprised he went so big with that sign." She winked. "It must have been a tough choice for him. I mean he could have put at least another five parking spaces there."

I laughed. "I think Gram's happy despite the mail and the checking account. She's preoccupied now with her birthday party."

"She lives in two conflicting worlds. She knows what they're up to, but the Riorden rush is seductive. I take it you weren't invited."

"No, no. Gram says it's a secret, that a certain someone isn't supposed to know."

"Meaning you?"

"I guess. Gram never said. She loves a good secret."

"She's not ready to give up the illusion." She paused to searched my eyes.

"What's on your mind?" She shook her head. "What? Tell me."

"Cheyla came by the kiosk earlier this week." She rolled her eyes. "By the time Cheyla and the Riorden guild are done circulating their lies, those lies will damn sure be somebody's truth!" The waitress placed two plates of omelets. "I asked her why they kicked you out."

I took a deep breath and waited. Maire loved intrigue. I knew this couldn't be good. "And?"

"She said they kicked you out because you were abusive." She blew smoke into the air, her eyes never leaving mine.

I met her gaze. "Saying it doesn't make it true."

"It does in our family."

"That's exactly what Ralph said to Seth."

Maire pushed her omelet around the plate with a fork. "Hun," she drawled, "warm this up, please." She handed her plate to the waitress and turned back to me. "Cheyla and the Riorden guild," she raised her brow for emphasis, "are God's most prolific gossips. They may not start out malicious, but they become intoxicated on their own drama. Their spin becomes their truth." She tapped her fork absently on the table. "If Bric or Acer or anybody wanted to spread that or any other rumor, they'd only have to leak it to their spouses. Within hours it would be accepted as fact."

"Why would they do that?"

"They have no boundaries. This family takes what it wants. You may be the only one in this family who has stood against it, well, except for Sean." She leaned forward, her voice low. "You've got your thumb in the dam and the force of the water you're holding back is about to blow you sky high!"

"She is their mother," I protested.

"She is nothing to them. Ralph said it months ago. She is a pawn." Maire pushed her plate away. "Look. I'll try to make this simple, because I know you are a logical person. Intrigue isn't necessarily your forte. Acer is trained to kill. He is trained to win."

"I thought I was the cynical one."

She slapped her hand on the tabletop. "It's not about you! It's not about Mom! Whatever Acer is after, he'll stop at nothing to get it. Acer believes that life is war and war is a game. He is playing to win! You were her primary caretaker. Do you think you would have had any defense if Bric reported that you doubled her dosage or drugged her?" Her words stunned me. "What would you have done if they argued that cancel- ing water therapy, the one thing she loved, cutting off her mail, disconnecting her cable and email and cance- ling her checking account were all done because you, the primary caretaker were abusing her resources?" She paused for effect. "That may be exactly what they are saying. After all, Cheyla didn't tell me everything she came to say because I stopped her. What if they planned to accuse you of every evil action they had taken? What if they claimed they assumed power of attorney to protect their mother from you!" My mind was on overload. I wanted her to stop talking. I knew that she was determined to make me hear and under- stand. She continued. "No matter what the politi- cally correct position is, everyone believes women are fragile. If Acer can get you to show emotion, it will validate his claim. If you cry, it proves you are weak. If you are angry, it proves that you are volatile. If you are stoic, it proves that you are calculating." I realized she was trying desperately to protect me the only way she knew how. Her weapon was her insight. She was a Riorden. I forced myself to focus and listen. "Of course, Acer's biggest challenge is Mom."

"Gram?"

"Oh, yes!" Maire waved her cigarette in the air, flicking an ash. "Ben Annan taught her to be nice, but Ida taught her be strong. She is strong! Dad couldn't break her. But beware! Acer is more dangerous than Dad ever was. He's got Riorden anger and military discipline. You and Mom are just collateral damage."

"That's what I don't get. Why go after their mother now? The land is already in a trust."

"Whatever his agenda, he needs you out of the way. Mom is strong, but she does have a breaking point. They haven't broken her yet, but they will. Dad couldn't do it, but Acer will use her love for him. And he will use your love for her. He'll break you both if he can!" Maire threw her arms up in conclusion. "You are the most dangerous opponent they have faced yet. You know why?" I shook my head. I didn't know. "Because you're smart and you will see through the lies. Acer must break you before that happens."

"How?"

"Figure it out," she answered impatiently. "You were the sole caretaker of their parents. Do you get it?" She counted on her fingers. "Dad fell while in your care and wouldn't let you touch him. They will say he was afraid of you."

"That's ridiculous."

"He told people that you were keeping him prisoner."

"Oh, my God!"

"Now you see. Your grandmother didn't make a move without you. She was never diagnosed with Alzheimer's, but Bric had to take over her checkbook, her accounts and her mail. They will say you were instructing her, controlling her. They will say you caused her to be agitated, so of course they had to sedate her. They will say you imagined everyone was against you. They will say you convinced Grace of that! They will say Grace lost her trust in her own children. They will say you isolated yourself and your grandmother. You said it yourself, isolation is the first act of intimidation."

"I asked for their help, often."

"So you say. Listen to me. Mom is just a pawn. You are Acer's target."

"Are you saying I should run away?"

"He's locked and loaded. If you stay you will have to fight. If you fight, he will pursue you until he beats you down. For Acer, life is war and war is a game."

"Being a member of this family is mind-numbing."

"Get away. Get on with your life. That's what I plan to do. Hey! It's a beautiful day. Let's take Mom to the pumpkin patch."

The big bus glided through a lush prairie fen as my thoughts twisted through a dark, muddled quagmire. I closed my eyes but I couldn't close my mind. Does the turtle choose the river because it goes in the direction it is headed or does it follow the river trusting in the journey? I drifted into sleep.

I dreamed I was back on the farm. I saw my grandfather in the cab of the gleaming green John Deere Tractor, the loader raised recklessly high above

the machine. The only sound was Chester's muffled barking from somewhere in the tall weeds. My
grandfather's head was bodiless. The loader lowered
to the ground and bit deep into the dirt, then heaved
skyward, unearthing not mounds of dirt, but more
bodiless heads flying through the air! As I watched
in wonder, I realized that I recognized the expressionless faces. There was Mary Caye, Crystal Ann, Acer,
Quin, Dierdre, Aiden, Ralph, Ward, Bric, Seth, Riley,
Lyssa and Ursula. They tumbled and bounced and
ricocheted randomly, expressionless, bodiless, across
the circular gravel drive in front of the farmhouse. I
woke with a start.

G race did have her birthday party. I decided I
would phone her a day or so after the party. She
would be the center of attention now and she could tell
me about that later. I thought I might offer to have a
private party with Maire at Royal Court. I never got
the chance to make that call.

Sometime after the lavish birthday meal, the singing of the birthday song, the opening of expensive
gifts and the loud silly jokes, the daughters and grandchildren withdrew to the sunroom and Grace's sons
loomed over her like tall dark shadows. Acer leaned
down closely into his mother's face. "We're not
going to talk about this. Understand? There will be
no commotion." Grace looked at the stack of papers
and nodded. She was caught in the Riorden rush.
She trusted and she obliged. The signing done, the

families made a hasty exit leaving her suddenly alone. It was a beautiful autumn day but as she watched the last of them drive away, she could feel the chill of winter approaching.

I stood in the small post office on Main Street in Ronan's village. The clerk leaned across the desk.

"Good morning, Elle. How's Ronan Doyle treating you?"

"Just fine, Ian. Happy Thanksgiving."

"And to you, my girl. I've got a special delivery here. You'll have to sign for it. Say, we'll sure hate to see you leave this town. Doyle's Pub won't be the same without you about." He handed over the envelope. I tore it open. My mind raced as I read quickly through the page. I did it! I landed the job. My cell phone beeped as I climbed the wide steps of the Victorian house.

"Elle? Where are you?"

"Gram! Happy Thanksgiving. What are your plans?"

"They're taking me to Blackwater Manor to hear a presentation," she whispered urgently.

"A presentation? What does that mean?"

"My sister, Jacelyn, is going to talk about her life. They want me to have lunch and then visit her husband, Claude, in the memory care ward."

"How do you feel about that?"

"I'm not going! They can't make me go there."

"Be very careful, Gram. Do what you think best and remember, they want you to live there."

"I'm not going! I'm still their mother!"

Thanksgiving came and went. The family descended on Grace so I stayed away. I sat in the alcove of the Victorian house, reviewing plane schedules and real estate listings. The message light blinked on my phone. It was Gram's number. It was marked urgent. I dialed back. Acer answered. "You flagged your message as urgent?" I asked. "What's wrong?"

He chuckled. "We were cleaning the garage at the house and found boxes of things that belonged to you.

"You're at the house? I have nothing there."

"We'll bring it to you. Where are you?"

"Just leave it. It's not mine."

His voice grew impatient. "Then we'll put it in storage. Where shall we send the bill?"

"It's not mine." I hung up. It rang again. This time it was Liam.

"I have the keys to your storage area."

"It's already in storage?"

"I have the key. I'll help you."

I drove to the North edge of town and pulled into a large commercial lot, filled with moving vans. "There must be lights," Liam exclaimed, searching along the wall for a switch. He disappeared down the hallway, then reemerged with a flashlight. He stopped and unlocked a padlocked door. A jumbled mass of garbage bags tumbled out. There were buckets of debris, broken and discarded holiday ornaments and used lumber. "What's this?" He kicked at one of the bags, causing it to tumble forward and spill out into the hallway. We stared at the mess and then at each other. "It's garbage!" His face fell. "Its just garbage!"

I laughed. "Well, that's one way to clean the garage!"

He turned a dark face toward me. "This family owes you an apology."

By nightfall I was again sheltered in the warmth of the crackling fire from the open fireplace of the Victorian house. I welcomed the safety but I knew I couldn't stay. I had nabbed the elusive job.

Thanksgiving turned to Christmas and I joined Maire after her shift at the mall for a late night dinner at the Texas Roadhouse. She lit a cigarette as the waitress poured two cups of dark, aromatic coffee. "I know exactly what Acer's doing. He wants to prove to you that he's in control, that he can make you jump. He thinks he's knocked you down and he wants to rub your face in the garbage, literally. He made you clean out a storage unit filled with trash. If he'd asked you to clean out the garage for him, you'd have told him to go to Hell. In the end he got you to carry away his trash anyway. You got caught in the Riorden rush! There are no rules and there are no boundaries. It's an addiction."

"You think this is the behavior of addiction?"

"Absolutely. Why do you think it's called it the Riorden rush? To the Riordens, all abnormal behavior translates as normal."

"What do you mean?"

"The Riorden rush is the highest of highs. It's ecstasy. Abusive behavior is the drug of choice." She reached for a cigarette. "Without the behavior, the ego feels deprived. And that's trouble."

"You've just described Grandpa Jack!"

"Dad was a pathological narcissist. His grandiose sense of self-importance, his fantasies of unlimited success and power, made him as ruthless as a junkie looking for a fix. I know. I was there. He was envious, arrogant, mean and demanding. He was praised by the community for keeping his large brood in line. Meanwhile, every day was torture for us. There were no boundaries, no rewards and no way out. It was like a cult without intervention." She sipped slowly on her coffee. "Our only defense was to be invisible. That's how we survived. That's who we are. You won't like what I'm about to say." She paused again and ran her finger around the rim of her cup. "Maybe it's time we leave Grace to her family." I stared in disbelief. "She raised them. Maybe we just leave her to her fate and, using Ralph's expression, just get on with our lives." I shook my head, overwhelmed with sadness. She continued. "I mean, I can barely make it from one day to the next as it is. I don't need this stress. Neither do you. You need to get on with your career. Maybe the best thing to do is just call it good and step aside. Think about it." She raised her cup in a toast. "At any rate, Happy Christmas! Whatever this next year brings, I'm sure we'll have a good story at the end of it."

That night I collapsed across the cozy bed next to the warm fireplace. Mentally sapped, I slept soundly. Then I woke with a start. There was a chill in the room. I sat up and looked around. The fire was out. Moonlight backlit the snow covered elm and cottonwood branches just outside the window. I swung my legs over the side of the bed and stood up. I padded barefoot across the wood floor from room to room, finally standing at the kitchen sink, looking out on the snow capped lawn, brightly lit by the luminous moon. Then I recalled the dream that woke me. I was running from Acer. He was chasing me through empty streets. I ducked into a church. A priest was celebrating Mass on the altar. I walked up a side aisle and sat in a pew close to the front. Acer slid into the pew next to me. He reached across my lap and clutching my wallet in his hand, grinned at me, stood, turned and walked away down the side aisle. A nun blocked his exit. Without speaking, she reached out her hand and snatched my wallet from his grasp, walked toward me, handed it over and led me out. Then she put a small leather bound prayer book into my hand and motioned for me to go. Without looking back I ran, frantic for a place to hide. I came to a glass door. I broke the glass and crawled through the jagged hole into a stairwell. I grabbed the stairwell railing and bounded up the stairs, but was stopped at the top by a brick wall. Trapped, I crawled back down the stairwell, back through the broken glass, back into the empty street. There on the sidewalk in front of me lay the leather bound prayer book. I picked it up, turned it over and stared at the title. Then I woke.

I was not the only one awake that moonlight night. Grace also woke with a start. She held her hands up to her face in the dimly lit room and stared at her fingers and arms. They itched and burned. She called for the aide.

"What is it?" The aide complained. "You can't be ready to get up."

"Hand me the lotion. My skin is dry."

The aide transferred her to the power chair and steered it to the bedroom door. "Here, can you drive through the door to the kitchen? We'll have some tea." Grace looked around and didn't move. She shook her head. "Grace, I think you are a little confused."

"I'm not confused. I asked you for lotion. Why don't you get it for me? Why are those lights blinking?"

"Here. Let's put in a DVD. How about I Love Lucy?" The aide inserted the disk, but nothing happened. She pushed the eject button. The DVD came partially out then stuck. She ran her finger across the counter. "It feels damp. Where are you going?"

"I'm leaving. There are bugs in here."

"Come to the table. Let's look at the newspaper." She scanned the headlines. "Katy called while you were resting. Aiden and the kids were planning to stay here tonight. They thought they would stay until Saturday. I called Bric and Doreen to tell them. Apparently there's some reason they can't stay here, so they'll stay there. They'll be here on Friday." She placed a cup of tea in front of Grace on the table. "Oh my gosh! There are bugs in here! She ran to the pantry to get a swatter and returned to the table, slapping the swatter furiously. Then she cupped her hands and began clapping them in the air. "I've killed five already! Where are they coming from?" She stepped back and gasped. "There are black bugs and ants everywhere!"

As Grace lived her own nightmare, I stood at the kitchen sink in the Victorian house looking out the window over the moonlit lawn, reliving mine. The sound of my cell phone brought me back to reality. It was Maire. "What is going on with Mom?"

"What?"

"She sounds sad and distracted. The aide says she can't swallow, not even water. What is going on?

She's telling me about flying bugs and ants and lights flickering. The house seems to be filling with moisture and there's a persistent gas leak."

"I'm on my way." I looked at the digital clock on my cell phone. "It's midnight! Where can we meet?"

Meanwhile, Grace's home health care aide mobilized the Riorden guild hotline. She called Bric. Bric called Doreen. Doreen called Cheyla. Cheyla called Quin. Quin called Acer. Acer called Delilah. Delilah called Kristin. Kristin called Seth. Seth called Lyssa. Lyssa called Bric. Bric called Acer. Acer called Crystal Ann. The plan, outlined on the lawn outside Grace's kitchen window the day of Jack's funeral was in motion. The toothy-grinned leprechaun piped a jig into the dark night sky as Jack's cunning spirit was about to release the Devil one last time.

"Happy New Year, Ma." Grace sat in the front foyer smiling broadly. Her lipstick was perfectly applied and Estee Lauder Beautiful lingered in the air around her. Maire leaned down and gave her a warm embrace.

"Oh. Your hands are cold!"

"You'll have to warm them up for me," Maire grinned and bustled past the home health care aide standing next to Grace. "We're having strawberries and waffles for a New Year's brunch." She lifted a gleaming steel waffle maker from a Macy's bag on the floor. "Here is your new waffle maker, just like at Royal Court."

"Oh!" Grace exclaimed, running her hand over the shiny cover. The aide picked up her cell phone and stepped away.

"What the hell?" Maire whispered to me. "Does she intend to report our every move?" Grace leaned over to whisper.

"Will you make me an egg? These girls won't cook for me."

"At your service, Ma," Maire gestured in a broad stroke, wrapping an apron around her waist at the same time. We ignored the aide. She stood aside, not helping, not interfering.

"Who is training these people?" I asked as Maire served up plates of waffles with strawberry and whipped cream topping. She turned to the stove. Grace cut out a bite of waffle with her fork and savored each taste. The aide jumped to her feet as a car pulled into the drive and hurried to the front door. Maire rose and cleared the table, leaving a dish of strawberries and refilling Grace's coffee. The doorbell rang and I answered.

A stern faced woman pushed past me. "I'm Jessica, director of Ania Care. I'll take over from here." She spoke inaudibly to the aide, who backed away and stood by the door. "I'll get right to the point." I guessed she wasn't much for small talk. "The girls aren't going to use this." She pointed to the waffle machine. Then she turned to the aide. "Don't document any of this."

"She loves waffles," Maire responded immediately. "All the girls have to do is put it in a bowl, measure the waffle mix and stir."

"Our instructions are to clean and keep things neat. Is that clear?"

"Not exactly." Maire was amiable but firm. "Who prepares her meals, if your aides do not?"

"You'll have to take that up with your brother. We take our orders from him."

"In that case," Maire turned directly to Grace, "we'll eat out often!" Grace laughed. Jessica was not amused and left abruptly. The aide handed the phone to Maire.

"It's for you."

"Happy New Year, Bric." Maire's voice was clear and firm. "Yes," she answered into the phone, "we are having breakfast. Yes, I did make her an egg and now we're having waffles." Her mouth tightened as she listened. Her forehead furrowed into tiny ripples and her eyes grew dark and narrow. "You're joking." Her face went dark. Her voice was even darker. "Listen, little brother, you may think yourself to be a god in your own world, but in mine, you have no power. If I want to fix an egg or a waffle for my mother, no one, especially not you, is going to stop me!" Her face was tense as she listened again. "Well, come on, boy. We'll be right here." She hung up the phone and stared at me.

"What was that?" Grace asked. "What were you talking about?" Maire smiled and sat at the table next to Grace. "Bric told me I need ask his permission to visit you. I told him that wasn't going to happen." She smiled at Grace and kissed her cheek. Grace turned to me.

"He chased you away, didn't he?"

"I'm here, Gram. They may kick me out of your house, but they can't kick me out of your life."

"Good." She nodded solemnly. "I'm depending on it."

Maire looked from Grace to me. "So much for getting on with our lives."

January turned to February and the wettest March on record. A large upper level storm system moved in, bringing heavy spring rains mixed with intermittent snow. It was Easter Week. A brightly colored van displaying the friendly faces of The Steam Team across its exterior pulled up to the curb at the back of the house. The technician trudged through the mud and snow to French doors at the lower level entrance. He pulled massive hoses from the van through the yard into the great room. He sloshed through standing water and pushed furniture away, hooking up the hoses to industrial vacuums and blowers. He worked quickly, spraying an antimicrobial solution through the rooms. Hours passed. When the carpets were sucked dry, he replaced the hoses with large powerful dehumidifiers.

Bric stood in the doorway. "I want your van out of the driveway. These machines have to go."

"Well, someone ordered this contract," the technician replied. "I'm just doing my job. This much moisture requires a couple of days to dry out." Bric walked from room to room. He stopped at a bulge in the wall and reached out to poke at it with his finger. "Don't touch that!" the technician warned. "That whole wall could come down."

"No. That's just overflow from the gutter," Bric scoffed. "It'll dry out."

"It's more than that. There is water in the wall from the ceiling to the carpet. The trim and the base on the backside of the mopboards are black with fungus. The southeastern walls and windows are covered with it. You need to call the mold guys. Here's their number."

Bric shook his head. "We called you to dry out the water from the rain."

"This is more than gutter overflow. This is serious. You could be putting Grandma in danger. She could become ill."

"Who are you?" Bric demanded.

"I'm Rory, your nephew." He removed his mask and gloves. "I'm Maire's son, Rory."

Thrown for a moment, Bric stepped back. "I forgot you worked with this company."

"You should call the mold guys. This is serious."

"It'll be fine. It'll dry out."

"Tell Grandma I'll be back to look in on her."

"No. No, that's fine. We won't need you anymore."

"She is my Grandmother. I'll be back."

Maire and I accompanied Grace to Ash Wednesday service. Grace proudly displayed the crisscross of ashes on her forehead. When we returned to the house, Doreen was there, lining the baseboards and counter tops with ant traps, spraying bug spray around the exterior and in the garage. "We'll go now, Ma," Maire said. "Why don't you lie down for a nap?"

"No!" Grace answered. "There are bugs in there." Acer and Bric stood on the front lawn. She propelled the power chair forward. "Acer, I won't be in there with those bugs."

"Well, then, how about a trip to the farm?" he suggested amiably. Grace agreed, happy to be included. "First I must speak with Bric."

Acer and Bric strolled across the lawn to the back of the house. Grace followed them through the lower level entrance, trailing behind as they entered and inspected each room. "Mom, back that thing up," Acer complained. "You're underfoot, here." She paused, then moved forward again to follow them. Acer flipped a switch. The lights dimmed, then glowed brilliantly. Bric stepped back, nearly sitting in Grace's lap.

"Mom! That chair is a tank! Back it up!" She sat still, refusing to withdraw any further. They continued through the bedrooms. She followed like a shadow. Bric pointed out a bulge in the ceiling. Acer touched the wall. It was damp. He gave out a low whistle. Then he reached to poke at the bulge.

"Don't touch it!" Grace cried out. "It'll burst!"

"Move away!" he growled. "There, over by the bed. Get back. I'm going to end all this commotion!"

Maire glanced at her watch. It was nine p.m. Macy's was closing. She had an hour left to get the towels and bedding organized for the next day. A young girl stood at her side. "May I help you?" Maire asked.

"Do you have mattresses?" The girl didn't look at her. Her eyes searched the aisles.

"Mattresses? No. May I help you find some bedding?"

"No. Thank you. My mother will take care of it," the girl replied absently as she disappeared around the corner into the bedding area. Maire followed. There was Doreen.

"How can I help you?" Maire asked again.

"We have it covered," she answered without looking up.

Maire backed away. "Either they are belligerent as hell or they don't recognize me," she thought.

Doreen divided her list, barking orders to her children. "You get this. You get this. I'll get this." They darted through the aisles, grabbing sheets and towels and pillows as they rushed past.

Maire walked back to Belinda, her coworker. "It looks like they're on a scavenger hunt. It's too late in the season to be school shopping. You know, they're being so damn rude, I'm not going to wait on them."

"Anyway, we have a rule against waiting on family," Belinda answered.

"Then I'm going to have a cigarette."

"Go on. I'll ring them up."

Maire finally clocked out at ten-fifteen. She strolled through the patio door of her apartment, kicked off her shoes, dropped her coat and stopped to gaze absently into the recesses of the refrigerator. She turned and looked back out the patio door to the streetlight glowing across the quiet street. She could see the outline of the mall. Something was wrong. She could feel it in her spirit. She picked up the phone. There were no messages. She could not shake the feeling of dread. She grabbed her car keys and drove back to the empty mall parking lot, past the entrance of The Royal Court. One car was there. It was Grace's Cadillac. Maire shuddered. She knew The Royal Court had been closed for over an hour. She walked to the front door and looked in. To her surprise, the door opened and a young man in an apron ushered her in. "You're looking for Grace?" He stepped aside and motioned for her to go on through. "She's here. We're done cleaning and we're waiting for her to leave so we can go home." Maire stepped into the empty dining room. The lights were dimmed for the night. The tables were empty. "They're in the back. They're waiting for you."

"They're waiting for me? Who's waiting for me?"

"She's with her son."

"I don't see anyone."

"They're way back." Then he whispered. "We're ready to leave now. We're closed." Maire moved tentatively past empty tables into a secluded meeting room. Grace was seated in her wheel chair at the end of a long table. Acer jumped up. "Welcome. Join us. We'll get you something to eat and drink. Coffee?" Maire brushed past him to her mother.

"Hi, Ma," Maire whispered and kissed her cheek. Grace did not respond. Maire's mind raced. The restaurant was closed. What was Acer doing here? She took a closer look at her mother then walked around the table and circled behind her. 'This is eerie,' thought Maire. Grace was stone silent. Maire sat at the table, directly across from her mother. "I'm glad to be here with you. Did you have something to eat?" Grace stared straight ahead. Maire pulled her chair around the table, closer to the side of the wheel chair. She took Grace's hand gently in her own. Grace pulled it back, grimacing. Her hand was stiff and rigid. Her eyes were glazed. Her face was ruddy, like it had been scrubbed with sandpaper. Her hair was matted and messy. "Ma, where is your hat? It's cold out tonight. Where is your jacket? You have no lipstick on. Where is your purse?" Grace looked at her. It was then that Maire saw that her glasses were bent and cockeyed across her nose, pressing into her cheek. "Ma! What's going on? You like you've been hit over the head by a 2x4. Grace looked into her eyes and moved her lips. Maire leaned in close. Acer stood rigid.

"Never mind right now," Grace said. Maire understood. This was Grace's way of protecting herself from further harm. Grace spent her entire life dodging abuse. Silence was a language she spoke fluently.

Maire realized there was an aide present. "Hello. What's your name?" The aide did not reply. "Are you new? Is this your first day?" Acer moved to the far end of the long table.

"No," the aide finally responded. "I've been with Grace a little over a week."

Maire looked down the table at Acer. "We have to consider a better way for Mom to travel. Look at the way she's sitting in this wheelchair. What's wrong with this seat? Her knees are scrunched up above her hipline and that's not good." Acer moved quickly, extending his hand as if in a handshake, but pushing it into her face.

"I'm Acer Riorden. I'm the number one son."

She glared at him. This seemed perverted, even for Riorden behavior. How dare he pretend she were a stranger and speak to her as if this were a joke? "I know who you are, Acer. You're the number one sumpin' sumpin'!" He pitched backward, steadying himself on the back of a chair, grabbed his cell phone, turned quickly and scuttled into the bathroom, dialing frantically. Maire turned back to Grace. "Ma, it's time for you go home. You're looking a little tired, there, honey. I think we'd better go now." Maire rose and pulled the wheel chair back away from the table. She adjusted Grace's foot pedals and pushed the wheel chair toward the door. "What's wrong with this wheelchair? The wheel is wobbling."

Acer darted across the room, pushing Maire aside. "I'll take that," he ordered, jostling Grace through the double doors, tipping the chair backwards, as if she were a kid on a joy ride. Grace gasped as she bounced across the rubber and metal threshold. Two waiters gratefully and swiftly locked the doors behind him. Acer's face lit up in the moonlight. He spun the chair in circles, calling, "Wheee!" Grace braced herself, clinging to the arm rests. Acer circled the lot, popping wheelies, racing past Maire and circling again, faster.

"What the hell are you doing?" Maire demanded.

"Stop! I'm sliding out!" Grace's voice split through the night.

Maire jumped to stand directly in front of the chair. "Stop!" she screamed. The animated glow disappeared from Acer's face. As if in a trance, he wheeled the chair to the passenger side of the Cadillac where the aide stood by the open door.

"Stand up," the aide ordered.

"Stand up?" Maire bristled. "That's what you're here for!" Maire peered into the window of the car. "Where's the gait belt? Where's her walker?"

"She knows how to do this," Acer commanded. "Watch!" He pulled Grace's arms. Grace winced as she stood stiffly beside the car, clinging to the cold metal frame. She obediently inched herself forward, sliding her body along the side of the vehicle.

"That's enough!" Maire shouted. She elbowed her way between Acer and Grace. "Here, Ma, lean on me."

"I can do it myself. I don't need your help." Grace shot her a stern look. Maire stepped back, shocked at the change in her mother. Then Grace softened. "See? I'm fine. I'm too heavy for you. You barely weigh a hundred pounds. I'll hurt you."

Maire persisted. "Lean on me, Ma. We'll do this together." She inched her mother forward until they reached the passenger seat. Grace slowly swiveled her body into the car. Maire lifted her legs and tucked them into the foot well. She carefully buckled the seat belt around her, kissed her mother and gently closed the car door. Then she turned her fury on the aide. "You need to go away and never come back. You should be fired!"

The aide looked defiantly past her to Acer. "I'm just doing what I'm told."

Maire glared at Acer. "That is what I am talking about!" Acer smirked mischievously in the fluorescent overhead light and slid into the back seat, motioning to the aide. The Cadillac backed out and disappeared around the corner, leaving Maire standing alone in the Royal Court parking lot.

I curled up on the couch in the quiet house in Ronan's quiet little town knowing he was across the way in his own house, ever the vigilant guardian. It was time to say evening prayers. I dialed Grace's number. There was no answer. Where could she be? Just then my phone beeped. "Hello?" There didn't seem to be anyone on the line. "Hello?"

"Hello." The voice was expressionless, mechanical. "Your mother would like to speak to you."

"OK. Who is this?" There was no response.

"Hello?" Grace's voice was soft and calm and yet the sound of her voice caused me to sit straight up. Something was wrong. I looked at the clock again.

"Gram! How are you? Are you all right?"

"Where are you?" she asked in a distant voice. "Will it take you a long time to get here?" I rose from the couch, slipping into my jacket.

"Do you need me there now? Are you all right?" I threw my bag over my arm and grabbed my keys.

"I'm all right."

"Do you want to say prayers with me?" I was behind the wheel, starting the car.

"Yes, we always say our prayers." I listened beyond her words, beyond the sound of her voice, beyond the tone. She was trying to tell me something, but what was it?

"Are you alone, Gram? Is someone else there with you?" I slowly drove through the quiet, tree-lined street.

"Acer is here."

"Is he there beside you?"

"He's right here."

A cold dispassionate voice interrupted. "Acer Riorden here."

I guessed I was on speaker. He was monitoring his mother's call. "Hey, Acer. Elle. How are you?" The entrance ramp was just ahead.

"We had a wonderful evening," he answered. His voice was artificial, mechanical, scripted. "We went to the farm. We have a new tenant, you know. We had to check on the carpet being replaced. Then we drove to Seth's, but he wasn't home. So we came back to Royal Court. Now we're back home having a little ice cream."

"It's a little late for Gram to be up, isn't it?"

"I'll put Mom back on," was all he said.

"Gram, are you all right?"

"I'm all right now." She was trying to tell me something. Why was I so dense?

"I love you, Gram."

"I love you so much. When will you be here?"

"I can be there in an hour."

"Tomorrow's fine, sweetheart. I'll look for you then."

"You call me if you change your mind, Gram. You have my number right there by the phone. Just dial and I'll answer."

"OK, dear. Good night. Thank you."

I hung up and dialed Maire. She answered on the first ring. "Maire, I just got a call from Gram. Something is very wrong."

"I know. I was just about to call you. I just saw her at Royal Court. She looked like she had been beaten. She had no hat, no jacket, no purse. Her face looked like it had been scrubbed. She could not raise her arms to the table. She could barely speak. She told me to 'Never mind.'"

"That's her code."

"That's all she would say! The really eerie thing is that her aide and Acer were as evasive as Grace was unresponsive. They are hiding something. I think Mom will tell me later, but she sure didn't want to talk about it in front of them. It scared me to the bone. I think she's in danger. I think she has been warned not to say anything." She finally took a breath.

"I'm just about to get on the Interstate."

"It's late. Tomorrow is a huge sale day at Macys. I'll be working from seven in the morning until ten tomorrow night. I'll check in on her after that and call you with whatever I've found out."

The next day Maire clocked in at Macys. She was in bedding, folding towels when the call came. "Maire, this is Crystal Ann. Mom has been taken to the hospital."

"What's wrong?"

"She has an infection. They thought she had pneumonia. It's probably just a urinary infection."

"I'm no nurse, Crystal Ann, but even I know there's a big difference between pneumonia and urinary infection. Cut the crap and just tell me the truth. Why pneumonia?"

"She had trouble breathing and a white infection in her throat."

"Well, what is it?"

"They don't know. Don't make a fuss. They gave her antibiotics, but they are going to keep her a couple of days."

My cell phone rang. "You need to get here. Mom's in the hospital. I don't believe what Crystal Ann is telling me."

I stared at the phone in my hand and dialed. "I'd like to speak to Jessica, your director. Not available? I'm calling about my grandmother, Grace Riorden. I'd like someone to tell me what happened yesterday."

The person on the other end was abrupt. "There's nothing I can tell you. Anything you need to know you can get from the power of attorney." The phone went dead. I redialed.

"Please tell me you did not just hang up on me."

"Whatever you need to know you can get from the power of attorney."

"Perhaps you would be more comfortable telling it to a home health care investigator?" Again the phone went dead.

The next day I walked through the long corridors of St. Christopher's Hospital. I waited outside her room as nurses and medical staff hovered over her with quiet determination. A nurse placed Grace's chart into a file holder on the wall next to me. I flipped it open and scanned the pages. Quin suddenly appeared from around the corner. He stared at me, then down at the chart. "I've heard that you are calling for an investigation." His voice resonated with controlled anger.

"If you think I'm a problem," I answered, "you'd better look behind you. I'm the least of your worries." He turned to face Maire, charging headlong toward us.

She seized his elbow. "Forget her!" she ordered. "I want to know!" He cowered from the venom in her words. "What happened to my mother? The hospital said she had pain and swallowing difficulty. You conducted a swallowing study. Then you filled her full of antibiotics, calling it a localized pneumonia. You said you saw spots in her left lower chest. Then you called it urinary infection. Is it that you don't know or is it that you're making it up as you go along?"

I left him in Maire's grip and returned to Grace. She stood bracing herself against her walker. "No!" Grace stiffened. "No! That's how I got hurt. I'm not going near that bed!" Lyssa stood by, coaxing her. "No!" Grace repeated, her body rigid, resisting with all her might. Mary Caye, Crystal Ann, Ralph and Ursula gathered in the hallway.

"How did you all get here so fast?" Maire asked no one in particular as she strode through the hallway. "Don't most of you live across the country?" She moved past them to join me. "The Riorden guild hotline must have been burning the airwaves."

"I know you!" gushed Mary Caye. "We go way back."

Maire bristled. "We go way back? Mary Caye, we're sisters!"

Ursula joined them. "Maire, I was wondering if you could tell me something."

"Sure," Maire answered, "but don't know what happened and apparently no one is saying." She glared at Quin, who ducked past and walked directly to the nurses' station. Mary Caye flitted away to join him.

"Oh, of course. No. That's not what I was asking. I was wondering if you could tell me about the train accident." Maire stared at her, dumfounded. Ursula was the youngest. She was about the same age as Maire's oldest daughter. Maire guessed that these words were the most she and Ursula had ever exchanged.

"Why are you asking about that now?"

"No one else will talk about it," Ursula pressed.

"Excuse me," Maire said. "I think Elle needs us." I stood in the doorway of Grace's room. "Why are people so damned fascinated by that train wreck?" she muttered, peering past me to the chaotic scene inside. "What am I saying? This family is a train wreck!" Grace was surrounded, penned in by a nurse, a nurse's aide and Lyssa. "I don't blame her for asking. No one else will talk about it. When the Riorden's get an order to bury something, they obey. That story will be in the vault forever. No, it's all right. Ursula is like you. She is all about the truth. With her there are no secrets." Maire looked over my shoulder at the scuffle ensuing. The struggle to get Grace into bed was intensifying. "What can I do?" Maire asked.

"Get Ursula," I answered. Without another word, Maire turned and crossed the floor to Ursula, standing alone where she had left her.

"Elle needs you. Now." Ursula brushed past her to the doorway in one effortless motion. I stepped aside as she stood silently taking in the scene. Once she assessed the problem, she slipped off her shoes and leapt into the bed, holding out her arms to Grace. Grace eyed her suspiciously. She sat up and smiled softly. "Come to me, Mom. Sit right here. I'll be right here waiting. I won't let you fall."

"I didn't fall!" Grace stated firmly.

"OK!" Ursula answered. "This time, I'll be right here. I won't let anything happen to you." Grace eyed her apprehensively. Ursula offered a firm and steady arm as Grace took a step, pivoted her body around and settled into Ursula's lap. Ursula slipped out and back. Grace was finally safely seated in the bed. The aide reached down to swing her legs up onto the bed.

"No!" Grace stiffened.

"I'm right here," Ursula repeated. She slid to the center of the bed and lay flat, her hand reaching out toward Grace. Grace leaned back on her elbows and the aide swung her legs into the bed. Ursula slid back out of the bed as Lyssa backed away, teeth clenched, jaw tight and rigid.

"Don't leave me," Grace pleaded.

"I'm right here, Gram. Don't worry. Just rest." I settled her head into the pillows. Maire stood at the foot of the bed. Mary Caye and her husband, Clay stood behind Maire. Ralph joined Lyssa and Ursula. Grace's children huddled and whispered while their mother lay silently watching and listening.

Maire moved to the side of the bed to hold Grace's hand. "Ma, how do you feel?"

"My neck hurts. My shoulders and my arms ache and my knee has a shooting pain."

The others moved out of the room. I stroked Grace's cheek. "Did you bite your tongue? It looks swollen. What's this? There are punctures on your left arm."

Grace looked up at me and then straight ahead to the foot of the bed and the wall beyond. "Do you see it?"

"See what, Ma?" Maire followed her eyes to the wall to a solitary crucifix.

"What is it?"

"Do you see it? It's a waterfall. It's golden. The water is gushing out of that cross. It's sparkling gold. It's coming right at us."

It was impossible to understand. This wasn't Grace's usual code. She was reliving some terrible sight. It was real and it was vivid. Maire took Grace's hand in hers. "I will not let anything harm you, Ma. I'm right here."

"You don't see it?" Grace whispered. "The water is sparkling, glinting gold."

I wanted to know what she was seeing, but I didn't want to draw attention. "Gram, just rest now. When you have rested, tell us again what happened. You can help us understand. OK?"

"OK," she answered and closed her eyes. Maire and I sat silently as she drifted to sleep.

"Morphine?" I asked.

Maire shook her head. "She's trying to tell us something. Something happened. It had to do with water. They're going to try to keep it from us." She stared at the wall, deep in thought.

"Crystal Ann said she had an infection?" I asked. "They thought she had pneumonia?"

"She had a white spot on her lungs," she answered, annoyed. "They filled her full of antibiotics and sedatives. They're going to keep her here a couple of days."

"Then what is Gram telling us about a waterfall?"

"We may never know. We are in Riorden territory, the land of many secrets." She shook her head in thought. "Bric is haunted by Dad. Acer is drunk on his own power. The rest have reason and conscience all their own."

"The Riorden rush!"

"Exactly. Just be careful," she added. "Behind power, reigns terror. They fear the secrets you might uncover."

Saturday morning dawned. Grace was restless, coughing, confused and drowsy. A woman breezed in. "Grace? I'm Mallory. I'm a social worker." She pulled a chair close to Grace's bed and recited a litany of questions. Grace slept through most of them. Mallory wrote that Grace was disoriented. The med nurse came in to administer pills. Grace couldn't swallow. Mallory wrote that Grace was unable to follow instructions.

I called every day. Each day there was a reason I couldn't speak with Grace. Finally on Thursday morning a nurse handed her the phone. "How are you, Gram?"

"When can you be here?"

"I'll be there tonight."

"Do you promise?"

"I promise. Have you eaten?"

"No. I can't swallow."

"Will you try? For me?"

"Yes, I will." Grace hung up the phone and pushed the button for the nurse.

"Can I be of assistance, Grace?"

"Elle said I should try to eat. I am hungry. I'll try some jello."

By Good Friday, the family converged again. Mary Caye arrived, then Bric, Doreen, Lyssa, Seth, Ralph and finally Quin. I found them gathered in the corridor.

"She's having a chest x-ray and after that was scheduled for physical therapy," Mary Caye offered. "We are hoping she might be able to stand."

"What happened?"

"Oh," Crystal Ann interrupted. "No one knows."

By evening her catheter was out and she was dressed for church. Lyssa, Ursula and the aide rode down the elevator with Grace to the small hospital chapel. The priest stepped onto the altar. Lyssa had alerted him that the queen mother of the Riorden family was in attendance. The priest placed his hand on the front pew and looked directly at each of them. "Welcome, Grace." He reached to hold her hand. "We gather tonight on the eve of the Resurrection. The story is told by four faithful servants of Christ." He paused and scanned the group. "Or were they?" Grace shot him a quizzical look. "On this night, Jesus' heart was full of sorrow." He patted Grace's hand and stepped into the aisle. "Every step He took was labored. He suffered under a terrible burden. His two companions supported Him or He would have fallen." Grace listened intently. "Christ desired his family of disciples near Him that he might endure the coming conflict with the powers of darkness. Christ's soul was filled with dread. His spirit shuddered. Satan taunted him, saying, 'Your number one follower denies You.'" The priest searched their eyes with each new statement. "Christ's whole being abhorred the thought that those whom He loved so much should unite in evil plots against Him." The priest circled the span of the pews and returned to center, standing before Grace. "The human heart longs for sympathy in suffering. Christ yearned to hear words of comfort from those He had so often blessed, comforted and shielded." The priest moved from pew to pew. "He would have been comforted if he found them praying with him." The priest spread his arms wide, his white cassock draping like angel wings. "Instead, He found them sleeping." The priest dropped his arms to his side and stood for a moment in silence. Then he gazed at Grace. "Obstinacy and malice conspired to confuse and overpower Him. He was like a reed beaten and bent by the angry storm. He spoke his entire life in words of courage and tenderness and praise. Now he spoke in human anguish. Yet even in His great agony, He excused their weakness." Grace sighed.

The priest returned to the pulpit. "Angels beheld the agony. Heaven was silent. A light shone forth amid the stormy darkness of the crisis hour, and the mighty angel who stands in God's presence, came to His side. The mob, armed with self-righteous entitlement, bound and railed against Him as they would against a thief or a robber. This was the hour of darkness."' The priest raised his hands, palms together in prayer. "Let us pray."

After Mass, the family gathered around Grace in the foyer of St. Christopher's Hospital. "Are we going out to eat?" Grace asked.

"Yes," Crystal Ann answered. "You'll come with me. The others will follow."

"Oh, good. Are we going to Royal Court? I'll need my hat and purse."

"We'll bring those things later," Crystal Ann tossed over her shoulder. The night was brisk. Grace felt a chill as she sat patiently in the passenger seat of the Cadillac. Crystal Ann drove determinedly through busy traffic.

Grace stared at the lights of convenience stores, fast food drive-ins, strip-malls and gas stations flashing past her window. "Where are we going? This isn't the way to Royal Court."

"I thought we'd drive around for a while," Crystal Ann answered. The car sped past a cement plant and several large car dealerships and a Target parking lot, now empty. A stream of cars exiting the shopping mall crawled past Grace's window.

"Where are we? This is the wrong way. I thought we were going out to eat. I want to go home." All

Grace could see was the deep night sky. Then she saw a large stone building and a black canopy. "That's Blackwater Manor! I'm not going there! Crystal Ann! I'm not going there!" She gripped the door handle furiously. Crystal Ann turned the Cadillac into a wide circle, slowed and then sped out of the parking lot back into the thoroughfare.

"We'll drive around a bit more. Let's see the lights of the city." The car sped back into four-lane city traffic. Airport lights flashed in the distance.

"Crystal Ann, I want to go home," Grace stated firmly. The car slowed and circled and parked again under the black canopy. Acer stood there waiting. He smiled broadly, rocking back and forth on his heels. Grace felt absolute terror. She could not control this by saying nothing. This would not blow over. This was different. She suddenly pictured Chester, looking up from the weeds at the hook of the deadly cycle mower veering toward him, helpless to escape the slash. She clung to the rosary in her pocket and prayed fervently. "Hail Mary, full of grace…"

"Here we are," Crystal Ann announced sharply, staring straight ahead.

"I want to go home," Grace said weakly.

"This is your home now," replied Crystal Ann.

I phoned the house at Scanlon Circle. There was no answer. I dialed again. It was too late for Grace to be out. I dialed her room at the hospital. No answer. I dialed the nurses' station. "Oh, she was dismissed," came the cheery voice. I dialed Maire.

"I know," she said immediately. "The phone was disconnected."

"What on earth? Where did they take her?"

"I'm guessing she's at Blackwater."

"I'm on the way."

Maire entered Blackwater Manor but was directed to Lonan Wing, a short term health care wing for Blackwater residents. She found Grace sitting alone in the hallway. "Ma! What's going on?" She leaned down and kissed Grace's cheek. Grace clung to her sleeve. Her knuckles went white with the grip. "Ma," Maire said softly. "No matter what, it's all right. We'll make it be all right." Grace watched a flurry of activity down the hallway. Maire followed her gaze. There was Dierdre, Quin, Cheyla, Crystal Ann, Lyssa and Bric, pulling furniture out into the hallway, hauling furniture in from a truck at the ambulance entrance.

"Who wants cappuccino? Do you want sandwiches or pizza?" Dierdre called as she headed toward the exit. A resident peered out from her room. Other residents closed their doors to shut out the noise. Maire stared aghast at the melee. Quin, Cheyla, Lyssa, Bric and Crystal Ann bustled in and out in a clamor of high-pitched joviality.

"Looks like the Riordens are having a party." A nurse stood beside Maire. "I'm Aubery, the RN on duty."

"Looks more like a circus than a party," Grace quipped.

"Don't worry, Honey," Aubery answered. "We'll have you settled in no time."

"Her name is Grace," Maire shot back.

Cheyla strode toward them. "We'll take it from here." She grabbed the handles on Grace's wheelchair and swung her around. Crystal Ann and Quin stood waiting.

Grace pointed her finger at the two of them. "You did this!"

Crystal Ann glared at Maire. "You can go home now."

"I'll go home when I damn well please!" Maire fired back. "I'm here to be with my mother."

Grace looked up at Maire. "Where's Elle?"

I turned off the Interstate and looped around the city bypass. My phone beeped. Grace was sobbing inconsolably. "Where are you?"

"I'm just minutes away, Gram. I'm coming around the city. I'll be there in fifteen minutes." Someone said something in the background; then she was on the phone.

"You'll have to phone her," the nurse explained. "She's not allowed to make long distance calls. I made this call for her because she insisted on speaking with you. In the future, you'll have to call her."

"Put my grandmother back on the phone," I said flatly.

"Elle," she stifled a sob. "I think I made a terrible mistake. They made me sign a paper at my birthday party. I think that was wrong."

"It's all right, Gram. It's not your fault. They seduced you. You trusted them."

"Can you find me? They won't chase you away from here will they?"

"Gram, I'll be there soon. I won't leave you. I'm right here." But I knew it was too late. The children she loved, raised, protected from Jack, had swiftly and without warning kicked her to the curb. Ralph said it all when he said he had to get on with his life. Her children no doubt saw her as Jack did, just a pawn in the Devil's game. What was the prize? I wondered.

Just blocks away from Blackwater Manor a party raged in a run-down never land between adolescence and adulthood. Two young teens moved through the shadows. Stormy's eyes flashed as she pushed through the crowded room.

"Call the roll!" breathed Neka.

Stormy broke into a group huddled near the fireplace. A slender male shook back a mop of tousled hair. Stormy stepped high to straddle his legs and plopped onto the coffee table in front of him. He brushed her away. "Awright." Stormy glared at them. "The Riorden twins are too good for us." He ignored her. She sauntered away, smoldering.

Neka pulled her to the door. "We gotta get to work."

"Yea," Stormy shot back, "to some pain in the ass drooling in the hallway, waiting to get sloughed off to bed."

I arrived at Blackwater Manor. The great stone entrance was vacant except for a lone woman at the front desk. She remembered me from the tour and gave me a card with my mother's room number and a map of the building. I hurried down stone hallways, past empty dining rooms, past closed doors and across the courtyard. Security doors opened onto Lonan Wing. I stopped at a door. The room was small and dark. Maire sat rigid in the shadows. Grace lay in a small single bed. She clung to a rosary, her eyes fixed on a large white poster board fastened to the wall. It was plastered with photos of the family. Jack grinned impishly back from a large framed photo on her bedside table. I leaned down and gave her a warm embrace. She untangled her small hand from the blankets and gripped mine.

"Look, there." She motioned to the pictures. "There's Jack."

"Do you want me to move these?" The pictures overshadowed her. "There's no room for you here."

Her eyes fixed on the framed photo. "He told me this would happen. He told me they would do this."

"How about we get up and take a shower?" I looked at Maire. She didn't move. She appeared to be as stunned as Grace. "Do you even have a shower? Have you eaten?"

"No." There was no expression in her voice. "No."

"I'm so sorry, Gram. I'm so sorry I couldn't protect you from this." I was struck with the awareness that this was the behavior her children expected from her. They counted on her not fighting back. Grace had her entire married life hid in the shadow of her husband's cruel indifference. Now her children lurked in that shadow.

She tightened her grip. "Don't leave me."

"I'm not going anywhere, Gram. I'm right here."

"Hail Mary, full of grace, the Lord is with thee," she prayed. Then she cried herself to sleep, murmuring, "Yes, I will. I'll be there soon." I sat in a straight-backed chair next to her, listening, holding her hand as it draped across the side of the bed. Maire watched in silence.

"Where are we?" I asked, confused. "This isn't assisted living. This isn't the apartment we toured. This is a 12 by 12 room with a toilet. What is this?"

"They call this a health care wing," Maire said quietly. "The apartment in assisted living was the first lie. I'm sure there will be more to come."

"So this is how the Riordens celebrate Easter with their mother," I answered, eyeing Grace, asleep in her cramped bed, lying uncomfortably on her plastic covered mattress. "Gram may one day forgive them, but her God never will."

"Heaven is silent tonight," Maire said grimly. "This is the hour of darkness."

"We love you, Gram," I whispered. "You are not alone. This is not over. You are not done."

Her eyes fluttered open and she whispered sadly, "Leave the light on."

The big bus jostled and rocked me back from my thoughts. There was Bridezilla, Elvira, Cat Woman, the tattooed ironworker, the scrap metal collector, the researcher, Ancient Eyes and Sonja. Yoki met my gaze. "Where do we find the balance?" I asked. "Where do we get the strength to go on?"

"From knowing we are not nothing." The ironworker answered quietly.

The scrap metal collector patted her hand. "Knowing we are loved gives us hope."

"Yes," I agreed. "Love is energy."

"Love means keeping our promises," Sonja added, glancing up from her laptop. "The story won't be done until our promises are kept."

"Our story is about the promises," Yoki concluded, gazing into space.

"Tell my story," Grace whispered.

The bus sped on through the dark night, the rhythm of the rain beating on the roof, lulling me back into a deep sleep. I dreamed I was swimming in murky green water. There were two others swimming with me. A light beckoned through the unfathomable void. I saw a glimmer through the depths, a glint through the surface of the water and finally a flicker through the trees at the water's edge. An image, at first indistinguishable, grew clearer as it loomed closer. Brilliant blue eyes twinkled with mirth. Rosy cheeks grinned from a face framed in an amber glow. The eyes widened and stared. The face drew back, grinning from ear to ear.

I jolted awake, recoiling from the dream. Shaking off the image, I scanned the faces of the travelers on the bus. It occurred to me that for all the drama, the crisis and the heartbreaking struggle, life is as surreal as an impish phantom, as fleeting as the ever-changing landscape outside the window of the bus. Through it all, each spirit moves on a steady continuum like the turtles following the river. The second of Jack's strange riddles beat a steady cadence in my brain. *What is the pleasure that yields only pain?* I shook the thought away. "What have I done, Grace? We're stuck on this bus. We're stuck in our thoughts. We're stuck with our dreams. God," I prayed, "end this obsession."

If I ever leave this world alive
I'll take on all the sadness

Grace by Greyhound

That I left behind

The madness that you feel will soon subside
So in a word don't shed a tear
I'll be here when it all gets weird
If I ever leave this world alive

The Road Of No Return

Follow the leader, stay in the lines
What will people think of what you've done this time?

Go with the crowd, surely somebody knows
Why we're all wearing the emperor's clothes
Play it safe, play by the rules
Or don't play at all - what if you lose?
That's not the secret, but I know what is:
Everybody dies but not everyone lives

The bus rocked through the night as I drifted into a new dream, where I rode, nestled into the soft leather seats of a limousine. The limousine glided to a stop beneath a black canopy. Ronan, dressed smartly in a black tuxedo, stood at the curb and offered his arm. Diaphanous shadows filled the large foyer. The banquet room glowed in flickering candlelight. Masked faces turned, mid-sentence to stare. We found two seats at the end of a far table. A waiter handed me card with the word Grace lettered on it. The card burst into flames that leapt at my face, then raced down the length of the table. Ronan reached for me. Then I woke. Dazed, I struggled to regain clarity. Adjusting my jacket behind my shoulders, I turned my thoughts back to Grace and Blackwater Manor.

Maire stood beside Grace's bed, fluffing her pillow. The soft contoured spa pillow she slept on in her own bed was replaced with a generic industrial one. Maire sniffed it and wrinkled her nose. "I'll bring you your own bedding tomorrow, Ma." She dimmed the lights and sunk into the blue upholstered recliner next to the bed. Grace followed her with her eyes. They sat silently for a moment. Then Grace spoke.

"Where's Elle?"

Maire sighed. "She'll be here, Ma. Don't worry."

"Maire?"

"Yes, Ma."

"It's just you and me here now?"

"Yes, Ma. It's just you and me." The room grew quiet again. "Ma?"

"Hmm?"

"Am I yours?"

"What do you mean?"

"I don't know, Ma. Most of my life I have wondered."

"Weren't you there?" Grace asked, her voice thin and distant.

"Yes. Maybe. Hell, I don't know."

"Oh, sure. You were there."

Maire leaned forward and peered at her mother. "Ma! You're teasing me!"

Grace met her gaze. "Sweetheart, I don't care who you think you are, or who you think I am, just as long as I can trust you and you're here when you promise to be."

"I understand, Ma. I understand."

"Do you promise?"

"I promise."

"Maire?"

"Hmmm?"

"I love you so much."

The room was silent again. Both Maire and Grace dozed. Then Maire woke suddenly to a shadow moving through the room. Aubery stood over Grace. Before Maire could shake herself awake, Aubery slapped on a blood pressure cuff on Grace's arm and began pumping. Grace woke, startled and alarmed, pushing her away with her hands. Aubery stuck her elbow directly into Grace's chest to hold her down.

Maire bolted from the chair. "Aubery, wait!'

Aubery spun around, stumbling backwards.

"What are you doing?"

Aubery trembled. She hid her face in the shadows. Her voice shuddered. "I forgot to give Grace her pills at supper." She steadied herself and reached again for Grace's arm.

"Amelia gave Mom her pills at supper," Maire stated evenly.

Grace looked up at Aubery, looming over her. "Why don't you just tell me, wake me up softly and tell me what you want?"

Aubery produced four pills in a cup. The cup shook as she slid the pills to the spoon.

Maire interrupted. "At least raise her head up. She's flat on her back. Where's the water?"

Aubery stumbled to her feet and left the room.

"This has been a long day," Grace sighed. "I think if I just rest, everything will be all right." Her eyes closed. Maire tiptoed to the door. Aubery stood in the hallway next to the med cart.

"Aubery, Amelia gave Mom her pills."

"No. No, she didn't."

Maire opened her journal. "I was there, Aubery. Six o'clock p.m., I went to the table, Mom had no food yet. Six o-five, Amelia gave her the pills, all the while carrying on some kind of flaky, flip narrative, insisting Mom must have had twins because nobody would want to be pregnant that many times. Mom was put off by her insolence, but Amelia persisted and said, 'Oh, Grace, you know you want to line me up with your boys.' Mom pushed her away and said, 'What are you saying?' I was so upset by Amelia's cheeky behavior I left the room before I said something I would regret, but I kept thinking something's wrong here. I went outside and thought about it. Then I came back and said, 'Amelia did you take her blood pressure first?' She said, 'No, I'll get it later. I just wanted to get the pills out of the way.'" Maire looked up from her journal. Aubery was shaking. "Which means, Aubery, that the pills were given twice and now here you are taking her blood pressure in the middle of the night!"

Aubery opened a drawer in the med cart. "Look here. The pills are still in the med card."

"Then what did you just give her?" Maire tapped the page in her journal. "I'm writing this down for Mom's protection." Aubery stiffened, staring at the book. Maire threw up her hands and headed for the exit. Minutes later my cell phone beeped. She spit the words as fast as they would come. "Aubery is shaking like a leaf. She seems to be moving in slow motion, as if her brain and her body aren't in sync. Something is seriously up with that woman. I don't know what it is but it reminds me of someone on speed and then on Valium. This is the RN? Elle, I'm scared to leave Mom alone with them. It makes no sense. Here is a woman who exercises all the time, doesn't touch alcohol, has a normal weight and eats healthy. What do they think is wrong with her?"

"If they're giving her an antidepressant they're probably looking for her blood pressure to elevate. They're looking to see if it drops at night."

"They're sedating her?"

The big bus rolled on. I shifted my body in an attempt to find some comfort despite the cramped leg space and unforgiving molded seat backs.

"It's good, now, isn't it, Sweetheart?"

"Yes, Gram. It's good now."

"Sometimes it wasn't so bad. Sometimes it was all right. You and Maire made it all right." She was quiet for a while. Then she added, "There were days that were rough, but we're all right now." She was momentarily quiet again. "That door in the back is making a racket. It's not shut tight."

"Do you want me to try to latch it?"

"No. Not tight. We need a little light. Would you say a little prayer with me?"

"Of course."

"How about the Jabez prayer? If I miss one little part, you can say it for me."

"We'll say it together." The sound of her voice and the Holy Spirit filled my soul as the smooth rhythm of wheels on highway lulled me back into the dream.

Flames raced across the tables as the group moved trancelike to a viewing room. The lights dimmed. I perched on the soft arm of a blue recliner. Ronan stood leaning against the mantel of a large fireplace, staring into space as others chatted around him. He glanced toward me and winked. The room went dark. As a movie screen came to life, the wall to my left opened, propelling me onto a surging sea. The chair swiveled and lurched upon the foam, blasting across the choppy waves, making hairpin turns in circular motions. Wind whipped at my hair. The chair rose on a wave and transformed into the stern of a boat. The Riorden siblings stood together at the bow, staring back. A sudden spray drenched me. "This is magnificent!" I exclaimed. My words were swept away on the wind. Crystal Ann glared at me, shouting furiously. Her voice was swallowed by the gale. I turned my face to the storm, exhilarated. Then a thought occurred. "What am I doing? I can't swim! If this family over-powers me, I'm done for." I awoke, stunned. Yoki and Ancient Eyes were both watching me closely.

"What?" I asked. "Was I talking in my sleep?" Yoki shook his head.

Settling my shoulders against the molded seat on the bus, I strained to see past the window, the rain and beyond. Life is hard, I thought. Grace's life certainly was. The bus turned off the Interstate and rolled to a stop under near the pumps of a gas station. A slender young woman trudged up the aisle carrying a baby in a carrier. She raised the carrier, trying to see past it. "No hay asiento"! She sounded tired. She rested the carrier on the arm of my seat. "Con permiso por favor. Con permiso, por favor."

"If you don't get settled, I'll put you off the bus!" the driver barked. I glanced up, surprised by his threatening tone.

"Necesito un asiento para mi bebe," she protested. "El Bus esta lleno, no es facil pasar."

A man boarded and reached forward to coax her. "Pasa, pasa, adelante."

"No. No." She tried to turn around but the aisle was too narrow and she was too small to lift the heavy carrier above the seats.

"She's stuck," Grace stated matter-of-factly. She can't go back. She can't go forward. Help her." I stood, motioning to her to take my seat. The driver fixed a stony glare on me, then turned briskly to slide behind the steering wheel, closing the doors with one swift stroke of the lever. The scrap metal collector reached up and caught my elbow. The bus lurched and I fell into him, tucking my bag into the two-inch space behind my legs.

"The ultimate gift of generosity," he said, "to give up prime legroom."

"Show compassion," Grace whispered. "It's important."

I nodded. "I hear you, Grace."

"What?" he asked.

"Nothing. Thank you for the seat. I'm Elle."

He shook my hand with a bear-claw grip. "I'm Jerry. That was a good thing you did just now."

"She was stuck."

"Hmmm," he answered. "Aren't we all!"

I pulled a throw from my bag and tucked it around my shoulders. The touch of it on my cheek brought my thoughts rushing back to Grace.

Now she saw the lie. She knew the choices her children made put her and them on a road of no return. Still she believed that her vessel was strong enough to balance her burden with patience and love.

Sunday morning dawn burst through Grace's window. Maire squinted to see the round-faced clock across the room on the wall. It was five or five thirty. Grace cried out in her sleep. "I'm here, Ma. I'm right here."

Maire dozed off again but was awakened by a large dark shadow moving quickly through the door. The round-faced clock pointed at seven. The shadow moved to the bed, jostled Grace awake, slipped an arm under her head and put a Dixie cup to her lips. "Sip," she ordered. "It's your Boniva." Half asleep, Grace obeyed.

Maire shook herself awake and leapt from the blue chair. "You need a full eight ounces of the water with the Boniva. She needs to be sitting up."

The shadow darted out as abruptly as it came.

Maire stared at the door. "What the hell?" She knelt by Grace and lifted the Dixie Cup to her lips, but Grace was sound asleep. Maire stared at her mother. "Oh, my God. What should I do? She didn't swallow that pill." Panic stricken, Maire paced as her mother slept.

A sharp knock echoed through the room. Clover came through the door. The hands of the round-faced clock pointed to eight. "We're here to help her get dressed and get to the toilet."

"I'm awake," Grace responded sleepily. Clover positioned herself in front of Grace. She took both her hands and pulled her straight up, then swung her feet around. "Ouch!" Grace pulled back. Be careful. What are you doing?"

"Wait!" Maire bounded forward. She grabbed the gait belt from the hook on the bathroom door and reached for the walker. Clover ignored the walker but leaned forward and fastened the belt around Grace's waist. She grabbed the belt with one hand, her arm linked under Grace's armpit and lifted straight up.

"Ow!" Grace recoiled.

"Please be careful," Maire warned. Clover pushed Grace forward, past Maire and into the bathroom, shutting the door in Maire's face. Maire opened the door and determinedly placed the walker inside. Clover pushed Grace against the wall, forcing her hands around the grab bar next to the toilet.

"Ouch!" Grace cried out again. Maire paced outside the bathroom door. At a loss for what to do next she stepped into the hallway, scanned left and right down the empty corridor, then flipped open her cell phone and dialed.

"The only support they give her in the bathroom is the grab bar. Twisting her body 180 degrees to sit on the toilet causes shooting pain in her arms and knees." A woman fumbled with the doorknob at Grace's door. With hand on her cane, she pushed against it with her hip. "Hold on," Maire said. I waited on the other end. Maire walked toward the woman. "Hi, what do you need?"

"I don't belong here. I belong with my hubby at Pine Haven. I'm not going to stay here. I don't belong here." The woman moved on, stopping at each door she passed, jiggling the knob, muttering her forlorn, singsong monotone.

Clover stomped out of Grace's room with a Dixie cup full of pills. "Why are you taking her pills away?" Maire asked.

"I tried. She refused."

"You tried to give her pills while she was on the toilet?" Maire shot back. "Mom is a private person. She would think that barbaric." Clover pursed her lips and turned away.

Maire found Grace trembling in the middle of her room. "Are you cold, Ma? I'll get your sweater. Would you like to wear a skirt today?" Grace's face brightened. "How about that gray wool skirt Ward sent to you? There's a beautiful silk blouse to go with it. How about this soft white sweater over that?" Grace smiled bravely. Fierce loathing erupted inside Maire. She stuffed it down. She would never forgive the family for forcing this existence on their mother. Maire reached for the hat rack and the mirror. "Which hat would you like to wear today?" Grace positioned the soft black rim just over one eye, fluffing the grosgrain ribbon. Maire and Grace strolled through the indoor village, stopping at a mirrored window. "Who is that beauty in there, Ma?"

"Oh, you!" Grace smoothed the soft woolen material of her skirt.

Maire pushed the wheelchair up the long ramp to Chez Clair. The tables at Chez Clair were dressed in bright tablecloths with linen napkins and centerpiece settings of fresh flowers and whimsical birds in nests. The silverware gleamed and the crystal water glasses sparkled under the chandelier. "I'm hungry," Grace said as she closed her eyes and savored the warm aroma of the Sunday buffet. Residents stopped to chat as they passed, introducing their children and grandchildren. "Do you know my daughter?" Grace asked proudly. Wheels on chairs touched like friends shaking hands. Waiters stood by. Maire glanced through large bay windows in the atrium across the courtyard to Lonan Wing. It might as well have been in another country. The difference was that great.

As they strolled back through the hallways, Grace asked, "Where are my children? Where are all my grandchildren? Call them, Maire. Tell them where I am. They must be worried not knowing where I am."

Maire knelt in front of her mother. "What do you mean, Ma?"

Grace looked intently into her daughter's eyes. "They must not know where I am. That's the only reason I can think of that they are not here."

March blustered into April. Grace woke to a strange elf-like figure bouncing around her room, opening drawers, touching her things. Her hair was streaked with strips of orange, yellow, white and black. She stood over the bed looking down at Grace.

"Are you ready to get up?" Stormy tossed the question over her shoulder as she turned and flung the curtains aside to look at the falling snow.

"That would be fine," Grace answered.

"Well, then?" Stormy cocked her head, hands on hips.

"Well, what?"

"Well, get up then."

"I'm afraid I'll need your help. My knees aren't strong. They pain when I stand."

"Whatever!" Stormy rolled her eyes and looked around, spying the wheelchair. She rolled the wheelchair to the side of the bed and reached out her hand to Grace. "Hang on. I'll pull you up." Grace stared at her as she stared blankly back. "OK. Hold on," she said finally. "I'll get help." She disappeared into the hallway. Soon she was back. "Nope. No one there. We'll have to do this on our own. If I pull you, can you lean on me?" She began to tug.

Grace grimaced and pulled back. "Stop. They told me how to do this in therapy. I can manage." Grace buried her fists into the mattress next to each hip and pushed herself up. As she came forward, her knees buckled and she pitched headlong toward Stormy.

"Whoa!" Stormy exclaimed as she caught Grace's shoulders, spun her around and plopped her into the wheel chair. Neka breezed through the door. "Finally!" Stormy threw her hands up. "What took you so long?"

"This entire wing's just a bag of pants. I'm the only one out there!" Neka sized up the situation. "I would have thought you two would have been all right, you and Mrs. R." she smiled mischievously.

"Don't even!" Stormy shot back.

"Mrs. R?" Neka repeated with emphasis. "R, as in grandmother to the Riorden boys?"

"No way." Stormy's eyes widened. "Well, what now?" Her eyes scanned the room. She spotted the hat rack and jewelry armoire. She turned to Grace and smiled sweetly. "Grace! Let's dress up." She rummaged through the closet, pulling out a silk blouse and knit pants, tossing them into Grace's lap. Neka tugged on the sleeves of Grace's pajama top. Stormy continued to rummage through the room. "Grace, I totally love your hats and your jewels are the best." She plopped the turquoise hat onto her own orange and yellow streaks, dancing about in front of Grace. "Anything you want, Grace, you lend me your stash, and I'll be your proxy."

"Give me that." Grace reached for the hat. "Stop that. You'll ruin it." Stormy's mood turned from coquettish to impish. She slid her fingers down the gold chain hanging around Grace's neck.

"What's this, Grace, a locket?" Grace pulled back. Stormy flipped the locket open. "Who's this, Grace?" Grace didn't answer. "What's the matter, Grace? Can't remember? Got Alzheimer's? If you can't remember, you might as well give it to me."

Neka froze. There in the doorway was Maire. Maire pushed past her, snatching the hat from Stormy's head. "Are you drunk?" Stormy dropped the locket.

I stepped in behind Maire and kissed Grace's cheek. She patted my hand softly, then gripped it firmly.

"We're getting your mother ready for breakfast," Stormy announced haughtily. "You two need to leave."

"Leave?" Maire seethed. If you ever put your hands on my mother again, you'll be the one leaving.

Stormy stumbled back. She hurried out the door, calling over her shoulder, "I'm getting the social worker!" Neka followed close behind.

I looked closely at Grace. "Gram, where are your glasses? I know you can't see without them." Grace gripped my hand.

Maire cut in. "Where are your teeth? Your hair hasn't been combed. Have you even been to the bathroom?"

"No." Grace shook her head, bewildered. "Those girls caused such a commotion. There wasn't time."

Maire reached for the nurses' call light. "We'll get someone in here to help you."

I steered Grace's wheel chair toward the bathroom. "In the meantime, we'll get started." I leaned down and smiled at Grace. Then I looked up at Maire. "I'll make a bet. I'll buy breakfast if someone comes to help before we are finished." Grace shook her head and smiled wistfully.

"Oh, you girls!"

The Lonan Wing dining room was a large beautiful dining room with an inset domed ceiling panel. A golden chandelier hung from the center. I steered Grace's chair toward an open table. "Grace goes over there," Amelia called from the med cart. The room was cordoned off into two sections by a long row of large rectangular urns holding tall ferns, creating a visible, physical separation. I wheeled Grace to her table.

"Family doesn't eat with residents," Stormy declared.

"You're joking." Maire stood over Grace.

Amelia moved to Stormy's side. "We want the residents to assimilate and socialize."

"Again, I ask, are you joking?" Maire looked around the table. The woman on Grace's left babbled and drooled. The woman on her right slapped out at Grace. Grace pulled back in alarm. "My mother should be at a table on that side." Maire pointed across the fern barricade. Residents chatted, read newspapers, sipped on tea or coffee or juice. "That's socializing."

"She's not capable of feeding herself."

"Who told you that?" Maire demanded.

"Family says she needs pureed foods and assistance eating."

"I am family!" Maire snapped. Amelia backed away. "I'm telling you the only assistance she needs is transferring. She has a bone density of minus-four. You are paid to keep her from falling and to administer medication. The rest is bullshit!"

"You should leave now." Amelia answered.

"What is this?" Maire challenged.

Amelia lowered her voice. "It is important to keep her mainstream. The Memory Care Unit is for low functioning people who cannot socialize properly."

Maire bristled. "Memory Care Unit? What the hell are you talking about?"

"No...I didn't mean to say...She's not ready for the memory unit yet," Amelia sputtered. Maire's eyes blazed. Amelia spoke hastily. "This is an opportunity for us to make new correlations for her."

Maire shot her a staggering look. "That's what this is about?" She stepped into Amellia, forcing her to back away from Grace. "My mother is here for assistance transferring. Osteoporosis is the one and only one diagnosis documented." She glared at Amelia.

"The rest is a lie! If you want her mainstream, seat her over there with fully functioning adults. As for me, I'm not going anywhere." Then she pulled a chair to the table between Grace and the angry resident pounding the table on her right. "Correlations!" Maire muttered. "Her correlations are on Scanlon Circle!" She turned to Grace. "Let's have some eggs, Ma."

"Don't leave me," Grace whispered.

The next morning I called Grace from the car.

"The girls fastened me down," she cried. "I haven't seen anything of any of them since. "It's not right!"

"Gram!" I exploded. "You have to tell Quin you want to go home. Tell him now." Then her words registered. "Fastened you down?"

"Two girls reached down and pulled me off my pillows and used the thing."

"What thing?"

"They taped me in. I'm still that way now."

"Tell me what it looks like," I prompted.

"The two girls banded me and tied me to the seat of my chair. The walking belt is clear around my chair! I can't breathe."

"I'll call Maire. She'll come to help you." Fury crashed in waves against my brain. I dialed Maire. "I'm a half hour away. She needs you as soon as you can get there. I'm calling Quin."

Grace sat wedged in a corner by the fish tank, under a blaring TV. Tears streamed down her cheeks. "Ma!" Maire rushed to her side. "What is this?"

"I'm stuck!" A gait belt lashed her to her wheelchair. A two inch strip of Velcro wound around her waist, circling the back of the wheel chair and fastened at the side, beyond her reach. Stormy stood three feet away, smirking.

"I called and called but that girl over there wouldn't answer. I can't keep calling when no one answers. They'll think I'm crazy!" Maire handed her a tissue. "These belts are too tight. I can't breathe."

When I arrived I found Maire pacing outside. "They won't let me near her," Maire fumed. "I don't know how far I can push them without getting thrown out. She's strapped in with not one, but two belts! Her clothes are soaked and smell of urine. This is jacked!"

I was beyond rage. I was lightening strike, white zone calm. I pushed through the doors and past the nurses' station. I threw my arms around Grace, unbuckling the gate belt and ripping the Velcro off in one deft pull.

Stormy put her hand out to stop me. "You're not allowed to take those off." She pushed at my hand, the gothic streaks in her hair flapping about her face. I shoved her tattooed arm away. "Abuse! Abuse! She hit me!" She looked around the room for an audience. A gaunt man in a wheel chair folded his newspaper, shook his head, turned and wheeled away down the hall.

"Take what off?" I handed the gait belt to Maire and rolled the Velcro into a tight ball and slipped it into my bag.

"Your family has given strict orders."

"Family?" Maire was inches from her face.

"I mean it's doctor's orders."

"Which is it, family or doctor? Let me see the order!" Stormy stepped back, stumbling into Delores who suddenly appeared from around the corner. Maire turned on Delores. "Are you telling me it's doctor's orders to strap my mother to her chair this way?"

"We take it off every two hours for fifteen minutes."

Maire was livid. "What are you saying? You are doing this every day? How is that possible? I'm here every day!"

"We're supposed to take the belt off before family gets here," Stormy retorted defiantly.

"Do you think she's some kind of animal you have to break?" Maire stopped suddenly, her eyes flashed with intensity. "That's behavior therapy. Dr. Corbin would not write that order. She's here because she can't stand without support. It's ridiculous and cruel to restrain her. Where do you think she's going? She can't push the wheels of her own chair. Who wrote the order to restrain her?"

"Her power of attorney," Stormy tossed back boldly. "One of your own."

"My own?" Maire's voice was fire and ice.

"One of the mighty Riordens."

"That's enough, Stormy." Delores came forward. "That's fine. Forget the belt. I'll look into it. Go. Enjoy your day."

"Enjoy my day?" Maire pointed a rigid finger in Delores' face. "When was the last time you took my mother to the bathroom? You make her beg for her basic needs, you ignore her and now you have her in a double restraint!" Alivia passed by and stopped.

"Grace must have spilled her glass of water."

"Are you people nuts? She can't reach the water!" Delores stared back grimly. Maire took hold of the wheelchair handles and steered Grace down the hallway to her room. She stopped at Grace's door. The room reeked of urine. Maire stepped in, leaving Grace in the hallway. Towels and pajamas lay crumpled on the floor. She picked them up and sniffed.

"I'll help Gram get freshened up," I offered, steering Grace into the bathroom.

"Yea," she said, handing me an outfit from Grace's closet. "Then call Wheelchair Direct. We're taking her out of here." She went into the bedroom where she leaned down to sniff the coverlet on the bed, jerking it back. She pulled it from the bed and felt the pillows. She pulled off the sheets. Then she darted from the room, straight to the laundry room. There she found Lidia, the laundry supervisor. "Come with me," she ordered. "Now!"

Lidia stared at the mess. "This can't be. No bedding ever gets that soaked. Something spilled on it."

"Smell it," ordered Maire.

Lidia sniffed and pulled away. "This is too strong. It's almost like a bedpan has been dumped here!" She started to remove the soaker pad. "What's this? Another one underneath?" She removed that pad and found another and another and another. She was hot with anger. "How many pads are on this bed?"

"I count five," Maire said flatly.

"Five!" Lidia grabbed the walkie-talkie clipped to her belt. "I'm calling the housekeeper." Soon there was a middle-aged woman standing sheepishly in the doorway. "Is this how you train your people?" Lidia demanded. "There are five soaker pads on this bed! Why are there dirty pajamas lying in the bathroom?"

"The pajamas are not in the hamper because Crystal Ann didn't want to come every day to do laundry."

"Please, God, let's not inconvenience Crystal Ann." Maire held up one of the wet sheets. "What is the reason for the soaker pads? Is that so staff is not inconvenienced, having to take her to the bathroom?"

"These pads were not put on the bed by me." She turned defensively to Lidia. "I'm proud of my work."

"All right," Lidia interrupted. "That's fine, but I expect this room to be spotless whenever I check it, no matter what time of night or day, understood?" The woman gathered up the wet load and hurried down the hallway to the laundry.

"Wheelchair Direct is waiting," Maire said, lifting a hat from Grace's hat stand and a small beaded bag from the bureau drawer. Lidia walked with her back down the hallway. "Do you think this could be a trick one of the staff played on Mom? Could they be doing this just to be mean or to get even?"

Lidia gave Maire a long sideways glance. "I can't imagine anyone being that shameful, especially to someone as sweet as your mother." She waved to Grace in the lobby. "I'll keep watch, though." She nodded thoughtfully. "I'll keep watch."

Wheelchair Direct arrived. The driver lowered the hydraulic lift and waited. Quin approached from one wing and Maire charged toward him from the other. "You tell me what is going on here!" she demanded. He turned away from her and reached down to kiss his mother. Maire would not be put off. "What is this business about strapping her in?"

"They say she's trying to walk without her walker," he responded evenly.

"Well, of course she is!" Maire exploded. "You've taken away her power chair so now she has to be pushed wherever she wants to go and no one will do that. They park her out of reach of her walker, the call light, food and water and her phone. She can't even get to the damn bathroom when she needs to."

Grace looked up at Quin and smiled appealingly. "Quin, Dierdre's son, Ethan, will be married this month in the Cathedral. I can't go to a wedding wearing that thing around me. People will think I'm deranged."

Maire eyes blazed. Her fury burned into Quin. "Is that your plan, little brother?"

He shrunk back. "Your ride's waiting, Mom," he muttered. She accepted the kiss he gave her but watched with sad eyes as he turned and strode down the hallway, not looking back.

Maire negotiated her shifts at Macys. She would work late night shifts in exchange for mornings off. For a week she stood guard while the aides transferred Grace. She sat with Grace at breakfast. She stood by while Grace struggled through physical therapy. At the end of the week Amelia stopped her at the nurse's station. "You'll need to sign in when you arrive and when you leave."

"What's this about? Is this a new policy?"

"Yes'm," Amelia answered, handing her a blank sheet of paper.

"If this is a new policy, why don't I see any other names here?"

"Because its not our policy. It's a Riorden policy."

"Excuse me? What does that mean?"

"Bric told us to phone whenever either you or Elle arrive and to document everything you say or do, especially things that rile your mother." She shrugged. "We can't always get him by phone, so we decided to just have you sign in."

Maire leaned over the counter and pushed the paper away, unsigned. "Have a nice day!" She walked across the hall to the therapy room. "Good morning, Ma. How are you?" Grace looked up proudly.

"Grace walked from the bed to the bathroom," the therapist offered. "With the walker, the gait belt and her walking shoes, she is making great progress. That's enough for today, Grace. See you again tomorrow?" The therapist leaned close to Maire. "Grace is increasingly tired in the morning."

"Is the therapy too much for her?"

"It has nothing to do with the therapy. She comes alive when she exercises. I'm wondering. Are they giving her something for anxiety?"

"Did you ask the nurses?"

"Well, I did, sedatives are not always documented here."

Emily approached. "Let's give Grace her pills now."

"Didn't she have them at breakfast?"

"No, there's no record of that." She held a teaspoon of pudding to Grace's mouth. Grace pursed her lips and shook her head.

"What's this?" Maire asked.

"We find that pudding makes pills go down easier."

"First of all, Mom doesn't like pudding. She never has. It makes her gag." Emily lowered the spoon impatiently. "Secondly, how will she know what pills she's taking? Have you stopped explaining to her the pills you administer?"

"That's not necessary. They're all physician ordered."

"Except the ones at your discretion. She has the right to know."

Emily rose defiantly. "If she won't take them, I'll write refused."

"Really? That's your answer?"

I heard Maire and Emily arguing as I came through the door. Grace reached for me. "Oh, Sweetheart, where have you been?" I leaned down and kissed her cheek as I opened the corner of a gift bag. "Oh!" she exclaimed in delight. "Red! My favorite color!"

A woman and a man sat nearby, sipping from small bottles of wine. "What have you got there, Grace?" The woman waved her wine bottle.

Maire offered her hand. "Hello, I'm Grace's daughter."

"I know all about you and your mother and your big family," the woman sniffed. My husband taught most of the doctors." Maire opened her mouth to speak, but the woman cut her off with a wave of her hand. "We're past that now. What's wrong with your mother?"

"What's wrong with this staff?" Maire shot back.

"We're all very proud of the staff here," the woman countered. "We're patrons. Blackwater's rated the best in the city."

Cassie and two staff members stood behind the man and the woman, miming fall-down drunks gulping from bottles. Cassie caught us watching and motioned for the other two to move out of sight. They disappeared in peals of laughter. "So you're saying this is as good as it gets," Maire countered. The woman sniffed arrogantly. We turned away and wheeled back down the hallway to Grace's room.

Maire inspected the mattress and pad and sprayed the room with air freshener. I opened the bag. "Gram, it's time for a room makeover!" Her eyes twinkled in anticipation. I pulled out a new mattress pad and a red quilted bedspread. Next came soft ivory colored cotton sheets, lace trimmed pillowcases and a throw appliqued with cardinals perched on branches.

"Oh." She ran her hands slowly over the lace trim.

"We're going to move everything in this room to the exact spot you want it. Who cares what's going on in that house on Scanlon Circle! Here is your own cozy place where you say what goes where." We worked side by side as we positioned each piece of furniture, each photo, each lamp and candy dish exactly where she directed.

Then Grace pointed to the phone. "Put that where I can reach it." She looked around. "Now if I only had my red address book. It's at the house, but I can't get anyone to bring it."

"Well, how about a new one? I wrote all the names and numbers in it for you."

"Oh, thank you, Sweetheart. Now I can phone my children and tell them to come here. Why aren't they here?"

Maire winced and looked around the room. "Anything else you see you want changed?"

"Move that." Grace pointed to an ornate crucifix, hanging barren and stern over the head of her bed. "Crystal Ann put it there. It makes me feel like I'm in a coffin. Put our wedding picture there so I can see it. Weren't we a handsome couple?"

"Maire," I whispered. "What do you notice about this crucifix?"

"It's the happy death cross. It's been hanging in their bedroom for years. I haven't seen it since Dad died." She glanced at Grace, preoccupied, arranging jewelry in her new jewelry case.

"Look again," I prompted.

Maire's eyes flew wide open. "It's not the same one."

"Right. It's new." Maire's eyes fixed on mine, then shot to Grace, still engrossed in the sorting of her jewelry.

"Ma said a golden waterfall gushed from a cross. I could see her mind racing to piece the puzzle together. "Maybe she didn't get hurt at the farm."

Grace looked up. "What are you girls talking about?"

"Ma," Maire asked, "What happened at the farm?"

"At the farm?"

"The night I found you at Royal Court. Acer said you went to the farm. Did you get hurt there or somewhere else?"

She lifted a corner of her sweater and wrapped it tightly around her arm. "It twisted me like this. I couldn't move. I told Acer to take the hammer and put the board like this and pound up. You have to pound up to loosen the nails."

"Is that how your arm got punctured? Is that why your knees pained and your shoulder and arm ached? Who else was there?"

Grace looked away. "I'm not supposed to tell you. I'm tired now."

Maire reached for the call light.

"Don't put on the light," I said softly.

"Yes, let's have one night without commotion," Grace sighed. Maire helped Grace into her pajamas. I transferred her into warm, clean sheets. Quiet blanketed the room.

Grace's voice drifted through the darkness. "Are you still there?"

"Yes, Ma," Maire answered softly. "We're here."

Soon we heard the deep even breathing of Grace sleeping. Maire motioned for me to move into the hallway. "Maybe it happened at Scanlon Circle." She glanced furtively down the empty hallway for eaves-droppers. "Rory said the entire ceiling was blown out. That same night Doreen and her family were frantic to buy bedding. They were even looking for mattresses."

"Gram said Acer couldn't get the board off. She had to tell him how to get the nails pounded back."

"She is locked away here to cover it up. She may be lucky she's alive."

During the following weeks of therapy, Grace learned to trust her legs again. With Maire cheering her on, Grace learned to walk again with the walker. Maire snapped photos, posting them in a frame on Grace's wall. The legends read: Grace walked 252 feet this morning at 9:30 a.m. Grace walked 156 feet at 11 p.m. Grace walked 262 feet at 9:20 a.m. It only took her 12 minutes!

"You are doing the impossible, Ma!" Maire exclaimed proudly. "You get all your strength from God almighty. Satan is strong, but God has author-ity. You might as well be walking on water!" Grace looked up from her walker to manage a smile. "Soon you will be walking the length of this corridor!"

"When I get to the end," Grace stated, "I'm going home." Maire felt a chill run through her bones.

The bus rolled as Grace whispered her prayers. "Angel of God, my guardian dear, to whom God's love commits me here, ever this night be at my side, to light and guard, to rule and guide, Amen."

"Amen, Gram."

"Oh that Thou might bless me indeed, and that Thine hand might be with me."

"Amen."

"My brother taught me that prayer."

"I know."

"I believe it, don't you?"

"Yes, I do."

"Keep me from evil that it may not grieve me. God bless you Elle. God bless Maire."

"She's waiting for you."

"That will be good, won't it?"

"Yes, it will. You'll love the ocean."

"Get some sleep now. Are you going to wake me or will I wake you?"

"How about whoever wakes first wakes the other?"

"Thank you." Her voice drifted off. I looked across the aisle. The Hispanic woman cradled her baby. Yoki slept. Ancient Eyes tranquilly and methodically looped yarn over needle. Sonja, deep in thought, studied something on the Internet. The researcher pondered his notes. 'We are a family of travelers,' I thought, 'remote from power and mostly unknown, left to reason and conscience all our own.'

A bright spring morning dawned over Blackwater. Grace woke in a stupor. 'It must be those pills they give me in the night,' she thought. 'I'm not going to take them anymore.'

"It's time to get up for breakfast, Grace." Three huge women towered over her. They looked like mammoth crows. Behind them loomed a menacing machine. The crows clawed at her.

Angry and confused, she fought back. "No! No!" Raven seized her wrists, pulled hard and wrapped a strap behind and around Grace's waist. "Stop! I'll call the police!" she screamed. Then she braced herself against the pain and prayed.

While Grace struggled against the straps of the big machine, her care conference was in session without her. Bric was ordering Lonan Wing staff to document anything Maire or Elle might do to irritate, confuse or tire Grace. "Specific quotes would be helpful." Then he added, "You don't need to phone Elle to say evening prayers with Mom every night. Your aides should learn the prayers and say them with her."

"We tried that," Candy said. "Grace refuses. She says we aren't Catholic and we don't know the prayers. She wants Elle."

Demaris reported that Grace had a pretty new look to her room. Crystal Ann declared that red was a terrible color. It agitated Grace. It should be removed.

"You'll never get that quilt away from Grace." Demaris answered. "Elle made that for her."

"Mom doesn't need those things in her room," Crystal Ann sniffed. "They just get in the way. And remove that curio that Elle put in the bathroom."

"It has her perfume and special things from home," Delores argued.

Raven glared at Delores. "It's in the way. There's no room to turn around."

"Remove it," Crystal Ann ordered.

The crows steered the big machine down the corridor, leaving Grace alone in her room, broken, trembling and sobbing. Cherilee tossed a faded pair of slacks and a wrinkled T-shirt into her lap.

"I don't want to wear that," Grace protested. "Those are not my clothes. They're wrinkled and smell bad. Throw them away. Look in the closet. I have nice things to wear.

Cherilee kissed Grace on the cheek. "Oh, Mom, you look just fine."

Grace pulled away. "I am not your mother."

"Sure you are. Don't you remember? You said I could be number seventeen."

"No, I didn't. That's a lie." Grace pushed her back.

"OK then, have it your way." Cherillee steered her chair into the day room next to the nurses' station, reached overhead and switched on the television, cranking the volume to high and left giggling.

Maire entered Blackwater through the front foyer of the assisted living wing and strode past the chapel. A steady stream of residents rolled past.

"What's going on?"

"Staff Appreciation Day," a resident answered.

"Have you seen Grace?"

"Who?"

"My mother. The lady in the hat."

"No," a woman pushing a walker answered. "She didn't come to lunch, either."

While Maire was searching for Grace, I was dialing Lonan Wing.

"Grace's not here, "Liddy answered icily. "Everyone's at a program in the chapel."

"So Grace is at the program?"

"Oh, sure," Liddy chirped back. "We took her there." Then she stopped. Maire stood glaring at her from across the counter.

"Liddy?" I called through the phone. "Are you there?"

Maire took the phone out of her hand. "Call you right back, Elle," she said and handed the phone back to Liddy. "Busted!" Maire turned her back and walked the three feet past the nurses' station to Grace, who was sitting alone in the TV room. The TV blared over her head. "Ma!" she blurted, "what are you wearing?"

"I told the girl I didn't want to wear this. She just laughed at me and pushed this shirt over my head and pulled these wrinkled pants on."

"They dress you this way to give themselves permission to hurt you," Maire muttered under her breath. "Ma!" Maire hugged her softly. "Why aren't you at the program?"

Grace looked dejected. "They wouldn't take me. I've missed it now."

"Oh, no. You have not. There's time. Let's go." Maire wheeled her quickly away, smoothing her hair and spritzing on a bit of Estee Lauder Beautiful. She helped her change clothes, wrapped a soft sweater around her shoulders and held out a pink felt hat with a grosgrain ribbon around the brim. "Ma, when was the last time your teeth were brushed? Let's just rinse them off so your mouth is fresh and clean." The chapel filled as Maire wheeled Grace into a spot near the center aisle, then stood back near the doorway.

Mallory joined her. "You shouldn't help anymore."

"Then who will help her? You? I found her abandoned in front of a blaring television. You know how much these programs in the chapel mean to her. Why was she left there?"

"She refused to take her Actonel."

"You mean Boniva?"

"Actonel, Boniva, whatever. She refused. We told her she could go when she took it."

"She's over eighty years old. What's to be gained by forcing her to choke down Boniva, Actonel, Fosamax or whatever you have in your drawer to give her with barely half a Dixie cup of water?

"Her care is decided in care conference. It is not your responsibility."

"It certainly is my responsibility. You can be sure I will be at the next care conference."   The CEO took the microphone at center stage. "Welcome to our Staff Appreciation Program. It's good to see so many familiar supporters from the community here. Since our program falls on April Fools' Day, we've prepared a special skit for you."

Grace looked tired. "It's just a program, Ma. It's not music. Do you want to leave?"

"No," Grace insisted. "It's the only entertainment this week. I want to see it."

The CEO turned as staff members walked onto the stage. The administrators dressed as farmers, in bib overalls and straw hats. Staff dressed as pigs, with pink snouts and curly pink tails. Others wore potato costumes. The characters romped and rollicked through a series of skits. The farmers pinned blue ribbons on the potatoes for keeping the pigs contained. The pigs rooted in corners of their cages, squealed for attention and foraged for food, leaving a trail of waste behind. The baked potatoes helped themselves to the drugs. Others were dressed as peanuts. The farmers said they'd like to crack those nuts. Everyone laughed. A farmer hung a banner over the barn that said *WHEN PIGS FLY*.

Grace listened quietly, frowning. Then she turned to Maire. "This isn't good. I don't think this is funny." Maire pushed Grace out into the hallway. Stormy stood blocking the doorway, an eerie spectacle; her blonde hair streaked with strands of shocking blue and black. She stepped aside, leveled her eyes at Maire and smirked.

"They didn't tell you about this in the brochure?"

Maire stood on the sidewalk puffing on a cigarette and muttering furiously. She snuffed out her cigarette and dialed. My phone beeped. "I took time off from work and hurried across town just so Mom could be subjected to this? The CEO, the director of nursing, all the staff participated. Members of the board of directors sat in the front row looking on while staff mocked residents and families alike. Well, that skit says it all. Mom comes here in relatively good health, relatively good spirits and what do they see? They see a groveling animal. So they rope her, tie her and throw her on the truck. No medical facility should permit this! No family should permit this! This is beyond demoralizing. This is dehumanizing."

"I can be there in an hour."

"Tomorrow's another day. I'm just ranting. I'm just saying that every second of every day now is a precious memory that will be soon lost in a sea of painful ones. We need to devote as much time as we can to creating joy."

I suddenly dropped my phone and doubled over. I couldn't breathe. "God! What's happening?" I gasped.

Maire also dropped the phone, suddenly gripped by an eerie premonition. She hurried back to Grace where she found Aubery crouched beside her limp body slumped over the arm of her wheelchair. Maire lept to her mother's side, brushing Aubery back. "Ma? Ma!"

"I can't breathe." Grace fought for breath. "Help me."

"Aubery, what happened? I just left her!" Aubery stared blankly. "Get help!"

Aubery balked. "No. We have an order not to resuscitate."

"What the hell are you talking about? She's not comatose. She's asking for help." Maire spotted the phone in the corner, the cord wrapped around the receiver. "Why is her telephone disconnected?" She reached for it. Grace clung fiercely to her sleeve. Maire tugged the chair and Grace with it, knocking Aubery back on her heels. She plugged in the phone and dialed. My phone rang.

"Call 911!" I ordered. "Do it now. Hang up and dial." She hung up. I dialed Lonan Wing. The phone on Aubery's belt rang. "Aubery? Elle. Put my grandmother on the phone."

"We're not supposed to," Aubery argued. Maire grabbed Aubery's phone and put it to Grace's ear.

"Go ahead, Elle. She can hear you."

"Gram? I'm right here. Don't try to speak. Just be calm. I'm right here, Gram. I'm right here." Maire came back on Aubery's phone.

"They're here. She's got oxygen and they're wheeling her away."

"Go with her, Maire. Don't leave her side." Maire jumped into the back of the ambulance, Grace still gripping her hand, leaving Aubery at the exit, gaping.

As the ambulance sped through the night. Maire stared in anguish at her mother. She was living a nightmare! Then, to Maire's amazement, Grace slowly reached her hand to her face, pulled the oxygen mask away and smiled wearily up at her daughter. "Your hands are cold."

"Ma! You scared me to death!"

Grace smiled weakly and winked, patting Maire's hands. "I'm not done yet, Maire. Not yet."

The emergent care nurses met them at the door and hustled Grace into ER, crushing against Maire, pulling Grace's sweater over her head and unfastening her bra. Grace screamed. Maire pushed through. Grace clutched her bra to her chest and cowered. "That's what they do at Blackwater. Why is everyone grabbing at me?"

Quin appeared. He stepped aside as the physician on duty moved through the doorway and took over. "Did she fall?"

"Uh, no," Quin stammered. Maire glared at him. Quin recanted. "Did she, Maire?"

The young doctor looked quizzically from Maire to Quin. He draped a blanket around Grace and spoke softly. "I believe we can back off these medications."

He took her hand gently in his. "We'll keep you here overnight, Grace. Get some sleep. You'll feel better in the morning."

Grace watched him go. Then she pointed at Quin. Her voice pierced the room. "You! You did this to me." He stared at her, dumbfounded.

Maire's eyes burned into him. "Since when is there an order not to resuscitate? I know for a fact that neither Dad nor Mom wanted that." She stepped closer and lowered her voice. "I know. I was there."

"I didn't fall," Grace said matter-of-factly. "I didn't fall at the house. I didn't fall at the farm. I didn't fall tonight."

The next day Crystal Ann posted an email telling everyone in the family that their mother and grandmother had been hospitalized with a slight urinary infection.

I found Maire and Grace in her hospital room. "Gram, why are you still here? What are they telling you?"

Grace shook her head. "They hooked me up to monitors, they put metal probes in my scalp, they covered my hair with sticky goo. I don't know what they were doing. I asked the doctor, 'What do you see?' He said everything is where it should be."

"Was he patronizing?"

Grace shook her head. "I said, 'Be serious. I have a right to know what you're doing.'"

"It sounds like they were testing you for Alzheimer's," Maire ventured. "Did the doctor give you a diagnosis?"

"No. The doctor said there was nothing I should be worried about."

A nurse interrupted. "We're ready for you, Grace."

"Where is she going?" Maire demanded.

"They have scheduled me for a CAT scan," Grace called back as a technician wheeled her away.

"Do they still believe she fell? I'm calling Quin." Maire searched the room. "Why is there no phone in my mother's room?"

"Family's orders," the nurse answered, glancing at the chart.

She threw her arms up, exasperated. "Again with the telephone!"

Maire and I waited to hear the results of the test. The discharge nurse told Grace that the combination of medications must have caused complications. They saw nothing else.

"No urinary infection?" I asked.

"The nurse shot a quizzical sidelong glance. "That wasn't an issue."

"No diagnosis of Alzheimer's?" Maire asked.

The nurse dismissed her questions impatiently and spoke directly to Grace. "You are cognitively healthy, Grace." Then she turned to Maire. If your mother did fall, there's no injury. We've backed off most of her meds. She's exhausted now. She should rest."

I drove through the night, furiously chanting the prayer of Jabez as the miles raced by. When I arrived at the Victorian house, the sky was an endless sea of twinkling stars. I threw my bags on the floor, slipped into my running shoes and headed into the night, jogging through the streets under a rustling canopy of cottonwood and elm trees. The moon leapt ahead of me like a Shotokan tiger. Dread loomed stealthily in the shadows. Finally winded, I stopped, kicked off my shoes and gave my body over to the quiet trance of a ceremonial kata. I kicked and punched at the night air, moving in slow, quiet rhythm and motion until my body and mind were one and at peace. Then I walked slowly back to the house. Ronan was there waiting. "Long week?" He plopped comfortably into the sofa, arms spread across the back. "Do you want to tell me about it?"

"No."

He rose from the couch and rummaged through my CDs. He waved a disc over his head and popped it into the CD player. The energy of Santana soothed my senses. He grabbed my hand and whirled me in circles from room to room, laughing, rocking and spinning me along with him until the music stopped and we stood suddenly suspended in time. Then he abruptly pushed me away.

"I'm sorry," he said. "I'm not who you want me to be."

"Who are you?" I barely got the words out. "Tell me."

He placed his hands on my shoulders. "Not who you want me to be."

Numb, I felt the urge to detach. Yet, having come from a family of a thousand tiny secrets, so prolific that even the big dangerous lies were no longer discernible, I was grateful to be in the presence of someone I could trust. In my world, that made him as close to being a hero as anyone could ever get.

The bus rolled along, following the river, crossing the vast chasm from where I had been to where I was going. I scanned the quiet travelers, each engrossed in his or her own quiet thought. Except, that is, for the odd, hollow looking woman that had scampered ahead of me just before I boarded. She stared as if looking out from a deep, dark void. I turned back to the window. An eagle soared calmly over a distant butte. 'On eagles' wings,' I thought. Then the shadows pulled me back.

Maire juggled her days between Lonan Wing and Macys. I juggled my time between weekends at Lonan Wing and weekdays in Chicago, where I was the strategic planner, the critical thinker. There I stood on higher ground. Yet my mind wandered. Between meetings, I reached for my cell phone.

"Lonan Wing nurses' station. This is Aubery."

"Aubery, this is Elle Riorden. I'd like to speak to my grandmother, Grace."

"I'm at the other end of the hall. I can't look for her right now. You 'll have to call back."

I called an hour later.

"Grace is at Bingo."

"Grace doesn't play Bingo."

"We're busy now. Call in an hour."

I waited as long as I could and dialed again.

"Grace is at supper."

"Already? Isn't it early for supper?"

"There's a concert in the chapel. We're getting supper out of the way early."

"She won't want to miss a concert."

Back at the hotel I paced, unable to concentrate. I dialed again.

"Everyone's coming back from the concert. We're busy now," came another unidentified voice.

"I've been asking to speak to my grandmother since before lunch. I'll wait while you go to her room and hand her the phone."

There was a pause, then footsteps, then I heard pounding and crying.

"What's going on?" I called through the phone.

"Grace is gripping her phone and won't let go. I can't transfer the call to her phone."

"I want to speak to my grandmother immediately. Give her your phone." I heard Grace sobbing. "Gram, what's wrong? Tell me."

"They locked me in my room. I pounded on the wall and called but no one came." She gulped for air and continued, sobbing. "I knew they were going to the program. I could see them passing by in the hall-way. I called and pounded but no one would stop and help me. I want to go to the chapel. The concert isn't over yet."

"Gram, let me speak with the aide."

"She's not here. She handed me the phone and left. I got to the side of the bed, but can't get my feet to the floor."

"Gram, don't move! You'll fall! I'll get help." I dialed the nurses' station.

"Yello!" came Amelia's flippant greeting.

"Amelia, my grandmother watched people go by and had no way to get to the concert. Why would you do that?"

"Someone would have taken her if she'd asked."

"Amelia, she's sitting on the edge of her bed, trying to get to her wheelchair. Someone needs to go to her now."

"No can do."

"Amelia, if my grandmother falls, I will hold you responsible." The phone disconnected. I redialed. After 15 rings, the phone disconnected again. I dialed Grace's phone, praying she still had the phone near.

"Oh, Sweetheart."

"Gram, I'm going to stay on the line with you. I don't want you to stand up unless someone comes to help, OK?"

Grace turned to the squirrels racing across the limbs of trees, the birds scratching at the bird feeder and a rabbit in the underbrush. She wondered who would tend the tomatoes and the roses in her garden at Scanlon Circle. I described the traffic and the lights of the city. I wondered how I could keep her from harm from so far away. Finally I heard voices in her room. Then an aide came on the phone, telling me they would transfer her safely to her chair. Grace had missed the concert. She was at the mercy of contempt and indifference, but she knew she was not alone. And for now, at least, I knew she was safe.

The next morning brought Chicago sun and Chicago bustle. As my taxi sped through downtown traffic, I dialed again.

"Lonan Wing, this is Aubery."

"Aubery, this is Elle. May I speak with my grandmother?"

"Well, I don't know where she is. There's a phone her room. Did you try dialing her room?"

"Aubery, you know Gram can't push her chair. She can't reach the phone unless someone helps her. Please go to her room. I'll wait."

"This is a 22-acre facility. We can't possibly be expected to know where our residents are."

"Are you saying you do not regularly check on the wheelchair-bound residents in your health care wing?"

"Well, let's see." She whistled as she walked through the hallway. She stopped to speak to someone then she exclaimed, "Oh, here she is. She's right around the corner. What's the matter, Grace?" I could barely hear Aubery over the blare of a TV. "Grace is just sitting here enjoying the day and watching TV. I'll put her on." The TV blared, drowning out her voice. She couldn't hear me. I hung up and redialed the nurses' station.

"Aubery, my grandmother is in tears."

"Cindy," she called out, "take the phone to Grace." Cindy must have turned off the TV. I could finally hear Grace and she could hear me.

"Gram, what's wrong?"

"Oh, Sweetheart, I'm stuck!"

"Where are you, Gram?"

"I'm parked in front of the fish tank by the nurses' station. I can't move and no one will help me. I'm tired. I want to lie down in my room where it's quiet."

"Do you want me to ask the nurse to help you?"

"Yes, they won't listen to me." She called out to someone passing by. "Hello. Can you help me? Hello?"

I hung up and redialed the nurses' station. "Aubery, my grandmother wants to get to her room."

"No, she's fine. She's visiting with the others."

"She's not visiting, Aubery. She's crying. She wants to go to her room. She's calling for assistance."

"Oh, they all call for help," Aubery answered.

"Aubery, please take my grandmother to her room."

I dialed Lonan Wing from the hotel. "Lonan Wing nurses' station. This is Sharla."

"Sharla, this is Elle, Grace's granddaughter. I'd like to know that my grandmother is resting. Did someone finally get her to her room?"

"I haven't seen her since breakfast. I didn't see her at lunch. I'll walk down to her room." I waited. "She's not in her room. She's not in the dining room. Has anyone seen Grace? She must be strolling around."

"Sharla, she's in a wheel chair. She can only be strolling around if someone pushes her. Has Grace's family come to visit?"

"No family. Well, maybe her daughter, Maire, is with her."

"Maire is working. Sharla, you need to find my grandmother. Please call me when you do." I packed my bag. Then I dialed again.

"Lonan Wing nurses' station. This is Amelia."

"Amelia, this is Elle. I'm calling to see if you've found my grandmother yet."

"No'm. Sure haven't."

"Amelia, are you not concerned that you have lost a resident? Should I be speaking with your nursing director?"

"Yes Ma'am, you can if you like. I'll transfer you." The phone rang through, then a second time, then a third, then a fourth. I hung up on the tenth ring." I dialed Macy's.

A din of voices and music drowned out Maire's voice. "Elle! I'm buried here. Can I call you back?"

I put down the phone, grabbed my bag, descended to the lobby, turned to take one last look at the Chicago skyline and hailed a cab. As the cab sped to the airport, I prayed. "Hold on, Gram. Hold on."

Maire's shift was finally over. She wove through traffic to Blackwater Manor. The door was open to the street. 'So much for security,' she thought. Aubery was at the nurses' station, engrossed in paperwork. "Who is that screaming?" Maire asked. 'Why are you ignoring that woman?' Her blood ran cold. Those screams were coming from Grace's room. She sprinted the rest of the way and pushed open the door. The television blared. The room was empty. The screams were coming from the bathroom. Maire pulled on the door. The bathroom was pitch dark. She flipped the switch. Grace lay face down on the bathroom floor, fully clothed. There was no walker, no wheel chair, no gait belt. Maire gently lifted Grace's hand. It was limp. Her face was hot to the touch. Maire cradled a towel under her face. Grace stifled her screams in agonized sobs. Maire ran screaming down the hallway. "Aubery! Come! Now!"

Aubery turned Grace over and tugged at her arms to lift her. "Stop!" Maire ordered. "She may be hurt."

"I don't know what else to do." Aubery answered, shaking.

"Get someone! Get anyone!" Aubery darted from the room. Maire cradled Grace's head, soothing her neck and face, caressing her temples with a cool damp cloth. The round faced clock on the wall seemed to be frozen in time. Maire looked at her watch. "Where are they?" Aubery finally came back through the door with Louis, the security guard. "Be careful," Maire warned. Louis gently and effortlessly lifted Grace from the floor. Maire rolled the wheelchair close to where he stood and he placed her into it. Grace reached for the cold cloth, leaned over the side of the chair and heaved. Maire snatched a waste basket and looked around for Aubery to help, but Aubery was in the hall speaking frantically to someone on her portable phone. Caught in Maire's glare, she put the phone into her pocket and returned, pulling out a blood pressure cuff and reaching for Grace's arm.

"Why are you doing that now?" Maire challenged. "She's throwing up!"

"I have to take her blood pressure." Aubery leaned across Maire's arm, into Grace's face. "I'm going to give you something to sleep."

"No!" Maire held Grace close to her. "You are not going to sedate my mother. She could have a concussion!"

Aubery shook. "Our procedure is to give people who fall something for anxiety."

"I didn't fall." Grace choked back her sobs.

"Who authorized that?" Maire challenged.

"Bric said it's our discretion," she retorted. Then she abruptly turned away and looked around the room. "I'm going to unplug the phone."

"Forget the phone! Forget the drugs! Help me take care of my mother!"

Sue, the CNA on duty, appeared in the doorway and rustled through Grace's closet. She pulled out a pair of pajamas. Maire exploded. "You people are just now realizing she is not ready for bed?" Sue tugged at Grace's arm. Grace winced and pulled away. "What's the matter, Ma? Are you hurt?" Maire turned to Sue and Aubery. "You've been ignoring her screams for what must be hours and now you want to medicate her and dress her in pajamas? What is wrong with you people?" She turned to Louis. "Please help me transfer my mother."

"You should leave," Aubery began.

"Don't even think about it!" Maire hissed. "I will stay with my mother. Someone needs to be sure she's safe!" Aubery backed into the hallway. Sue followed. Maire stroked Grace's temples. "What happened, Mom?"

Grace shook her head. "There was a concert. I wanted to go. That blonde girl pushed me into the bathroom and said, 'Stay out of the way.' Then she slammed the door and kicked it. She shouldn't even be working here." Aubery and Sue, listening in the doorway, came back into the room.

"Who, Ma?"

"She was angry at me but I didn't do anything! She shouldn't even be working here."

Aubery and Sue again retreated, whispering, to the hallway. Maire sat with Grace, stroking her hands, softly reciting prayers until she finally relaxed into sleep. The round-faced clock on the wall marked midnight as it came and went. Questions raced through Maire's mind. "Certainly Aubery could hear Grace screaming. Why hadn't she responded? Why hadn't anyone else responded?"

Shortly before 1:00 a.m. there was the rap of knuckles on Grace's door. A muscular man with a military buzz strode forcefully into the room. "I'm Sol Bump," he announced, his angular jaw flexing in determination. "I'm Blackwater Manor's administrator."

"Shhhh!" Maire held her fingers to her lips. She shielded her eyes from the light streaming from the hallway through the door as he held it open wide.

"I need to talk to you," he barked.

"Wait in the hall," she whispered. "My mother's sleeping." She left Grace's side to join him. "She's had a bad day."

"I know all about that." He looked past her, down the dark hallway, avoiding eye contact. "You cannot be in this room anymore."

"Why not?"

"We're trying to get her to meet and socialize with other people. She can't do that if you're always hovering."

Maire stared at him in disbelief. "Socialize? Are you drunk? My mother has been locked in a bathroom for hours. She has fallen and been stuck face down, screaming for help! None of your staff responded! If I hadn't walked down that hallway, she may still be there! What if she'd had a stroke or a heart attack from such a horrific experience?"

"That be as it may," he began dismissively.

"She has been traumatized!"

"That be as it may," he continued arrogantly, "you cannot be here. You cannot be with her at meals and you cannot stay overnight."

"I have every right to be here!"

"If you wish to stay here; if you wish to spend any amount of extended time here, you'll have to pay."

"Are you nuts? We're talking about my mother, a woman who is paying out of pocket to receive assistance transferring from the bed and to the bathroom. That's it! That's the only reason she's here. Your staff can't even manage that! She's been locked in a dark bathroom all day without her walker or her chair and fell when she no longer had the strength to stand!"

"They all fall," Sol interrupted. "It's a fact. She was probably just trying to get back to bed from the potty."

"Listen, Sol!" Maire jabbed her finger into his plastic gold-plated name badge. That's what I'm telling you! She's wheelchair bound. She has a minus-four bone density. She's here without her power chair. She can't push the wheels on that buggy. She can't move without one of your staff assisting her. The only way she could have gotten to the bathroom is if someone put her there!" He turned away dismissively. Maire wasn't finished. "Your staff takes hours to answer her light when she needs to go to the bathroom, but locks her in when she doesn't!"

"Grace was listed as incontinent when we admitted her. We can't be running to get her to the bathroom every time she pushes the button."

"She can't get to the damn button! She can't move her chair to reach it! Get this! She is not incontinent. Who signed that document?"

"Grace's daughter Crystal Ann, when Grace's sons, Acer and Bric admitted her."

"You don't have a doctor's signature?"

"They are doctors! They should know."

"That's irresponsible!"

"Are we done here?" He asked condescendingly. "Are we agreed?"

Maire reached for the phone in her pocket and dialed. My phone beeped. My plane was still idling on the runway.

"I'm in the hallway outside Mom's room," she said. "Sol Bump is kicking me out."

I stared out the small oval window of the plane cabin, helpless. "Who's Sol Bump?"

"The administrator."

"What's the administrator doing there at two in the morning? Wait. What are you doing there?"

"When I got here last night, Mom was face down in the bathroom. I think she had been there all day. I heard her screaming when I came in the back door. I know Aubery heard her but she didn't move until I ordered her to help. I got her into bed and I'm with her now but Sol Bump says if I stay with Mom I'll have to pay."

"That's outrageous. Is he still there? Put him on the line."

"Sol Bump here," barked an abrupt voice.

"Sol? Elle Riorden. I want a copy of Blackwater Manor's policies and procedures emailed to me immediately."

"Who are you? I cannot possibly provide you with that."

"I'm Grace's granddaughter, Elle Riorden. Why not?"

"It's a big document."

"Then copy it and give it to Maire."

"Not possible."

"Then send me just the policies which apply to families. And Sol? For Christ's sake, leave my Aunt Maire alone and get the hell away from my grandmother's door. It's two in the God damn morning." I put down the phone. The flight attendant stood in the aisle blinking at me in polished disapproval. I turned off the phone and stared again out the small oval window into the night.

When I turned my phone back on, there was a memo on Blackwater letterhead listing just two policies. The first was that family could stay over with advanced notice to staff. The second was that staff would check on residents a minimum of once every two hours. It was signed by the CEO of Blackwater and dated that morning. 'Odd,' I thought. 'It's now three a.m. What's the CEO doing at the office sending out memos?'

Hours later, I walked through Lonan Wing. Grace lay in bed, wide-awake, watching for me. She stretched to reach me. I wrapped her in my arms and she buried her face in my chest, sobbing. "I want to talk to that woman."

"Who? Who do you want to talk to?"

"Crystal Ann. She put me here."

"Crystal Ann put you in the bathroom?"

"She put me here. I want to talk to her. I have something to say."

"Tell me, Gram."

Grace told and retold a story about Raven and Dimmea and another 'fat crow.' They held her down. They tied her to a machine. Then they tied her to her chair. She missed breakfast. She missed lunch. There was a concert in the chapel. She called out to people passing her doorway. She wanted to go but no one would stop for her. Then the tall blonde girl, dressed in black, came in and pushed her into the bathroom and told her to stay there and closed the door. She was alone in the dark with nothing to hang onto but the grab bar. She clung to the wall for as long as she could, but the blonde girl came and kicked the door, saying, 'You stay there.' I listened in horror.

Grace grew quiet and calm. Then she said, "I'm hungry. I didn't get to eat today."

I brought a bowl of chicken noodle soup and fruit from Café Sofie. She sipped on the soup, deep in thought.

"What is it, Gram?"

"Teach me about karate."

"You think you can fight them off?"

"Probably not. No. Probably not."

"Gram, what I know about karate, I learned from you."

"Me? No."

"Yes, Gram, my whole life I watched you calmly standing against the storm." Her eyes widened in surprise. "But now I realize you didn't stand against the storm, Gram. You were one with the storm. That's karate."

"Oh." She nibbled on a grape. "Will karate help me stand against the girl in the chair?"

"What girl in the chair?"

"The girl that sits in that chair, sometimes all night long. Sometimes she stands over my bed. Sometimes she holds me down."

"What?"

"She looks like a boy. She sits in that chair."

Grace clung to my hand as she dozed. When she woke again the round faced clock pointed at four. I pushed the call light. Sue and Ivy, chatting in the hallway, ignored it. I transferred Grace from the bed, laced her shoes and wheeled her into the bathroom. Finally Ivy poked her head around the door and ducked back out.

Julia came through the door next. "Grace is scheduled for a shower before supper. Do you want to wait here?"

"No. I'll go with you." We wheeled to the shower room.

Clover burst in behind us. "Julia, what are you doing?"

"I'm giving Grace her shower."

"You have no business giving anyone a shower. You are the only one taking care of this wing! Lights are flashing up and down the hallway!"

"Grace is scheduled for a shower."

"Leave her. Go answer the call lights." Julia dropped the towel and hurried out the door. Clover rolled her eyes at me and stomped after her, leaving Grace sitting naked on a plastic shower chair. I closed the door after her and for a moment we simply stared at each other. Then I reached for a large towel and draped it across the front of her body, covering her back with another. The door opened again. It was Julia.

"Will you stay with Grace?"

"Of course. Close the door."

I put the shower wand in Grace's hand. "How's this? Right temperature? As if I would leave! God! Who are these people?"

Maire sat at a table in the Lonan Wing dining room, waiting. Grace reached for a kiss and then pointed past her. "She shouldn't be here. She locked me in the bathroom. She shouldn't be working here." We both turned to look. There was Poppy, bouncing through the dining room, her bleached blond ponytail bobbing behind her. Silver and gold bangles jingled on her wrist. Her perfume wafted through the air as she passed. Her Yorkie pranced around her. "That one," Grace insisted. "She kicked the door and locked me in. She should not have been working there." I looked past the barricade of greenery-filled urns dividing the two sides of the room to tables of four where residents chatted. I looked past the scurrying brown-clad kitchen staff, carrying plates to and from the tables. I looked past Amelia standing at the med cart. The only other blonde was Mallory, the social worker. She chatted with one of the residents.

"It's that one, right there, with the square shoulders." Grace said impatiently.

Maire scanned the dining room. "I don't see anyone else, Ma."

Bric, Crystal Ann and Lyssa stood at the nurses' station. "I'll go," Maire said flatly. "I've got this one." I watched as she sauntered to the counter. "What's up?" she asked, flicking her words at them like she was flicking an ash from her cigarette.

"I've come for the curio in Mom's bathroom," Crystal Ann declared smugly.

Maire's voice was cold and level. "That curio isn't going anywhere."

"It's in the way," Crystal Ann argued.

"In the way of what?" Maire volleyed. Crystal Ann's eyes narrowed. Lyssa left them and strode toward Grace. Maire turned to Bric. "In the way of what?" Bric didn't answer. "That's a very beautiful, very expensive cabinet, Bric. You didn't pay for it. Crystal Ann didn't pay for it. Lyssa didn't pay for it. Elle paid for it. Mom loves to look at her things through the beveled glass doors. You want to take it away from her? I'll tell you what. Let's take Mom's wheelchair into the room and measure around it. Let's just see how crowded it is." Crystal Ann turned on her heel and huffed away.

"That's not necessary," Bric conceded. He signaled to Lyssa, who left Grace and joined him. "I'm sure it's fine where it is."

"Yea, little brother," Maire whispered as she watched him drive away. "It's just fine where it is."

That afternoon, Liam stopped by. Grace basked in his presence. Maire left them alone to visit, but waited in the hallway for him.

"Do you know what happened at the farm?"

"What?"

"It seems that this all started with Acer's trip to the farm. What happened?"

"I don't know," he answered.

"How did this all move so quickly from that night at the farm to here at Blackwater Manor? How was it that her telephone was disconnected the very day she was admitted to the hospital?"

He stared back at her. "I don't know."

She threw up her arms. "What do you know? I don't have a medical degree, but I know that it was not a urinary infection."

"We won't point fingers," he said quietly.

"So!" Maire faced him squarely. "We are all expendable pawns in the Riorden game? What about the oath to do no harm? Why is Aubery on the phone taking orders from Bric at midnight? Why are you the only one in this family who comes to see her?" Grace pretended not to hear, but caught every word. Maire stopped abruptly as Crystal Ann charged headlong toward them. "Christ! I need a cigarette." She moved aside to let Crystal Ann pass but Crystal Ann pivoted mid-step, following her to the exit.

"She didn't fall," Crystal Ann snarled.

Maire turned to face her. "I thought you left."

"There's nothing in the documentation about her falling. She didn't fall."

"Crystal Ann, I was here. I was the one who picked her up off the floor. She was locked in a dark bathroom for probably most of the day, while the entire staff was not even pretending to look for her." Crystal Ann glowered, speechless. "I was here! Don't tell me she didn't fall. If Aubery didn't document it, take it up with her, and get out of my face!" Maire flicked her cigarette. "What do you know about how she got here?"

Crystal Ann bristled. "Bringing her here was the hardest thing I've ever done."

"You brought her here? You did? How did you convince her?"

"I didn't." Crystal Ann reached for the door, trembling.

"You just said you did!"

Crystal Ann shook her head. "She wouldn't get out of the car. I drove around and around and around the city for hours. Finally, I just brought her to the front door and Acer and Bric took her inside."

Maire stared at her. "You are all nuts! You are completely out of control! She is our mother! What was so important that you had to get her out of the way at any cost, even if it meant hurting her?"

"She didn't fall," Crystal Ann repeated weakly.

"Stop saying that! It makes you look stupid." Maire snuffed out her cigarette with the toe of her boot. "Devils!" Maire opened the side door, ignoring the sign, which read

PLEASE PUSH BUTTON BEFORE ENTERING. She left Crystal Ann sputtering as she walked back through the corridor to the earsplitting screech of the security alarm. Liam kissed his mother goodnight as Maire approached. Aubery stood in the doorway.

"Aubery, my sister was here. Did she ask about the fall?"

"No, but she took the nurses' notes."

"Is that legal?"

"Bric was there with her, so I suppose it was all right."

Maire turned to Liam. "I'm sorry, Liam. You are a good and true son to your mother. I shouldn't take my anger out on you. I think you and I both know that this family needs to stop gaming and by God start thinking about what they are going to do as daughters and sons for their mother."

Maire drove furiously with one hand, dialing my number with the other. "They're going to kill her. I've got to stop this if I have to kidnap her myself!"

Listening to Maire, I realized that the April Fools' Day skit was an omen. Lonan Wing, I discovered, was as full of fools as it was of danger. I phoned the next morning. Amelia answered.

"She's still in the dining room."

"It's nine-thirty. Was breakfast late?"

"Don't know. Can't say."

"May I speak with her?"

"She's in the dining room."

"The dining room is less than ten steps from you, Amelia. May I speak with her?" She breathed an exaggerated sigh. Then I heard Grace's voice.

"Oh, Sweetheart."

"Why are you still in the dining room?"

"I'm waiting for breakfast."

"Isn't the kitchen closed?"

"There's someone back there, cleaning."

"Didn't anyone bring your breakfast?"

"I asked for a scrambled egg. That was a long time ago." I hung up and redialed.

"Yello!"

"Amelia? Elle. My grandmother has not had her breakfast yet."

"Oh? She's right there in the dining room." Just then Cecilia passed by the nurses' station. "Go help Grace," Amelia ordered, pointing to the dining room. Cecilia shrugged and unfastened Grace's bib.

"No," Grace clutched the bib to her chest. "I'm waiting."

"Let go, Grace!" Cecilia commanded impatiently. She grabbed the bib, twisting it from Grace's hands. A spoon clattered against the wheel of the chair and fell to the floor. Grace reached for a second spoon, lying on the table. Cecilia wrenched it from Grace's hand. "What are you doing, Grace? Stealing silverware?" Grace pulled back, shaking her head.

Maire found Grace sitting in the dining room, holding her arm, wincing in pain. "What's this? What's the matter, Ma?"

"I'm waiting for a scrambled egg." Maire turned to face Cecilia, the napkin still in her hand.

"Cecilia, what's going on here? Why did you take my mother's napkin? Why is she still waiting for her breakfast?"

Cecilia opened the napkin and abruptly dropped a stainless steel teaspoon onto the counter. "She's stealing silverware."

"What the hell?" Maire exploded. "Are you crazy? Get your administrator." Minutes later Sol Bump walked stiffly around the corner, his right hand pressing a button on the pager clipped to his belt. "Explain this to me!" Maire waved her hand at the spoon, the napkin and Grace sitting in the dining room.

"She's stealing silverware," Cecilia blurted out.

"She's got a houseful of beautiful things. Why would she want your old bent spoons? She's not stealing anything. She's sitting at the table waiting for an egg."

Sol interrupted. "Why is she taking so long to finish her breakfast?"

"She's waiting for breakfast!" Maire exclaimed, exasperated. "Do you think she can get it herself?" She threw up her hands. "Is anyone in charge here? Not only do you not feed her, but you ignore her and then you insult her! My mother deserves an apology."

Sol turned to Cecila. "Go back to work." Then he turned to Maire. "Is that it? Are we done here?"

"Done here? No, we're not done here. This is the second time you have completely blown me off. My mother has been subjected to indifference, insults and contempt and all before her breakfast."

"To your point," Sol bristled, "breakfast was at eight. If she chose to sleep in or refused what she was served, then she will find lunch at noon. As for the silverware, we'll keep it here in the dining room." He straightened his shoulders and pushed the button on his pager. "I'm glad we agree on this."

"This place is out of control!" she shot back as he strolled away. "There is no one driving this bus!" Maire turned back to Grace. "Never mind, Mom.

We'll eat at Café Sofie. We'll find a cup of soup and a sandwich and real silverware."

"Don't forget to come back for pills before supper," Cecilia called as they wheeled away.

"Jesus! Help us!" Maire muttered. Grace stared quietly ahead.

Maire and Grace arrived at Café Sofie just as Grace's sister, Jacelyn arrived. "Oh Grace," Jacey called, "I'll join you."

Maire bristled. "You refuse to sit with her in Lonan Wing dining room but you will sit with her here?"

Jacey averted her glare. "Lonan Wing is just for..." she stopped. "The seating is assigned."

"Residents are joined by family members every day there," Maire challenged. "You are family, aren't you?"

Jacelyn pursed her lips into a pout. "You never did like me, Maire. I don't know what else I can do."

"You can show my mother the respect she deserves from a sister," Maire snapped. "You can join her for breakfast or lunch or an afternoon snack or for just a walk in the garden. You can earn your $750 referral fee."

Jacelyn sniffed and strutted away then stopped and turned back, pulling out her camera. "Take a picture of us."

"What? No."

"You'll be sorry!" Jacelyn whined. "You'd better take a picture now, or it will be too late."

"Too late? What are you saying? What on earth does that mean?"

"You'll be sorry. It'll be too late."

Grace tugged on Maire's sleeve. "Let's just go."

"All right, Ma," Maire acquiesced, steering her away to a table in a bright corner of the atrium. Maire and Grace spent an hour over the white-meat sandwich and chicken noodle soup watching squirrels dart through the branches just outside the window. They lingered, savoring each bite of a chocolate brownie and sipping on warm, strong coffee. Then they strolled through the corridors from wing to wing, viewing the gardens, barely awake from winter's sleep, marveling at the squirrels scurrying over the slippery rooftops. There would be just enough time to change into a silk blouse and soft woolen sweater before the concert.

Grace positioned a pink pillbox hat on her head before Maire pushed the chair back to the nurses' station. Emily stood at the med cart, flipping through the resident charts. Then she impatiently pushed a Dixie cup against Grace's lips. Grace choked and shook her head. "I don't have time to wait," Emily ordered. "Just swallow it." Grace shook her head. Emily tipped the cup to her clenched mouth, spilling water down the front of the ivory silk blouse. Grace stared at her, stricken. Maire snatched the Dixie cup and dabbed at the stain with a soft towel. Emily threw up her hands and backed away. "Refused."

"They're mean here," Grace whispered.

The bus slid around sleet-covered curves, jogging me from my thoughts. The Interstate was leading us up hills and through snowy passes. We rode a steel turtle, safe in its shell, following the course of the river. Coyotes cried in the distance. 'Turtles annoy the hell out of coyotes,' I thought.

April wasn't done. A late spring blizzard brought the city to a standstill. I dialed Blackwater Manor to ask if there would be a program in the chapel.

"No'm. There's nothing on tonight."

"May I speak to my grandmother?"

"No'm. Not right now."

"Why not?"

"She's far away. Down the other hall."

"Put my grandmother on the line, Amelia. I'll wait."

Maire inched across town through one-lane side streets. She hated driving in this weather, but her heart ached with a premonition of evil. She slid into the back parking lot of Blackwater and hurried through Lonan Wing to Grace's room. The door was closed. The TV blared. She pushed the door open. The drapes were shut tight. Grace was sitting in the dark. A big bowl of chips was on the table in front of her, out of reach. Her wheelchair was turned away from the TV. Maire reached over and touched her hand. Grace looked up, helplessly.

"Ma, are you all right?" Grace didn't answer. "Ma, what can I do for you?"

"I need to go to the bathroom," she said in a weak voice. Maire pushed the call button and then spun her mother's chair around. "I don't know how I can help you, Ma. I'm not strong enough to lift you like Elle does, but I'm going to try." Then she saw the belt. Her mother was again cinched into her chair, the Velcro belt wound around her waist, around the chair and again around two of the metal bars under the arm rest. Maire strode from the bathroom down the hallway straight to the nurses' station. "My mother needs to go to the bathroom. She's parked in the dark, out of reach of her call light, strapped to her chair, which is ridiculous because she cannot move without someone helping her and the TV is blaring so loud no one can hear her call for help. You help her now or I will by God hire someone who will!"

I was still on the phone. "Hello? Is anyone there?"

"It's me," Maire answered. "I'm with Mom."

"How is she?"

"She's emotionally and physically worn."

"It must break her heart to be locked up like an animal."

"I found an aide to help her in the bathroom. She said she called out her 'yoo-hoo' until she was exhausted, but residents and staff alike just passed by, ignoring her. Here's another thing. I tried to help her with her sweater, but her arm was sore and bruised! Forget lifting it."

"Did she say what happened?"

"She's telling me about a machine. She says it feels like they broke her back. I don't know what that means. There's something else. She said the aides taunt her, insisting that Grace isn't her name. That's malicious!"

"They're messing with her. What machine? Is she talking about an exercise machine? We have to find out what she's describing."

"Whenever I press her for more, she says she's been warned not to make a commotion."

I could hear bustling in the room and then a sharp cry from Grace. "Ouch!"

Then I heard Maire call out, "You are supposed to use the gait belt and the walker. You're pulling her arms straight out to lift her. Why are you doing that? She can barely lift her arms and you are pulling her weight from her arms to stand her up? Is this the way you've been trained to transfer?"

The aide's voice crackled in the background. "Why don't you wait outside?"

"Here's the gait belt," Maire countered. "I'm not leaving my mother. Mom is in her stocking feet. She can't walk simply because you push her. How is it you do not know this? Where's the walker?" Maire paced in the hallway. "I'm back. I'm reading the Bill of Patient's Rights hanging here on the wall. I wonder why they bother to post it when they obviously ignore it." Then she interrupted herself. "Gotta go."

"Ow!" Grace's voice came through the bathroom door as Maire opened it a crack. "Careful! That really hurts."

"Well, if your daughter hadn't opened the door, I wouldn't have jumped and hurt you," the aide snapped. Grace faced the wall, gripping the metal grab bar to the side of the toilet.

"I told you to be careful of her right arm," Maire warned. "She's been hurt. She can't raise it."

"You will not be here next time," the aide warned. She placed Grace's hands on the walker and steered her to her chair waiting by the bed. Maire followed her into the hallway.

"Just a minute. I need to talk to you."

"Not now. There are lights flashing up and down this hallway."

"I want you to know that Mom sits strapped to her chair, calling for help while staff ignores her. Did she even get to the bathroom today?"

"I don't know about that. I came on at two. As for her yelling, she's been told to put on her light."

"The call light is across the room. She can't move without assistance. How long have you been taking care of her? Why don't you know this? And, by the way, a big bowl of potato chips? Who's are those?"

"I don't know anything about that. That wasn't my shift."

"That seems to be everyone's excuse!"

I stared through a sleet covered window helplessly listening to Maire's anger and frustration. Then she was back on the phone with me. "There are bruises and abrasions on her forearms, her knuckles and her shins. Why are we the only ones noticing this?"

"Either they are trained to treat patients like that or no one one's trained them at all and they're learning from each other."

"I thought you said that they discontinued Mom's physical therapy."

"That's what they told me. She was doing so well with the walker, but suddenly they refuse to give her physical therapy or water therapy or any other kind of therapy."

"Well, she's talking about a machine."

"What is this machine?"

"Mom described it. She said there are arms that come out and grab her."

The next day Mallory, the social worker, phoned Maire. "You asked me to tell you when the next care conference was scheduled. There's a care conference this afternoon."

"Am I allowed to go?" Maire asked, surprised to be included.

"All members of the family are welcome at care conferences," Mallory answered.

Maire raced through the morning and worked frantically through lunch, checking the clock repeatedly against her progress. She sped across town and arrived at Lonan Wing to find Crystal Ann waiting for her in the foyer. "I just need a minute to freshen up," Maire called, motioning to a nearby restroom. As Maire walked away she heard Crystal Ann's voice echoing through the atrium. Maire guessed she was on the phone with Bric.

When she emerged from the bathroom, Crystal Ann was gone. Maire crossed through the foyer to the conference room, but Mallory stopped her. "I'm going to the care conference."

"I know. Please come with me." She waved Maire toward an office across the hall.

"Great!" Maire muttered. "Now what?"

"You won't be allowed in the care conference," Mallory replied flatly.

"You told me that family was welcome."

"Yes, but in this case the power of attorney has restricted attendance. I don't know why."

"That's ridiculous! You invited me. I took off work to be here."

"I'm sorry. We have no consistency."

"Oh, I disagree," Maire snapped. "Inconsistency is the one consistency Blackwater can claim!" Furious,

Maire dropped into an overstuffed wing chair in the atrium.

My phone beeped. "There's got to be reason they don't want you in there, beyond Crystal Ann's usual ploy for power," I offered. "Do you know who else is there?"

"Yes, I can see them coming out. They're walking right past me. They're so full of themselves they don't even see me." She paused. "They're gone. It was just Crystal Ann and Doreen. Mom wasn't even there."

"Well, that's it then. Bric doesn't want you to know that his wife speaks for him as power of attorney. Talk about a violation of HIPAA. The one person Gram would never allow access to her information is Doreen."

"War is a moral contest. It's won on principle before it's even fought. Acer claimed his victory the day the family stood on her lawn and voted to kick her out of her own home."

Early Sunday morning I again sped along the Interstate. The thought of Lonan Wing knotted my stomach and tightened my throat. Maire met me there and we walked through the double security doors together. Liddy stood at the desk. "You can wait for your mother in the Day Room," she ordered. We walked past, ignoring her. "Wait for her in the Day Room!" she ordered, reaching for the phone.

Screams pierced the hallway. Maire and I froze, then bolted to Grace's room. My heart was in my throat as I burst through the door. Grace hung off the bed, her face contorted in terror and pain. Her shrieks slashed through the room. A grotesque machine had her in its jaws. A two-inch wide belt stretched from a center beam of the machine and looped around Grace's frail frame, cutting into her waist. Raven stood with her hand firmly on the lever. Two other giant women towered ominously above their prey. Then Raven flipped a switch and a single strap around Grace's back jolted her precariously forward. Shrieking in agony, she clung in desperation as her body jerked forward then flung upward. The pressure on her frail legs and fragile joints twisted her body to the left and then rotated her to the right, pulling on her wrists, strapped to the arms of the machine. Her arthritic knuckles, taut and white gripped the bars. I shot past Maire, past the big women and past the machine. I threw my arms around Grace's waist, lifting the weight off her legs, holding her against me.

"You need to leave the room," Raven hissed.

"Are you on drugs?" Maire shrieked. "What are you doing?"

I held Grace firmly in my arms, releasing the belt from her waist. Grace's pleaded with feverish eyes, her face white and drawn with horror. My heart bled. She looked like quarry caught in a death trap. As I loosened a strap from her wrist she threw her arm around my neck, burying her head in my shoulder. Her muffled screams resonated in my bones and seared my soul. Raven reached across the machine to stop my hand from unbuckling the second strap. Our eyes locked. She froze and backed away. I rocked Grace in my arms as she shuddered in terror. Her body was rigid and her mind, I feared, had gone deep into hiding.

"Gram?"

She lifted her head and searched my eyes. Then she tightened her grip around my neck and buried her head again, quivering with each anguished breath.

"Gram?"

She lifted her head again and stared, first at me, then at Raven, then back at me.

Maire came closer. "Ma? Mother?"

Grace stared at Maire and back again at me. Then she blinked and brushed my face with her fingers. "Gram? I'm here. Look at me, Gram. You know me. Look! Here I am."

"Mother," Maire whispered.

Grace looked again at Maire, then back at me, then she collapsed, sobbing. I motioned toward my purse, lying open on the floor where I dropped it.

"What?" Maire looked around frantically, then nodded and flipped open my cell phone. Raven snarled as Maire aimed the camera and snapped a shot. Raven grabbed for the phone.

"Get out!" Maire growled. "Get out of here and take that machine with you."

"This is an appropriate machine," Raven lifted her chin defiantly. "The doctor ordered it."

"Then you'd better produce a script." Maire flared, snapping another shot of the machine. "Get out of here or I'll have your license."

"And I'll have you both removed," Raven threatened, still eying the phone. Maire raised it in her face and clicked. Raven stormed out the door. The other two followed.

We stared at the machine, gaping down at us. "Can you dial?" I whispered. "She's got a death grip on my hands." Maire quickly tapped in a series of numbers and put the phone on speaker.

"Cheyla, Elle. I'm here at Blackwater with Maire and Gram. There's been an incident and I need to speak with Quin."

"Quin's on call this weekend. I'd rather not disturb him. Can you tell me what the problem is?" She sounded ominously calm.

"I'd rather speak to Quin directly."

"Just tell me what's the problem and I'll call Doreen and she'll relay your message to Bric."

"I can do that myself, Cheyla."

"Maire tapped in more numbers and pushed the speaker button. Doreen answered.

"Doreen. It's Elle. Is Bric there?"

"He's right here. He's expecting your call."

"Interesting," Maire whispered. Bric came on the line. His voice was evenly modulated.

"Hello?"

"Bric. It's Elle and Maire. We're here with Gram. Maire and I found her strapped to a lift machine, screaming in pain. It's nothing like the sling seat that Grandpa used. This machine is a dinosaur. It hoists her forward putting all the weight on her legs. She's here because she can't tolerate weight on her legs! Her arms were strapped to bars. She is covered with bruises and gashes. Her body won't tolerate this abuse. She won't last the week if this continues." Grace lifted her head. "It's Bric," I said. I held the phone out to her. Grace tried to speak, but no words came.

'It's Bric, Mom. Can you hear me?" She did not respond. "Mom?" Grace pushed the phone away stifling her sobs in my shoulder. "I'll be right over," he said and hung up.

Bric did not come alone. Doreen's shrill voice penetrated the room before she got through the door. "Grace? Grace! Do you know who we are? Do you want to get out of bed and go to church this morning?"

Grace glared at her. "I can hear you, Doreen. I'm not deaf."

Maire steered Bric into the hallway. "Look at your mother, Bric. Before she came here she was in good health and of good spirit. You lock her in here, tie her down, and hoist her onto a machine like a carcass at slaughter. I don't know of any medical facility that permits that." She leaned in nose to nose with her brother. "I don't know of any family that permits that."

I joined in. "What went on here this morning was vicious. I need you to tell me that you did not order that machine."

"No. No, I certainly did not." His eyes were wide and steady. I watched his reaction closely.

"If she is subjected to this terror again, she won't last the week."

"I will take care of it."

"She's a frail woman with osteoporosis and arthritis. If the staff is not capable of transferring her safely, she needs to be somewhere that can."

He started down the hallway. Maire followed him. "This is abuse and malicious intent."

He nodded impatiently. "I'll take care of it."

We returned to the room. Doreen, Raven and Luella leaned over Grace. In the short time we were in the hallway, they had changed her pajama top for a sparkly sequined shell.

Maire immediately faced off with Raven. "Why are you still here?"

Bric headed toward the nurse's station. Maire positioned herself on the bed next to Grace. I stood outside the doorway watching as Bric grinned broadly, wrapping his arm around Liddy's waist. Liddy smiled and leaned into him. 'Odd,' I thought.

I turned my attention back to Grace. Doreen was urging her to stand. "No," Grace stated flatly. "Not while these girls are in the room. They're mean."

Cassie, the CNA with the perpetual tan, strutted in. "You'll all need to leave the room now."

Maire faced Raven. "Just a week ago you had double restraints on her to keep her from using her walker. Not less than an hour ago, you hoisted her to her feet with a crane because you believed that she could not stand on her own. Now you insist she stand without assistance. I'm asking you again. Why were you using that machine?"

"Because she didn't want to get up." Raven retorted defiantly.

"And you think that answer is acceptable?"

"The doctor ordered it." Cassie interrupted.

"Did Dr. Corbin order that machine?" Maire demanded.

Doreen slipped into the hallway and motioned for Bric to come back. He hurried through the door. "Please leave us, Cassie."

Cassie spun around defiantly, a surge of anger forcing a tinge of redness to her tan as she bared her white teeth. She tossed back a lock of ice blond hair, turned on her heel and snapped angrily over her shoulder as she left the room, "This is ridiculous!"

Bric and Doreen followed Cassie down the hall back to the nurse's station. Maire spoke quietly, still stroking Grace's arm. "This is a test of wills. For what purpose?"

"They are on a timeline," I guessed.

"We hire them to care for her." She looked across Grace, past me to the doorway. "I'm afraid to leave her alone with them."

"Cassie's remark is surprising," I said. "No other physician would tolerate that insolence from a CNA."

"Unless they have some other arrangement," she concluded. "I'm thinking Bric approved that machine and is telling them to just wait until we are gone." She stared at Grace's arm. "Oh, my God!"

"Calm down," Grace scolded. "Be careful." Two-inch bruises circled each of her forearms. I lifted her pajama leg. There were similar bruises and abrasions on each chin and a bump on her ankle. Maire strode into the hallway and waved Bric back.

Bric leaned in close to look. "I'll order something for these abrasions. Don't worry. I'll take care of it."

Grace met his patronizing tone with a withering stare. "Do you promise?"

"I promise," Mom. He kissed her and walked into the hallway where he stood leaning against the wall, staring at his phone. Maire joined him. "I told them to let her sleep in the morning," he said. "They don't need to rush to get her out of bed."

"Why is it so hard for her to wake in the morning?" Maire countered. "What is your position on sedatives?"

Bric straightened. "There are no sedatives authorized."

"Aubery tells me that they sedate Grace at their discretion." She studied Bric's face for the effect of her words. There was none. "After twenty years in AA, I know the signs, Bric. She's sedated, probably so they can manipulate her. No wonder she's in tears all the time. In all my life I've never seen my mother cry." Maire pressed closer. "Until now. Is this what you want?"

He studied the screen on his phone. "I think what you're seeing is the symptoms of aging."

Doreen joined in. "I know about these things. I had two aged aunts. Both hallucinated."

"This is not hallucination, Doreen," Maire countered.

"I need to go," Bric said abruptly. "Are you staying?"

"Yes, Bric. We're staying." Maire stared in disbelief.

Grace waited quietly for Maire to return. "They really can hurt somebody with that machine," she said heavily.

"Have they used that machine before, Ma?"

"I'm not supposed to tell you." Dark fear flashed across her face.

"Bric promised there would be no more machine, Ma."

Grace clasped both our hands in hers. "How long can you stay?"

"I can stay all night if you want," Maire answered.

"No, just until I get to sleep," she answered bravely. Then she smiled weakly. "Maybe a little bit after."

Early Sunday morning I joined Maire and Grace for Sunday TV Mass. Then we joined the other residents for coffee and cookies. "She has weathered insurmountable storms in her life," Maire whispered as we stood back, watching. "None can know the dysfunction that is this family. It is well concealed by a unified front. As she spoke, her gaze followed Grace's sister,

Jaclyn, moving through the room like a politician, shaking hands and firing off humorous one-liners.

Grace turned to a woman on her right. "Hello. I'm Grace. Who are you?"

Jacelyn leaned over the table. "Don't pay any attention to her. She says that to everyone." Jacelyn rolled her eyes and made circular motions with her fingers. Grace stared at her sister in shame and disbelief.

"Every time we turn our back, she is met with humiliation and contempt," Maire seethed. "No one should have to endure that. Her family portrays her as demented and you and I are portrayed as misfits for befriending her."

I moved to Grace's side. "I'm Elle, Grace's grand-daughter. Grace is a resident here. What's your name?" The woman smiled and extended her hand.

Grace also smiled, determined to overcome Jacelyn's snub. "Here is my daughter. She works at Macy's and makes chocolate."

Maire slid in next to Jacelyn, crowding her back with her shoulder. "Busted!" she whispered.

The women chatted with Grace about family and grandchildren and Sunday brunch at Chez Clair. One said she would save her a place for coffee at her table after every TV Mass.

We left them and rolled Grace's chair away. Jacelyn scurried to catch up with us. "I'll join you later for brunch, Grace."

Maire turned and leveled her eyes. "What game are you playing?" Jacelyn gaped wide-eyed, caught in Maire's fury. "I've got your number, Jacey. I'm watching you."

Then as easily as changing her jewelry, Maire changed her mood. She waved her hand at the span of wheel chairs parading ahead of us. "These residents can't teach, work, golf, bowl, swim, dance, run, drive, knit or a hundred other things they did yesterday. They are on an uncharted course." She nodded down at Grace. "Nothing Ma did in her lifetime prepared her for this. She is at the mercy of egos. Staff and family alike want her to sit in the corner, remember the past and stay out of the way. In my opinion, remembering the past is overrated. Ninety percent of the thoughts we think are the same thoughts we thought yesterday and look where that gets us. No! Let's look at this differently than we ever have before. She's lost her home? We are her home. She's lost the use of her legs? We are her legs! She's lost her water therapy and exercise? We are her exercise. We are her therapy. She can't get the nourishment she needs to be healthy? We'll bring her food. They mock her beauty, rummage through her jewelry and taunt her? Well, I know what Uncle Sean would say. This is going to change. Things are going to be different!" Maire looked at Grace defiantly. "Enough is enough, Ma. Things will be different!"

Within a week Maire walked through Blackwater with her daughter, Celia and her two young grandsons. Behind them followed a frizzy-haired clown. His brightly colored suit billowed and his mouth grinned into a wide smile. He sat next to Grace and blew long, angular balloons, deftly forming a heart and a bear. Grace beamed. He honked his bicycle horn and turned to go. She stopped him. "Please, will you entertain the others? They need to see you." Residents crowded into the room, circling, as Grace turned to her great grandsons. "You are a blessing. I love you so much." The little boys beamed.

Maire brought a surprise nearly every day. She presented Grace with a bright pink To Do List. The jaunty letters bounced across the plaque reminding all who read it to sing, smile at strangers, keep learning, notice kindness, eat ice cream, hope, count blessings, laugh, love and love some more. She presented Grace with a vibrant green and white jacket and pants and a matching ribboned hat. They strolled the grounds for hours. Residents passing them in the courtyard outside of Café Sofie called out, "Love your hat, Grace!"

Grace spotted seven mallard ducks stepping gingerly across the patches of snow on the lawn. "Oh!" Grace exclaimed. They've survived the winter!"

"Yes," Maire nodded. "And so have we!"

Maire stood guard, challenging anyone to stop her as Grace peddled the recumbent cycle in the empty therapy room. She wheeled Grace to a weekly sing-along where Grace warbled familiar songs and tried some new ones. Before Grace had only heard the sound of Jack's voice. Now Grace heard her own. During a stroll through the myriad of hallways and courtyards, they came upon a dining area for one of the assisted living wings. The fireplace crackled. Residents waved them in. There was a tall mesh net filled to overflowing with bright colored balls. "Oh, Ma," Maire called. "Let's play ball!"

Grace reached into a bowl of fruit on a side table and plopped a banana into her bag. "They're always out of bananas in Lonan Wing," she scoffed. Then she turned with her hands outstretched, a broad grin on her face. Maire plucked a bright blue ball from the net and held it high over her head. She swung it low and pitched a lob into Grace's lap. Grace grasped the ball, took a wide swing of her own and hurled it back.

"Yea Ma!" Maire cheered. "The exercise is paying off!"

Grace spotted me coming around the corner and bounced the ball a second time between my legs. I scrambled after it. Grace bounced and laughed and frolicked for over an hour. Soon the dining room filled with residents. It was time to dress for dinner and escape to Chez Clair.

At the end of the day we knelt with Grace in prayer. Maire held her mother's gentle hands. "Behold, I give you power to tread on serpents and scorpions and to overcome all the power of the enemy. Nothing will harm you."

Grace looked deep into her daughter's eyes and nodded. "Thank you, Maire. I'm depending on that."

Macy's buzzed with talk of a fashion show. Maire's friend, Jane, planned the event. "We'll stage our show at Blackwater Manor. It's an elegant place. The residents are the most prestigious in the city. I'll develop a unique 'older women' wardrobe." She smiled. "Your mother is there."

"Yes," Maire agreed. "She would so enjoy being able to attend."

"Attend? No!" Jane ran her fingers through the shawls and scarves near the hat section. "She will be on the runway!"

"She's wheelchair bound," Maire reminded her.

"Exactly! We'll show wheelchair fashion!" She clasped Maire's hands and laughed out loud. "No one else has done it! We'll be sold out!"

Maire took the day off from Macy's. She spent the morning with Grace, giggling behind closed doors, curling hair and polishing nails. Just before lunch Grace looked at the clock. "Where's Elle?" Maire froze. She forgot to make the call. My phone beeped.

"I can't get there in time," I answered. "I'll never make it."

"I'm sorry, Elle. What am I going to tell Ma?"

"Put her on the phone. I'll tell her."

"Sweetheart, where are you?" Grace's voice was filled with joy and anticipation.

"I'm so sorry, Gram. I'm away and can't get there, but I want to hear all about it this weekend."

"Oh, are you sure you can't make it?" Disappointment crept into her voice.

"I'm going to imagine you wheeling down the runway, waving just to me, Gram."

"Really?"

"Take lots of pictures. I want to fill a book with your runway debut."

She giggled. "Do you think I can do it?"

"Of course, Gram. You're a super chick!"

"Oh, you!"

"We're going to be late, Ma." Maire stood by the doorway.

"Whatever," Grace retorted.

Maire laughed in feigned shock. "Ma, where did you learn to talk like that?"

"From you girls," she said matter-of-factly. "Just because my knees don't function, don't think my ears don't." Maire laughed so hard she fell back against the door. Grace giggled, too. The dimples in her cheeks danced.

Maire and Grace wheeled down the hallway, past Millie, waiting in her doorway. "Millie," Maire called, "you and Mom are always the last to be helped. Do you want me to push you?"

"No, thank you," she replied quickly, glancing furtively the length of the hallway.

"Don't you want to go to the fashion show?"

"I would like to go to the show, but they won't take me."

"Well, just insist on it," Maire responded.

"Oh, no." Millie shook her head. "If I insist, they'll get even."

"Come with us," Grace offered. "Just don't say anything. No one will even notice."

"Well, if you think so." Millie held out her hand and took hold of the armrest on Grace's chair. Maire steered the two chairs as they rolled in tandem down the hallway toward the chapel. The chapel was adorned with sprays of spring flowers and colorful banners. Maire parked Mille at the center aisle and steered Grace away. "Where are you going?" Millie called.

"You'll see," Grace called back.

Lights dimmed in the crowded chapel. Models strolled to a bouncy beat. The audience applauded each new suit, dress, scarf and string of beads. Finally, the curtains parted and Maire and Grace rolled onto the stage. Grace wore a stunning velvet hat with a satin ribbon and a lacy silk shawl. Maire wrapped and draped the shawl to show how many ways it could be worn. Then Jane said, "I'll bet most of you here know this model."

Millie called out from the back, "Grace!" Others in the crowd called her name. "Grace! Grace!" Maire wheeled Grace forward, down the center aisle and around the side aisles. Women held out their hands to touch her. She reached for them and waved.

Maire leaned close to her mother's ear. "Ma! You're a rock star!"

"Oh, you!" Grace patted her hand and beamed.

Mother's Day was approaching. The Riorden guild sprang frantically into last minute action. Lyssa phoned to reserve the dining room at Chez Clair but she was too late. Urgent wheedling got her a small meeting room. Crystal Ann emailed last minute invitations.

The email machine in Grace's room spit out an invitation. "Will you girls be there?" Grace turned expectantly to each of us.

"Yes, Gram. We'll be there," I answered.

"Really?" Maire asked. "I don't think they're going to want you there."

"That's too bad. They've got me," I replied firmly.

Grace chuckled. "You girls!"

"Gram, you deserve one excellent day."

"Oh, Sweetheart," she answered, "every day with you and Maire is an excellent day. I love you both so much."

I arrived at Maire's door at 6:00 a.m. "Why so early?" She handed me a coffee to go.

"I intend to get there before they even think of rolling out that lift machine. Nothing is going to ruin this day for her."

We walked through the quiet halls of Lonan Wing. Grace was awake, waiting. Maire browsed through her closet, selecting the soft white sweater and the gray woolen skirt. Grace put her arms around my neck and we swiveled easily and painlessly to her wheelchair. Maire dressed her and applied blusher and a spritz of Estee Lauder Beautiful. Grace reached for a white hat with the polka dot ribbons and a flirty feather. As we rolled out of her room, Novalee, Triston and Cassie averted their eyes.

"Why aren't they speaking to us?" Grace asked.

"It's just as well they aren't," Maire whispered. We want this day to be one of..."

"Pleasure," interrupted Grace.

We rolled into Lonan Wing dining room for breakfast. "I'm Doris," a woman said softly. "You may not remember me. My husband was your obstetrician."

"Oh," Grace exclaimed. "What a wonderful doctor."

"Where are your children?" She looked around. "It's Mother's Day."

"They will be here," Grace announced proudly. "My family will be here today."

After breakfast and TV Mass, we strolled the hallways. Residents stopped to visit. "What are you doing for Mother's Day, Grace? Will there be a party?"

"Oh, yes," responded Grace. "My family will be here. It will be a wonderful day!"

When we reached the meeting room, it was dark and empty. Maire flipped on the light. "There is no one here," Grace said, not hiding her disappointment.

Maire went to work immediately. "Let's get a head start. Elle and I brought decorations." She winked at Grace. "Just in case." We strung bright ribbons and tied balloons. Maire placed centerpieces on the tables and pinned a corsage on Grace's sweater. Grace beamed. An hour passed. Grace watched the parking lot closely. Through the wide windows she saw families with mothers in wheel chairs, mothers pushing walkers and mothers walking arm in arm with children who cared.

Maire hovered close to Grace. "Are you hungry? You must be. You didn't have lunch. We should have eaten by now."

"No," Grace replied firmly. No. Llyssa said not to eat. There will be Kentucky Fried Chicken."

Maire's eyes blazed. "Let's open a present or two," she said cheerily.

Grace smiled wistfully. "We can do that." Maire placed several bright packages in front of Grace. Together they unwrapped and examined each one carefully. Nearly two hours had passed. Still no family.

I walked to Café Sofe and returned with a white meat sandwich, a banana and a cup of coffee. "Take a bite, if you like, Gram. You must be hungry."

Suddenly there was a bustle of activity in the hallway. Dierdre and her family jostled through the door, unloading buckets of Kentucky Fried Chicken, mashed potatoes, gravy and biscuits onto the table. Llyssa brushed past them to kiss Grace's cheek. "Sorry we're late, Mom. We were all at Bric's and lost track of time." Bric sauntered through the doorway with his two sons and daughter close behind. Acer and Delilah arrived.

Acer held out his hand to Bric, giving it a hearty shake and turning to Bric's sons. "Well, if it isn't the Riorden boys!" He slapped them each on the back.

The waiter from the kitchen appeared carrying pots of coffee and pitchers of juice. "We called ahead to tell them we'd be late," Doreen announced.

Maire's eyes flamed. "Mom waited here for two hours without a word from you or them."

Llyssa stood over Grace. "What are you doing, Mom? I told you not to eat! I told you we'd bring Kentucky Fried Chicken." She took the sandwich out of Grace's hand and threw it in the trash. The small room soon filled with piercing laughter and raucous chatter as three generations of Riordens shared stories and filled plates. Grace sat alone as they towered above her and crowded around her. Maire set a plate of hot food in front of her. She pulled up a chair, but Llyssa slid into it, clutching Grace's arm with a firm grip. She motioned for one of her daughters to sit on Grace's other side, while she regaled the children's latest triumphs and accomplishments. Grace lifted a chicken leg, then put it back on her plate and listened patiently. Another hour passed. Grace had not yet touched her food, now cold. Teens and tweens and twenty-somethings shifted and moved about the perimeter. Grace's sister, Jacey, joined the group. She chatted with everyone but Grace.

Liam arrived and embraced Grace warmly. "Happy Mother's Day, Mom."

Grace brightened and laughed. "Today really is Mother's Day."

"Every day is Mother's Day, Mom."

"Bless you, Sweetheart." She patted his hand. "I love you so much."

Maire stood at my shoulder. "Not one of them brought a gift."

Liam looked back at me. "I know you and Elle are the movie makers. Do you have something for us today?"

"How did you know?" I asked, surprised. Grace smiled in anticipation.

"Attention, everyone." Liam clinked a glass. "Mom has a movie she would like us to enjoy." Doreen, Cheyla, Kristin and Delilah huddled and whispered. Crystal Ann moved to a back corner table next to her husband. Dierdre clenched her teeth, squared her shoulders, crossed her arms defiantly and glared. Llyssa moved a chair to the doorway. She sat there, rigid, glaring back at the roomful of faces as they watched the screen. Grace studied her daughter and then looked sadly up at Liam. Liam slid in next to Grace as the rhythm of the music carried her story from days with the red bird at Scanlon Circle to days with Maire at Blackwater Manor. A song, The Voice, swelled in the room to a photo of Grace pointing her finger at them from the screen. I scanned the faces in the room. Lyssa glared. Dierdre seethed. Acer looked on, impervious. Then I saw Bric. Tears streamed down his face. Llyssa followed my eyes and abruptly cleared her throat. Bric looked up. She jerked her eyes toward me. He brushed his face with the back of his hand. Doreen pushed her chair back, stood and strode from the room. The Riorden teens took that as their cue to escape. The movie ended and Liam stood to applaud.

Then, as quickly and noisily as it filled, the room emptied. The noisy clamor of voices receded down the corridor as Maire and I cleared the tables. Grace sat silent. "Where did everyone go?" She shook her head and searched the parking lot through the window.

"I guess that's it," Maire stated flatly. We stared at each other in disbelief.

We left the room and strolled with Grace through the corridors, past the village windows, past the library and through side gardens, trying to bring some joy back to the one day that was set aside to honor her. Grace certainly deserved that. When we rounded the corner to Lonan Wing, the security doors swung open to familiar high pitched giddy laughter.

"What's going on here?" Maire gasped. Bric and Doreen blocked our way. Furniture stood in the hallway behind them. Maire pushed past. She stood gaping at Lyssa, determinedly rearranging Grace's room. Dierdra drug a dresser past us toward the exit. Crystal Ann clasped Grace's photo books and the green address book tightly to her side.

"What are you doing?" Grace demanded.

"You'll have more room this way," Crystal Ann replied, tucking the photo album and the address book into her bag.

"Stop it!" Grace cried out. "Put that red bedspread back."

Maire followed Crystal Ann as she hurried out through the exit. "Where do you think you're going? Crystal Ann! You made your mother cry on Mother's Day!"

"She had a perfectly nice day," Crystal Ann sniffed.

"Crystal Ann, stop being you for a minute and try being her," Maire countered. "She's banished from her home and deprived of her mobility. You refuse to bring her power chair. Instead she's got a wheel chair she can't push or maneuver. Therapy is denied her. She's at the mercy of caregivers that don't respond. Now her children take her things while she looks on."

Bric and Doreen pushed through the doors. Lyssa followed. Maire turned on them. "Why would you make your mother cry on Mother's Day?" They walked away from her. She followed, determined that they hear. "Don't you understand? Whatever your issues are, Mom doesn't give a damn about the past. She's clinging to the present and struggling with every breath she takes toward the future because she needs to believe that she has one." They continued walking, intent on escaping her words. She stood aghast. "Stop your gaming! She gave you the one thing you needed most in life; that's love. You get back in there and act like the children she deserves!" Car doors flew open and tires spun on the gravel. Maire watched them drive from the parking lot.

I found her there, staring down the empty street. "Not too long ago, they doted on her," she reflected. "Now they scorn her."

"It's eerie, isn't it?"

"It's plain damn evil. There's right and there's wrong, but this will stay wrong no matter what they say to cover it up. Why did this family turn on her? She didn't change. Why did they?" Her eyes were drawn to what I was holding. "What have you got there?"

"It's an envelope of Gram's favorite recipes, in her own handwriting. Lyssa must have lifted them from Gram's kitchen but in her hurry to get out of here, she left them behind. Wait until she gets home and realizes that."

"Busted!" Maire sneered.

A week passed. I arrived at Lonan Wing at noon on Saturday to find Grace sitting at the dining room table staring out the window. Amelia passed by.

"Amelia, has Grace eaten?"

Amelia shrugged. "She refused."

I kissed Grace's cheek. Doris was slumped in her chair, her hand covered in syrup. Her face was raw and red. She drooled from the side of her mouth. Her glasses were missing. Her eyes stared vacantly. "God!" I shuddered. "She looked wonderful on Mother's Day."

We sat in a sunny window outside Café Sofie. The squirrels and rabbits frolicked across the yard outside. Grace finished off a full plate of roast and vegetables, then chocolate cake and ice cream. I pulled a book from my bag. "Gram, I have something for you that I couldn't give to you at the party."

"There was too much commotion," she agreed. I handed her the book. "The Secret Garden," she read. Her eyes sparkled in anticipation. "Will you read it to me?"

"Yes, let's read a little bit every day. It'll be our secret. OK?" She smiled. Gram loved a good secret.

Maire joined us then and we strolled past the empty beauty salon, past the library, closed the night, past the chapel, standing open and quiet, past the elevators to the assisted living wings and finally returning through the glass doors to Lonan Wing and

Grace's room. Maire slipped her arms through the sleeves of Grace's pajama top and buttoned up the soft lacy front. "Ma, why is your skin peeling? The skin on your hands is blistering and tearing away."

Grace tucked her hand up inside the sleeve of her sweater. "Just get me some lotion. Stop fussing." Outside Grace's door there was a buzz of voices.

"We just love your mother," a woman said, peering through the doorway. We adopted her. We have to look out for each other here, because no one else will."

"I'd like to shut this place down," one of the them added angrily. "My sister has doctors and nurses to take care of the cancer. All she wanted was a blanket, but no one came. She tried to reach it herself and fell out of the bed. She got caught on the call light cord. When I found her she was strangling and crying for help." She glared the length of the empty hallway. "The light is on right now and still no one comes!" Mahlon, a resident from across the hall, wandered into the hallway, pants unzipped, falling from his hips. Jasmine, parked sideways in the corridor, slid precariously forward out of her seat, one shoe and sock on, one shoe and sock off. Sheridan, another resident, wandered aimlessly. Isabel wheeled from her room, crying. Aubery pushed the med cart through the double doors at the end of the hall.

"What's wrong, Isabel?"

"My son was here. Where did he go?"

"He went home," Aubery tossed back over her shoulder. Isabel dropped her face into her hands, crestfallen.

A man and two young children hurried through the doors. "Don't cry," he hurried to calm his mother.

"I told Aubery we'd be right back." He wrapped his arms around her.

I stared at Aubery. "I'm sorry, Gram," I whispered. "I'm sorry I can't take you away from this."

She looked up wearily. "Tomorrow's another day, Sweetheart." I reached for a small hand-crafted book of her favorite prayers as Amelia came through the door.

"I forgot to give her meds. There was a problem with Doris. I was called into Loree's office. They've been interrogating me all this time. Meanwhile, no one covered for me. There are lights flashing up and down the wing! Thank goodness she's not asleep yet." Amelia put down the Dixie Cup and grabbed the prayer book from Grace's hand.

"What are you doing?" Maire crossed to them as Grace tugged back on the book.

"We don't let her have her prayers. She might get a paper cut." Amelia answered, holding firm to the pages.

"A paper cut?" Maire exploded. "Her skin is shredding and no one cares! A paper cut?" Amelia dropped the book and exited as abruptly as she entered. Maire chased after her.

Grace nestled into the pillows and patted my hand. "Read to me. We'll say prayers later."

"This is the story of an orphaned girl," I began, "who found a secret key that unlocked a secret garden of hope and life. The manor she came to live in was old, like a castle. Most of the rooms were shut and locked up."

Maire returned and settled into the blue chair, her hand on Grace's. Grace closed her eyes. "Go on," she urged.

I continued. "You'll have your own space, the girl was told. Outside you may go wherever you please, but inside you must be quiet and stay out of the way."

"Sounds like Blackwater Manor," Grace mused.

"The garden gate was locked. No one had seen it in years."

"How could anyone shut up a garden?" Grace wondered, drowsily. "You should always be able to walk in a garden."

"It was a strange place," I agreed. "As they walked through the long hallways, the little girl searched for the door to the garden."

I read, as Maire closed her eyes and Grace drifted into sleep. Then I sat watching the two women I loved. "Please, God," I prayed. "Let this moment last." I realized then that any moment in which we find peace, silence, clarity of thought and love for others is a moment of creation and connectedness. That must truly be the gift of the Holy Spirit.

Aubery entered abruptly, her flashlight swinging by her side. "I was thinking right about now I should be wondering where Grace was."

"Keep your voice down." I stood, forcing her back to the doorway.

"There's no need to be hostile," she snapped.

"Don't you think it's a little late for you to be looking for her?"

Beads of sweat broke out on her forehead. She laughed nervously and her face reddened. Then she grew defiant. "Did you put her to bed?"

"Grace has been sleeping for nearly an hour."

"That's not your job," she sputtered.

Maire woke and pushed past me, planting her Mary Janes toe to toe with Aubery's Dockers. "Look, Aubery, the call light has been on for an hour. Do you really imagine that you are now going to engage in a confrontation over who helped this woman to bed? Not going to happen." Aubery backed away begrudgingly. Her flashlight sprayed long strips of amber light as she disappeared around the corner.

"Let's go," Maire sighed, exasperated, with a lingering glance back at her mother, sleeping soundly. "Texas Roadhouse is waiting. I need a strong cup of coffee."

We settled into a comfortable booth. Maire stirred her coffee, pondering a thought. "We may never know what happened to Mom that night with Acer. Acer said he was replacing carpet on the farm. You saw puncture marks on her arm. Were they carpet tacks? Did something fall on her, knocking her out of the chair? Rory said something exploded at the house. Did the ceiling fall in on her? The waiters at Royal Court were waiting for someone, certainly not me. But when I showed up, Acer had to abort his scheme. I think he threatened Mom. She was frightened. That much I know. I thought maybe the one good thing about her being at Blackwater would be that she might be safe from her family. But now I see she is trapped in a more terrifying kind of danger."

"How does Lonan Wing staff get away with this behavior? This place is rated the best of the best in the city? This place should be closed down."

"They think they have Acer's blessing. They don't know Jack!" she sneered. "Acer wears the mask of Grace, but that mask hides the eyes of Satan and the grin of a Leprechaun. Acer will use these people until he's done with them and then kick them to the curb like everyone else. We are all expendable."

I guess that's why Liam said, 'We won't point fingers.'"

"The Riordens live by fear. But you do not. You're a warrior. If I had just met you, I'd keep walking."

"Thanks a lot! As I recall, Maire, that's exactly what you did. When I asked you for help, you blew me off."

Maire nodded thoughtfully. "We Riordens behave as we want others to see us. You are not like that. You are impenetrable. What others think of you is not your concern."

"Am I fearless?"

"I watch you with Grace. You are her barefoot champion. Mark my words. There is a war. It's a deadly game between fear and faith. For you and me, losing is not an option. We promised Grace. She trusts us. Although, I don't know where we'll find the strength to see it through. I'm exhausted."

"I know," I said. "There are days when I don't recognize myself! If I'd just met me, I'd keep walking too. Whoever I have become, though, I know there is no turning back. We are on a road of no return. I don't know why just yet, but, no matter how desperate it becomes, I know we have to let Acer's game play out."

The conversation with Maire streamed in a con-
tinuous loop through my head as the bus rocked
in steady rhythm. I looked around the cabin. The
young Hispanic mother nuzzled her infant. Jerry
stared out at the landscape beyond his window. Yoki
and Ancient Eyes chatted. The tattooed iron worker
bounced her head in rhythm to the beat on her head-
phones. The researcher scribbled in the margins of his
notebook. Sonja scrolled through her email. Suddenly
a thought flashed through my brain. I bolted upright
in my seat. I knew the answer to the third riddle!
What rights nothing that is wrong? I couldn't believe it.
It was so simple.

"Isn't this nice?" Grace's voice chirped joyfully in
my ear.

"Yea, Gram," I answered. "We're all finding a
way to get unstuck!"

I wish we could have worked it out
I wish i didn't have these doubts
I wish i didn't have to wonder just what you are doing now
I wish i didn't know inside
That it won't work out for you and i
I wish that i could stop this wishing and just say my
last goodbye

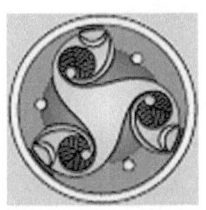

A Bump In The Road

It's been one of those days for a lot of days now
I need a day when the world can take care of itself
This isn't what I wanted how I thought my life would turn out
And I wonder if it's like this from here on out
Sometimes life gets you, but we go on
Sometimes life gets you, we're still going on

"It's just you and me, now, Grace." Stormy grinned mischievously as she grabbed Grace's hand, twisting the gold and diamond rings from her fingers.

"No," Grace protested. "No, please." Stormy bounced across the room to Grace's hat rack, plucking the turquoise straw hat and plopping it on top of her own streaked strands of hair, dancing around Grace as she sat captive. "Those rings are all I have left of Jack." Grace reached precariously from the edge of her seat."

Delores stood dark and threatening in the doorway. She snatched the rings from Stormy and retrieved the hat. "It's all right, now, Grace. We'll go to break-fast." She turned on Stormy. "You have fifteen minutes to get out of this building. I've seen enough of your tricks. You're done." Grace reached again for the rings. "These rings have attracted quite enough attention for one day, Grace. I'll just keep them safe for you."

"No! They're mine!" Grace insisted. "I want them now."

"You're upset, Grace." Delores pushed her out into the hallway. "Let's have breakfast and your morning pills and we'll talk about it."

Later that afternoon I dialed Blackwater Manor. Amelia answered in a falsetto voice. I shuddered to think what that meant. "Grace is here by the nurses' station, holding a baby."

"Holding a baby?"

"Yes."

"Someone is there with a baby?"

"No," she laughed, her voice shrill and tinny. "It's the doll, Annabelle." She handed the phone to Grace. "Here, Grace. Your granddaughter's on the line."

"Gram? It's Elle."

"Oh, Sweetheart." Her voice was distant.

"What are you doing?"

"Someone gave me her baby."

"Is it a real baby or is it a doll?"

"No, the girl said it is a baby. Its eyes are moving and its mouth is a little open, but its hands are cold. It needs another blanket."

"Gram, is it a doll or a baby?"

"I did ask the nurse that, because at first I thought she was tricking me. She said I should know a baby when I held it."

"Who brought it to you?"

"One of the girls said it was all alone. It needed me." Her voice drifted away. "There, there. Smile, you can do it." Then she came back to me. "Her eyes are wide open. She's looking right at me. Her mouth is moving. I think it is real."

"Gram, how was your day?" I backed the car into the street.

"Not so good."

"What happened?"

"Three big crows clawed at me." Her voice drifted off again. "I'm all right now."

My senses signaled red alert. 'The lift machine,' I thought.

"They accused me of being pretty tough. They just want things easier for themselves. I told them they should keep things quieter." Her voice trailed off.

"Gram?"

"A lot of prayers are needed. Some people were very, very bad. I need protection. So I'm praying. If it gets much worse, you'll hear me above everything else."

"I'm on the way, Gram."

"It's very close."

"Amelia said you were by the nurses' station. Where are you?"

"I'm in the room that locks and unlocks."

"You're locked in a room?"

"It's the room they lock us in with the dog."

"The dog? Who is that screaming? It sounds like Sybil. I'll get the nurse and get you out of there."

"That's good. I'm very hungry." Then she called out, "Maam? Can you hear me?" No one answered. She called louder. There was no response. Then came the inevitable "Yoo-hoo!" Waves of anger crashed against my soul. I knew that Amelia was nearby. Grace's voice suddenly switched tone from distant to urgent. "When can you get here?"

"I'm on the way. It'll take about an hour."

"Not until then?"

"Gram? Should I phone Maire?"

"I'll watch for you."

I dialed Maire. "She's in danger, Maire. I'm sure of it."

Her voice crackled in and out. "I'm trying to get across town in this traffic," she yelled into the phone. "I've got Celia's children. She's on her way to the airport. I'll check in on Mom as soon as I can."

Maire pushed through the Lonan Wing doors, setting off the alarm. She strode past the empty nurses' station, down the vacant hallway to the double doors of the TV Room. There was her mother, locked behind the glass doors, crushed wheel chair to wheel chair against residents in chairs. Poppy's terrier scratched and jumped at the legs and feet that dangled helpless to kick it away. Maire rattled the latch and flung the doors open. "Get my mother out of there, now!" An aide suddenly appeared and quickly wheeled residents one by one into the dining room. Sybil, naked except for a diaper drooping around her legs, clung to Grace's arm. Maire grabbed Grace's chair and spun her away into the corridor. Aubery rushed to stop her.

"You can't go to her room just yet."

"Why not?"

"The janitor is cleaning it."

"Now?"

"There was an incident."

Livid, Maire reached for her phone and dialed. My phone beeped. "There's lipstick smeared all over her carpet. They are telling me she did it! They say she must have had some kind of fit! She can't get out of her chair! How is she going to get down on the carpet and smear lipstick? I can't leave her here alone anymore. They wait until we are gone to make their move. I'll have to change my work schedule. And get this! Her rings are gone! And she won't let go of the damn doll! None of this makes sense." Then she whispered, "I think she's been drugged."

"OK," I answered, trying to make sense of it. "Take a breath. Put Gram on."

"Oh, Sweetheart," Grace cried.

"I'll be there soon, Gram. What can I do to help?"

"I'm hungry."

"Maire's right there. She'll get something to eat. OK?"

Maire interrupted. "Something crazy happened here. I've got to check on the grandkids, but I'm going to come back so I can be sure nothing else happens tonight. There has been a 360 degree turn between yesterday and today. Yesterday we walked through the dining room and Mom pointed to a frail woman sitting alone in a chair and asked me why she was holding a doll. She said it looked ridiculous. Now she is that woman. She may be lonely and they may be playing on that. She appears to be drugged. They may be manipulating her into submission. I don't think she's getting to eat. Whenever Raven, Aubery and Amelia are on duty something vicious happens. Raven was on this morning. Delores was on this afternoon. Amelia was on tonight. Aubery is on now."

I listened as I sped across the Interstate. With each dark mile, I sank deeper into sadness. Finally, overwhelmed, I pulled the car off the road to the shoulder and stepped out onto the asphalt. The air was crisp and bit at my nostrils as I reached my arms to the empty darkness. But the prairie is not kind to those easily overcome or defeated. My cry was swept away by a sudden gust of wind.

My cell phone beeped. This time it was Zia. She had tried to call from Grace's phone, but it wouldn't work. So she called me from her own cell phone. "I care for your mother," she whispered in broken English. I want her to be at peace."

A convoy of eighteen-wheelers shook the road as I stared into the distant haze of ambient city lights while together Grace and I recited the Angel of God, the Lord's Prayer, the Hail Mary and the prayer of Jabez. "Thou would keep me from evil, that it may not grieve me," she whispered. I sang to her, then all was quiet.

"She's sleeping," Zia's voice whispered through the darkness. I wondered in amazement at those words. Where did Grace go to find her peace? It must be a secret place that only she and God knew. The staff intimidated and overpowered her. Was the doll a hateful distraction to further confuse her and to cover something more terrible? Bric promised the lift machine would not be used but he was a Riorden and that was a lie. When staff didn't use the machine, they pulled her by the armpits and dragged her across the floor. They put their faces in her face and taunted her. They deprived her of personal care and food just as cruelly as her own children deprived her of her own home. She had learned in her marriage that survival was made possible by submission. That was the behavior her children depended on. Sol Bump hid behind Bric, Quin and Acer. Bric, Quin and Acer hid behind the law. The law hid in the shadows of a society that accepts exile as punishment for aging. This was the wilderness to which she was abandoned. What could I do but walk it with her?

The next morning I dialed Bric. "I am aware," he said. "I've already spoken with Crystal Ann. I asked her to look into having those rings resized."

"Resized?"

"Well, if they're slipping off..."

"Slipping off?"

"But Crystal Ann's out of town," he continued. "Would you be willing to take the rings to the jeweler?"

This was an odd comment, I thought, coming from a guy who had been overtly adversarial. What was he up to?

"I'll need authorization. We don't want someone to think I've stolen them."

"I'll leave a note with the rings." He laughed. Why did he laugh? I hung up and dialed Blackwater.

"Lonan Wing," a voice answered. "How may I help you?"

"Who is this?"

"Who is this?"

"This is Elle Riorden. May I speak with Grace?" There was a long pause. I heard footsteps on tile. I heard a door open and close.

"There's no Grace here."

"Who is this? Do you know where Grace may be?"

"No. Not here."

"Is there an activity? Is she in the bath or the beauty salon?"

"No. Not today."

"Who is this? I need you to find my grandmother so I might speak with her."

"There's no Grace here. You'll have to call back."

"Listen. She's one of your residents. She's in a wheelchair that she cannot move herself. The only way she can be gone is if someone took her away. Do you have a record of that?"

"I don't know where to look."

"It's on the counter at the nurses' station. It's a large notebook. Who is this?" There were more footsteps and shuffling papers.

"There's nothing here in the book. You'll have to call back."

I dailed Maire. She burst out laughing. "When they say there's no Grace at Blackwater, that's as close to the truth as it gets."

I chuckled, but then dread took over. "How could they lose her? She can't go anywhere without their assistance. She can't even reach the phone if it rings, or the call light if it's out of reach. Do you think they have her locked away again?"

"I'll get there soon," she answered, breathless, still chuckling.

The Blackwater Manor tour van idled at the Lonan Wing ambulance entrance. Jacelyn and Crystal Ann stood by. The driver pushed Grace's wheelchair over the threshold and onto the lift. Other residents filed past, filling the seats. "Where are we going?" Grace asked in anticipation.

"We're going on our monthly tour of homes," Jacelyn chirped. "Today we're going to yours."

Grace's heart raced as the van pulled off the highway, onto a cul-de-sac. The monument on the corner read Scanlon Circle. There was her home. The van pulled into the drive. Jacelyn stood in the aisle and clapped her hands. "Everybody, this is where Grace lived with her wonderful husband, Jack. Grace's beautiful home is now cared for by her children."

"What?" Grace shook her head, puzzled. Jacelyn quickly descended from the bus to the front walk. Grace thought she saw the curtains flutter. The door opened. Acer walked out. He spoke as Jacelyn threw back her head and squealed with shrill laughter. Grace touched her hand to the window. Acer disappeared back inside the house. Jacelyn bounced back to the bus and reclaimed her seat, beaming.

"All right," the driver called over his shoulder as he drove away, "our next stop will be the falls." Grace stared at Jacelyn, chattering at the front of the bus. Acer didn't even come to the van. Crystal Ann sat stiff and motionless in the back like a guard. The rest of the ride was a blur.

When the van finally turned into Lonan Wing ambulance entrance and residents exited, Crystal Ann was the last to get off. Grace caught her sleeve. "Crystal Ann, I want to go home." Crystal Ann pulled away and walked across the parking lot to her car. Grace watched her go, overcome by a feeling of terrible darkness.

Maire grabbed her coat, cashed out her register and sped through town. She found Grace bound to her chair in the middle of her room. The curtains were closed. I Love Lucy blared from the TV. Maire rushed to her mother's side and ripped at the Velcro. It wouldn't budge. "Devils!" Maire muttered as she grabbed a scissors from Grace's bureau. She snipped and rolled the strip into a tight ball, tucking it into her bag. Then she flung open the curtains.

"Oh, Maire!" Grace cried. "I knew you would come. I wanted to watch for you, but I couldn't move."

"Ma," she said, kissing her mother, "who left the TV blaring?"

"They turn it up so no one hears me calling." She looked into her daughter's eyes. "I like I Love Lucy, but not all the time and not so loud!" Maire handed Grace her lipstick and a mirror. "Besides, if I'm going to be shut in here with a movie blaring, I'd rather watch The Flying Nun."

"Really?" Maire spritzed Estee Lauder Beautiful on Grace's wrists. "Why?"

"Because the little nun is always happy. When something really bothers her, she just flies away!"

Grace's eyes and her dainty mouth curved into a sad smile. "That's what I want to do."

Maire picked up the DVD. "Ma, I've never seen this here. Where did you get this movie?"

"The little nun brought it."

"A nun? Are you sure? What nun?"

"The little nun."

"Did you know her?"

"Of course. I've known her since you were born."

Maire looked closely at her mother. "Did something happen today to make you want to fly away? What am I saying? Everyday must be like that."

Grace's eyes blazed hot with the pain she tried to convey. "Maire, I know where they are."

"Who, Ma?"

"The children. I know where they are. They're at the house. I saw Acer at the house."

"You were there?" Maire didn't understand. Then she did. "The van ride. They took you past your own house?"

"Jacelyn showed them the way."

"Jacelyn paraded them by your home?" Maire's heart fell like a stone. She wrapped her arms around her mother. "Oh, Ma!"

"The others were there behind the curtain. They didn't know I was there. Call them, Maire. Tell them where I am. Surely if they know..."

"Ma, they're not coming."

"What? Why?"

"Ma, it breaks my heart to say this, and I can only imagine what it will do to yours, but they don't care."

Grace gazed into Maire's eyes, then she sighed and said simply, "I thought they were smarter than that."

My phone beeped. "They can all rot in Hell!" Maire blurted.

"How is Gram doing?"

"She's OK now, but get this. She's wearing her rings! I took her to the salon, but we just got settled there when Amelia came to find me. Guess what she asked me? She wanted to know if I was here last night."

"Odd. So you said yes?"

"Amelia said that Mom had gone missing and so had the rings so she thought she would straighten out the details so there wouldn't be a problem with me."

"What on earth does that mean?"

"I don't know. I told her to ask the nurse on duty. She said that was Delores, but Delores is no longer working there. I don't know why. I think she wanted to distract me, because when I turned back, Cassie was walking away. Mom's mouth was full of something. She gagged and upchucked it all. Oh boy! There was pudding and pills all over the floor, all over Mom, everywhere. I grabbed Miss Thing in the hallway and said, "You realize, I'm sure, because we've discussed this before, that pudding makes Mom gag. She cannot swallow all those pills at once. Still you force them down her throat."

"What was Cassie's reaction?"

"She glared at me, threw down the towel and walked off, leaving the mess! I followed her and said, 'What about her pills?' She just tossed her head and said that she left them with the beautician. She said, 'If she doesn't finish them, I'll write that she refused.'"

"Yikes. These people are getting more contemptuous every day."

"Meanwhile the beautician shut off the hairdryer so she could finish the pills. Now we are really late for lunch."

"Wait a minute. Are you telling me all this was taking place while she was under the dryer?"

"Yea! At that point I just told myself, 'Lighten up. Just cruise with it. If she has to go through it, I sure as hell can. I'm just hanging out with her. Just tagging along. She's the one going through it.'"

"Who finished giving her the pills?"

"The beautician! She had them in her hand and popped them in one after the other."

"The beautician? Under the hairdryer?"

"Yea! Crazy, huh? This place is out of control."

After lunch, Maire wheeled Grace back to the room for a nap. Two aides came quickly and the transfer was easy with the walker and the gait belt. Maire shook her head and chuckled. 'You just never know what you'll get when that door opens,' she thought as she nestled the edge of a soft blanket under Grace's chin. Then she sat back in the blue recliner. Grace slept for hours. When she woke it was time for dinner.

Chez Clair was warm and welcoming, the food was inviting, the uniformed staff was friendly and cordial. On the stroll back to Lonan Wing, Grace looked up and asked, "Where did that baby go?"

Maire pulled the wheelchair to the side of the hallway, just next to the little boutique. "Ma, that was a trick they played on you, and I'm very angry about that."

Grace's gaze was steady and sober. "What do you mean?"

"Well, what did the girl say to you?"

"She asked me to hold her baby."

"It was a doll," Ma. "She was making fun of you. They want naughty laughter." She looked softly into Grace's eyes. "It hurts me to tell you this, Ma, but I will not have anyone laughing at you."

"It was a doll? Oh my God." Her eyes narrowed as she processed the thought. "They lied. Why couldn't I see it? My head was so fuzzy!" Then her eyes filled with tears. "Oh, they did lie. They did." She looked heartsick. "I feel so foolish."

Maire put her arms gently around Grace's shoulders and kissed her cheek. "Well, we'll just not play their game anymore. When they do that again, we'll just say, 'No thank you.' We'll just keep our eyes open for those kind of things." Grace sat straight up in her chair and took Maire's hand.

"Yes, we will. We'll be on guard all the time." Then she looked intently into Maire's eyes. "Why didn't I see that then?"

"Because they're sedating you, Ma." Grace's eyes went dark. Her fingers closed into a tight fist.

"You deserve better, Ma." Maire lifted Grace's hand and placed it on her open palm. Like a blossom opening to the warmth of the sun, Grace automatically stretched her clenched fingers open, resting each finger on Maire's small ones. 'I want to remember this moment for the rest of my life,' Maire thought. 'No one can take this from me. No one can steal this from her.'

They stopped in the doorway of the chapel, where a concert was underway. After the concert, they filed with the group out into the hallway and back to the

Lonan Wing. Sybil sat alone in the TV room, rocking back and forth in her wheelchair. "Please help me!" she wailed.

Maire stopped next to the woman. "Sybil, they are going to help three people and then they will come to help you."

"Will it take a long time?"

"Yes, it probably will, but it is our job to be patient." Sybil closed her eyes and waited. Mallory passed by.

"We're going to hire you."

"Jesus," Maire thought to herself, "why don't they give Sybil the damn doll?"

Friday afternoon I found Grace sitting in the Lonan Wing dining room alone, staring out the window. "Oh, Sweetheart!" She began to cry and reached out for a kiss.

"Did you have something to eat, Gram?"

"I had a piece of cake, but she took it away." A brown clad kitchen worker stood next to Grace, spraying the table with solution from a spray bottle.

I looked across the urn barricade to a table of residents still eating and chatting. "Why aren't the tables on that side of the room being cleared?" The kitchen worker ignored me, moving to the next table. I reached for Grace's hand. It was wet. "Gram, did that worker spray your hands with the stuff she is spraying on the table?"

"Yes, she sprayed it right at me and told me to move, but I can't move this chair without help."

The kitchen worker stood at the nurses' station, engrossed in conversation with Alivia and Cassie. I steered Grace's chair toward them. "Jasmine won't leave," I heard her say. "She won't allow anyone to take her back to her room." The kitchen worker saw us coming closer and leaned in to Alivia to whisper. Alivia pushed her back with an arrogant lift of her chin.

"Good God, girl, just speak up or keep it to yourself."

The kitchen worker choked back her embarrassment. "Someone put Jasmine w-a-a-a-y back in her bathroom, pushed her down, shut the light off, shut the bathroom door and left her there in the dark!"

"Maybe we'd better speak in here." Alivia motioned to the nurses' office.

The kitchen worker glared defiantly and continued. "Jasmine couldn't get out and had no way to get help. Now she won't let anyone take her back to her room!" The kitchen worker threw down her towel and motioned back into the empty Lonan Wing dining room where Jasmine sat quivering, her white knuckles gripping the table.

"My God! Gram," I whispered. "That's exactly what happened to you."

"I told you," Grace answered quietly. Alivia glanced witlessly from the kitchen worker to Grace to Cassie and back to me. Then she hurried across the dining room to Jasmine.

"Gram, can you forgive me for being so stupid?"

She placed her soft hand on my cheek. "You are not stupid. You are my granddaughter."

"I love you, Gram."

She sighed and smiled. "What's in the bag?"

'Where does she get her strength?' I wondered. "I brought apple pie filling and pie shells and ice cream," I said. "We can bake a pie later."

Cassie grabbed the bag out of my hand. "We'll put it in the resident refrigerator."

"Hey!" I chased after her and retrieved the bag. She stood back defiantly, hands on hips, glaring at me. 'What a strange place this is,' I thought. 'It's fraught with confrontation. The issues surface so fast it's impossible to keep up.'

Grace was quietly taking it all in. "I don't want to be anywhere near those girls, she whispered. They are bad girls." I nodded. Grace smelled as if she had not bathed. Her eyes were dry and matted. She was dressed in a wrinkled shirt over pajama bottoms. She looked as debilitated as her children had described her.

"Gram, who helped you get dressed this morning?"

"The fat crows."

"Were they mean to you?"

"I don't want to talk in front of them."

I wheeled her back to her room. Her toothbrush was dry. Her washcloths were unused. "You said they took your cake away. Is that all you've had to eat today? Are you hungry?"

She nodded. "I'm very hungry." I helped Grace bathe and change into a comfortable sweater and casual slacks. We strolled through the hallways and the courtyards to Café Sofie. "I'd like a white meat, white bread sandwich and chips," she said to the clerk at the counter. I smiled. She only made her sandwiches with Wonder Bread and turkey. I selected a banana and a small dish of ice cream as well. She ate slowly and eagerly, enjoying every bite. She sipped her coffee. "That was a good lunch," she said. "I didn't offer you a bite." I laughed. She had not lost the instinct to make sure everyone else at the table had something to eat. She looked at me with a meaningful gaze. "I was very, very hungry."

I made the afternoon last as long as I possibly could. "Do you want me to help you into bed before I go?"

"No, I'll just sit here by the window."

"Are you sure? I don't want to leave you alone here."

"No. I'll sit here. Maybe one of the children will come by for a visit."

"All right, then. I'll call from the road. Here's your phone. Push this light if you need one of the girls to help you. I love you."

"I love you so much." Grace watched as I walked away. I turned back reluctantly. "It'll be all right," she called to me. I blew her a kiss as she smiled bravely and waved.

Three finches and a yellow cardinal gathered to scratch at the bird feeder outside her bedroom window. The round faced clock ticked on as the light faded across the distant sky. Grace dozed. Then the knob on her door rattled and the door burst open. A girl stood in the door, eyes blazing, fists clenched. She darted toward Grace's wheelchair. Grace pulled back to protect herself.

"What do you want?"

"Was that your mom with you?"

"No. That was not my mom."

"Yes, it was. Don't lie! Now that your mom isn't here, I can get you. I can get you this time!" She jabbed at Grace's leg.

"You get away from me," Grace yelled. She pushed back with her hands. "Get away!"

"No one can stop me now! No one is here to stop me!" The girl grabbed a tube of lipstick from Grace's bedside table. Then she opened a drawer from the jewelry box and dumped it out on the floor.

"Stop!" Grace shouted. She reached down to push her away. The girl scratched at Grace's legs and arms. Grace screamed in pain. The girl laughed and screamed louder to mock Grace's screams. Suddenly a tall shadow of a man appeared in the door. His long arms swept the intruder back. He gave a light kick with his polished shoe and she skittered away down the hall. He moved in closer. He had a kind face.

"What was that all about? Where is staff when this kind of thing happens?" Grace trembled, rubbing her legs. They ached now and so did her temples. "Come across the hall with us for a bit. We can watch Lawrence Welk on TV. Grace shook her head. "Come on, now. You shouldn't be alone." He pushed her chair into the hallway. "I never leave my wife alone. Come. Sit with us for an hour."

An hour later I dropped my bags and sank into the couch, staring into the soft fireplace glow. I absently fingered through a few pieces of mail. The return address of one made me sit up again and flip on the light, tearing open the flap. Chicago wanted me back. I stared into the fire. Chicago wanted me back. Glancing at my watch, I dialed Blackwater.

"Aubery, It's Elle. I'm calling to say goodnight to my grandmother."

"She's visiting."

"It's late. Who is with her at this hour?"

"She's visiting with other residents."

"Please let me speak to my grandmother."

Aubery heaved an exasperated sigh. I heard her moving, then I heard her say, "Grace, your granddaughter's on the phone."

Grace was barely audible. "Help me, Elle. I'm stuck."

"Stuck? What does that mean?"

"I'm trapped. I can't get out." There was noisy activity in the background.

"Are you in the TV room?"

"There are eight people surrounding me and I can't move," she cried. "I'm very, very tired."

I picked up the landline phone and dialed the nurses' station. "Aubery, can you find someone to help my grandmother to bed?"

"I thought you were on the phone with her."

"She's on my cell phone. I'm calling you on my landline."

"We're short staffed tonight. She can visit for a while."

"Aubery, she's not visiting. She's crying. My grandmother is tired. It's late."

"Yes, she is tired." Aubery's tone was dismissive.

"Will you make sure she gets some assistance?"

"All right. I'll see about that."

I hung up the landline. Grace was still there on my cell. "How can I help you, Gram?"

"Come here. Come here now."

"I'm an hour away. Would it be helpful if Maire would come?"

"That would be very helpful."

'Typical of Grace,' I thought. She was trying to tell me something without saying too much. She didn't have to say it. I could hear that she was in trouble. I dialed Maire.

"I'm on my way," Maire shot back as she dashed to her car.

Maire entered Grace's room to find Ivy standing over Grace. Startled at the sight of Maire, she jumped back. "I'm going to go get an aide." She pushed past Maire and ran frantically down the hallway.

"What in the hell is wrong with that girl?" Maire asked, but Grace didn't answer.

Ivy hurried back into the room with Alivia close behind. "You need to leave," Alivia demanded.

Maire stared at the two. "I'm not leaving. Why should I?"

"You'll have to leave now!"

"Why?"

"Because we're uncomfortable."

"All the more reason for me not to leave! Why is my mother crying?"

"I'm OK," Grace interrupted. "It's OK." Maire looked closely at her mother and then warily at the two aides. She nodded and walked reluctantly into the hallway. Alivia slammed the door behind her. When they came out they whisked briskly past Maire without a word or a glance and disappeared around the corner into the adjacent wing.

Maire grabbed her phone and dialed. "Mom's in bed now. She's OK."

"What does that mean?" I asked. "What happened?"

"Her leg is hurt."

"What on earth is going on there?"

"I have no idea. Let me put her on speaker phone."

"Hi Gram."

"Oh, Elle. Are you home?"

"No. I'm on my way back to you."

"I'm OK now."

"What happened tonight, Gram? What happened after I left you?"

"There was a red headed girl. She was mad-wild! She looked like a boy. She was strong like a boy."

"What? A girl that looked like a boy? Was she there when we talked on the phone earlier?"

"No, that was before. Then a man took me away to hear the music."

"Was there a concert tonight?"

"No. It was on the TV."

"Oh, OK. Is that where were you when we talked on the phone?"

"No, you don't understand," she sighed.

"OK. I'll just be quiet and listen. You tell me."

"We were on the cement. They told me to step over the ledge. I knew if I stepped over the ledge, I would have to stretch too far. The pain in my leg was too much. I thought I could stand it but I couldn't and I fell down."

"You fell?"

"My head hit the cement."

Maire's voice broke in. "She has told me this story three times."

"Did this happen tonight, Gram?"

"It happened tonight. I was trying to get over the ledge. No one knew how to get me up out of the cement. I had to take a step, a wide step. I knew I couldn't jump so I had to take a wide step, but I knew

I couldn't make it and my leg pained and my head crashed."

"You fell?" I repeated. I couldn't make sense of it.

"My head crashed on the cement."

"I'm baffled, Gram."

Maire interrupted. "I'm going to stay right here to make sure nothing else happens."

"Jesus! I've only been gone an hour!"

When Grace finally succumbed to sleep, Maire tiptoed out of the room into the hallway back to the nurses' station. I arrived to find her there squaring off with Alivia.

"What time did you come on?" Maire demanded.

"Two or two-thirty, I guess."

"What time did Mom fall?"

"Fall? What are you talking about?

"Mom fell tonight. What time did she fall?"

"I don't know. She didn't fall that I know of. You'll have to ask Aubery." Her jaw clenched. Her neck reddened.

"Liars," Maire muttered as she turned away. I followed her as she searched the hallways for Aubery. Finally, Maire spotted the med cart outside a resident's room. She waited until Aubery appeared. "Aubery, what time did Mom fall?" she demanded.

"Uh, it was eight-fifteen, I guess. It was somewhere in there, right after she talked to Elle." Maire stared, dumbfounded.

"Why did no one tell me that when I got here?"

"I called Bric." Aubery's voice trembled. Her hands shook. "The only reason I left her alone is because somebody died. I had to hurry."

"Somebody died?"

"Yes, I had to leave Grace and take care of him. I had to hurry."

"He's dead! What do you have to hurry for? Are you telling me that in less than an hour someone died, my mother fell and the aide on duty knows nothing about it?" Maire stopped. Suddenly she realized what Aubery was saying.

"Hold it! You left Mom sitting alone in her room after she fell?"

"She wasn't in her room!"

"Of course not! She was corralled in the day room with eight other wheelchair residents. Maybe you were on your break? Maybe you were having supper? What the hell? They're not going anywhere!" She planted herself squarely in front of Aubery. "Only something went wrong, didn't it?" Aubery tried to look away, but Maire had her in her sights. "How did she fall, Aubery?"

"Well, she must have slipped out of her chair."

"Slipped out of her chair?" Maire blasted back. "You've got her strapped in!" Then another thought flashed into Maire's head. "One of those residents trapped in the TV room died right there in front of her, right? They were all helpless to do anything, right?" Beads of sweat appeared on Aubery's forehead and ran down her cheeks. "So Mom did what she has done her entire life. She reached out to help. Only in doing so she got her own leg tangled up. Right?" Grace's words echoed in Maire's head. "Then she crashed headlong to the floor!" Aubery flushed. Maire stepped forward menacingly. "Am I right?" Aubery reached for her flashlight. "That's why Alivia was in a panic when I walked in."

"It was Ivy."

"What?"

"You mean Ivy," Aubery corrected her.

"Whatever!" Maire shouted. "Your staff changes hands so fast how can anyone keep up? What would you have done if I had not walked in tonight? Would you have left her there alone in pain or would have sedated her, strapped her into the lift machine and tossed her into bed crying?"

I listened, numb from the impact of calamities and confrontations transpiring in relentless rapid succession. Maire was right. It was out of control. There was nobody driving this bus!

It was nearly midnight when we finally stood alone at the exit door. "I think if I hadn't called Gram to say evening prayers, we would never have known."

"To think I sat outside her room leaving her alone with those two devils and I had no idea she was hurt. I should have demanded that someone examine her. When Aubery told me she called Bric, she was probably lying. I could see that she was lying about something."

"They are lying about everything. They're lying about using the machine. They're lying about sedating her. Aubery lied the very first night when Gram fell. When Aubery's on duty, things happen."

"What's so hard about caring for these residents? You show respect. You keep them safe. What the hell is the problem? If you don't have sufficient staff to do that, contract with another business to come and help. What's so difficult about that?"

"God! Why is she here?"

"Aubery needs to stay out of that med room. Watching her swinging that flashlight all night long, up and down hallways gives me the creeps. She shakes all the time. I know a user when I see one. That's an addict, and she's not the only user walking these halls." Maire was on a roll. "That belt that is strapped around Mom, the lift machine, the doll and the sedatives are all part of Acer's agenda. She is told to keep secret whatever it is they are subjecting her to when we're not here. That is a secret that will kill her. They know it. And they know we can't stay ahead of them. I'm so damn tired, Elle!"

The next morning I dialed Bric's number. "No," he said, "I was not informed that she fell. I appreciate your telling me. I'll call her physician this morning. She should have an X-ray."

I hung up the phone. "Liar."

Just after lunch I phoned Grace. She said she was in terrible pain earlier but didn't have any now. "Did you take any pills?" I asked. "Do you feel sleepy?"

"Yes, and dizzy."

An hour later, I slipped into Lonan Wing unnoticed. Grace sat slumped in her chair, holding the doll. "Gram?" Grace looked at me through hazy eyes. I wheeled her to the nurse's station. Giselle stared back from behind the counter. "You sedate her and then give her a doll to pacify her pain? This is beyond losing your license!"

"We have a order from Dr. Corbin."

"Then let me see it." She stared stubbornly back at me. "You cannot produce a script, can you? Why did you medicate my grandmother this morning?"

"Sedatives are at the discretion of Blackwater staff," she answered mechanically.

"Well, at least you admit you're sedating her. Why? Is it because you are forcing that archaic lift machine on her?" She glared back at me, tightlipped. "Deny it if I'm wrong." She stared belligerently.

I wheeled Grace back to her room, tossing the doll into the doorway of an empty room as we passed. Then I cradled Grace's head on my shoulder as I dialed. "Acer? Elle. I am sitting with your mother. She is sedated, abandoned to her room with a plastic doll, which the staff insists is a baby. Is this what you want for your mother?"

He didn't hesitate. "Oh, Elle," he cooed, "you are such an advocate. We all appreciate that."

I interrupted him. "Why is she here, paying out of pocket in a temporary care facility, Acer? Grandpa faithfully paid his insurance premium to ensure she would have quality care." He was silent. "Unless you let it lapse." He remained silent. "You let it lapse."

"I have absolute faith in Blackwater," he responded firmly. "She needs to be left alone there to rest."

"She's suffering, Acer."

"You need to get on with your life. The longer you're out of circulation, the harder it will be to get that job you want," he answered and hung up.

"He didn't want to talk to me?" Grace sighed. I tucked a soft woolen wrap around her small frame and reached for The Secret Garden.

"Then she saw a high wall covered with ivy," I read. "It was a long wall. It seemed to go on and on. Over the top she could see treetops and birds flying. One bird, a red-breasted robin, sat staring down at her. The friendly bird whooshed down and circled. It burst into song and landed on a branch right next to her."

Grace listened intently. "A secret friend from the secret garden," she murmured wistfully. Her words were to me like a drop of rain that falls on a vast angry sea at the height of a hurricane. 'If a soul cries out in the wilderness,' I wondered, 'does anyone hear?' I studied her face as she watched the squirrels scurry across the rooftops outside. Here was a woman who knew how to stand against the storm. Faced with the unnamed shadow before her, she refused to back down. She was determined to take one more step. I thought of her words, 'When I've reached the end, I can go home.' I rested my head against her shoulder. She patted my face. "Read," she said.

"With a chirp the robin set out, flying toward the gardens. The robin landed on a branch and sang, bobbing his head from side to side. Then the robin took off again, landing on another wall across the way." Grace's eyes moved across the page as I read. I paused and her eyes searched mine.

"More," she said.

"One day as the little girl searched through the long hallways, she heard a strange sound. It sounded like the wind, but it wasn't. It was the sound of someone crying!"

"Oh, my," Grace exclaimed. "Just like Wanetta crying next door!"

I nodded. "She could smell the earth warming all around her. She couldn't remember being this excited about anything in a very long time. She stood with her eyes closed and her face toward the sun. Suddenly she heard the soft rustling of tree branches and the sound of a bird chirping. She knew it was her robin. The little girl opened her eyes and saw him hopping on a nearby branch. She clapped her hands. The robin flew so close to her it made her tremble with excitement."

"He came back," Grace whispered.

"The robin flew to a branch high overhead and perched on a branch. 'Don't leave me,' the girl called. The robin bobbed his head and trilled into the wind. Then he fluttered to a branch in a distant tree, where he perched, bobbing and trilling."

"Oh," Grace interrupted, "the robin is calling her."

"She followed the robin from tree to tree until finally he landed on the ground beside a tiny mound of earth. There in the clump of earth was the glitter of something buried. It was a key. Could it be the key to the secret garden?" Grace grasped my hand. I reached to kiss her cheek.

"I'm so grateful that you are here," she sighed.

We sat with our heads together in the peace of the moment. I savored the scent of her perfume and her soft touch. I whispered softly into her ear, "Oh, my Jesus, bless us more. Fill us with the Holy Spirit. Keep my grandmother from evil. Grant my grandmother whatever she asks, and when my grandmother speaks, let others listen."

"Is that how the prayer goes?"

"It is now. We can pray it however we want."

"That's good," she answered.

I continued to read. Grace nestled next to me in her wheelchair. The warm sun through the window made her drowsy and she dozed off.

Emily came through the door. Cherilee followed. "Will you sit with Gram a moment?" I whispered. "I'll slip around through the side door and fill the bird-feeders on her window." Emily shrugged. I walked quickly through the corridors and through the doors to Grace's garden to stand just outside her window. The curtains in the window jerked shut. "Now what are they up to?" I muttered. I filled each of three small feeder wells and hurried back around the corner to see the girls scurrying down the hallway. "Where are you going?" I called after them. They didn't look back. Grace was sitting on the side of her bed staring at the closed curtains. "I'm here, Gram." I reached and flung the curtains aside to reveal a dozen finches scratching and nibbling at the new supply of seed in the window feeders. "Obstinate!" I muttered. "Who are these people?"

"I'd like to go to the bathroom," Grace said softly.

"Oh, OK. Wouldn't the girls help you?"

"They tried to give me a pill but I wouldn't take it so they left."

Café Sofie was closed for the evening so we wheeled into Lonan Wing dining room for supper. A well-dressed gentleman hobbled through the doorway next to us. A brown-clad kitchen worker motioned for him to sit on the other side of the barricade at a table with three other men.

"I don't want to sit there," he said flatly. "That gentleman right there has been sick and coughing and I don't want his germs."

"Well, there are plenty of people who don't want to sit with you, either," the kitchen worker retorted. His eyes widened in embarrassed surprise. I motioned for him to sit at our table.

"Join us," Grace offered. "Just don't be crabby."

He pulled a chair to the table. "I don't need to be insulted by a staff waiter. I was only making the point that I couldn't afford to be sick. That man has been coughing all week long."

"Maybe she just misunderstood?"

"Maybe," he conceded.

Maire joined us. "Who is training these people?" She tugged a chair from another table and pushed it in between the man and Grace. "We should place an ad. If you are insolent and arrogant without any discernible people skills, you too can work for Blackwater Manor." The man slapped his hand on the table and hooted. The kitchen worker scowled. Grace smiled and shook her head.

After supper Grace settled back quietly into her pillows. "Read to me from The Secret Garden. I'm not sleepy yet."

Maire curled up in the blue chair by the window. "Where did you leave off?"

"They found the key and they were looking for the garden," Grace prompted.

"Yes, here is the page." I read on. "The little girl skipped around the perimeter, following the robin. 'You showed me yesterday where the key was,' she called to him. 'Can you show me where the door is today?' Then she laughed at herself. How could a robin know what she was saying? The robin chirped at her and flitted from branch to branch. Finally he stopped and perched, bobbing and trilling down at her. 'What's in there?' the little girl asked. The robin bobbed and trilled as the girl pushed the thick ivy away from the fence. 'Nothing can keep me out. Show me the way,' she said."

Suddenly a cry came from the room next to Grace's. Grace tugged at the wheels of her chair. "There. Push me in there." I pushed her chair forward, across the threshold into the hallway, around the doorway and over a second threshold into the next room.

"Wanetta, why are you crying?" Grace patted the edge of her bed. "This is such a dark place. You need to go outside."

"No, leave me alone," she wailed.

Grace held her hands over her ears. "Well, it's not her fault she's stuck in here with no help to relieve her pain and no one to care for her. Don't you think that people would be much better outdoors in the garden, watching everything grow?"

The next morning Maire's words resounded through my phone. "Mom is sitting in the hallway across from the nurse's station, under the poster board. Her wheelchair is back to back in a queue with ten or more other residents in wheelchairs. They look like cattle in a chute." Then she was talking to Grace. "Ma, where are your teeth?" Then she was talking to Cecilia. "Cecilia, how do you expect her to eat without her teeth?" Then she was back to me. "Do you believe this? She just blew me off and walked away." Then she was back with Grace. "Well, we'll just go back to your room."

"Maire? Are you still there?" She was gone. I hung up my phone. They were together. Grace was safe. I would be there soon.

Maire wrapped her arms around Grace. "I love you, Ma."

Grace looked up, tears streaming. "I love you so very, very much. It's so important that you are here."

They strolled back down the hallway to the nurse's station. "Mom is ready for breakfast," she said.

"She had breakfast," Clover snapped. "She had sausage, eggs, toast and juice."

Maire leveled a cold stare at them both. "How was it possible for her to eat without her teeth? You understand what I am saying, right?"

Clover tilted her head and rolled her eyes. "Well, I wasn't on duty."

Cassie interrupted. "She refused to put her teeth in. We could hear her screaming all the way down the hall."

Maire faced Clover. "You weren't on duty but you know for sure what she ate?" She turned to Cassie. "You heard her screaming all the way down the hall?" Maire moved in ready to pounce. "Did you go to her?"

Cassie backed away. "You can see how busy we are."

"All I see is you three gossiping," Maire fired back. "God help the resident that gets in the way of that."

"Let's go, now," Grace whispered. "That's enough."

Poppy stopped them in the hallway. Her Yorky's wide eyes peeked through wisps of hair which had escaped from a bright pink bow. "Come to our bake sale. We have chocolate fudge and brownies."

"Let's go on," Grace urged.

"We'll come back later," Maire answered. "Mom's had a difficult morning."

"I know." Poppy's silver bangles jingled as she leaned forward to pat Grace's hand. She scurried down the hallway, calling, "Come to our bake sale!" A waft of heavy perfume followed. The Yorkie jingled along behind, scurrying to keep up.

"You know?" The words stuck in Maire's brain like an axe in her forehead. "You know?"

When I arrived, I found them in the hallway with Anthia. Anthia carried a cane, but rarely used it. "You missed my birthday party, Grace. I turned 93. Would you like to come to my apartment and see my angels?" Anthia pointed to her ankle. "I have a pedometer. It's exactly one-quarter mile from Café Sofie and Chez Clair to my front door. I figure with lunch and dinner, I walk a mile a day, at least!" She laughed and paused to allow for Grace's full appreciation.

"Oh, my. That's a lot," Grace exclaimed. Anthia nodded and the two women moved through the hallways, chatting easily, touching hands to emphasize a word or thought, engrossed in each other's company.

Anthia proudly led us through her apartment, reading to Grace from poems she had written, handing her an angel from her collection. "Do you have a collection, Grace?" She placed a tea cup, a silver spoon and a linen napkin on the table. Grace smoothed the lace on the napkin.

"Oh, my, yes," Grace answered. "I have an angel collection at home."

"You should be going home, soon," Anthia said. "Most residents don't stay long in Lonan Wing. When therapy's done, they go home."

"My children don't want me there, I'm afraid," Grace replied. "My children have taken everything. All I have left is a wall of photos staring back at me." Anthia chuckled. Grace blinked in surprise. "That amuses you?"

"Oh, Grace, I'm over ninety years old. I know the only value our children see in us now is the value of our assets."

"I should go," Grace answered. Beyond us, through the large atrium windows, loomed Lonan Wing.

The bake sale was in full swing in the activity room. "Let's buy some brownies, Ma." Maire reached for a plate.

Grace clicked open her purse. "I don't know if I have any money."

Maire laughed and knelt beside her chair. "Ma, you have money."

Grace looked at Maire with sad eyes. "No, it's all gone."

"Ma! It's all yours," Maire laughed.

"They took it, Maire. I have nothing."

I opened my wallet and pulled out some bills and stuffed them into her hand. "Here, Gram. What's mine is yours."

She smiled and grasped my hand. "And what's mine is yours." She tightened her grip. "I mean it. Remember that. Both of you. It's important."

I leaned in and kissed her cheek. "Right now, this is all that matters, Gram. Just seeing you smile makes me happy."

"Are you ready for a nap?" Maire asked.

"Yes, I'm tired now."

I moved toward her. "Would you like to go to the bathroom first?"

"Yes, I need to do that." She held the brownies from the bake sale firmly in her lap. "We need to take these with us."

"Into the bathroom?" Maire questioned.

"The girls are tricky here, Maire. They take things." Maire flipped the call light and Clover and Luella came through the door. Luella grabbed for the plate. Grace pulled it back. Clover demanded that she let go. Grace gripped it tighter. Clover wheeled Grace into the bathroom and Luella closed the door. I leaned my head against the cool wall.

Maire sighed. "They could hear her screaming all the way down the hall. They're using the machine on her again. She's drowning here in Blackwater, clinging to anything that reminds her of her former self, even if it is just a plate of brownies." I opened the bathroom door. Clover spun to face me. Grace looked up, tears streaming down her face. I stepped in.

"You'll need to leave," Clover hissed.

"This is jacked!" Maire snarled.

"What?" Luella snapped.

"Step back," I sighed. "I'll do this." I leaned down and reached around my grandmother. She tilted her head to rest on my shoulder and with one easy motion, I had her out of the chair and positioned on the toilet. "I'll be right outside, Gram. Just let me know when you're ready." She nodded. I leaned back. Something scratched at the window. There in the bird feeders, little gray finches fluttered in the warm sun. I wondered at the simplicity of life, so strong, yet so fragile.

Maire watched me, still fuming. "What the hell is their problem that they cannot or will not allow her the smallest bit of compassion? Those devils torture, torment and trick her all day long. I wouldn't cooperate with them either!"

I sighed. My gaze circled the room, settling on the large framed family photo. "Where are they? Why are you and I the only ones here to defend her?" I peeked into the bathroom. Grace still clung to the brownies. I smiled. Despite everything, my grandmother defied them all to stake her claim, even if only to a plate of brownies.

Forty-five minutes later Grace was in bed, asleep, the brownies on her bed side table. I reached above the headboard to shut off the call light, not that anyone on duty was paying attention. Maire leaned back into the blue chair, watching the finches scratching at the window. "Do you remember stories of the chickens on the farm?" I nodded. "I was still very small," she said. "I wanted to help, but I was terrified of those chickens. They ran and flopped and scratched, stirring up a huge clouds of dust. I usually ended up in the doorway, helpless. One day Mom said, 'I'll show you how to lull them.' She picked one up, tucked it's head under its wing and swayed it back and forth. The chicken immediately went into a trance. One by one she lulled those chickens into submission. Then one by one she either collected their eggs or chopped off their heads. The ones that were still alive didn't stir at all until they heard the rooster crow." Maire gazed across the room at me and then back at Grace, sleeping peacefully in her bed. "We used to call it 'hypnotizing the chickens'. Sometimes I think that's exactly what Acer is doing now. He's hypnotizing his chickens."

The next morning when I arrived at Lonan Wing Grace was awake and waiting for me. I pushed the call light button. "Are you comfortable, Gram?"

"Yes, quite." She smiled gratefully.

"Let's read some more from The Secret Garden while we're waiting." I flipped through the book to the marker. Grace looked on in anticipation. I marveled at the strength of her spirit against daunting odds, her hope so eagerly rekindled by the simplest gesture of love. "She saw little green shoots poking through the earth," I read. "She leaned down to clear a place for the tender growth. She decided she would come back every day and do more."

"Yes," Grace nodded, gazing out the window. "You have to attend to your garden faithfully, every day."

Cassie bustled through the door. "You'll have to leave."

"I'm good right here. I'll stay."

"I'm not going to fight with you today," she snapped and left.

Minutes later, Giselle came in. "You'll have to leave," she ordered, tapping her fingernails on the door.

"There's no aide to assist my mother and there's no reason to leave."

"I will get the aide." She left the door ajar and disappeared.

I smiled at Grace and turned back to The Secret Garden. "She went from place to place, digging and weeding. She enjoyed the day so much she completely lost track of time. She forgot lunch."

The round-faced clock ticked past 9:00 a.m. Mallory came in. Ignoring me, she briskly and silently wheeled Grace into the bathroom. Then she quickly wheeled Grace out of the bathroom and left. Grace applied her lipstick, straightened her hat and spritzed on a bit of Estee Lauder Beautiful. Then we wheeled to Lonan Wing for breakfast. Brown clad kitchen workers bustled around us, clearing tables. One brought a plate of toast and jelly and a banana. It was enough. Grace nibbled on the banana, savoring each slice. I wondered how anyone could be cruel to a soul as gentle and congenial as Grace.

After breakfast, we wheeled through the hallway and out a side door into a small garden. The crocuses peeked through the snow. We paused in a sunny spot. I pulled The Secret Garden from my bag. "The sun shone down for nearly a week on the garden. She decided to call it her secret garden. She liked having a secret, but most of all she liked the feeling she got when she went into the garden. She felt free to do whatever she pleased. It was a magical place. She knew that when unattended, roses run wild. The thorny tendrils coiled and curled, winding through the underbrush, taking over the garden and choking out the more tender plants. The little girl knew that with care and sun and spring rain showering them with joy, the roses could be made to blossom."

"Like the girls here," Grace mused. "Most just run wild, choking life out. One or two are good, though. One or two could blossom."

"What an interesting, thought, Gram."

Clover passed by. "Are you going out today, Grace?"

"No," Grace responded. "We're going to lunch at Café Sofie." I shook my head in wonder. Taking her out of Lonan Wing or even out of the building was of no concern to staff. Yet, when in the confines of Lonan Wing, they repeatedly insisted that I leave the room. What were they afraid of?

The next morning I walked into the Lonan Wing about a quarter after seven. Grace sat at the day table next to the nurses station. Her hair clung to her face, wet and uncombed. A towel lay damp and rumpled under her elbow. I leaned down to give her a kiss. She looked at me through dazed eyes and shivered.

"Gram, are you cold?"

"Yes," she said.

"Gram, where are your teeth?" Shell-shocked, she didn't answer. "Let's get you a sweater." I backed her wheel chair away from the table and past the nurses' station. Cassie looked up absently. "Cassie, I don't understand how you expect her to eat her breakfast without her teeth."

Cassie turned back to her paperwork. "She refused."

Back to Grace's room, I handed Grace her teeth and dried and styled her hair. Then we wheeled back to the breakfast table. A brown-clad kitchen worker placed a tray without silverware in front of us. I stared in disbelief as the aide walked away without a word. Another worker parked Sybil next to us. Sybil stared blankly at the table. A server put half a peeled banana in Sybil's hand. It slid out of her hand onto the floor. Raven watched from across the table.

"Raven," I asked, "did you give my grandmother a whirlpool bath this morning?"

"Yes," she replied, expressionless.

"Why is my grandmother's hair wet? Why was she shivering?"

She glanced at Grace. "We had an episode."

"What does that mean?"

Raven tossed her head, her fat cheeks jiggling. She groaned and shifted her large body away from the table. "She was agitated."

I turned to Grace. "What happened, Gram?"

Raven stood abruptly and pulled a baggie from her pocket. There inside was Grace's pearl wristwatch. The diamond-encrusted face was broken. Pearls from the bracelet lay loose in the bottom of the bag. "Her bracelet broke."

"How did that happen?"

"She took it from me while I was in the whirl-pool," Grace said quietly. "She put it on her fat wrist and it broke."

I looked from Grace to Raven, who dropped the baggie on the table. "You were wearing Grace's watch?"

"We were just fooling around, having a little fun."

"You were fooling around while Grace was in a whirlpool, helpless to stop you?"

Raven shot a steady, stern look at Grace. Grace met her glare straight on. "It was just an accident, Grace. You have it back now. You'd better hurry up with your breakfast or you'll miss your appointment with the beautician."

Grace's eyes grew dark. "It wasn't an accident."

As the bus wound around the river's edge, the road rose toward the mountains. A heavy fog descended. It occurred to me that unraveling the confusion of the present and solving the riddles of the past would be like trying to see clearly through the stealthy mist. My thoughts were interrupted by the voice of the bus driver through the overhead speaker. "We'll be delayed at the next station, folks, but only those changing buses will get off. Everyone else stays on the bus." A din of disgruntled moans and angry retorts rose up. The driver scowled back at us from the rear view mirror and continued. "There's a pile up ahead. The Interstate is closed." The angry moans became hushed whispers. Passengers peered through the windows as the bus slowed to a crawl, weaving past ambulances and tow trucks and police vans. Orange and yellow-jacketed firefighters and road patrol waved lanterns. The amber lights faded and then brightened, appeared and then vanished eerily in the dense fog. I lay my head back on the seat rest and gazed into the haze outside the window. I heard Grace's voice.

"We're safe here."

"Yes, Gram. We're safe here."

The bus lurched as the driver pulled into the Maverick Country Store. A slogan splashed across the window in bright yellow letters touted proudly that *FILLIN UP YOUR GAS TANK AND YOUR BELLY IN THE WILD WEST IS A BREEZE.*

"Here's where I get off," the researcher announced, tapping the back of my seat. "Did you solve the clues?"

"I'm working on the fourth one," I answered.

"What is it?" He pulled his bags from the overhead compartment.

"What measures a man's girth but only on earth?" I asked.

"That's simple," he answered. "Look around you." He swung his bag over his shoulder. "Don't give up on the clues," he said. "It's how you find your way. Remember the turtles and follow the river."

The riddles danced in my head like the leprechaun's jig. *What's more blinding than the break of dawn? What is the pleasure that yields only pain? What rights nothing that is wrong? What consumes what it abstains? What measures a man's girth but only on earth?* "Gram?" I whispered. "Did you know what your children were up to?"

"I knew," she answered. "But I hoped they'd be smarter than that."

A man and his teen-age son boarded. The teen slumped into the seat ahead of me. "Boy, is this day gonna suck!"

As sirens pierced the quiet, I thought of Wanetta's piercing wail, echoing against the walls of the corridors of Lonan Wing.

"That will go on all night," Maire scowled. I watched Aubery busily sorting pills at the med cart. "That poor soul should not be here. But then, either should Mom." My phone beeped with a text from Crystal Ann.

> *Llyssa and Diedra would love a little thank you from you for all they did for the Mother's Day party.'*

I stared at the screen. "Are you kidding me?"
"Elle!" Maire screamed as she rushed to Grace's side. "Gram? What is it?"

"I have a pain." Grace could barely speak. "It's sharp."

"Where?"

"It cuts like a knife from my jaw to my ear."

"Christ!" Maire muttered. "What are the chances Aubery will be of any help?"

I scanned Grace's jawline. I could see no bruise or abrasion. "I'm calling Bric. He should get someone to look at that." It went to voicemail. I left a message.

Maire held a warm washcloth to Grace's jaw. Grace nodded, tears streaming down her cheeks. Aubery, still in the hallway, next to the med cart, brought a Tylenol. Grace tried to open her mouth but clenched her lips in pain. Maire and I crouched over Grace throughout the night, repeatedly replacing the hot packs until she finally succumbed to exhaustion and slept.

By morning a small lump had formed on her left jaw. I dialed Bric. It went directly to voicemail. "Bric? Elle. I called last night about Gram's jaw pain. I now see a lump forming. Whatever this is, it is growing fast." As I spoke, a brown-clad kitchen worker handed me a plate of hard toast and two links of sausage. I handed it back to her. "She's not able to chew this. Can you find yogurt and a banana?"

"We don't have that today," she replied in broken English. "We have this."

"Go to Café Sofie if you need to!" I ordered. Grace shook her head and winced, her hand flying to her jaw. "Just think of me as your warrior granddaughter, Gram." Her eyes crinkled. I couldn't tell if she was laughing or crying. "Battle!" I whispered.

"Oh, you!" she sighed.

I found Cassie at the med cart. "Cassie, my grandmother needs something for a sharp pain."

"Not now. I'm giving new meds."

Grace held her hand against her jaw, unable to hold back her tears. Her hands were raw. The skin was peeling. I took her hand in mind. "I don't want to fall apart now," she sobbed. "I'm not done."

I put my arms around her and leaned my head against her shoulder. "Oh, that Thou would bless me indeed, and that Thine hand might be with me." She nodded. I redialed Bric. It went to voicemail. There was a squeak of wheels moving behind us. Dimmae, tugging the blood pressure machine behind her, stared at Grace.

"Oh, my God! What's wrong with your face? Your hands!" Grace turned away, startled and embarrassed. "Well, I was just so shocked by what I saw!" I grabbed the handles of her wheel chair and backed it away.

"Oh, Sweetheart, who can stand to look at me now?" Grace sighed.

I gazed into her sad eyes. "Gram, I think you're the most beautiful woman I've ever seen."

"Oh, you," she sniffed and attempted a smile.

We found a quiet table in the atrium outside Café Sofie next to wide windows overlooking a garden. Baby squirrels frolicked along the branches of a massive oak tree. I held a spoonful of warm egg to Grace's lips. She took a small bite, winced and took the spoon. I studied her hands. Her flawless, silken smooth skin was shredding and tearing away, leaving raw red wounds. What was that? The warm late morning sun drifted across the room. Grace tilted her face and smiled weakly. "Will you read to me about the garden?"

'Here was a woman,' I marveled, 'hungry and in pain, still instinctively rising to one ray of hope in a very dark wilderness.' I reached into my bag and pulled out the book. "There behind the ivy growing down the wall was a door," I read. "She took the key out of her pocket and turned it in the lock. She couldn't believe it. She was standing inside the secret garden."

Grace looked to the budding branches outside. "It's a secret."

"Everywhere she looked, she saw empty flower beds and leggy rosebushes. She wondered if the garden would bloom again if someone would tend it properly."

Nicole and Christina, two new trainees passed through the atrium and stopped. Nicole stared at Grace's cheek, then reached to probe the lump. "Don't touch her jaw," I ordered.

Nicole pushed in. "Would you like to go to the bathroom, Grace?"

"Yes, that would be good," Grace nodded, looking at me for assurance. I followed them to Grace's room. Nicole turned an arrogant shoulder and impatiently rocked the walker up and down in front of Grace's wheelchair. "Your granddaughter's waiting, Grace. Let's stand up. Don't keep her waiting." Grace's face went dark. I could feel the defiance rising in her. She looked around the girl, entreating me with her eyes. I stepped in.

"Do not speak that way to my grandmother." I turned to Grace. "Take your time, Gram. You decide when you are ready." Grace's face smoothed and she stood carefully, slowly, determinedly. Once standing, she smiled weakly at me. She was summoning all the energy she had. She turned and slowly walked the ten steps to the bathroom. I followed, close to her elbow. Nicole pushed past and slammed the bathroom door with a loud snap of the latch. When they finally emerged again, the two girls wheeled Grace ahead of them into the hallway. I sprinted to catch up, handing Nicole the foot pedals. "She'll need these to protect her legs and feet."

"Did you find a lotion without alcohol in it?" Nicole flippantly tossed back over her shoulder.

"What are you talking about?"

"It was reported in care conference that you are using an abrasive lotion on your grandmother. We were told to remove it."

"Are you saying these skin tears are from lotion? That's absurd. That's the same lotion she's used for years."

A man sat crumpled in his chair, moaning in pain. Cassie left the nurses' station to go to his side. "What's wrong, Neil?"

"I have an insufferable pain," the man groaned. "Can you give me something?"

"Oh, Neil, you are the insufferable pain!" Cassie motioned for a brown-clad worker to wheel him away.

I took hold of the handles of Grace's wheelchair. "Let's go, Gram. This is not the place for you." We left them to find a quiet corner by a window in a quiet nook. I poured Grace a glass of water. She took a sip, winced, held her jaw and pointed to The Secret Garden, peeking out of my bag. I opened it to the bookmark and read. "Every day she wondered about the mysterious garden, but she still could not find the door. 'There has to be a door,' she thought." I paused while Grace attempted another sip of water. I noticed a brown-clad worker moving from table to table, spraying each table from the same orange-labeled bottle I saw before, leaving puddles of liquid behind. Someone called to her from the kitchen. She placed the spray bottle on a nearby cleaning cart, peeled off the protective gloves she was wearing and dropped them into a nearby wastebasket.

"I'll be right back, Gram," I whispered. I lifted the spray bottle and read the label. "Oh my God!" I exhaled and glanced around. Moving quickly to the copy machine behind the nurses' station, I lay the bottle, label side down onto the copy bed. The light from the photocopier scanned the label. A single piece of paper shot out the side tray. Hearing voices, I quickly retreated to the cart and replaced the spray bottle, tucking the piece of paper under my sweater. The brown-clad, ruddy-faced kitchen worker hurried back and wheeled the cart away. I pulled out the crumpled paper and read it again.

> *HAZARDS TO HUMAN AND DOMESTIC ANIMALS CAUTION:*
> *Harmful if inhaled or absorbed through skin. Causes mucosal eye irritation. Avoid breathing vapors and contact with eyes, skin or clothing. Wash thoroughly with soap and water after handling. Remove contaminated clothing and wash clothing before reuse.*

Grace waited patiently for my return. She didn't see the person moving in behind her. Suddenly she felt a pair of strong hands grab at her wheelchair. Her chair swung around and she sped down the corridor into the atrium. "Who's back there?" she called. "Stop that. Where are you taking me?" The wheelchair turned into a side office. A stranger waited there. Crystal Ann came around from behind and stood next to him. "What's this about?" Grace demanded.

The man spoke to Crystal Ann. "Lonan Wing is not meant for long term care."

"She has nowhere else to go," Crystal Ann responded.

"She has a home," the man argued.

"She's not going back there," Crystal Ann answered. "That's not possible."

"Then where will I go?" Grace asked, bewildered and dismayed.

Crystal Ann pulled out her cell phone and walked into the hallway, speaking quickly. She listened intently as she stared at Grace through the window. Then she motioned for the man to come into the hallway. He took the phone and he also spoke, then listened, looking back at Grace. Then they both returned. The man closed his file and left the office.

"I should go home, now," Grace stated firmly. "The man said so."

"You're not going anywhere," Crystal Ann retorted flatly.

"It's my home, Crystal Ann."

Crystal Ann gripped the chair. "You signed the documents. You agreed."

Grace gasped for air but the oxygen had been sucked from the room. She felt herself drowning in blackness. "Please, God," she prayed. "Not now."

I folded the paper and tucked it into a pocket and returned to the nurses' station. Grace was gone. I scanned the adjoining hallway. I searched the dining room. I ran to the activity room. I looked in the beauty salon. I pushed open the door to the whirlpool room. I hurried down the corridor to her room. There she was, staring back at me from the shadows with a sad, shocked expression.

"Gram! What happened? What's wrong?"

"Where will I go now?" she asked, breathless.

Maire came into the room. "What's going on here?"

"I left her for only minutes and when I returned, she was gone. Now she's back in her room. Was she with you?" I demanded.

"Whoa! Back off!" Maire countered. Then she thought a moment. "Crystal Ann drove away as I drove up."

"Crystal Ann? I didn't see her."

"She must have been in stealth mode," Maire said dryly. "Ma, was Crystal Ann here?"

"Yes," Grace replied, struggling for words. "She and a man were arguing in the hallway."

"A man?" we repeated it in unison.

"He wasn't her husband," Grace went on. "He wasn't an appraiser and he wasn't a realtor."

Maire and I exchanged surprised glances. "Why do you think he may have been a realtor?" Maire pressed.

"No," Grace shook her head impatiently. "He wasn't a realtor. Crystal Ann said there should be no commotion. I'm worried. Where will I go now?"

Maire's arms flew around her mother's shoulders. "If I have to, I'll take you home with me. What's mine is yours, Ma."

"And what's mine is yours. Remember that. It's important."

'Where does the courage come from,' I wondered as I wrapped her in my arms. "Gram, you know we won't leave you. We will always be together. We are three cords of the same braid. We cannot be separated."

"Do you promise?"

"I promise, Gram." I transferred her to her bed and fluffed the pillows under her head.

Grace pushed herself up on the pillow. "You girls are so good to me."

"We love you, Ma," Maire answered.

"Well, I want to give something to you," she said, reaching for the top drawer of her jewelry case. She lifted out two pink envelopes. The envelopes were sealed. Across each back flap was a note written in her even steady handwriting.

> *Elle, thank you for all you do. I love you so much. What's mine is yours. Love, Grandma.*

> *Maire, thank you for the girly girl times, the giggles and the gossip. I love you so much. What's mine is yours. Love, Mom.*

Maire settled back into the blue chair. Grace settled into her pillows, her grip loosening on my hand as she drifted off to sleep, smiling. Maire headed for the door. "I need a cigarette."

"Go ahead. I'll meet you outside," I sighed, reaching for my bag. I walked past the nurses' station, through a set of security doors and into the vast, elegantly decorated foyer, past the swimming pool and exercise area, past the brightly striped awnings of Chez Clair and Café Sofie, to a small computer room. Within minutes a screen came to life and a site popped up for the State Department of Health and Human Services. I dialed the number.

Maire was waiting for me under the canopy behind Lonan Wing. "What do you think is in the envelopes?"

"Probably the last couple of dollars she had in her purse," I chuckled.

Maire flicked an ash from her cigarette and blew a puff into the crisp morning air. "They declare her incompetent, steal her home, lock her away from her friends and all the things she loves and threaten her not to talk about it? That's not crazy, that's sinister. She stared through the dark windows into Lonan Wing dining room. "You asked Bric to examine her jaw. Instead, Crystal Ann shows up to threaten her. Meanwhile, this thing is still growing inside her and no one has come to her aid. I will never, as long as I live, understand children who refuse to stand by their mother. Where are they? I'm going to the next care conference," she declared firmly. "They won't keep me out of the next one. I was raised to not ask questions. Well, I'm asking questions." She gazed back into the darkness of Lonan Wing. "The specialists and the primary care doctor relegate her care to her family. The family delegates her care to Blackwater Manor. Blackwater staff want her to be invisible until she dies so they can replace her with someone else who is invisible until he or she dies. If necessary, they'll sedate her to make it all go more smoothly. And they all pat themselves on the back. That's the politics of caregiving."

Grace woke to an empty room. She turned her eyes to the window where the finches scratched noisily at the bird feeders and the squirrels chased across the branches of the big oak tree. Loneliness overtook her. She needed her girls. She looked toward the door and waited. "I'm not done yet," she whispered.

Maire rushed through the door to her side. "No, Ma, you're not done. Not by a long shot. We're going to get you out of this dark tunnel and into the fresh air. Do you want to go outside?"

I pushed her wheelchair through a side corridor, into the shadows of an empty room. Across the room beckoned French doors covered with heavy curtains and blinds. "Where does this lead?" Grace asked. Maire pushed past us, reached for a cord and pulled. The curtains flew back and the blinds flipped open, flooding the room with light. A tumble of weeds and unruly trellises covered the walkway outside. Maire reached for the gleaming gold handles and pulled. The doors were locked.

Grace scanned the edges of the doorframe. She pointed to a key dangling from a hook. "Look there," she said. Maire placed it in the lock and turned the knob. The latch clicked. The doors opened. I rolled

Grace's wheel chair over the threshold. A squirrel scurried through the underbrush. A single robin sat high in the branch of the budding tree, overlooking Grace's bay window. Withered vines overtook little shoots in the underbrush.

"Look! Look what we found!" Grace breathed. "Life!

I reached down to whisper in her ear. "We'll bring it back, Gram."

"What are you doing out here?" Poppy stood behind us.

Grace turned defensively. "It's my garden. I found it."

"Why is it locked away?" I asked.

"The resident gardener died last year. We closed it up."

"It's just outside Gram's window. We'll plant some things so she can see them from her room." Poppy shrugged and retreated, her Yorkie bouncing behind her.

I reached to uncover a garden hose, half-hidden in the underbrush. "Gram, do you see this hose?" She reached to hold the nozzle. "When our thoughts and hearts get twisted and kinked like this hose we cannot function as we are meant to be."

She turned the nozzle over in her hand thoughtfully. "Yes, I see."

"And your point is?" Maire asked.

"My point is that Crystal Ann and Bric and Acer and all the rest do their best to twist and contort Gram's spirit." I smiled at Grace. "It is our job to stay calm and fluid, so our energy can flow."

"Hmmm," Maire answered. "I don't know about your hose theory, but I do know that we have work to do before this garden will function."

"Let's call your faithful gardener," I exclaimed.

The next afternoon Liam appeared. "Happy Mother's Day, Mom." He embraced her with a hug and a kiss.

"Mother's Day is over," she smiled.

"Every day is Mother's Day, Mom."

"Oh, you!" She attempted a smile as her hand flew to her jaw. She winced, tears streaming down her cheek. Liam studied the lump.

"Let me take a look at that."

Grace's eyes widened with mischief. "First I have to tell you a secret."

"What's that?" He grinned and leaned in closer.

"I've stolen a garden!" She lowered her voiced. "But I think it's mostly dead."

Liam pushed her through the French doors. There stood a bag of seeds and gardening tools. "Do you think this will help?"

"Oh you!" Her hand flew to her jaw again. "You knew?"

Liam spread his arms wide and turned in a wide circle. "This garden's not dead! It's as alive as you and me!"

"Can we make it bloom?"

"I bet my reputation as a gardener! Soon you will look through your bedroom window and see blooms full of life."

"I have my own secret garden." Grace beamed and her hand flew to her jaw.

"Why don't you and I take a look at that bump while Elle and Maire get things ready?"

"All right," Grace agreed reluctantly. "You girls can get started, but don't do any planting without me."

"We won't, Gram."

Liam gripped the handles of the wheelchair. "Has anyone else come to examine her?"

"You are the only one who has responded. Something is very wrong."

"Yes," he said. "I'll take a look." He leaned in to study Grace's face.

She looked at him quizzically. "Liam, how will I pay you?"

"You know, Mom, all I ever need is a hug and a banana!" She nodded and smiled. "You are a good son."

The warm sun shining through Grace's window lured us every day to her garden. Grace, bundled in a warm woolen shawl, proudly displayed her strawberry patterned garden gloves. She scooped up the soft dirt, dropping it into a nearby pot, patting it firmly around the base of each new plant. She still could laugh, gingerly holding her jaw as two squirrels played hide and seek under the tree and rabbits chased through new shoots of grass. She scraped at the dirt around a clump of crocuses peeking through. Each day when the sun set and it was time to come inside, Grace turned back for one more look. "This is good," she whispered. "I'll come back every day and do more," she said to the little plants. "I promise."

Grace's garden was as close to magic as she could get without flying away. She spent hours gazing at the clouds, soaking up the sun. It was there that her countenance became serene and the gaunt, pained look diminished. "I would like to live in this garden," Grace sighed. "Its so peaceful here, so full of pleasure." I grabbed the camera from my bag and let the shutter click happily away as Grace moved from leafy plants to blossoms. The green straw brim of her hat blended with the colors around her as she became one with the garden. The door to the garden was Grace's way out of the wilderness. Although she found rest for her spirit, she unfortunately, could find no rest from the pain. Still there was no appointment made to examine the thing growing in her jaw.

As the pain grew in intensity Grace and I developed a rhythm to minimize her need to speak. When she needed to transfer, she extended her hand, I placed her arms around my neck, she leaned forward and rose. Although the aides watched us together, they defiantly did not change their behavior.

One afternoon I had just left Grace in the bathroom, leaving the door ajar, when Tillie and Novalee slipped past, slamming the door in my face. 'Very well,' I thought. 'Let's see how you manage.' I opened the door and looked in. Tillie was demanding that she stand. She could not. Novalee was arguing. She ignored her. They knew they couldn't force her while I stood there. Finally Tillie stepped back and asked me to help. I placed Grace's arms around my neck. She leaned forward and I eased her back into her chair. It took minutes. Then Tillie wheeled Grace back to her bed. Novalee braced herself in front of the walker.

"Shall we stand up?" Novalee demanded.

"Well, you can stand if you want to." Grace answered.

"Shall we get into bed?" Tillie ordered.

Grace's eyes darkened. "Well, you two get into bed if you want to get there so badly."

Novelee rolled her eyes impatiently and changed her tone from impatient to patronizing. "We'd like to help you if you'd just cooperate, Grace."

"Do what you want. Do what you want." Grace turned her gaze to the window.

Novelee turned to me in desperation. I followed Grace's gaze. The branches of the trees moved slowly with the wind. The squirrels performed a balancing act as the robin looked on from the fence. I waited. When Grace finally placed her arms around my neck, I eased her up, being careful not to brush against her jaw. She wiggled her right foot around and pivoted into the bed. When she could feel the bed against her leg she reached with her left hand, touched the bed and sat down. It was a textbook maneuver. Then Tillie suddenly grabbed Grace's ankles and lifted her legs high, twisting her body onto the bed. Grace clenched her fists and stifled a scream, grinding her knuckles into her forehead. I brushed Tillie aside and threw my arms around her.

"Gram?"

Grace nodded valiantly. She unclenched her fists, put her hands softly against each side of my face and offered up a weak smile. I positioned her back against the soft pillow.

Maire stood in the doorway, watching the scene. She lay a warm wash cloth against her cheek. "Every day, Ma, I pray to God to remove this thing; to give unto you power to tread on serpents and scorpions, and over all the power of the enemy and nothing shall by any means hurt you."

Grace patted her hand. "Thank you, dear."

Maire fell to her knees at Grace's bedside. "I know God's word is. I know you have God's favor. You should be healed. Have I said the word wrong?"

Grace smiled softly. "No, dear. We can be hurt. What we pray for is that our spirit will be strong." Grace gazed upon her daughter's face. "What do you think heaven is like?"

Maire, shocked by the question, recovered quickly. "Ma, I see you running through grass, barefoot like Elle, as carefree as the squirrels and rabbits."

"Or flying," Grace added, "flying free with the red bird and the robin."

"I love you, Ma."

"I love you so much," Grace whispered and closed her eyes. "Let's say our prayers now."

"What do you want to pray for, Ma?" Maire asked.

"I pray for myself," Grace answered.

"Really, Ma?"

"Of course. If I don't, who will?"

"Ma," Maire smiled, "you never cease to amaze me. How about you, Elle? What will you pray for?"

I moved to Grace's side. "Let's pray for rain so we don't have to water the tomatoes!"

Maire burst out laughing. Grace attempted a grin. "Oh, you girls! I'm so glad you're here."

I arrived Sunday to accompany Grace to the TV Mass. The round-faced clock pointed to 6:45 a.m. Grace was still asleep, despite Wanetta's screams shrieking through the hallway. Six forty-five turned to seven fifteen. Maire came through the doorway. "Raven's down the corridor. She's avoiding us. I think she's frustrated. She would have had Mom strapped into the lift machine by now, hoisted into the air and dragged to the bathroom by her armpits if we weren't here."

"Well, we are here and it's not going to happen."

"Right. Unfortunately, that means she will probably miss that TV Mass."

"Right about now, I'm thinking Grace has God's every blessing. She doesn't need to go to a TV Mass to get that."

"Well, then we'll just sit here and watch the birds." Maire sighed. "I think the birds must be God's way of apologizing for what we have to go through here."

When Grace finally woke, we transferred easily and found soft comfortable clothes to wear. She was in intense pain. She sipped on apple juice, but struggled to swallow. She was withdrawn and disoriented. Maire frowned. "It's like a tomb in here." I flung the curtains open. Warm sunshine streamed through the room. Grace immediately brightened. "Here is a woman,' I thought, 'hungry and in pain, still struggling to find her way in a very dark wilderness.'

Later that evening Grace made a valiant effort to attend a concert in the chapel. "Where shall I go?" she asked. "Right up here? See them? Watch there. This will be nice tonight. Very good." Maire shuddered and moved in close, tucking a warm woolen throw around her shoulders. Grace smiled and continued with her discourse. "See her there with her pink jacket? Now he's walking out into the hall." Her thoughts were disjointed and scattered, but she fought through the haze to find normalcy. "That's all right, then. We'll do this together. We're together now."

Wheeling back to the Lonan Wing, we stopped at the library. I picked up *Healing And The Mind*, by Bill Moyers and read aloud. "When the mind is present in the heart, we call it happiness." Grace smiled. I paused as I scanned the next words. "I can see you gather, such an unlikely family, and I know I can find my way home." I read on. "We know that anxiety aggravates illness. We cannot just prescribe medication and walk away. This is medical neglect. Touch is medicine's real professional secret. Families can interfere with medicine or they can be the medicine." I stopped to gaze at Grace, who was listening intently. She nodded and patted my hand.

"That's you," she said. "You are good medicine."

I continued. "The terrible doctor robs the patient of hope." I stopped and leaned forward to kiss her cheek. "Remember what Liam told you, Gram." She smiled and nodded again.

"It'll be all right," she murmured. Then she looked into the distance. "I miss my grandmother."

The next morning I received a call from Giselle. She said that Grace threw up all night. I grabbed my bag and headed for my car. When I walked into Grace's room, I found Nicole and Christina, a new trainee, leaning over Grace, poking at the lump on Grace's jaw. Grace tried to push her away. Christina brushed Grace's hand back. "Don't touch it," I ordered.

"You should leave," she blurted back.

"Unless you are a registered nurse, and qualified to examine my grandmother, I will stay and you will leave," I bristled. Grace grasped my hand. "Have you been throwing up, Gram?"

"I'm all right now," she whispered.

"Would you like to lie down?" She nodded, her sad eyes fixed on mine. I lifted her to her bed and nestled her into her pillow, caressing her forehead. She lay ominously still. I recalled words from the book. 'It is important to become partners with those for whom we care. We should be able to do that better now because we understand so much more about not only the body but also the mind.'

Thoughts of Grace lingered as the big bus lumbered through the dense gray mist rolling past my window. "What keeps us going?" I asked aloud. Jerry leaned his back against the window, pondering the question. "Fear of letting someone down. Fear of letting ourselves down."

The tattooed iron worker leaned forward and rested her chin on the top of the seat, her graceful arms draping forward. "The promises we make. Knowing other people depend on us. Knowing we are not nothing."

Jerry nodded. "Knowing we are not alone. Knowing that someone cares gives us strength to fight harder to be the best we can."

"Do you think if our lives were easier, if the road wasn't so steep, we would be the same people with the same stories?" I asked.

Jerry looked away. "No, but I sure wouldn't mind coasting downhill for a spell." We laughed and with laughter, the conversation turned. He hummed an old

Gospel tune. She harmonized. I joined them. Three heads together, we sang softly, almost at whisper level. Despite the large sign at the front of the bus stating *BE CONSIDERATE. KEEP YOUR MUSIC AND YOUR CONVERSATIONS TO YOURSELVES,* no one in the bus asked us to stop. Grace sang along, like a little bird chirping in joy.

Sometime during that night I fell into a deep sleep. As I slept I drifted through an unfathomable void. An image grew from the far reaches of the darkness, at first minute and indistinguishable, then looming forward. His hat was cocked over one eye. His eyes were a brilliant blue, twinkling with mirth. He was handsome with a lilting smile. His nose was strong and straight. His hair was thick and curly, tumbling onto a prominent brow. His cheeks were rosy and full of life. The face moved closer. Finally, his nose nearly touching mine, his eyes widened as he stared intensely into my own. Then he suddenly drew back, grinned from ear to ear and exclaimed loudly, "Do you like my shoes?"

I woke with a start. "No offense," Jerry said, "but you're as tense as a stone. Why don't you let me give you a shoulder massage?"

"That's all right," Grace whispered. "That's fine."

"That's fine," I nodded.

"Where are you headed?" he asked.

"Oregon."

"It must be good to know where you are going."

"You don't know where you're going?"

"The landscape has changed." He dropped his hand from my shoulder, lifted a bag from under his feet and settled it on his lap. "I get off at the next stop." We both stared out his window at the murky mist as the tattooed iron worker hoisted her bags to the front of the bus. He followed her, stopping in the aisle to turn back. "Maybe the journey never ends. Maybe it just keeps changing direction. Life is more random than we know."

"Be careful," Grace called after them. "Take care of yourselves and don't get hurt. What was that boy's name?"

"That was a girl, Gram. She just looked like a boy. Her hair was pulled back and she was all tattoo and muscle. I don't know her name." I thought about that. I grew close to them both in such a short time and I didn't even know her name.

"Being with you made them feel good," Grace said. I smiled at the thought. Sonja glanced over the top of the book she was reading and smiled back.

The driver turned to scan the faces from the front to the back of the bus. "Next stop is Billings, folks. We'll be delayed there until the connecting bus arrives."

Sonja reached over the aisle to touch my sleeve. "We'll be stuck there for hours. Are you going to dinner?"

"Oh, yes!" Grace answered. "Let's go!"

I arrived at Blackwater Manor to find Grace in the dining room alone. "Gram, did you have anything to eat?" She looked up at me wearily. "Never mind," I said. "We'll go over to Café Sofie."

We passed by several staff workers including the physical therapy assistant standing in the hallway. They averted their eyes. "They don't speak to me anymore." Grace whispered.   Seated in the atrium outside Café Sofie, Grace sipped on orange juice and water. There was a bruise and a large knot on her finger. There were more skin tears on the palms of her hands. An aide sauntered past, her long curly ponytail jauntily flipping from side to side.

"Excuse me. Can you find a nurse to examine these skin breaks?" She shrugged and bounced away.

"See?" Grace said. "That's the way they are."

I reached for the brightly striped tote bag I had packed that morning. Maire had phoned to tell me to take a camera and a pocket tape recorder. "Find some surveillance equipment," she suggested. "Surveillance equipment is the size of an eraser and totally cordless."

"Gram, do you mind if I take a picture of your hands and arms and legs?"

"Why?" She asked warily.

"I want to document what you are going through."

"OK, then," she answered.   "That's all right. That's good."

By late afternoon the pain hit her hard. Grace couldn't get her thoughts around standing up. "I'm afraid of it," she whispered.

I found Liddy at the nurses' station. "That's a job for an aide," she sniffed impatiently. I gingerly transferred Grace to the bed. We sat together, helpless against the pain. An hour passed. Jansina came through the door, stared blankly at Grace and left. The round-faced clock ticked on as Grace slept. The door suddenly flung open again with a bang. An aide

I didn't recognize walked directly up to Grace and reached over her to clumsily fasten a silver clip and a cord to her pillow.

"What?" Grace woke, startled.

"What are you doing?" I demanded. "She was sleeping."

"Well, we have to make sure she doesn't roll out of her bed," she argued.

"I'm sitting right next to her. Besides, that doesn't keep her from rolling out. It only alerts you when she does. Let her rest."

Grace drifted back to sleep. It seemed that we were both drifting through an endless dark, vaporous tunnel.

The door again swung open, flooding the room with light from the hallway. Aubery flashed the bright beam of her flashlight directly into Grace's eyes. Grace woke again with a start. Aubery leaned into her face. "We just wanted to make sure you were sleeping, Grace."

"Well, I'm not now," Grace replied. "Go away."

As the days passed, Grace fought valiantly to break through the darkness closing in. Maire arrived to take Grace to a concert in the chapel. Grace placed a pink hat on her head. Then she took it off and replaced it with the turquoise one. She peered at her reflection in the mirror. Then she took the hat off and reached for a third.

"Ma! We're late," Maire urged. "You don't need the hat."

"Yes, I do," Grace replied calmly.

Maire stared at her mother's reflection. The growth on her jaw now distorted her mouth, pulling it to the side of her face. "Ma! You're beautiful without it."

"They need to see me in my hats."

"Why?"

"They need to see that our lives are important, that we matter."

"Take your time," Maire whispered. "We've got all the time in the world."

On the way back from the concert, Grace reached her hand out to touch hands of residents passing by. Maire realized just how foolish we were to imagine we could control this angry force consuming her. Her hat covered the mind-shattering scream rising up from her soul. She reached out in the hope that she might comfort others passing through that void. When the two got back to Grace's room, there was a note from Quin.

> *Hi Mom. Sorry I missed you. You were at*
> *the music concert. See you tomorrow.*

Maire stared at the note. The color drained from her face. She grabbed her phone and dialed. My phone beeped.

"This has been going on for over a month! Quin finally shows up and doesn't stay because we are in a little concert? This is bullshit! How do we know that this thing growing inside her mouth isn't a result of the Fosamax or Boniva or whatever else they are giving her with just a Dixie cup of water? How do we know this can't be fixed?"

"What are you saying?" Grace looked up annoyed. "Don't talk about me. I'm right here!"

The light on the email machine flashed. Maire reached over to pull an email from the print tray.

There was a photo of Grace wearing the green hat, sitting by the tree in her garden. "You and I took this picture," Maire said into the phone. Then she read from the email.

> Hi Mom,
> I will be coming tomorrow to take you to the clinic. I will ride with you in the wheelchair van to the doctor's office. It will be early in the morning. I will come to your room and I will be looking for you, the beautiful lady in the pretty hat.

"Mom has been waiting for months for this appointment. Neither Quin nor Crystal Ann bother to come here and tell her personally. What a strange family you have, Ma."

Grace wrinkled her nose. "It's your family too."

"How unfortunate for all of us," I answered back through the phone.

"Do you want to read Crystal Ann's email?" Maire held the paper out to Grace.

"Not really," Grace shook her head.

"Shall I just put it in the waste basket?"

"No," Grace answered. "She'll ask if we threw it away. Just put it on the edge there. That's what I do. It'll just fall into the basket on its own."

"Ma," Maire laughed. "Every day I learn something new about you."

"Oh, you," she scoffed. "Shhhh! Here comes the fat crow. Don't let her hear." Dimmae and Sol Bump headed toward them. Raven was not far behind.

"We're taking Grace to her bath now," Dimmea announced.

Maire stared at Sol. "Why are you here? Certainly you are not going with my mother to her bath."

"No, no," he sputtered. "Crystal Ann phoned. Grace needs to be ready to go in the morning."

Raven joined in. "Crystal Ann doesn't want any delays."

"Battle," I whispered into the phone.

Maire circled her arm around Grace's shoulder. "Mom is ready for bed. She's finally had something to eat, no thanks to your staff. She will not be taking a bath at this late hour." She eyed Raven and Dimmea. "And she doesn't need any more trauma." Dimmea stiffened and stomped away.

Sol moved closer. "Hello, Grace," he offered flatly. She looked past him with disinterest. He shrugged and left. Raven followed.

The next morning Maire stood with Grace as Crystal Ann rounded the corner. "We'll take you to the clinic, now, Mom," she announced. Grace stared at her. "I'm here to take you to the clinic, Mom," Crystal Ann repeated. "Do you remember? I know you got my email."

Grace ignored her patronizing tone. She held her jaw and spoke slowly. "Crystal Ann, I'd like to stop for ice cream on the way back from the clinic. I have money in my purse. I'll buy."

"Oh, that's not necessary, Mom. We'll be in a hurry to get there and back."

"No, Crystal Ann, we'll stop for ice cream. I'm looking forward to it." Grace smiled and patted Maire's hand.

"It may soothe her throat," Maire added. "She may be able to swallow it."

Crystal Ann pushed Maire back. "Maire's not going. There's no room. It's just us, today, Mom. Maire can wait here if she wants. Just us, Mom," she repeated. Grace tightened her grip on Maire's hand.

"I'll be right, here, Ma," Maire assured her.

"All right, then," Grace loosened her grasp. "We'll go." She looked back through the window, waved and smiled as the van pulled out of the parking lot and down the street. Maire reached for her phone and dialed.

"Meet me at Perkins," she said quietly. "We'll have lunch while we wait."

I found Maire in her favorite booth. She pushed a paper across the table. "This is what I pulled out of the email machine."

Subject: Mom's issues

About four weeks ago, a small lump developed on Mom's left side of her face, below her ear, in the area of her jaw bone. Dr. Corbin prescribed two different antibiotics for possible infection. The lump did not respond to that treatment, and continues to grow. She has been able to wear her dentures, and has had no trouble eating or talking. She does get Tylenol for occasional pain. An ultrasound was done last week, revealing some cellular growth and accumulated fluid. Mom is to have a CT scan, a needle biopsy and fluid drainage. The material

*will be tested for cytology and cultures. Bric
and Lyssa will be with her during and after
the procedures. We will keep you updated
as more information becomes available.*

Thanks, Crystal Ann.

Maire fumed. "Mom saw Dr. Corbin? She's been taking antibiotics? She has no trouble eating or talking? She's wearing her dentures? An ultrasound was done? Liars!" The people in the next booth turned to look. She waved apologetically.

When we returned to Blackwater Manor, we found Grace at the dining room table in tears. "What happened?" Maire asked, scanning the room. "Where's Crystal Ann? Didn't you stop for ice cream?"

"No, the driver of the van ordered it through the drive through. She wouldn't have any. She just put it into the freezer and left me here."

Maire headed for the hallway. "I'll go get it right now and we'll have our treat together, just us girls." She returned seconds later, her face flushed with anger. "This is what you ordered?"

"No." Grace's disappointment was clear. "Crystal Ann said we should have Jack's favorite, instead."

"Who could be that cruel to her own mother?"

"Never mind." Grace held her jaw. "You're here now. It's all right."

Maire knelt beside her mother. "Tell me, Ma, what did Dr. Corbin say about that lump on your jaw?"

Grace looked stricken. "I didn't see Dr. Corbin."

"What?"

"The nurse took a biopsy. They talked to each other, but not to me." She sighed and shook her head.

Supper was something chopped up on a plate. Maire mashed it and Grace nibbled a bit. Then we strolled through the hallways, past the stained glass windows of the cool, quiet chapel. We stopped to admire the blooming plants along the walkways leading to Café Sofie where Grace ordered the ice cream that Crystal Ann had denied her. We sat in the atrium savoring the sweet cool treat and each other's company. Then we wheeled back to her room. The email machine was spitting out a new message. Maire scanned the paper.

Subject: Mom's biopsy results

Mom's biopsy tissue pathology report showed the presence of lymphoma. Her primary doctor will consult with Bric and Quin and oncology specialists to determine possible treatment. Bric and Quin welcome your phone calls if you have questions.

Maire stuffed the paper into her bag. She stared at me then she turned to Grace. "This is how they tell her?"

The morning after the Grace's appointment at the clinic, she woke in the grip of pain. Maire stood at the nurses' station. "Liddy," can you give Mom something for the pain?"

"No," she answered dryly. "I have to work myself up to do that."

"Liddy," Maire shot back, "this isn't about you. My mother needs help."

An hour passed and again Maire strode to the nurses' station. "Will you call whoever is in charge of her care and ask what can be done?" Codi stepped up to the counter.

"We gave her five milligrams of Oxycodene yesterday. That seemed to work." She poured the red liquid into a cup and tipped it to Grace's lips.

Another hour passed as Maire and I wheeled Grace through the atrium. We took our time strolling back through the indoor village, past shop windows and the beauty salon. When we finally returned to Lonan Wing we were met with a flurry of activity. Nurses, CNAs and aides scurried in and out of doorways.

"What's going on?"

"Who knows? These people are out of control." Maire pushed open the door to Grace's room, then recoiled from a stench of excrement. Through the dark I saw a shadow of a figure in the blue chair. I flipped on the light. An aide knelt in front of a large muscular girl. Two more aides pushed past us.

"Adesea is aggressive," another aide explained. "Keep Grace back."

Gram had described her accurately. She looked strong like a farmhand. "Her room is nicer than mine," she growled. "I'm going to stay here." Giselle, Codi and two aides looked on, helpless.

"How many times has this girl been in my grandmother's room?" I demanded. "She's defecated in the chair!"

Maire stood at my side. She turned on Giselle. "You blamed my mother for lipstick smeared into the carpet? You laughed when she talked about a girl in her room. Now here she is! You knew about her all this time and didn't tell us. Instead, you made it look like Mom was the one that was unstable."

Codi spoke into a two-way radio. "We found Adesea. Bring a security guard and some cleaning solution. We have a problem here."

I reached across Adesea to a little flower pot holding several pens wrapped in green ribbon and pink velvet roses. "Take this with you back to your apartment, Adesea. See here? It's a pen."

Adesea snatched it from my hand. "I know what that is. I saw them here before. I already took one."

I turned to Giselle and Codi. "She is angry and strong. She could easily have hurt my grandmother or scared her terribly. Is she a resident?"

"She is tricky," one of the aides whispered to me. I thought of all the times that Grace used that word to describe what had happened.

Grace watched from the doorway. "Gram, has this woman been here before?"

"Yes," Grace nodded firmly. "I told you. She was mad-wild." Suddenly Adesea stood, holding the rose firm in her grip, and lumbered out the doorway. Codi followed her out as the aides hurried to clean the seat of the chair. "Good riddance," Grace gasped. "She stinks."

We left them to their work and headed through the corridors to Grace's garden. Quin met us in the hallway.

"How are you, Mom?"

"Not so good."

He chuckled, hands in pockets. "You know, it's been a tough year for everyone." He rocked on his heels and made his voice sound like an old farmer.

"The tractor broke down, the mower quit." He flashed a foolish grin and rocked back and forth on his heels.

She looked at him in disbelief. "What are you saying?" Quin just chuckled and rocked.

"What's your plan?" Maire moved to stand squarely between them.

"The plan?"

"The care plan for this growth on her jaw. It has been months now."

He dropped the comedy routine and his voice was taut. "I met with the oncologist. There is a better treatment; one that can be injected once a week. We think she'll tolerate that much better than chemo."

"Are you saying now that it is cancer?"

"Well, no, it's not...It's a difficult thing to know," he stammered. With that, he backed away, turned and disappeared through a set of glass doors, out through a side garden to the street.

Stunned, Grace let out a piercing scream. "Oh, no! No! No! No! Quin! No!"

Maire thrust the doors open and I pushed Grace through. "Quin!" I called across the garden. "Stop! She's not ready for you to leave."

He knelt beside her chair. Shaking and sobbing, she turned her face to his, clinging to him with one hand, holding her jaw with the other. "Is this cancer?"

"No, we don't think so. We don't know."

"Can you fix it?"

"Yes, but it won't be easy. It may take surgery."

"I am strong, Quin. Do whatever it takes to fix it."

"I need to leave," he said quietly.

She grasped his hand, pleading. "When will you come back?"

"I'll be back soon."

"Do you promise?"

"I promise."

"Will you fix this?"

"Yes."

"Do you promise?"

"Yes, I promise," he answered quietly.

The three of us watched him walk away. I turned her wheel chair toward a side garden. There we met a woman, strolling. "I love your hat, Grace," she called. Grace brightened, tears streaming down her cheeks.

The next morning I found Grace in the beauty salon. She held her jaw and stared straight ahead. "Gram?"

"It's very painful."

Amelia walked in with red liquid in a cup. "What are you giving her?"

"It's Oxy."

Loree, the nursing director, came up from behind. "I understand you are trying to tell my staff how to lift Grace."

"What? Where is this coming from? We are talking about pain medication."

"I'm talking about the instructions you give my staff."

"They cannot lift her from under her arms and drag her to where they want her to go. She is in excruciating pain. It is pointless for your staff to argue with her." Her eyes blazed but she remained stoic. "I realize it is frustrating for your staff to stand by when they have an obviously tight schedule, but they cannot be impatient with her."

"Their level of frustration does not come from Grace," she spat out. "It comes from you and Maire."

"I'm telling you the reality of the situation. Grace is a two-person lift and you do not have enough staff available."

Maire came through the door behind her and stepped beside me. "Your short career is full of violations, Loree. I'm sure you don't want any more."

Loree squared her shoulders. "It's obvious I can't discuss this with you when you are this hostile."

I stepped between them. "We're not hostile, Loree. We're watchful. Maire's mother, my grandmother, is in desperate need of care and this facility is not capable of providing it."

"I think we're done here," she snapped.

As Loree huffed away, Cecilia appeared. "There's no one to help me take her to the bathroom," she announced. "You'll have to help me."

Maire shook her head in disbelief. "Really?"

Cecilia squared off in front of Grace. "Stand up, Grace. We can't lift you. You'll have to reach for the bar. Stand up, now, Grace." I slid between them. Grace reached for me and I easily transferred her.

"See? I can do it if you help me," Grace said to Amelia. Her voice was soft but firm. The transfer from the toilet to the chair to the bed also went without mishap and was nearly complete. Grace was still wearing her hat. I was thinking that I would remove it when her head was on the pillow, but Cecilia reached over my arm and snatched it. Grace clung to the brim, pulling it down tight to her head. Cecilia pulled harder. Grace pinned her elbows tight to her side, gripping it with all her might. I took a deep breath and again stepped between them, placing my arm behind her head as she settled into the pillow.

"Are you comfortable?"

Her lips pursed. She glared at Cecilia and then at me and then at Maire. I placed her rosary in her hands. She rolled the beads between her fingers. That calmed her. I placed her hat next to her on the bed and put a CD in the player. Soft music filled the room. Her eyes closed.

I watched her as she slept, clinging to her rosary with one hand and her hat with the other. My heart ached. 'If serenity awaits her,' I thought, 'she no longer has the energy to reach for it. God will have to bring it to her.'

The next morning Maire and I found Cecilia forcing a large pill, buried in a spoonful of pudding into Grace's mouth. Grace gagged, winced and held her jaw. Minutes later the pill and pudding were down the front of her blouse.

"What did you give her?" Maire demanded.

"Tylenol."

"So you're back to the Tylenol now?" I asked.

"It's our discretion."

"You do realize she can't swallow?" Maire charged. I turned the wheelchair away.

"Grace ruined my shoe!" Cecila called after us.

"What?" Maire spun around to face her.

"Grace rolled her wheelchair over my foot and ruined my shoe. What are you going to do about it?"

"Are you kidding me? How can she run over your foot when she can't move her own chair?"

"She ruined my shoe!"

"Oh, for heaven's sake. This is pathetic. Here's a twenty. Go buy another sneaker."

Quin stood watching from the nurses' station. "The nurse said she was fine this morning," he muttered. He turned to Grace. "Are you in pain?"

"Yes, terrible pain," she cried.

Quin turned back to Cecilia. "Please assist my mother into bed for a nap. We'll wait here."

I waited impatiently in the hallway with Maire and Quin. Minutes later Grace shrieked in pain. Quin didn't move. "We'll wait," he said. Maire shuddered. Grace screamed again. I rushed to her door. Cecilia and an aide were dragging her by her armpits to her chair. I bolted in.

Stop! I demanded. Quin pushed past me.

Grace faced him. "You said you'd come back. You promised to help me."

He shuffled his feet and shifted his hands to his pockets. He didn't have to answer. Mary Caye breezed in behind him.

"Hi Mamma! I took your advice and cut my hair. What do you think?"

Maire leaned close to my ear. "That's a wig. Does she think we're idiots that we don't know that?"

Mary Caye wheeled Grace back into the hallway and down the corridor to Lonan Wing dining room. Quin followed Mary Caye. Maire and I followed Quin.

Amelia stopped me at the nurses' station. "Why didn't you tell me that Grace spit out her pills this morning? You should have told me. I'm the nurse in charge."

"Don't you instruct your staff to communicate with you?"

"I had to hear it from Dr. Riorden!"

"Then you have been informed."

"I should not have had to hear that from a doctor. You should have told me."

I stepped forward. "In what universe do you imagine it is appropriate for you to talk to me this way?" She backed away and I turned my attention to the dining room where Mary Caye cooed and Quin hovered. 'These are the children she raised,' I thought. 'She needs to be with them and they need to be with her. She knows their behavior cannot, at this late date, be altered. The time for that has long passed. She has to accept them for what they are.'

Quin and Mary Caye left as Maire's daugher, Celia, and her sons arrived. Not long after, Ursula and her children appeared unexpectedly. The grandchildren and great grandchildren nuzzled close to Grace, touching her hands and resting their heads against her knee. Maire circled the group, snapping photos. Ursula, immersed in a phone conversation, turned away from the camera.

"Who are you talking to?" Maire asked. Ursula cupped her ear with her hand. Maire scowled. "She hasn't seen her mother in months, but she can't be bothered to take a picture. She's been on the phone the whole time. Does she think Mom doesn't notice that?"

"Do you think it's odd that they all came today?" I wondered.

"I'm guessing the siblings are here because they are having some sort of family meeting." Maire looked back at the children gathered around Grace. "They are probably plotting how to divide up her things."

Mary Caye returned just as Celia and the boys and Ursula and her children were leaving. "I'm tired now," Grace said, rubbing her forehead. "My head hurts."

"Oh, Mama," Mary Caye gushed, "I'll push you back to your room. I have a surprise for you."

As the two of them entered Grace's room, we heard Grace gasp, "What is that?"

"What the hell?" Maire pushed past her and stood at Grace's bed. A huge bulge protruded from the red quilted bedspread. There was a red plaid flannel shirt stuffed with pillows. A John Deere cap crowned a pillow head which stuck up out of the red plaid collar.

"It's Daddy!" Mary Caye announced, clapping her hands.

"Take it away. Get it out of here! Now!" Grace demanded, her hand flying to her jaw. Mary Caye reluctantly removed the pillows, the shirt and the John Deere cap.

"I'm sorry, Mamma. I thought it would make you feel better."

"I'm tired," Grace sighed.

I stood at the exit, staring blankly after Mary Caye as she drove away. "Who are these people?"

"I think the Botox has gone to her brain," Maire said. "Listen, I have something to tell you."

"I have something to tell you, too," I interrupted, "but we never have a moment to talk." I pulled the letter from Chicago out of my bag.

She peered into the distant sky. "Celia is moving to the West Coast. She needs me to help her with the children. I don't know what to do."

"Oh," I said slowly, stuffing the letter back into my bag. "Well, you have to go." She shook her head. "What about Mom? Who will look out for her?"

"You and I have carried Gram this far. We'll cross this threshold together. There's no going back. You will always be with Grace. Grace will always be with you. You have to go. The good news is that you're not stuck anymore."

Maire shook her head, not convinced. "And the bad news?"

"The bad news is that we know how this will end, Maire."

"I should be here."

"You will be. Remember, a braid of three cords cannot be broken."

"We weren't the ones she wanted, but we were the ones she let in. Many are called but few are chosen. We don't need Crystal Ann's email machine to communicate. We don't need important labels like doctor, or nurse or number one son to feed our egos. We have no guarantees, but we have Grace."

"Freedom goes to the highest bidder," I said. "But, Grace doesn't bargain. I think she trusts us because we love her unconditionally."

Her eyes met mine. "I think she trusts us because we are the only ones here." She stared through the window, shaking her head. "I never meant to hurt her."

"What do you mean?"

"I never accepted that I was her child. I didn't look like her. I didn't fit in. I thought she always preferred to have someone else around. Now I know that although our life was far from perfect, we had the best life she could give us. I took it all for granted. She'll never know how much I love her."

"She knows."

"I can't tell her goodbye, Elle. You'll have to do it for me."

The bus rolled on as the past, the present and the future seemed to me like parallel rivers rolling into a wide sea. Yoki slid into the seat next to me. "The researcher said you were working on a riddle?"

"The sixth of seven clues."

"What is it?"

"*What exalts as often as it shames?*"

"Before this ride is over," he said, "I'll tell you a story that may help you with that."

She feels locked in her own life
Scared of what she might lose
If she moves away from who she was
And she's afraid of being free
There's a way she knows is right
And she can't feel the things she knows and so each step
she's taking
Is a step of faith towards who she'll be

The End Of The Tunnel

The lights go out all around me
One last candle to keep out the night
And then the darkness surrounds me
I know i'm alive but i feel like i've died
And all that's left is to accept that it's over
My dreams ran like sand through the fists that i made
I try to keep warm but i just grow colder
I feel like i'm slipping away

"Your grandmother wants to say her prayers," announced an unidentified voice.

"Who is this?" I demanded.

Grace sobbed into the phone. "She wouldn't listen. She wouldn't stop. She wouldn't stop."

I was already in the car, turning the key in the ignition. It was after 10:00 p.m. Lonan Wing doors would already be locked. I doubted they would let me in. Foreboding gripped me. "Gram, are you in bed now? Are you hurt? Do you want to say prayers?"

"That would be good," she sobbed.

"Angel of God," I began, struggling to hold back my own tears.

"That's right," she said. "That's right."

"Gram, do you want me to sing you a little song?"

"OK."

I sang softly. "You are my sunshine, my only sunshine." She became quieter. "Does that make you feel better?"

"No. Not tonight." She was sinking in a sea of pain and desolation. She was drowning in darkness. "No more. No more."

"I'll be there at sunrise, Gram. I promise."

"She wouldn't stop. She wouldn't stop!"

The phone went quiet. "Gram may forgive you devils," I hissed at the darkness, "but her God never will!"

I arrived at Lonan Wing at dawn, the sound of my grandmother's agonized sobs echoing in my head and in my heart. I slipped through a side exit to a terrifying awareness that her sobs were now echoing through the hallway. I rushed to her room. She wasn't there. Then I heard her cry out. I rushed in the direction of her voice, past the cold monster lift machine looming ominously nearby. I saw bodies huddled together by the nurses' station. As I moved closer, I realized that Grace was trapped in the middle. Tillie, Dimmae, Amelia, Cassie, Emily, Tristan, Giselle and Cherilee heckled and taunted, pushing the doll to her as she pushed it away. Her pajama top was pulled back to reveal her bare breasts. "Feed the baby, Grace. It's hungry. You know how," one of them jeered. She was trembling. Her body was rigid. Her face was taut with fear, shame and pain. Raging, I jabbed and grabbed and shoved them back, throwing my arms around her.

Grace buried her head against me, clinging, sobbing.

"They wouldn't stop. They wouldn't stop. Don't leave me."

"I'll stay, Gram. I'm not going to leave you." I turned to face them. They were gone. "Let's go to your garden, Gram. You'll be safe there."

Neither one of us spoke while I helped her with her bra, a silk blouse and soft cotton cardigan. I placed her favorite straw hat on her soft curls and handed her a tube of lipstick, reaching down to straighten her leg on the foot pedal. She yelped suddenly and lunged forward. I carefully lifted the hem of her pant leg. There was a deep, bloody gash oozing a dark stream of blood. Furious, I wheeled her back to the nurses' station.

Cassie's raccoon eyes stared coldly from her tan face. She flipped back her frosted blond hair with a wave of her manicured hand. "The nurses are bringing residents to breakfast. No one can look at it now."

"Cassie, get someone now or I will take her out of here."

She sniffed and looked away. "Do what you want. Nobody here can look at it."

I steered Grace away back down the hallway out the security doors to the village and followed the long hallways up to the ramp to Café Sofie. Two cabs idled outside the lobby doors. I stopped and stared.

"Do you want to get out of here, Gram?" I whispered. She looked up at me, eyes wide. I steered her chair toward the doors. Loree, the nursing director,

rounded the corner in front of us, balancing her breakfast on a tray.

"You were looking for a nurse?"

"My grandmother has a deep gash in her leg. I'll
take her to the hospital if I have to."

She stared impatiently at the breakfast on her tray,
rolled her eyes and walked past us to a table in the
atrium. "Take her back to her room," she tossed back.
"Someone will look at it."

"I've had enough of this!" I turned back to the
lobby but the cabs were gone. I stood staring at the
empty drive. I felt as trapped as Grace. I turned and
slowly wheeled her back down the corridor, past Loree,
past Café Sofie, past the shops in the village, past the
library, past the beauty salon, back to Lonan Wing,
back to her room. She was exhausted from the morning's onslaught and ominously quiet. I sat with her in
the silence of her room, stroking her hand. I would
have to think this through more carefully. The cab
would jostle her. I would need her walker for transfer. I needed Wheelchair Direct. I reached for my cell
phone. Where would we go? If I took her to the hospital, Quin would just send her back. What if I took her
out of town? Grace sat quietly, eyes closed. She was
trapped. She knew it and I knew it. I studied the lump
on her jaw, now the size of a lemon. It distorted her
face, stretching her mouth to one side. Where would I
find a specialist without alerting the Riordens? They'd
bar me from seeing her. I dropped my cell phone into
my pocket. It was too late. I had to let their game play
out to the end. I stared at the round faced clock. How
many lives had deteriorated here in this room while it

ticked off every painful minute as indifferent staff and family went about their lives outside this door? Grace slept in her chair, her head tilted onto her shoulder. I sat helpless as the round faced clock ticked on.

An hour passed before sharp knuckles wrapped on the door. Sol Bump swung the door open and strode in. I put my fingers to my lips. He ignored that. "I need you to leave the room," he announced. Grace stirred.

I stared back at him. "I'll stay."

"We have an agreement with your uncles. You should leave the room."

"Why would I do that, Sol?" My whisper was more of a hiss.

"The nurses need to examine Grace."

"I've already spoken to your nursing director. I'll definitely stay."

"We have an agreement with your uncle!" His voice ricocheted off the ceiling.

Grace's eyes flew open. "What's going on? What are you two arguing about?"

"Don't play that game with me!" I spit back. "I caught your staff humiliating my grandmother. Now I see that she has been badly hurt, probably by that lift machine that Bric ordered you not to use. I was standing right here when he gave that order. He also told me sedatives are not authorized. Yet here is my grandmother, sapped on sedatives. Any one of those things should put your license at risk, and yet you continue! I'll stay."

"You will leave!"

"Lower your voice," I repeated.

"What's going on here?" Grace straightened, wincing as she moved her leg. I leaned down close to her. "It's all right, Gram. The nurses are going to look at your leg. It's bleeding and they need to take care of it."

"No! I don't want those girls in here. Who told them?"

"I did, Gram. I'm sorry, but it's important for them to know that you've been hurt. If a nurse doesn't come soon, I'll take you to ER. It will be all right."

"Will it be all right?" I knew that wasn't a question. Sol abruptly backed out of the room and closed the door. The room was again quiet. The round faced clock ticked away another thirty minutes. Graced dozed again. I slipped into the hallway and headed towards the nurses' station. Sol emerged from a side wing, but quickly ducked into a doorway when he saw me. The nurses' station was empty. The corridors were empty. I doubled back to Grace. To my surprise, there was Sol, bent over Grace, probing the gash in her leg. She pushed him back, but he held her down with one hand.

"Sol! What are you doing! Where are the nurses?"

He moved quickly to face me. "Please understand that I ...that my hands are tied. I take orders from Acer."

"Understand this, Sol. I will find out how she got hurt and why medical care is denied her! I will expose this place for what it is!"

He backed into the hallway. I returned to Grace's side. She was again asleep. I wrapped a soft shawl across her shoulders. I held a warm wash cloth to her wound and wrapped soft gauze around her leg. She stirred, gazing into my eyes. "Oh, Sweetheart, I had a dream just now. I saw my mother. I cried out to her, but she just kept walking." Grace's eyes brimmed with tears. "She didn't answer me. She didn't even look at me. She just kept walking."

My heart ached. I held her trembling hands. "Gram, I am your mother and you are mine. We are daughters, we are sisters, we are the best of friends. You finish my sentences and I finish your prayers. When I look at myself, you are all I see. I will never walk past."

"Nor will I, Sweetheart. Nor will I."

"I love you, Gram."

"I love you so much."

Grace slept through lunch but we ate dinner at Chez Clair. Grace was subdued but welcomed the warm glow of the elegant restaurant, smoothing the crisp linen napkin on her lap. She licked mashed potatoes from the silver spoon and sipped water from the crystal goblet. Selma, Louise, Betty and Clarence stopped at the table.

"I'm taking carrot bars back to the apartment for a TV snack," Selma announced.

"I'll bet you have made hundreds of pans of these," Louise added.

"The secret," Grace offered quietly, "is in the cream cheese frosting. You have to soak the golden raisins overnight." I watched the exchange. Grace's face softened with the distant memory of desserts baking and secret recipes. That life was gone now. Now she lived on the edge of darkness. These friends were a brief glimmer of light. They welcomed her into their circle, into a community of changing weather and seasons, unconditional support and interests that included life outside Blackwater Manor. They comforted her maybe because of, or maybe despite their suspicions that each of them also was only one misstep away from being confined to Lonan Wing.

We strolled back through the village library. Grace spotted Jonathan Livingston Seagull in a stack of books on a side table. She opened the book and read slowly, delighting in the little bird learning to fly and soar. Quin rounded the corner and pulled a chair toward us. I stepped back into a stack of books and watched. Quin lifted the hem of her trousers. He applied a bandage and nodded as she leaned down to speak. He looked up into her sad distorted face, just inches from the thing growing on her jaw. Then he left. Grace dropped a quarter in the little basket on the table and tucked Jonathan Livingston Seagull into a small bag in her lap.

We wheeled back to Lonan Wing nurses' station, past Dolly, administering pills. As Grace opened her book and began to read aloud again, Sybil rammed into her, jamming the wheels of the two chairs. I jumped between them to break the wheels free. Sybil slapped at her and screamed "Blah! Blah! Blah! Blah! Blah!"

Grace pulled back. "What is she saying? She sounds like a sheep bleating." Dolly, less than three feet away, didn't look up.

Sybil screamed louder. "That's bullshit! That's bullshit! Get on with it! Get on with it! Just shut up! Shut up!" Dolly didn't move. Grace studied Sybil warily. I unlocked the wheels of the two chairs and steered Grace away. Sybil followed, again slamming her wheels into Grace's. Again I backed Grace away. Again Sybil followed. We were now inches from the nurses' station.

"Dolly, do something about Sybil. Grace has no defense against her."

Dolly looked up, exasperated. "You're her defense. Just stay out of Sybil's way."

"Let's go to your garden, Gram," I whispered. She nodded gratefully and patted my sleeve. We rolled down the corridors, through the shadows of the activity room and over the threshold into the warm smell of leaves and earth. I parked her under the sheltering tree.

"It's quiet here," she breathed. "Like a prayer. Maire would like this." She looked up at me. "Did you know that's how she got her name?"

"How?"

"Right after she was born, I was afraid for both of us. I prayed. The little nun took it as a sign. She named her after the prayer. It's a good name. It suits her."

"How did you get your name, Gram?"

She leaned her head back. A soft breeze played in the curls of her hair. "I was born in a fierce October snow storm. The roads were blocked and my mother was alone. She said that I was born by the grace of God."

"You are the grace of God, Gram."

"Did I ever tell you how you were named?" She brushed my cheek with her fingers. I gazed back at her. "When you were born, we didn't have a name, so Sean named you. He said it meant light."

"Does it?"

She touched my cheek. "It does now."

The next morning I arrived at Lonan Wing before seven. I found Grace in the dining room. Her hair was dripping wet and matted to her face. She wore a wrinkled T-shirt a size too small with a polyester shawl slung over her shoulders. One of the foot pedals was bent upward and askew. Her foot dragged on the floor. She was crying hard and trembling. I put my arms around her. "Gram, I'm here. Where are your glasses?" She clung to my hand. There on her plate was a slice of hard toast, two link sausages and a crusty turnover. There was a dish of cantaloupe chunks next to a small glass of juice. I put the glass in her hand. She sipped slowly through a straw. A brown-clad kitchen aide brought a dish of oatmeal. I handed Grace a spoon. She touched a morsel to her lips.

"It's cold." She sobbed quietly and held her jaw.

I found Amelia at the nurses' station. "When was Grace's last pain medication?"

She flipped through her chart. "It doesn't say. Either last night or this morning."

"So we don't know when she may have another?"

"You'll have to wait."

I returned to Grace. "Let's go, Gram. We'll find breakfast at Café Sofie."

Liddy suddenly appeared and stopped us, tipping a cup of red liquid to Grace's lips. A brown clad kitchen worker brought a banana. I mashed it and handed a taste to Grace. As she reached for the fork I stared at her hand. It was trembling. Her knuckles were raw and swollen. The skin was broken and red. I steadied her hand in mine. She winced. I looked closely at her fingers. Her right finger nail was torn away from her finger and hung loose.

"Amelia, my grandmother's been hurt again! Have you seen this? It looks like her hand has been smashed in a door!"

"No. I haven't seen that."

"Amelia, this is the second injury in two days!"

"I'll put in a call to Doctor Corbin to see if there might be an antibiotic."

"Antibiotic? Her nail is ripped off."

"I'll look in Grace's med drawer," she answered. "There might be something in there from a previous injury she might be able to use." She turned and left. She did not come back.

The round faced clock in Grace's room seemed to move slower and slower as morning turned to late afternoon and on into evening. I brought a cup of soup from Café Sofie. Grace sipped and then dozed in her chair. The red call light flashed on and off as the round-faced clock ticked away the time. No one appeared. Grace woke and I dressed her in her pajamas and transferred her to bed. It was easy with just the two of us. She dozed off again soon after her head touched the pillow.

I walked through the empty hallway, past the unattended nurses' station, and out to my car. I drove six blocks to a nearby Walgreens and bought an over the counter antibiotic and a nail scissors. I returned to Lonan Wing, walked back through the empty hallway, past the unattended nurses' station and back to Grace's side. I spread the ointment over the gash on her leg and gently trimmed the rip in her thumbnail. Grace slept quietly. It occurred to me that this may have been the first night in a week that I did not hear her sobbing. Had she become numb to the daily onslaughts? How much more could she endure? Her injuries were coming closer and closer together. I couldn't stop this deadly cycle.

The next morning I found Grace's room in a jumbled clutter, worlds apart from the peaceful room I had left the night before. Grace's pajamas lay rumpled on a side chair. Blankets and sheets lay in a heap on the floor. A soiled Depends lay on the bed. The wheelchair seat was gone. The wheels and chrome bars of her chair were spattered and wet. The foot pedal bent awkwardly upward and careened wildly off to the side. An aide tried to push past me. I stopped her.

"What happened in this room?" She aide averted her eyes and ducked out the door, hurrying down the hallway. Sue, the beautician, came through the door.

"Where is Grace?" I demanded.

"She's in the shower. I'm waiting for her."

"I thought she was scheduled for chemotherapy?"

"Oh, I don't think she has a chemo treatment."

"Are you sure?"

"I'll check."

She didn't come back. Instead, Sol Bump sauntered in. "Without going into any detail, without telling you things I'm not allowed to tell you," he began, "I will tell you that Grace is not having chemotherapy." I stared at him.

"Sol, you'd better drop the attitude and tell me right now what's going on.

"I'm just doing what Acer tells me to do."

"Sol, you want desperately to be a player, but you don't know the game. You don't even know the rules. You are just another Riorden pawn." His face went white. His arrogance seemed to dissipate as he turned and walked slowly away.

Four hours later, an aide walked through the door, carrying a thick ham sandwich. I handed it back to her. "Do you know that she is not able to chew?"

"No. No one told me."

"She hasn't eaten today. Can you bring a cup of yogurt?"

"It's not on my cart, but I'll see if I can find some." She did not return. Grace dozed in the sunny window as the round faced clock ticked the minutes and then the hours.

At 3:00 p.m. a brown-clad kitchen worker brought Angel food cake and coleslaw. I sent it back. "Just open a can of Campbell's Soup. It's not that difficult." She also went away. The round faced clock ticked on. Another hour passed and another aide brought chunky vegetable soup and mashed potatoes and gravy. Grace licked the potatoes and gravy from the spoon and then pushed it away, crying.

"This isn't right," she whispered through her tears. "Quin promised."

The next day I walked through the lobby of the State Social Services complex. A gray-haired woman led me through a maze of cubicles to a conference room. She motioned to a table. She sat, hands folded, facing me. "I've read your complaint," she stated simply. "While I appreciate your concern for your grandmother, I must refer you to her power of attorney."

My heart felt like a deep aching bruise. "Are you saying there is nothing the state can do to help a woman in harm's way? She's in danger. I've detailed incident after incident. Loree has a long history of tags. Is no one accountable?"

"I'm sorry." Her tone was clinical. "You tell me her power of attorney is informed. It's out of our hands."

"My grandmother needs medical care," I pleaded. "At the very least, we need communication." She excused herself and left the room. Her secretary ushered me out.

Stunned, I found myself back on the Interstate, driving blindly, defeated and alone. There was no one who would help. I returned to Grace with absolute clarity. I knew how this must end.

Grace rested fitfully, her hand clenched to her mouth. Pink crystal beads twinkled from the bracelet on her wrist. A rhinestone framed photo of Grace at eighteen sparkled next to a photo of Grace and Jack leaning against a tree on the day of their engagement. Porcelain angels stood guard from her bedside table. Tiny finches scratched at the bird feeders overhead in the window. Bright red geraniums bloomed bravely from the shepherds hook beyond in the garden. Gleaming red tomatoes hung plump and juicy along the perimeter, waiting for her to pluck them from the vine. Squirrels scurried over the tree branches beyond. Maire's little plaque stood simple and plain on the window sill, reminding all who entered that Grace's God is God. Grace stirred. "Where's Maire?"

I stroked her hand. "Celia needs her now."

"Will she be back?"

"They're moving to Oregon."

Grace sighed. "That's important, I know it is."

"We must let her go, Gram, but she is still with us. The three of us will always be together." Grace looked away, past the finches scratching at the bird feeder, past the geraniums, past the tomatoes, past the squirrels in the branches. "Look at me, Gram. Please look at me. I'm right here. I will not leave you. Whatever happens next, we'll face it together."

Sunday, late morning a brown-clad kitchen worker slipped into the room. "Would your grandmother like ham or roast beef?"

I turned away from her to gaze at Grace. "My grandmother is barely getting down chipped ice. Surely by now this must be documented somewhere." The brown-clad worker stared blankly. "Neither", I sighed, shaking my head. "Yogurt or broth."

Shayla brought a tray with chunks of watermelon and roast beef. I reached for my bag and pulled some dollars from my purse. "Can you get her some yogurt? She may be able to eat that." She went away, and brought back an egg. "Yogurt. Please." When she finally brought a cup of yogurt, Grace licked at the spoon, then winced in pain. "Shayla," I asked, "is it time for pain medication?"

Shayla stepped into the hallway. Cassie rustled through the chart. "What is she getting? Morphine?"

I joined them. "That's the third time I have heard a med aide say she was wasn't sure what to give my grandmother."

"It doesn't matter," Cassie snapped. "She'll refuse it."

"How do you know she'll refuse it?"

"She won't open her mouth!"

"She has a growth on her jaw that's stretching her mouth halfway around her cheek. Of course she can't open her mouth. She's delirious with pain. Find some other way to help her."

Amelia came next. She tried to wedge a straw into Grace's clenched lips. Grace winced and turned away in tears. Then she tried a plastic spoon. Grace shook her head and moaned. The round faced clock ticked on. Hours passed. Dolly came in and dripped the liquid from a Dixie cup onto Grace's lips while she was sleeping. The pink stuff ran down the sides of her face and onto the pillow and her neck. Grace woke, turned her eyes toward me, moaned and shook her head in pain and frustration, or perhaps disgust. Dolly left. The round faced clock ticked on. Four hours later Dolly returned.

"She'll just refuse again," Dolly argued, spoon in hand.

Grace clung to me with a vice-grip clench. My hand had gone numb hours before. Brown-clad kitchen workers brought trays of hard toast, hard boiled eggs and oatmeal without milk or sugar. There were no bananas. I sent the trays away giving them dollars and saying always the same thing. "Bring yogurt."

The round faced clock kept its vigil. I spooned yogurt onto Grace's lips. She licked it off and nodded, then winced. Finally, I resorted to chipped ice. Grace was struggling to take her last steps through the shadows of the dark tunnel. Her eyes filled with tears, pleading with me to help her. "Shall I say a prayer?" I whispered. She nodded. "Shall I say the Angel of God?" She nodded again, her eyes never leaving mine. I began. "Angel of God, My Guardian, dear. To whom God's love entrusts me hear. Ever this night be at my side to light and guard to rule and guide. Amen." Tears streamed from her eyes. "Shall I sing for you, Gram?" Her eyes attempted a sad smile. "No matter, what, Gram, I will always be with you." She nodded and I sang softly into her ear as I caressed her temples.

I''ll be calling you when the meadowlark sings.
I'll be touching you with every beat of its wings.
And when evening comes, you just close your
eyes and rest easy.
Love never dies.

Maire stared out the window of the Suburban at the changing landscape flying past as the family sped west. Celia was at the wheel. The two boys watched videos in the back. Her thoughts were with her mother. She couldn't say goodbye. Grace was asleep when she left. She had stood for a long time gazing upon her mother. The urge to stay was strong. She was detached and yet more connected than she had ever been to anyone in her life.

Thursday morning I found Grace wedged against a table in the day room next to Sybil. Sybil was spewing venomous curses and pounding the table, pulling on Grace's arm. "I thought I lost you," Grace cried. I backed her away and rolled her through the corridors to her garden, where we stayed nestled under the leaves of the big tree until lunchtime. Lunch was, unbelievably, a hard chicken breast with green beans. I sent it back. I reached into my bag for a container of

Jello. She licked the Jello from the spoon. Then she held her jaw and rocked in pain.

I rolled her to the nurses' station. "We didn't give her pain medication today," Dimmea reported. "We don't have any luck with pills."

"Dimmae, if you can't help my grandmother, I will take her somewhere that can."

I transferred Grace back into bed. Whimpering, she slept fitfully. The round faced clock ticked on.

Quin walked in. "I hear she's agitated."

"She's suffering agonizing pain, Quin."

"Well, let's let her sleep. I'll stop back later."

When Grace stirred again, I dialed Quin's number. It went to voicemail. I transferred Grace to her wheel chair and headed to her garden. A soft breeze played in her curls and stirred her senses. She reached to pluck a soft round red tomato from the vine. Quin found us there. I stepped away while he sat with her. Then he left. "How can you turn away from your mother?" I asked the empty doorway.

I spent every hour of every day that week at Grace's side, helpless as she fluctuated between anguished sobs and fitful sleep. Then Friday morning, before noon, Crystal Ann peeked into the room and motioned for me to come out into the hall. "Let's go to the cafeteria where we can talk," she whispered. We walked together through the long hallways leading past the quiet library and bustling hair salon. We turned and walked up the ramp to Café Sofie. I ordered two coffees. "I don't have money," she said flatly. I handed the clerk the cash. Crystal Ann was already seated in the atrium. I handed her the coffee.

"Aunt Jacey tells me you have been keeping Mom from TV Mass."

I sighed. Why was I even talking with her? "Crystal Ann," I answered evenly. "It's ridiculous to be concerned about TV Mass. Gram is suffering. Be concerned about that."

"What do you think of Mom's care?" She asked pointedly.

"She does not belong here. She belongs in the care of someone who can love and nurture her and see her through this time. She needs hospice."

"This is the only place for her."

"That's not true. St. Albert's has a health care wing. There are several hospice agencies in town. They will even come here."

"Hospice will take away her meds."

"Crystal Ann, she hasn't taken meds in weeks. She can't swallow pills."

"Hospice won't feed her. They won't even put her on a tube. She would starve."

"Crystal Ann, she's starving now."

"I don't know that."

"If you were ever here for more than a cursory visit, you would know."

"Hospice would deprive her of her pain medication."

"Crystal Ann, she's not getting pain medication. They don't know how to administer it, so they say she refuses."

"That's not documented." She retorted. "Blackwater isn't telling the family that Mom is in distress."

"Crystal Ann," I said quietly, "Sol Bump says he takes his orders from Acer. He is only obligated to communicate with him."

Grace's sister, Jacelyn hurried toward us. She stood over Crystal Ann's shoulder. My eyes were drawn to a laminated letter J dangling from her key chain. "I've got a hilarious story about Grace," she cackled. "You'll love this." She didn't wait for an invitation to sit. "I saw Grace squished up tight to a table at Lonan Wing. She was trying to get away, but she couldn't move her chair." Jacey threw her head back and let loose with a squeal of laughter. I stared coldly, shaking my head in disbelief. She ignored me, intent on telling her story. "So she tried to move the table! What a hoot! Isn't that hilarious? She tried to move the table!" I shoved my chair back and stood. Jacey stepped back. "Well, I didn't want to interrupt. I only wanted to tell you that story." She turned and scuttled down the hallway.

Crystal Ann motioned to the chair. "Please, let's talk more." I eyed her warily. "The last time I took Mom to her infusion, I found her slumped over in her chair next to the nurses' station with a spoon caught in the buttons of her front shirt. I could tell she was sedated!"

"This is not the place for her," I repeated.

Doreen strode towards us. "The party room is ready for the big party tomorrow. It should hold all of us."

"You are going ahead with plans for Gram's birthday party?"

"Of course," she chirped. "First we'll take her to her to the Cathedral for Mass and then the baptism, then onto Royal Court and a family reception in the Rose Room at Blackwater Manor."

"Crystal Ann, Gram can barely tolerate three minutes awake. She's not going to be able to tolerate that party."

"Mom was just fine the last time I saw her."

"Crystal Ann, she's right there in her room. See for yourself. Come with me now. I'm going back. She shouldn't be alone." Crystal Ann stood staunchly beside Doreen. "Are you coming?" I demanded. Neither one of them moved. "God," I breathed, "who are you people?"

When I got back to her room, Grace was awake and sobbing. A med aide was attempting to pry her clenched lips apart with the tip of a spoon. I stepped in and touched a bit of yogurt to her lips. She licked it. I lifted a straw and she took a sip of water. Then she shook her head. She couldn't tolerate more. I stroked her hand. She gripped my fingers. 'This family harbors a deadly lie,' I thought. 'They play a deadly game to lay claim to what would be theirs soon enough anyway'. Beyond Grace's window, out over her garden, perched in the ivy, sat her Robin. I wondered if he were waiting for her. I shook my head and wondered, 'Why break down the wall when you hold the key in your hand?' The ticking of the round faced clock was the only sound in the room. Footsteps came and went outside Grace's door, but none belonged to Crystal Ann.

Then Bric peeked in. He saw that Grace was sleeping and motioned for me to join him in the hall. "No," I whispered fiercely. "You come here. Gram's suffering terribly. She needs a hospice."

He came into the room and knelt beside her, checking her pulse. "Let's go to the cafeteria where we can talk," he said, moving back into the hallway. "I don't want to disturb her." I walked with him, just as I had walked with Crystal Ann earlier, through the long hallways, past the quiet library where Grace and I spent hours reading, past the hair salon with the chatty beautician and whirring dryers. We walked up the ramp to Café Sofie where I ordered two coffees.

"I didn't bring my wallet," he said, pulling his hands out of his pockets.

'What a coincidence,' I thought wryly. 'Either did Crystal Ann.'

I handed the clerk the cash. She smiled and winked. "Back again?" I nodded and walked to the atrium where Bric was already seated. I put the coffee on the table.

"What do you think of Mom's care?" he asked.

His words startled me. I wondered why he and Crystal Ann were asking the same question in the same way on the same day. It appeared to be scripted. So, I repeated exactly what I had said to Crystal Ann. "She does not belong here."

"This is the only place for her," he stated, repeating what Crystal Ann had said. The cup stopped at my lips, coffee spilling onto my hand. This was eerie.

"She needs hospice care," I said, regaining my composure. "She is suffering." Did they imagine themselves to be clever? "She needs her family with her now." He clenched his teeth and leaned back in his chair.

Doreen strode toward us, joining the conversation while abruptly pulling a chair to the table. "What you are seeing is symptoms of aging," she interjected. "I know. I've had grandparents in the same condition, whimpering, refusing to eat."

Bric nodded. "She looks decidedly different from the last time I saw her. She may be progressing faster than we thought."

"Bric, she has a growth on the side of her jaw the size of a lemon. She is suffering excruciating pain."

"It's probably not pain," he cut in. "It's probably advanced Alzheimer's. It's a natural progression. I will speak to the med aide and have her back off on the pain from every four hours to every eight hours."

"Bric, she's not receiving her pain medication on schedule now." I could hear my voice getting shriller. "Is there anyone paying attention?"

"We have absolute faith in Blackwater Manor," he answered. He turned to Doreen. "Are you ready?"

I watched them disappear down the corridor as my cell phone rang. It was a text from Crystal Ann. She had blasted the email to every other member of the family. The email read:

> *Elle,*
> *Aunt Jacelyn reports that Mom has not gone to Mass for the last three weeks, and is not taking communion. Is there some issue that is preventing this from happening? Please e-mail me.*
>
> > *Thanks,*
> > *Crystal Ann.*

"Bitch!" I muttered and flipped my phone shut.

The fiercer the grip of pain on Grace's body, the fiercer her grip on my hand. I lay my head next to hers and whispered. "What a blessed year we have had, Gram. Remember the ducks following the current and the kids in the boat at the park? Where do you think they were going? Remember the wedding in the gazebo along the water? The bride was angelic in her white gown. There was a little girl who stopped at the wheel of your chair. You gave her a cookie. There were two boys in a shiny red convertible. They offered you a ride." I stroked her hand and smiled. "Do you remember Gracie, the lady at Royal Court? You had the same name. She gave you a rosary. You and Maire and I were together every day." I imagined she could hear me, although all I heard were anguished whimpers. Her eyes met mine in a sad gaze. I continued. "Oh that Thou would bless me indeed, and that Thine hand might be with me, and that Thou would keep me from evil, that it may not grieve me." Her eyes glazed in pain and closed. Her grip tightened. "I am your voice, Gram. Fly away. I will be right here to tell your story." 'If a sparrow dies in the wilderness,' I wondered, 'who hears the cry?' I sang in soft melodious whispers.

I"ll be calling you when the meadowlark sings.
I'll be touching you with warm spring rains
I'll watch over you like the moon in the sky
For I know love never dies

Celia had been driving for hours. The CDs and DVDs were played out. The children squirmed impatiently. Celia pulled off at the exit. Maire stepped out to stretch. Celia pumped gas as the children looked for ice cream. Maire's thoughts turned to Grace. "They won't see people like her every day," she murmered.

"You're thinking of Grandma?" Celia stood at her side. "She's rare."

"One thing is for sure," Maire answered. "That's the closest Blackwater Manor will ever get to Grace on earth."

Saturday morning was a haze. Grace cried out in pain. I pushed the call light button. Deka stepped in, disappeared, and returned with ice chips. Grace licked the chips with her tongue and fell back asleep. The round faced clock ticked away time. Grace stirred and opened her eyes. "I thought you had gone," she whispered. "Don't go."

I rubbed her hands and lay ice chips on her tongue. An aide brought her a plate of breakfast. "Just bring her some yogurt," I whispered. "There's money in my wallet. Go to Café Sofie." She looked at me blankly and left, not touching the money. I mashed a little banana on the tip of a spoon. Grace licked it away. Her hunger was great but the pain was greater. She bit at the rough skin on her chapped lips. I applied a little Vaseline. She fell back asleep. The round faced clock ticked on as I watched the birds and the squirrels bobbing and dancing across the branches. I whispered to her as she whimpered in her sleep. "The small world we live in may not know or remember your life here, but your story will be told, Gram. Your truth will be known." I lay my hand against her brow. "You sacrificed your life for your family, Gram. Your children owe you an apology." She whimpered but her eyes remained closed. "Gram, I would trade places with you if I could." Tears streamed from her eyes. "Thank you for letting me into your life." She gripped my hand.

The round faced clock ticked away Grace's life in measured moments as the med aides came and went with pain medication and kitchen workers came and went with ice chips and yogurt. 'My grandmother had a garden,' I thought. I looked from her face, tight with pain, to the robin bobbing on the fence. I unclenched her fingers from my hand. Then I lifted her to her wheelchair one last time, bundled her into a warm blanket, and together we slipped unseen down the hallway, past the French doors and into her secret garden. There under a universe of stars we listened to the rustling of leaves of the big oak tree as I stroked her hands and arms and sang softly into her ear.

I'll be ever true like the northern star
So you can find my heart wherever you are

And when evening falls, you can close your
eyes and rest easy.
Love never dies.

The round-faced clock pointed to ten as I lifted Grace back into bed. Exhausted and emotional, I stared blankly out through the bay window, out across the silent sky.

Suddenly the door swung open, blinding me with a flash of light. Dolly stood over me. "You have to leave," she said bluntly. I stared at her shadow, illuminated by the neon hall light, towering grotesquely over us. "You have to go!"

Grace cried out and I turned my attention to her. One clenched hand was against her jaw. Her other hand gripped mine.

"It's an order from Bric," Dolly insisted.

"I don't believe you." I nodded toward my bag on the floor. "Hand me my phone." She reached down and pulled the strap of the bag toward me. I reached into the bag with my free hand and hit speed dial. "Prove it."

She took the phone and turned away, walking out into the hallway. The round-faced clock ticked seconds into minutes. Then she returned. "Bric said to let it go, he'll deal with you tomorrow."

"He'll deal with me? That's what he said?"

"That's what he said," she responded flatly.

I redialed as Dolly left the room. "Bric? Elle. Dolly tells me you have ordered me to leave but now you've decided that you'll deal with me tomorrow? What does that mean exactly?"

Bric's answer was cold. "The family agrees that she does better when she gets consistent rest so the attempt was to try and have her get consistent sleep without interruption. It was addressed as a medical issue regarding her fatigue. We're trying to give her consistent sleep."

"Bric, your mother is dying. Are you intent on her dying alone and in anguish?"

He ignored the question. "We talked about this in care conference. We do not think it is a good idea for her to be up all night."

"Bric, she's dying. You are concerned that I'm keeping her awake?"

"Is she sleeping?"

"Yes, she sleeps fitfully and then wakes in anguish, holding her jaw. She's in pain."

"That's not pain. That's the symptoms of Alzheimer's."

"Alzheimer's? Bric, her face is distorted and there is no room inside her mouth for her tongue, let alone her teeth. Why are we even having this conversation?"

"We agreed in care conference that she should be alone to rest." Abashed, my heart turned to stone. Then his voice boomed through my phone. "If you insist on staying I will have you physically removed!" My arm fell limp. I flipped the phone shut and dropped to my knees at Grace's side. Time stood still as I breathed in her sweet scent, memorizing her gentle face. Then I reached for my coat and bag and moved toward the door.

"Elle! Elle! Take me with you." I spun around, but she was not awake.

"Gram?" I whispered. "I can hear you! Come with me, Gram. Just let go and come with me." I softly stroked her temples and her fingers. "Come with me, Gram. Come with me now." Then I kissed her soft cheek for the last time, turned, walked into the empty hallway, down the empty corridor, past the empty nurses' station, out the double doors into the parking lot and into the crisp night air. My grandmother was broken. God's word was broken. This family was broken. I fumbled with my keys, then dropped to the ground. "I can't breathe," I gasped.

Her voice came to me again. "Elle! Take me with you."

Tears streamed down my face as I stared into an open sky. "Live in me, Gram. I am a strong vessel. I am your barefoot warrior."

As I turned the key, I saw a shadow moving through the halls, a flashlight beam moved from window to window. "Come with me, Gram," I whispered. "Come with me, now. No one will even know you're gone."

The next day I rose early and walked alone through Ronan's little town. It was her birthday. I stepped through the door of Doyle's Pub into a fray of angry voices. Ronan was locked in verbal battle with the neighbor who had encroached on his land.

"The city levied me with a fine!" the man screamed.

"I warned you!" Ronan roared back. "I told you to move your rubble or I'd have it hauled away."

"You think you own this town?" the man retorted. "Well, own this, ya dirty bastard!" He pulled a revolver from his jacket, but it caught on his pocket. He stumbled into a table and it went off, taking a chunk out of the table leg.

"Worthless drunk!" Ronan lept towards him.

"The Devil take you!" The man lurched at him as the gun clanked to the floor.

Ronan gave the gun a kick. It skittered across the wooden planks to land at my feet. "Get that thing out of here!" he hollered above the fracas.

I gingerly lifted the weapon and dropped it into my bag. 'The world has gone crazy,' I thought as I left the noise and headed for the woods. I walked for hours in silence. It was her birthday. I wanted to be alone with her. I thought I could hear her calling. "Gram, I am your vessel. Come to me," I prayed.

Early the next morning, I drove back to the city. I expected the family would still be hovering. I thought I might wait them out. The Walgreens on the corner was close by. I stopped there. The weather had turned quickly from the balmy last days of Indian Summer to the dangerous first blast of early winter. As I stepped into the street, sleet stung my face. It felt good to feel something besides the numbing ache in my soul. My cell phone beeped. I fumbled in my pocket. It was Acer.

"Hello!" Came his easy drawl. "How do you like this weather? I'm just driving across country and realized I'm probably in your neck of the woods. By the way, where is your neck of the woods?" Not knowing where I lived made him crazy. "Everyone's talking about Obama. Aren't you an Obama girl? But you Wall Street types probably aren't in favor of health care reform, are you?"

"What are you talking about?" I sounded like Grace.

"I imagine jobs are difficult to find now, even in Chicago. Of course there's always Omaha, if you like insurance, and Minneapolis, if you're into medicine. Are you into medicine?"

I imagined he thought himself to be very clever. Enough of this. "How was Gram's birthday party?" I asked.

"Good. Very good. Everyone enjoyed it. Do you have time for coffee? I'll meet you at Perkins."

I nearly dropped my basket. "No, actually, I don't."

"Yes," he rambled on, "Mom's birthday party went well."

Suspicion overtook anger. I stopped mid-aisle. 'Wait for it,' I told myself.

"I think her care is going well."

'Wait for it,' I breathed.

"There is something important I want to discuss with you."

There it was. I dropped the basket, shuffled through my bag, found my pocket voice recorder, clicked it on and held it to my phone. "What's that?"

"You should know that the family is saying that you doubled up on Mom's meds."

"That's ridiculous," I snapped. "Why would anyone think that?" A woman standing next to me quickly moved to the next aisle. My dream at sea flashed before me. I saw the family in the front of the boat angrily shouting at me but I heard only the roaring wind. I adjusted my tone to hide any emotion. "By meds, do you mean the Coreg? Perhaps you mean the multivitamins? Maybe the Boniva? Surely you don't mean the Dulcolax."

He didn't expect that. He tried to stay on point, but his pride got in the way. "No! No, of course I don't mean her vitamins. I mean...the family is referring to the Oxy and the Morphine."

His lie was clumsy and he was too eager to deliver it. "Acer, I wouldn't think I would need to remind you that the pharmacy as well as the med cart is locked and under supervision of a certified med aide and a registered nurse. If I remember correctly, controlled administration of her medication was your primary motivation for locking Gram away at Blackwater."

"We didn't lock her up," he snarled. I smiled. The green light on my recorder assured me I was capturing it all.

"So let me just tell you, for the record, that Gram's not able to swallow pain or any other medication, but if the family is saying that a med aide or a registered nurse gave me the key to the med drawer they should realize that would be a serious violation. The staff member you point the finger at would of course lose his or her license. I imagine the facility would lose their license as well." He was silent. "Or did you think you might accuse me of breaking into the med cabinet?"

"I'm just telling you what they are saying. I think it's documented."

"Are you saying it's documented that a med aide handed me the keys to the med room or are you saying it's documented that I broke into the med cart?" He was silent. "Look, Acer. You're the executor of this estate and an attorney. Surely you must realize the consequences of malicious prosecution." He remained silent. "Blackwater Manor doesn't document falls or injuries but they do document that she refuses her daily meds as well as her pain meds. I'll tell you another thing that's documented. Sol Bump says he takes his orders from you. He's very vocal about that. The staff, the med aides and the nurses take their orders from the director of nursing, who takes her orders from him. If the key to the pharmacy is not secure then they are either more incompetent than I thought, or it's all being done under your direction."

"Would you rather I didn't tell you what they're saying?"

"That accusation would be a malicious, capricious act which you should have stopped in its tracks. If I were you, Acer, I would instruct this family to be very careful."

"Well, there are rules set forth by an appointed patient advocate."

"What are you talking about?"

"You didn't get a directive from Mom's appointed advocate?"

"Advocate? There is no advocate. Your mother is dying, Acer. She needs hospice. Do not refuse her that." He was silent. I was surprised. That was the best he could do? "Thank you for calling, Acer. Always a pleasure to get a call from the Riordens."

"Sarcasm?" he spit back.

"Always a pleasure, Acer." I hung up the phone and clicked off the recorder. I was done with the drama and the orchestrated issues and the narcissistic self-driven agendas, but I wondered how crazy and just how dangerous he really could be.

My thoughts retraced the past year and the year before that, to when this all began. I could still see the moving van outside the gaping patio doors at Scanlon Circle. I could hear my Uncle Ralph's comment, 'She's just a pawn.' I recalled Cheyla's explanation of why they kicked me out. 'We had to get rid of her. She's abusive.' At the time I had dismissed it all as too absurd. Now I began to see a pattern forming. Acer's outrageous accusation rang in my ears. I scanned the street. 'It's very possible,' I thought, 'that he's not on the road at all. He may be right here waiting for me to come into sight.' I thought of Maire's warning, 'If he can get you to display anger it will validate his claim of abuse.' Then another thought crossed my mind. Why wait for him to pursue me? I tossed my bag into the passenger seat and slid behind the wheel.

Minutes later, I was parked next to the dumpster at Perkins. I eased around the building to the side windows. A streetlight shone behind me and a security light overhead, but the fluorescent lighting from inside was brighter. I would not be seen. I scanned the interior. There he was. "What are you planning, Acer?" I whispered. "Another ambush?" Acer systematically scanned the restaurant, watching the door.

Then he reached for his cell phone and dialed. My phone beeped. Gripped by sudden apprehension, I backed from the window to my car, dropping the ringing phone on the seat next to me. As I turned out of the parking lot, the traffic light flashed red. I stared into the four-lane highway that would take me safely away. 'Hypnotizing the chickens,' I thought. 'They will stay lulled until the rooster crows.' The traffic light flashed red to green. The car behind honked and startled me back to reality. "You should have gotten to know me better," I whispered and disappeared into the shadows.

The next Monday I received an email from Jacelyn. It read:

> *The day dawned with clouds, threatening a rainy day but by noon the sun broke through and we experienced a glorious sunny day.*
>
> *High Mass was at the Cathedral at the 11:00 AM. The music was Angelic.*
>
> *In attendance was the Queen, the Matriarch of the Riorden family, honored guest, Grace Riorden, in constant attendance her daughter, Crystal Ann. Also attending were her sister, Jacelyn, eight of her children and spouses, many grandchildren and spouses, three great grandchildren and other relatives and friends.*
>
> *Immediately following the Mass the procession led to an alcove off the church proper,*

where a baptism was held for the newest grandchild. The immediate family, the child, the child's parents and grandparents and close friends and relatives gathered in the alcove for the service. Following the baptism, the priest scooped the baby from the mother's arms and lovingly carried her into the church and placed her on the white linen of the altar and blessed her with the sign of the cross. It was so emotional.

The entire family exited to Royal Court for lunch before returning about 2:30 p.m. to the party room at Blackwater Manor for a reception. Food, food, food, and drinks, a small layered oval cake with a picture of Grace on top including candles, plus a large layer cake was waiting for us. Following the singing of HAPPY BIRTHDAY and blowing out the candles the visiting and picture taking began.

It was a come and go party and some had to leave earlier than others to get back to distant homes and school. My apologies if I missed mentioning someone as I didn't look at the guest book. Unfortunately, Grace had to go back to her room shortly after the birthday song and cake and ice cream. It had been a long day for her.

I read the email in horror. My heart was a black void. I dialed Maire. When she heard my voice, she shouted, "Crystal Ann took Mom from her bedside, dressed her in something sparkly and put her on shameful and pitiful display! Crystal Ann did this! She put the crown on her mother's head and paraded her around town. She dragged her to Mass. She made her sit through a family baptism. She paraded her in front of the chef and waiters at Royal Court, who knew her better than her own family. She held her captive and made her suffer a party at Blackwater Manor. Then and only then did Crystal Ann return to her room to be shut away, alone again while her family partied on. Shame! Shame! Shame! How closely their actions resemble the mob that crucified Christ. Mom has special favor for enduring this suffering!"

Listening to Maire I knew what I had to do. I had to go back. "Hold on, Gram," I breathed. "I'll be there in the morning." But the universe had other plans.

The next morning I woke to the high pitched whine of a ferocious wind tearing through windowsills and tree branches. I looked out to see a wide sea of snow. It was a total whiteout. A blizzard on the prairie at the end of October is not unusual, but I wondered at God's timing. I leaned my forehead against the frosted window and thought of the story of Grace and her grandmother and the false teeth frozen in the glass. I couldn't be with Grace but I knew that her grandmother was. I stared out across the frozen prairie, blanketed in snow. 'How easy it would be to get lost in that,' I thought. 'It would be so easy to forget this insane family and all that's happened this year.' I pulled a warm woolen blanket over my head and cried myself back to sleep.

When I woke again, the blizzard was over, but the Interstate was closed. I phoned Lonan Wing. Aubery answered. She passed the phone to Amelia.

"She's having an emotionally fragile day," Amelia stated bluntly.

"What does that mean, Amelia? Is she crying?"

"No, no crying."

"Is she striking out?"

"No, no she's not striking out."

"Then what are you referring to?"

"She's easily upset."

"Do you mean that you finally recognize that she's in unbearable pain and there's nothing you can do for her?"

"We're on top of it."

"She needs hospice care, Amelia. What are your general guidelines for calling in a hospice?"

"We're on top of it."

"No, Amelia. I'm asking you a question. What are your general guidelines for calling in hospice?"

Her voice became thin and crisp. "Our general guidelines are if she asks us for pain medicine or tells us she's in pain or if we determine that she's in pain then we will give her pain medication." I hung up the phone and dialed Acer's number. It went to voicemail.

"Right," I muttered and threw the phone down.

I phoned again that evening. Aubery answered. "Grace is doing fine," she answered in an artificially friendly voice. "She is sitting in the TV room. She just finished supper."

"Supper? In the TV room? She can't chew. She's in unbearable pain."

"She's fine," Aubery retorted. "She's sitting all alone in the TV room, rocking back and forth. Everyone else is at a concert in the chapel so she's all alone. She's fine."

'Rocking back and forth?' Her words tore at my heart. That was her intent, of course. I realized suddenly the power she must feel, knowing the punishment she could inflict on anyone who challenged her egocentric authority. I remembered what the residents at Lonan Wing had said. 'They'll get even.'

"You are telling me that Grace is still in the day room? Since everyone's at a concert, and you have the time, there's no need to keep her sitting there any longer, is there?"

"Are we done?" she spat back.

I shuddered at the steel cold contempt in her voice. "Come to me, Gram," I whispered. "Come to me." I stared at the blowing snow, the wind whistling in my ears until I could tolerate the wait no longer. I redialed Lonan Wing.

Dolly answered. "Calling to see how Grace is doing? Oh, she's doing fine. She ate supper."

"That's not possible."

"Yes, she ate supper at the table."

"Do you know what she ate?"

"No, I don't know what was served."

"Did you give her pain medication?"

"Well, I haven't given her any since I've been here. She'll tell us if she needs it."

"Dolly, have you actually seen my grandmother today?"

"No, not yet."

"Then how is it you can report these things? If she is fine, I should be able to speak with her now."

"Well, she's sleeping."

"Is she sleeping in her bed?"

"No. She's sitting here in the day room sleeping."

"I thought you said you hadn't seen her today?" Dolly was silent. "Dolly, can you hear me?"

Jacelyn's voice cut in. "Elle, listen. I've been sitting with Grace for hours. I asked if they were going to put her to bed and their response was, and I quote, 'when we get around to it.'"

"Jacey, what are you doing there? Nevermind. It's cruel to make her sit up in the dayroom in that chair."

"Do you want to talk to the nurse?"

"Yes, put Dolly back on the phone."

"We'll take care of it," Dolly responded abruptly. Then she hung up.

I called Lonan Wing early the next morning. Sally answered. She said Grace was doing very well and sitting at the dining room table eating.

"How can that be? Has anyone from the family been with her?"

"Someone came by. I don't know if it was family and I don't know if they stayed."

I called again just before lunch. Naomi answered. "You'll have to speak with the nurse."

Amelia came to the phone. She was excessively cheery. "She's doing fine, as usual."

"Amelia, I'd like to speak with her."

"I don't know where she is right now. I think she is getting toileted.

"Excuse me?"

"I think she's getting toileted."

"Did you say toileted?"

"Yes. Toileted."

"What an odd term."

"That's all I can say."

"Amelia, if my grandmother is as fine as you say, I'd like to speak with her."

"Oh, sorry, no can do. We'll call you when she's available." The call never came. I dialed every hour for the rest of the day and was given the same answer.

Sometime the next day Quin called. "Elle, Mom seems to be slipping into a different mode. She is refusing food and we've decided not to force feed her with intravenous."

"Refusing food? She can't swallow. What does that mean, no intravenous? She'll dehydrate."

"She has the pain patch so she will not be in any discomfort."

"Is anyone with her? Are you just leaving her alone to die? Where is hospice?"

"I will call you tomorrow to give you an update."

Quin phoned the next day. "Mom seems to be comfortable. She is in a place where she is slipping away. You should not worry. She does not seem to be in distress. I will call with any further updates."

"Come to me, Gram," I whispered. "Come to me. Just let go. Come to me. I'm right here. No matter what happens next, you are safe." Grace was dying. No one held her hand in comfort. No one was with her to say goodbye. "Oh, God," I begged, "don't let the light at the end of the tunnel be just a leprechaun with shiny buckles on his shoes."

Grace had always known that whatever her strengths, whatever her journey, she could not prevent the storms that loomed on her horizon, nor the dark shadows that would be cast on her path. The better part of Grace's journey had been beset with the mischief of the spirit of Jack, transformed by intent and word, shape-shifting into the children that would end her. Grace's spirit was not done, but her body was. She couldn't fault that. It had served her well but it was done. Stubborn wills, and malicious hearts filled with cunning had conspired to confuse and overpower her. She was beaten and spent. She could feel herself dissolving into nothingness. Her spirit tried to accept it, but her body fought violently against it. Her arms flailed furiously. She knew she could not withstand it. She moved toward one world looking back at another. This was it. This was the moment she had anticipated. Grace was no stranger to the abyss. She had faced it often. Now she turned as she always had to the strength of prayer. She prayed fervently in a still small voice. As she prayed, angels beheld her agony and gathered.

Beyond the dark recesses of the tunnel before her, she saw a radiant glow. She felt a soft breeze. Brilliance filled the darkness and the sky opened. A Cherub moved toward her, arms outstretched. The mighty angel who stands in God's presence, stood at her side.

"Where have you been?" Grace cried.

"Right here," the Cherub assured her.

Grace peered into the brilliance. "Where's Elle?"

The Cherub spread her wings. With a rush of wind, Grace lifted. She was at last free of Blackwater, free of the hold it had on her. With another flutter of the Cherub's wings, Grace looked upon her children, scattered and alone. "What is it, Grace?" The Cherub asked.

"What will become of them?"

Two giant Principalities moved forward, wearing crowns and carrying scepters, followed by a glinting, gleaming cross, immersed in a waterfall of glittering gold. "Their spirits are trapped," one said.

"Oh, no," protested Grace. "I must help them."

"They have received the Word, but have not heeded," the Principality answered. "They must remain bound by their choices."

"I must help them," Grace repeated firmly.

The Cherub reached her hand to Grace. "You have carried your journey to the end, Grace. You have God's great favor. What you desire will be done. You will be there, Grace. Do not worry. You will be there."

Grace stared in wonder. She felt no pain. The Cherub lifted and suspended her in time and place. "Come," she said sweetly in a clear melodious tone. "Come." Grace looked back again. Far across the prairie, across snow and wind and cold spaces, she saw her granddaughter on her knees praying. Farther in the distance, in the balmy morning sea air she saw her daughter tilting her face to the morning sun as eagles circled above her. "I can't leave them," she exclaimed. "They are as broken as I am."

"You must come with us," the Cherub insisted. "It's the only way the three of you can heal."

"How?"

"You will see. You have great favor. What you desire will be."

"Promise?"

The Cherub and the mighty angel answered in unison. "Promise."

Grace had faced her final storm. She would be made to endure no more winters. The freak prairie blizzard blustered through, followed by new fury as jagged sheets of rain swept the snow into the river. When that force was spent, howling winds conceded to a shroud of silence and I returned to Scanlon Circle.

I stood alone overlooking her garden, gazing across the lawn through hazy shadows, quietly safeguarding the memory of geraniums nestled under climbing roses. I tilted my head, letting the cool Autumn drizzle patter against my face like the gentle caress of her fingertips, releasing a flood of memories, tumbling and cascading through my brain. "Pray for rain," I sighed.

"So we don't have to water the tomatoes," Grace chuckled.

I spun around to see her smiling back at me. "I thought I lost you!" I cried.

"I didn't leave you," she answered softly. "I'll never leave you."

"I knew I would find you here, Gram. I knew it."

"Only you knew, my barefoot girl. Only you and the rain knew for sure." Dawn's ambient glow spread across the horizon. "I stole a garden," she giggled.

"I know," I smiled. The steady drizzle pattered against the edge of the wide cedar deck. A robin perched under the overhang, watching us.

"I never got to wish you Happy Birthday, Gram."

"Every day is a birthday, Sweetheart."

I nodded. The air was crisp with change. "Are you ready?"

She answered as she always did. "Where's your car? Let's go." She grinned mischievously. "No one will know we were here. No one will notice we're gone. Let's go!"

After all this has passed, i still will remain
After i've cried my last, there'll be beauty from pain
Though it won't be today,
Someday i'll hope again
And there'll be beauty from pain
You will bring beauty from my pain

Hurly-burly

Singled out for who you are,
Takes all types to judge a man,
Feel. It's all you can.

Fill your sense with biggest ears,
Hide behind their own worst fears,
Live. It's all you can.

Ah but don't, don't sink the boat,
That you built to keep afloat,
Ah no don't, don't sink the boat,
That you built...you built to keep afloat.

As my thoughts brought me full circle to the day I boarded the bus, I looked around the quiet cabin. 'Life is not a journey,' I thought. 'Life is a dark adrenaline-infused water ride on a careening roller coaster through a hurricane. When it slows to a crawl, we want it to move faster. When it's over, we don't want to get off.' I turned to the murky shadows rolling past my window and marveled at Grace's ability to withstand. The bus crept farther and farther away from Blackwater Manor as skilled hands deftly arranged the broken body of the late queen for her final party.

The bus pulled into the depot and Sonja rose from her seat. "Are we still going to dinner?"

The intersection ahead was brightly lit and alive with traffic. Vibrant Halloween costumes, laughter and music awaited us. The strumming of a guitar drew us to the doorway of a bistro on the corner. "Oh!" Grace exclaimed. "Let's go in there. I don't want to miss the music."

"What?" Sonja shouted, dodging traffic as she crossed the street.

"Let's go in there," I shouted back. The tantalizing aromas of fresh brewed coffee and spicy barbecue in the open buffet welcomed us. Fuzzy spiders lined the soup caldrons labeled eye of newt and frog soup. A sixteenth-century barmaid led us to a table. Freddie Kruger and a prom zombie stared, grinning. Frankenstein, a gorilla and a neon skeleton settled in at the bar. A werewolf wailed on his guitar and howled, 'My mamma told me not to come,' into the microphone. We lingered over our food, embracing the revelry. Finally the clock struck midnight, the bar dimmed and we wandered back through the dark streets.

Sonja pointed to a Starbuck's sign in the window of the Stone Court Plaza on the corner. "Shall we?" She pushed through the door. "That mess at the depot will still be there when we get back." The hotel was bright and inviting. Starbucks was closed, but there were open couches next to a large, warm fireplace in the adjacent hotel lobby. It was deserted. "Oh!" she exclaimed. "There is a God." She sank into the luxurious cushions. "And we found his hiding place."

Grace rolled her eyes. "Really?" I kicked off my shoes.

"What?" Sonja asked absently.

"What?" I responded, surprised.

She clicked open her laptop. "Maybe I can check my email while we're here."

The desk clerk looked around the corner and pretended not to notice as she typed methodically on her laptop. "I think she can hear me," Grace whispered. Sonja looked up and smiled and went back to her email.

I reached deep in the side pocket of my bag and pulled out my cell phone. There were three voice messages. Seeing the missed calls and messages waiting on my phone brought the chaos of the past days, weeks and months back into focus. "Don't worry, Gram," I whispered. "You're safe now." I rested my head against the soft cushion and stared into the flickering fire until my eyes could no longer stay open.

"Time to go." Sonja slapped her laptop shut, stuffed it back into her bag and stood above me, stretching her arms to the cathedral ceiling and pointing toward the door. We power-walked the few blocks through the night back to the neon lights of the depot, looking ahead for signs of busses ready to board.

Wait!" I waved her back. "Hold up!" There outside the revolving glass doors of the depot stood a dozen armed police officers, hands on holsters, ready for action. Neon red and yellow strobe lights flashed from patrol cars parked nose-to-curb. We slowed our pace and circled wide around them into a back alley where we stared through the high narrow windows of a delivery door. Travelers crowded shoulder to shoulder perched on luggage, huddled against the walls or stretched out on the floor. Others crammed into available benches. More stood in lines leading to the ticket counter. There appeared to be a scuffle near the front doors where the lights were flashing. Officers stood over a lanky body of a man curled into a fetal position. One officer sat on his back, pinning his arms. The officer standing above him yelled, "Get up!" and kicked him. The man didn't move. Another officer zapped him with a taser. The man's body jerked and went limp. Again the officer leaned down and yelled, "Get up!" But the man didn't move. Again he zapped him.

Sonja watched in horror, then she pushed through the door. "What's going on?" I followed her in as she shoved through the crowd.

"He was just lying there," a teen answered, holding his cell phone high over his head. "The clerk kicked him but he didn't move so he called the cops. When the cops came, the guy didn't respond so they blasted him. He came up swinging. They stunned him and he went down. He never moved again but they keep shocking him." He looked back over his shoulder at us. "I've got a feed on U-tube."

"That's enough." A man grabbed the teen's elbow and steered him toward the door. "I'm Kevin. This is my son, Chance."

"You're on our bus!" Sonja exclaimed.

Kevin waved us back. "We're done here. It's going to be morning before we're on the road again. Hell! It's already morning."

We scanned the depot. Bodies sprawled across the floor, heads propped against duffle bags. Sonja turned to me. "Let's get out of here. Let's see if we can get back into the hotel lobby. Maybe they'll just look the other way for another couple of hours. She scanned the room. Where did those two go?" As I looked around the room I spotted the hollow looking woman from the bus. She didn't have a jacket. She wasn't carrying a purse. She seemed to be in her own private world, unaware of the chaos around her.

We left the depot and retraced our steps, back down the dark streets, to the Stone Court Plaza. There was a single post-it note on the glass door. A smiley face directed us to the side entrance. We stepped around to the side of the building and turned the knob. It was unlocked. We stared at each other in amazement, then we slipped in quietly. The fireplace was glowing, inviting us to our previous spots on the couches. Grateful for the peaceful respite, we relaxed against the soft leather cushions. Sonja flipped open her laptop. I pulled out my cell phone.

"Hey. Where are you? Are you OK?" Hearing Maire's voice made me smile.

"I'm OK. We're stuck here for a while. Next time I call we'll be somewhere between Coeur de'Alene and Spokane."

"Have you heard from the family?"

"There are messages. I haven't checked them."

"Well, just get here. Don't think about them."

"Right. I'll call again, but we'll be going through the mountains, so there may not be coverage." I hung up. Then I retrieved the messages.

"You have three missed calls. First missed call..."

"Elle. This is Quin." His voice was dispassionate, controlled. "I hadn't heard from you at all. I'm still hoping that you will be able to come for the funeral. I think it is...it is important that you come if you could. I'd sure appreciate it. If there's anything I can do further, just give me a call. I'd sure like to see you. Thanks."

"End of message. To reply to it, press eight. To delete it press seven. Next message..."

"Hi, Elle. This is Ralph calling. Just calling to say hi and to see how you're doing. Um..the visitation rosary is today, of course. I just hope to see you there or at the funeral, so, please give a call."

"End of message. To reply to it, press eight. To delete it press seven. Next message..."

"Hi Elle. This is your uncle, Ward. I am so sorry I'm calling you so late. It's almost midnight. I just wanted to give you a call and let you know that I love you so much and I miss you and I just wanted to call and talk with you about your maybe coming to Mom's funeral. Uh..I don't know what's been going on but I know that she loved you very, very much and I know that you meant an awful lot to her, especially how you cared for her and took care of her..um..and Dad, really, and I just wanted you to know that I'm going to be there tomorrow. I'm here if you come tomorrow I would feel very, very honored if you would sit with me. So I hope you can come tomorrow."

"End of message. To reply to it, press eight. To delete it press seven. Next message..."

"Elle, this is Ursula. This is a bad connection...."

I flipped my cell phone shut and slipped it back into my bag. They meant well, I suppose. But hearing their voices left me feeling desperately alone. And where were these people when I was being dumped to the curb, my belongings loaded into a moving van? Where were they while their mother was being terrorized? I stared into the flickering fire. Acer's words flashed through my mind telling me the family accused me of drugging their mother. Maire said it was a war between fear and faith, darkness and light. How could I judge? I left her there and drove away.

"But we're OK now," Grace interrupted.

"Yes," I whispered. "We're OK now." I held my grandmother close to my heart and drifted into sleep.

Early morning fog hovered outside Starbuck's as staff bustled through the lobby. The pungent aroma of rich coffee filled the air. Sonja and I quickly gathered our bags and exited, coffee and muffins in hand. "I feel like a schoolgirl after a prank," she laughed. "Can you believe it? Nobody kicked us out! I just hope the bus is still there."

"Oh, don't worry. That bus won't depart for hours."

We stood outside the depot, eyeing the wide expanse of sprawled bodies inside. Kevin and Chance joined us.

"It feels like we're stuck in a dark gray tunnel," Kevin grumbled. "We're at the mercy of guards on night patrol! We've got no choice but to wait for the next bizarre thing to happen."

Chance flipped through the screens on his phone. "Bus service is slowly returning, as southbound buses are expected to leave the terminal late this morning."

Hands in pockets, Kevin headed to the door and then turned back, pacing a wide circle. "Why is this happening now?"

"It's not what happens that is important," Grace offered. "It's how you deal with it."

What?" Sonja asked. "Did you say something?"

"What?" I answered. "No."

"We do have a choice!" Kevin announced suddenly. "We can refuse to be stuck. We can rent a car and drive the rest of the way. Are you two game?" Chance reached for their bags. "No, not yet, son. We can get a car, but we can't go until the fog lifts." He peered into the murky distance. "I'm hungry. Anyone for breakfast? There's supposed to be a coffee shop just blocks from here." He eyed our cups. "Looks like you've already found one."

"We're in," Sonja answered. "I welcome any reason to stretch our legs and stay out of that trouble in the terminal."

Sonja followed Chance, who followed Kevin as they picked their way through the dense fog across the parking lot and down the next block. The hollow looking woman stood in the doorway. She pointed to my coffee and the bag with the muffin. "Oh. Are you hungry? Do you have any money?" She reached into the breast pocket of her blue flannel shirt and pulled out a wrinkled pack of cigarettes. She poked a slender finger into the pack and pulled one out, offering it to me. "No, no thank you. You keep that." I handed her the cup and the bag. She took it and stepped back into the crush of people.

Chance flipped through screens on his cell phone. "They say there is nothing suspicious about it. The bus driver they interviewed said because there were so many people sleeping on the terminal floor it was difficult to tell that the man was in need of assistance." He flipped to another screen. "Another driver said stranded passengers piled into buses until investigators finish at the scene. Others just left the terminal." He looked up as I joined them. "That's us!"

"Why do people just stand by?" I wondered out loud.

Kevin and Sonja were deep into conversation. "Where's your destination?" Kevin asked her.

"Not far," Sonja answered. "Idaho. It's our first anniversary."

"Congratulations."

"Thanks. I'm kind of nervous."

"You don't like to travel?"

"It's not that. We were married before he was deployed." She paused. "He was injured."

"Oh, that's terrible."

She leaned across the aisle and grinned self-consciously. "It'll be like a first date." She gazed out the window at the fog.

"Like a first date?" Kevin asked.

"We met on the Internet."

"No. Really?" Chance blurted. "Dad should do that."

"Why?" Sonja checked her words, embarrassed. "Sorry, I mean, it was right for me, but..." Chance nodded affirmation. She leaned over the table emphatically. "Forget what I said. You should get out there. Do it. There's no reason to be alone."

"I have to admit, it's been a while," Kevin answered slowly.

"How long?" Sonja sipped on her drink, studying him over her straw. "What was it? Divorce?"

"Mom was killed in the 9-11 attacks," Chance interjected.

The table went silent. "It's all right," Kevin added quickly. "Chance and I speak of it all the time. He unwrapped his breakfast burrito.

"I was supposed to be with her," Chance chimed in. "But she changed her mind."

"Thank God!" gasped Sonja. Then she checked herself again. "I'm sorry. I'm sorry."

"That's all right," Kevin assured her. "I got a call to meet with an investigator. I thought it was routine, but turns out, it was because she gave my son's ticket to someone else." Kevin stared at his burrito. None of us knew what to say. He fixed his gaze on his son. "I thought we were on a good course. Then we hit a bump in the road. I felt like that guy who got blasted with the taser, stranded and stunned."

Sonja reached across the table. "If we were to go through our life without any bumps, we wouldn't know our strength."

He suddenly withdrew his hand, stood and pushed his chair back. "I'm tired of waiting. Let's get the car and get the hell out of here."

We walked back to the depot in the quiet introspection. I stood by looking on as Kevin, Chance and Sonja loaded their bags into the trunk of the rental car and drove away through the heavy mist.

"You three be careful," Grace called after them. "You watch out for each other. Don't get hurt!" Sonja turned back, smiled and blew us a kiss. It occurred to me that being shut off from the truth is like being engulfed in that fog, searching for a way along an invisible river.

G race had traveled a very long way, on a journey that took her from gaslights to ringer washers, through pregnancies, hip replacements, broken bones, cancer, a crushed femur and an excruciating death. When Grace began her journey, there was a story already written. It began generations before her. Grace never claimed to be a wise person. She gave all credit to God and to others. She saw herself as a channel of peace for her children and grandchildren. She respected her elders as a repository for wisdom. During the last half of her life, she learned, much to her wonder, that women could be recognized for their own achievements. She had her own stories to share. The love she offered was a gift. She expected her children and grandchildren to share that love. She expected to have a place in their lives. Her journey was not over. She was more relevant at that point in her life than she had ever been. She expected her children and grandchildren to know that. They did not. She thought they were smarter than that.

Back on the bus, I settled my shoulders against the molded seat. She needed me but I let them chase me away. I left her. Yet, here she was with me. "Grace," I whispered, "you are a mystery wrapped in a riddle."

The faint whirring sound of the bus engine rocked my brain in rhythm to the renewed spattering of rain on the window. Soon I was lulled into the first deep sleep I had in over a week. The ache in my heart loosened its grip a bit as the bus carried me farther and farther away from the spiritual gutter of Blackwater Manor.

I dreamed a brilliant flash of lightening leapt through the sky, piercing the darkness like a meteor, igniting a prairie fire. The fire raced across the horizon, building fast, following the river to a solitary farm house. A windstorm whipped the flames higher. The intensity of the heat cracked the window panes. The glass shards flew through the air. There from within the darkness of the house, bodiless heads peered. Then the rain began. I woke, shaking my head to free my thoughts of the image.

"It's OK. We're OK now." Grace's voice soothed me.

"I'm so sorry I wasn't there, Gram. I'm so sorry I couldn't protect you. Why wasn't I stronger?" My cell phone beeped. "Maire?"

"Are you sitting down? What am I saying? You're on a bus. Of course you're sitting down."

"What? What is it?"

"Crystal Ann posted a photo of Mom in her casket!"

"Why would she do that?"

"It's surreal. Are you seeing what I'm seeing?"

I flipped through the screens. "What the hell! Is that a black wig? Where are her beautiful soft curls?" I held the screen to the light to get a closer look.

"Who would do that to their mother?" Maire seethed. "Get this. Crystal Ann included a picture of Dad. Even Mom's funeral had to be about Dad."

"Oh!" I shot straight up in my seat.

"You see it now?" Maire prompted me impatiently. "Her hands, her arms, her entire body is hidden up to her shoulders. She looks frozen. Her face is puffy. She's wrapped like a mummy. What does that mean?"

"Her hands should be holding her rosary." I zoomed in on the screen.

"What happened to her hands and arms? Why are they hidden? I cringe to think what that might mean. Why on earth would they put her in a wig? It's bizarre! The first thing I looked for was her rings, her rosary and her beautiful hands."

"Her hands and arms would be bruised if she struggled."

"Quin said he would not force feed her. Hell, she was already starving!" Maire blasted. "He said he'd put a pain patch on her. It was over twenty-four hours between the time he said that and the time he called to tell me she died." Maire was quiet. "She may have died in Grand Mal seizure! They may have restrained her. They've certainly done that before. Jesus! She was an animal in a trap."

"What is she wearing?"

She looks like a mummified queen that was bundled too tight."

"I wasn't a queen," Grace interrupted.

"Gram!"

"What?" Maire asked. "Who are you talking to?"

"They resent me because I couldn't stand up to Jack," Grace answered. "I wasn't strong enough."

"You did the best you could, Gram. What more could you do?"

Maire's voice came back through my phone. "Mom lived for her children and this is what she got for it."

"Remember the snapshot we took in her garden, Maire? That is the woman I remember."

"You're breaking up. I'm losing you. Can you hear me?" The phone went dead. The screen went dark. I jammed the phone into my bag. "Why does this madness continue?"

"Perhaps when you destroy those that love you, there is something you want more than love." I turned in my seat to see Yoki's brown, weathered face. He quietly eyed me from under the brim of his Stetson. I rose from my seat and moved next to him, taking in his words. He turned away to gaze beyond. Then he turned back to me. "Do you want to solve the riddle now?"

"Yes." I had forgotten all about the riddle. "I need a diversion."

"In that case, I have a story for you. Years ago I married a beautiful young woman. Not only was she beautiful, but she was also smart. I met her in law school. We had a daughter. I had a good job. She did too. She was a good mother and a good lawyer. I wanted to move back to the reservation. She didn't want that for her daughter, but in the end I won out and we moved. I sat on tribal council and she worked tribal court. Our daughter struggled in an inferior school system in an impoverished community. One day my wife came home to find her crouched and crying. She tried to comfort her, but all my daughter said was, 'He made me touch him.' My wife rushed through the house, searching for the intruder. She didn't have to look far. My brother lay on the couch, passed out in a drunken stupor. My wife raged with the fury of Haokah! She flew to the fireplace, grabbed a log from the embers and unleashed her wrath. When she finally stopped, his body was embedded with slivers of wood and covered with blood. It was then that I walked through the door." Yoki paused. He gaped into an abyss I sensed but couldn't see. "I did not run to help my wife. No. Instead, I turned on her. I told her it was her problem to solve. So she wrapped the body in blankets and dragged him to the car. The next morning, the front page news showed a photo of a man frozen in the snow in front of his own house. That was that. It was assumed he collapsed there, drunk. No one pursued it. But I did not let it end there. I threatened that if she did not pay me, I would turn her in. She would go to prison and our daughter would have no mother."

"Why would you do that?" I stared, incredulous.

"I was jealous. She had no right to be my equal! She was just a woman!"

"Go on."

"She moved away but her fear was so great that every month she sent money to keep the truth hidden. Many years passed. Then one day a beautiful young lawyer, probably the same age as you, faced me in court." He looked at me and then looked away. "She was beautiful and she was smart. She won the case.

She approached me afterwards, but she did not shake my hand. She handed me an envelope and told me it was the last payment I would ever receive from her mother."

I hesitated to speak. "I thought I was traveling with a sage," I finally got out. "Turns out you're struggling to find your way like the rest of us."

"The truth that I seek is my own," he said. "I was jealous, angry and greedy. I took everything from her until she had nothing more to lose. Now I am the loser. I thought what I owned was a measure of my worth. The punishment for my greed is losing pleasure in anything I gained."

I sighed. "Do you think your daughter will ever forgive you?"

"I'm afraid she will tell me that forgiveness is not hers to give. I know in my heart that forgiveness can only come from her mother. It's too late for that. Her mother is gone. I tried to make my wife feel shame—my shame. But I could not break her. The right choices lead us to life. The wrong choices lead us to death. I know you understand. I have watched you since the first day you boarded, dealing with your own demons."

"I thought on this trip I might see past the confusion," I answered. I looked beyond him through the window. The rain had stopped. "What is that?" I pointed. Yoki followed my gaze. Two eagles flew low. "Look!" I pointed again. One soared above the window. A long, waving tail hung from his beak.

"It's a snake," Yoki exclaimed. "That eagle is carrying a snake. Look how it's winding and coiling in the wind. Yoki laughed. "The second eagle is flying shotgun!" We laughed together and watched in wonder as the two eagles soared beyond a break of trees and the bus sped on. Yoki leaned back and sighed. "The eagle has great vision. He sees there are two ways through life. The way of self and the way of love. We have to choose. Love is selfless. Love accepts being slighted, forgotten, disliked even. Love accepts insults and injuries. Self is loveless. Self bids others to please it. Self likes to control and have its own way. Self finds reasons to be unhappy while love smiles through all things. When the storm breaks, each man acts according to his own vision. Some flee, some stand strong, some spread their wings and soar. That is the eagle's way."

"Some carry their enemies with them," I quipped. I thought of Kevin. "And sometimes the truth falls out of the sky." My cell phone beeped.

"Check your email," Maire blurted seething. I thumbed through the screens on my phone to email and uploaded.

"My email is jammed full," I mumbled. "I have to unblock it. What's going on?"

"It's full because Crystal Ann has sent hundreds of emails." "What is going on?" She stopped.

"What?"

"Elle, her rings are on the Internet!" Maire was livid. I listened, aghast. I couldn't utter a sound. Maire was not at a loss of words. "This is how the Riordens honor their mother's memory?"

Suddenly my screen came alive and I frantically thumbed through the images. I scrolled through the screens in stunned silence. My heart ached with a hurt so deep I couldn't fathom it.

"Jabez said enlarge my territory. He didn't say give me someone else's! This is ego plundering and pillaging to get its needs met," Maire shouted. "Ego thrives on attention. Well, they'll get plenty of attention doing this. Murderers!"

"Murderers?"

"What the hell else would you call it? You said when you left Mom, she couldn't eat, speak or move on her own. She was whimpering, at best."

"Yes."

"She should have been in the care of a hospice. Instead, they parade her around town, dressed like a queen with a crown of thorns, first to Mass at the Cathedral, then to a baptism, then to a family dinner at Royal Court and then to a reception at Blackwater Manor. That's degradation at it's cruelest. You know she had to have been sedated to survive that. Then they blamed you?"

"Family members see her for the first time in months, maybe for the first time this year. Acer or Bric or both whisper that I drugged her and the guild hotline spreads the word like a prairie fire."

"Jacelyn's email praises Crystal Ann for holding her hand the entire time. Bullshit!" Maire erupted. "The entire family looked the other way while their mother suffered. They shamed her."

"Then Acer set me up for an ambush. "Bastard!"

"Bastard!" Maire shouted over the air waves.

"Girls!" Grace scolded. "Settle down."

"I'm sorry, Gram, but in this family, bizarre is normal. Why would anyone behave like this?"

"Who are you talking to?" Maire asked. "Anyway, it doesn't matter, because she wasn't there."

"What are you saying now?" I asked.

"She left when I did. You were sitting with an empty shell."

"So you're saying the time I spent with her was... what? Inconsequential?"

"No, not inconsequential. I'm just saying she wasn't there."

My mind went numb. "I forgot," I whispered. "You are a Riorden. To you I am invisible."

"No, that's not what I meant."

"I am not invisible," I whispered. She was silent. I was silent. Yoki slept. Ancient Eyes knitted on a strand soft gray wool. The moon shimmered through the cold distant night. Shadows of buttes skimmed the horizon like the backs of huge serpents sleeping in the earth. Then a blue orb flickered in the darkness. It grew slowly, until it danced in the air next to my seat.

"Hey, look what I can do," Grace exclaimed, dancing around me.

"Gram!" The phone fall to my lap. I leaned my head against the cool window, watching the shimmering orb.

"You girls stop fighting," Grace scolded softly. "There is work to do."

"OK, Gram," I whispered, "but I am not invisible."

"I know," she whispered.

"Don't leave me Gram."

"I'm right here," she soothed. "I'm right here."

"The old spirits believed there is a rod chosen carefully from the tree of sacrifice," Yoki uttered, his eyes still closed.

I turned, surprised. "I thought you were sleeping."

"This rod, wielded by a faithful messenger of God can be made to reveal truths out of mysteries and secrets."

"Are you saying you wield that rod?"

"No, Elle. I am saying you are that rod."

"Me? I am no one. I am invisible."

"You may be invisible, Elle, but you walk with Grace."

I smiled. "Yes, I do."

I fell asleep to the warm smell of him next to me. I slept for a very long time. I woke as he tugged on my sleeve. "This is my stop."

"Where are we?"

"Washington."

"Find your daughter," I said, shaking myself awake.

He stood in the aisle, a bag slung over his shoulder. He leaned back over the seat top. "When you first stepped on this bus, you were troubled and grieving. The decision to follow your own vision is a choice. We call it finding your own buffalo." He turned to go and then turned back. "May I offer some advice?"

"Yes." I brushed the sleep from my eyes.

"Be careful of the game. The opponent you face may be yourself." I looked up at the big man as he turned to go. He turned back. "When you're in a tunnel the light at the end will always be a train." He smiled. "Because the light of truth comes from within." He patted my shoulder. "You are at the end of this tunnel. If you don't want to get hit by the train, it may be a good time to get off the tracks."

I nodded. He walked into the depot as the bus pulled away. I picked up the phone and dialed Maire. I needed accord after that last clash. Her voice exploded across the air waves. "It's bad. Very bad."

"Now what?"

"I am looking out the window across the back deck and the Fed Ex guy is surrounded by a pile of boxes. They all have Mom's return address! These people are just plain evil! I asked him if I could refuse them. He said no. All he could do was deliver them."

"What's in the boxes?"

"Junk. Just junk. These things should have gone to the dump or to a thrift store. It's the same old narcissistic game! We can't escape. Ten boxes! Ten boxes might suggest to someone there is something really important in there somewhere. All that is there is a slap in the face!"

"Doesn't any one of them object to this upheaval?" I asked.

"No one does. Apparently no one can," she returned. "We all just stand by and watch Acer plunder and pillage. Well, stubborn pride is going to get someone killed someday."

"Why do you think they are doing this?"

"As far as I can see, from here on out it's going to be a constant battle. They will go on blaming themselves and taking it out on everyone else, but they can't stop what they have put into motion. They have to bury themselves in this bruhaha so they don't think about what might come next. Guess what? They can run hurly-burly for a thousand years, but they cannot escape the truth."

"Hold on, I'm getting an email." I paused to read it. "Maire, turn on your computer and pull up your email."

"What are you looking at? Oh, I see." She gave out a low whistle.

"This email says Acer sold Scanlon Circle for a loss. Why would he lock up, abandon and disrespect his mother just to turn around and discard her assets? Who are these people?"

"I know exactly who they are. Mary Caye believes that with enough self-love, drugs and cosmetic surgery, her life will be satisfying. Crystal Ann exudes pride and envy, desperate to prove that she would be a better matriarch to this family than her mother ever was. Acer is driven by a lust for the power his father wielded. Quin is overshadowed by Acer's influence, so he hides his pain behind the mask of medicine. Dierdre is consumed by unfulfilled entitlement. She will steal what is not given to her. Aiden is enraged. He is neither the heir nor the spare. All the rest are irrelovent. Ralph hides behind normalcy of nine-to-five clinic life. Ward escapes to the virtual parallel universe of Los Angeles. Bric self-medicates to convince himself he is not invisible. Seth buys the homage he desires. Liam is steadfast, honest and straightforward. But if he doesn't join ranks, he risks being seen as weak. Riley is wise. He knows to stay off the tracks and out of the tunnel. Llyssa hides behind Bric, thinking the devil you know is better than the devil you don't know. Ursula is content to be content. I know exactly who they are and what they are doing. They welcome this clamor to affirm their existence."

"Portland is coming up next. I'll see you tomorrow."

"Yes," Grace agreed. "You girls should let this go now. Tomorrow is a new day."

I leaned back into the seat. How could I avoid the pull of the vortex? How would I find my way to that place in the sea where all things float? I thought of the researcher. "Don't give up on the clues," he said. "It's how you find your way." I thought of his parting advice. "Follow the riddle."

My phone beeped. An email from Blackwater Manor sprang to the screen. There was a letter from Mallory Patos, Director of Blackwater Social Services. I scanned the words.

> *May you find comfort in your memories as I*
> *hold Grace in mine. I don't ever see a lady*
> *in a hat that doesn't bring Grace to mind.*
> *There was much to celebrate in Grace's life*
> *and her spirit remains near and dear.*

I stared at the screen. Was she kidding? I hit delete as an image flashed through my mind. Did I miss the obvious? Mallory was a blonde. Mallory wore black. Mallory was always there when something went wrong. Mallory ambushed Grace in the hospital. Mallory reported our every move to the Riordens. Mallory escorted residents to every concert. Was Grace pointing to Mallory?

"Gram, did Mallory lock you in the bathroom and knock you down?"

My mind was caught in a spin. Yoki's words came back. "Be careful of the game. The opponent you face may be yourself." Ancient Eyes smiled quietly at me from across the aisle.

The landscape is changing, I thought, as I looked out through the bus window. The last of the seven riddles danced in my brain like the Leprechaun's jig. *What measures a man's girth but only on earth? What exalts as often as it shames? What fury wears the mask of mirth while it gives up to lay it's claim?* I couldn't sort it out.

"Show me, Gram," I whispered.

No matter where i put my head,
I wake up feeling sound again,
Breathe. Its all you can.
It's all you can
It's all you can... do.

Ah but don't, don't sink the boat,
That you built, you built to keep afloat,
Ah no don't, don't sink the boat,
That you built... you built to keep afloat.

A New Dawn

This is my brand new day starting now
I let go the things that weigh me down
And rob me of the beauty that's to be found
And life all around
And this is my prayer without ceasing,
the negative releasing
And as i rise above, my burden is easing
This is my brand new day starting now

Ancient Eyes slid into the seat next to me. "You had a dream." She watched me, waiting. I welcomed her warmth.

"Yes," I answered. "I dreamed I was suspended in time and space. A hurricane raged around me." I closed my eyes to recapture the image. "I felt myself evaporating, molecule-by-molecule, disappearing. Then I was gone." I stared at the vision replaying in my head. "Then I was gone." She nodded silently. "For what might have been a millisecond or a moment in eternity, I don't know which, I was my grandmother. I felt her isolation as her children exiled her. I felt her desperation as her caretakers abused her. I felt the pain that ached in her body and shot through her jaw. I felt the terror of being trapped in a violent struggle. Yet, at the center of the tempest, I knew that she was as still and as pure as a single drop of rain." Her unwavering gaze brought me back to present. "I believe my dream was a gift from my grandmother. She wanted me know. She wanted me to understand."

Ancient Eyes folded her delicate white hands. "Do you remember the story I told of the turtle and the shark? Like the turtle, your grandmother balanced the weight of good and evil. Like the drop of rain, her spirit transformed. You are the shark that guarded her passage. Your grandmother emerged from confusion to calm, from darkness to dawn. Your grandmother's body struggled, but her spirit was already free. Free is not finished. When you were physically removed, you were closer to her than ever before. Invisible is not ineffective. The warrior spirit, after all, has no form. The warrior spirit is motionless in motion. Your grandmother's spirit is no longer bound by pride, envy or wrath. Nor is it held captive by avarice, addiction or ambition. It is free from malice, entitlement and fear. It has attained harmony and intuitive knowledge. From your dream, you know the formidable effortless power of the still spirit. We should embrace the end of life, no matter how it ends, as another stage in a wondrous journey. That was your gift to your grandmother."

Ancient Eyes smiled. "The truth rises like a sleeping serpent. Your battle may not be over, but I believe when the serpent approaches, you will not avert your eyes. Instead, you will stand in exhilaration." The bus slowed and pulled off the Interstate. "This is my stop," she said, rising to her feet.

"Wait. I don't know your name."

"I am Mamori Kami." She bowed gracefully and stepped to the ground where she stood backlit by the early morning dawn as the bus pulled away. She was radiant.

"Gram," I sighed, "about these dreams I'm having, are you sending them to me?"

My grandmother's patient voice filled the void in my head. "Sometimes we meet the truth on the very road we took to avoid it."

The bus pulled into Portland. I gathered my bags, moved to the front of the bus, turned and stepped down the three steps to the street. I thought about all the people we meet and leave along our journeys. Some step to the side as we move on, etching their faces into our heart's memory, knowing we will never meet again. Others move on ahead of us, leaving us behind, anticipating a future time and space where will be reunited.

Exiting passengers collected bags and moved quickly to waiting vehicles. I stood in the quiet night air, face to face with the strange hollow-looking woman. Before I could speak, she shuffled past me, into the shadows. Then the clerk locked the depot doors and I was alone. I was invisible. 'Embrace the still spirit,' I thought.

"We'll wait," Grace whispered.

A cab turned the corner and parked at the curb. "I'm meeting someone," I called to him. I looked around. I felt like I'd just run a marathon and there was no one at the finish line.

"I'll wait with you," he answered. "No charge." I stood by the cab as he chatted about the neighborhood, the economy, his job, his life, the possibility of a black president and change. Celia's Suburban pulled up next to him. He tipped his hat and backed away. As he did, I thought I saw the glint of a toothy smile.

On the ride to the restaurant, Maire turned to the two boys and said, "This is Elle."

The youngest boy leaned over the seat and said, Grandma, who is she to me?" Maire, Celia and I burst into laughter.

"Good boy," Grace cheered.

The boys colored quietly at the table while Celia ordered from the menu. Maire launched into a conversation that had been interrupted weeks before. "I'm going to need a sign. I need to know that her sacrifice meant something." I watched the two boys nudging and giggling. Maire ran her fingers over the Crayolas, selecting a color. She drew broad strokes on her placemat. "Mom could have had a much different life. From the stories I heard growing up, she had another suitor when she met Dad.

"I remember Grandpa shouting his name like it was a curse," I laughed. "Chauncey!"

"Chauncey?"

"I met him. He looked like her brother Colin, distinguished, kind, happy."

"No!" She looked to the boys and back at me. "How ironic. She might have lived in a sleepy little town with her brother nearby, sharing holidays, family picnics, graduations and weddings. Instead she spent her entire life sheltering her children from the brunt of her husband's fury." She looked back at the boys, coloring at the table. "Imagine the life her children would have had. Those children would not have been raised like we were, in borrowed shoes looking through broken windows."

"Speaking of irony, remember Dachs Raben?"

"Dad's nemesis."

"Turns out, Dachs Raben left his entire estate to the church. Just imagine. If Grace and Jack had sold their land to him..."

"It would now be in the hands of God!" She laughed. "Now that's ironic!"

Listening to Maire's words, I realized that during these past days of introspection on the bus it was possible that I had learned no new truths. Perhaps I simply came to know some very old ones. I realized that the river that I followed here is the same river that I left behind, the same river waiting to take us to the sea. "Sometimes I feel like my heart is just one big broken window," I said.

"This isn't over yet," she answered. "I feel Mom moving around me. Sometimes when I speak, it's her voice I hear. I believe she must be very busy right now. She said she wasn't done. She has to finish her purpose on earth. Her spirit will nudge each one of her children. One by one each will feel the chill. One by one each will her hear voice. One by one each will come to terms with the deeds of this past year. One by one each will atone for the agony of her death. One by one each will be disrespected as they disrespected her. I know something in the spirit realm is about to take place. Mom saw her mother pass by without a word or glance. You can be sure that Grace Riorden's spirit will not pass by silently. I think we can look forward to some surprises." Suddenly, as easily as changing purses, she changed topics. "Tell me about your God."

"My God is a sudden breeze in tall grass, quiet mornings in the garden, a single drop of rain."

"My God is favor. I believe no matter who we are, what we believe or what our next move is, God has issued a Get Out of Hell Free Card for you and me. The rest of the family will have to fend for themselves."

I laughed. "I believe that. When Grandpa Jack died we chose to walk with Grace. Now Grace chooses to walk with us."

A smile fluttered across her face. "I'm happy you are here. We can drive to the ocean tomorrow morning and greet the dawn with Mom."

We drove through tree lined streets, covered with a carpet of brightly colored leaves. "I can't get my thoughts around the nagging questions," I mused. "What was that all about?"

"It's the Riorden rush," Maire answered. "They fly high, intoxicated by their own illusions. Anger, envy, greed, arrogance and desire for power are all super-sized. They heed no boundaries. They recognize no consequences. Now that she's gone, they can wax poetic about their beautiful mother, because that is what others want to hear. Whatever commitment they profess, it is a lie. A commitment is only a commitment when it has no expiration date. Acer, Quin, Crystal Ann and Bric signed off on a care plan that would break her. Certainly there was a prize. To win any war there must be commercial gain. All the rest was just noise to hide the real agenda. Each one of those boys think they are entitled to the farm land. This is their chance to beat the leprechaun out of the pot of gold. I knew it at his funeral. I saw them huddled together and I said, 'It's starting.' There were days when I pitied her. She asked over and over, 'Where is everybody? Why aren't they coming?' I said, 'They don't care, Ma.' She looked straight at me and said without hesitating, 'I thought they were smarter than that.' She knew it. She just wanted me to say it out loud. She accepted the truth, but it broke her heart. She loved us for sticking with her but no one would ever be as important to her as her sons."

Then she changed thoughts again. "I think that was Crystal Ann's issue. She wants the power a son would have, but she's just a woman. The next best thing is to take her mother's place!"

"Envy is a powerful force. It's one of the seven deadliest."

"Why do you think they abandoned her?"

"I think they were waiting for you to make a mistake," Maire concluded.

Celia returned to the table with a tray of food. "All it would have taken would be for you to give her a Tylenol. On top of the pain patch? Without a prescription? That would be a federal offense."

I stared at her. Maire jumped in. "Isn't that what Acer was accusing you of? I think Celia's right. After seeing her drugged up at her birthday party, all it would have taken would be for one of the staff to catch you giving her something, anything. But you never did."

"I couldn't get back to her."

"The pawn is the one player in the game that transforms when it reaches the other side. In the game of good and evil, Gram is on the other side, transformed."

The next morning as dawn burst over the shimmering horizon, Maire and I stood overlooking a sea as serene as infinity. Waves rippled like silk against the sandy shoreline.

"Is she in God's grace?" Maire asked.

"She is God's grace," I answered.

"Then by the Grace of God, it is what it is," Maire said quietly.

I gazed at the clouds floating overhead. "I have been blessed to have a life with Grace."

"We kept safe the one thing they couldn't steal from her," Maire mused.

"What's that?" The water lapped contentedly at our toes.

"We were lucky to have had her love."

The water caressed our ankles and receded. "I am lucky to have had someone to love."

"Mom's spirit soars with eagles above a sea without storms." Her smile broadened into a wide contented grin. "She is rooted in us while she soars beyond." Maire tossed a single rose onto a wave. Then bathed in the brilliance of a new dawn, we strolled together along the water's edge.

Life gives us a journey and many reasons to make that journey. There is rebirth, discovery, challenge and growth. Sometimes the journey is reason enough. The best we can do is hope and pray for the strength to follow a true path. The road may not be easy but we will know where we are going if we set our compass to the dawn, into new possibilities. Life with Grace taught me that each new day is worth living and that hope is worth keeping alive. I know now that although Maire and I stumbled and struggled to see Grace through the dark days of Blackwater, every move we made was the right one. I now know that I will look at life through the eyes of Grace, with a clarity that comes from peace and with a smile that comes from mirth. Because I know now, having survived the wilderness, the human condition is irrelevant. The spiritual condition is the essence of life.

By nightfall, I was again standing on the platform of the bus depot, bags in hand. "I wish you'd stay a little longer," Maire urged.

"I will be back soon. If I leave now I'll be able to attend the memorial for Sean's wife, Matty."

"I know it's important to be there, Elle. Matty and Sean were the only sane people in our lives."

"Matty and Gram died the way they lived. Matty died surrounded by love and prayers. Gram died standing alone against the storm."

"Even so, we can be sure that their spirits are free now and at peace."

As the driver pushed the lever and the double doors closed behind me, I thought of the last words of Mamori Kami. 'Your battle may not be over. When the serpent approaches, you will not avert your eyes. Instead, you will stand in exhilaration." I wondered what that meant. Her name rolled around in my head. Mamori Kami. What a beautiful sound.

When the bus stopped again, I looked down a mountain, across the tops of tall pines, as black as they were green. Below there was a cascading waterfall and a peaceful valley. I left my bags at the depot and walked the distance to a stone church nestled against a cove. The doors stood open. I slid into a pew at the back of the chapel unnoticed. The scent of burning candles mingled with the perfume of incense charged the room with the aura of Grace. The organist played a hymn. The priest lead the family in a processional. Mass began. I glanced around the church. I was the only member of Jack and Grace Riorden's family. How sad, I thought, after all Sean and Matty had given to us during our lives. There was movement behind me. Acer slid into a back pew. He stared straight ahead. He didn't see me. The priest spoke of a woman who loved her husband, loved her children, loved her community, loved her gardens. Matty was cherished. Grace was thrown away. The priest turned and raised his arms to the congregation and offered a final blessing to go in peace. The family filed into the center aisle and moved slowly in procession toward the back of the church. Matty's daughter looked up, burst into tears, left the procession, moved to where I stood and threw her arms around me. Looking over her shoulder, I braced myself, expecting to come face to face with Acer, but he was gone. There was only his coat lying on the pew. He had vanished. I looked toward the exit. I looked toward the back of the church. I looked toward the doors. He was gone.

I left the church and walked through the crisp autumn air, turning up an array of vibrant wet leaves underfoot. "He acted like he just heard his own eulogy and didn't like it," the voice behind me quipped. I spun around.

"Mom! You're here."

"I warned Acer he would face his actions one day," Faith answered. "Today he faced the light and he ran in fear. He can't run for long. He really should have gotten to know us better."

"Did you see him run?" A second voice startled me.

"Gram! You're here too? What are you two talking about? Why did Acer run?"

"He thought he broke you," Faith answered. "He told the family you were abusive, unstable, pushing pain killers on your grandmother. Yet here you are and Sean and Matty's family welcomes you with open arms. You proved him to be the liar he is."

"Or, it could be because he saw me," Grace interrupted.

"Gram?"

"When you look out through evil eyes, there's nothing more frightening than to have Grace smiling back at you," Faith laughed.

Grace chuckled. "He thought he buried me. Then for one terrifying second he saw me and I smiled and he knew he was in trouble." I could see the dimples playing in her cheeks. "Did he see you, too, Faith?"

"I made sure he did," my mother retorted.

"Gram! Mom!" I laughed. "What are you two up to?"

"I told you, Sweetheart, I'm not done yet."

"You're a super chick, Gram."

"Hey, what about me?" Faith pouted.

"The verdict's still out on you, Mom."

"You girls!" Grace answered.

A BMW slowed in the street and parked at the curb. Ronan slid out. "I have your car waiting at the station," he said. "I'll drive you there."

He handed me an envelope. "I thought you might like to read while I drive."

I stared at the package. "It's been with me the entire time?"

"It must have gotten mixed in with your papers when they kicked you out," he quipped.

Ronan drove while I settled into the soft leather seat and opened the pages of the ledger. Afternoon turned to evening as I studied the columns and rows. Ronan flicked on the reading light. I closed the ledger and reached for the Last Will and Testament of John Riorden. There was the codicil. There was a hand-written will tucked behind that. I looked up as Ronan pulled into a strip mall.

"I could use some coffee. Same for you?" The bright lights of a 24-hour Kinkos glared against the wet street lights.

"I'll just be over there," I pointed.

Back behind the wheel, Ronan sipped on his coffee. I dialed Maire.

"Maire, are you awake?"

"I am now," she answered faintly.

"Check your email."

"Now? What time is it?"

"I am reading Grandpa's will and testament and a codicil. Check your email."

"Where did you get that? Wait a minute," she answered, yawning. "Wha?" She was instantly awake. Her voice was clear and sharp.

"Check out the second page of the codicil."

"I see it. Wait a minute! Dad's signature in the codicil doesn't look like the signature in the will."

"Right. What else do you see?"

"I'm reading. Oh! The legal description is wrong! The amendments reference one section of land. The legal description in the original refers to another."

"Right. See anything else?"

"The dates don't match. The codicil references a will ten years earlier than the one attached. Wait. There's more. The date on the notary signature line is different from the date in Dad's signature line. There is no way Dad would have signed a document with that many mistakes in it."

"This document is dated four years before Grandpa's death. It doesn't make sense. Look at the two articles that are amended. The first deletes the clause that the title remain with Gram until her death. If Grandpa had removed that clause, Gram would have known about it. He taunted her until the day he died that her children would steal the land from her. If he had taken the land out of her hands, it would have been a closed subject. The second clause removes the cash gift to each of his children. If he had the article deleted from the will, he would have taken the money out of the CDs."

"That money wasn't cashed out until after Dad's death," Maire affirmed. "I know because I called the bank and asked what happened to it. The bank officer said the Trustee can do whatever the Trustee wants with that money."

She hung up. 'Does an error-riddled codicil affect the outcome of anything now?' I wondered. I refolded the papers and tucked them back into the envelope. This was all old news. A greeting card fell out and onto my lap. The whimsical drawing on the front flap was of two girls in the midst of a tea party in a garden. One wore a straw hat. Both wore heavy lace up shoes. There was a single robin perched nearby. I stared at the writing inside.

To someone very special,
and loving and kind.
Have a very happy birthday.
I love you very much!
Love, Gram

This was a card meant for me. The writing was unmistakable. It was from Gram. I looked up, expecting to see her looking back but she was hiding. "Gram, what is this?"

"I wasn't able to wish you a Happy Birthday," she whispered into my ear. "I wanted you to know."

"I know, Gram. I know."

"Keep reading."

I looked down. "What? What is it?"

"I made a mistake."

"What, Gram? What is it?" She didn't answer. She was hiding again. I leaned back into my seat, the birthday card in one hand and the envelope in the other. There was a folded paper tucked inside. It was the revocable living trust. The words jumped out at me.

...hereinafter referred to as 'Settlor'...Acer
Riorden and Quin Riorden as co-trustees...

shall pay the net income derived from the trust estate to the Settlor or as the Settlor shall direct during her lifetime...such sum or sums from the principal of the trust as the Settlor may request from time to time...in the event the Settler shall at any time or times be incapacitated, as hereinafter defined... Trustee shall use and expend so much of the net income as the Trustee may deem necessary...Settlor shall be Trustee during her lifetime excepting that the Settlor may substitute any other person or bank as trustee in her stead...in the event two registered physicians, one of whom should be the Settlor's personal physician, deliver an instrument... certifying that the Settlor during her lifetime has become incapable of managing her own affairs, the said incapacitated Settlor shall cease to be Trustee and the successor Trustee shall become sole Trustee without requiring any action or permission of any nature or kind whatsoever....

I stared blankly at the paper in my hand. There it was. There was the reason I had been searching for. I refolded the paper and stared out the window. The riddle hung heavy in my brain like a lead weight dragging my heart to the bottom of a bottomless well. "What is more blinding than the break of dawn?" I asked.

"What?" Ronan shot me a quizzical glance.

"A mother's love for her first-born son," I answered. "Gram gave her trust to her number one son and he wielded it like a sword to cut her down.

Now I understood why she was constantly in tears. Now I understood why she said she thought he was smarter than that. He was her son. She trusted him with her life. He saw that trust as a weakness. He used it to cut her down as swiftly as if he had used a knife or bullet. That was the reason he kicked me out. That was the reason he kicked her out. He had her permission." The blue orb floated and flickered around me. "Quit hiding, Gram," I whispered. "It's all right. I understand."

"There's one thing more," Ronan said. He tapped a leather bound journal.

"Where did you get this?"

"Your mother gave it to me for safekeeping when you were still very small. It's yours. She wrote it for you. I think now is the right time for you to have it."

Faith leaned across the seat. "Your Aunt Maire and I thought being invisible was our only defense. Watching you I have learned that power is not always visible. I have learned that in the midst of clamor, one can be deadly calm. The only thing you ever asked for was the truth. So, here it is. If, when you've finished reading, you still want me in your life, I will be there."

"Of course she wants us in her life," Grace answered. "Don't be silly."

I stared down at the journal. The words *Sheath and Knife*, penned across the front cover, stared back at me. What an odd title, I thought. It sounded like an Irish song or poem or legend. I unsnapped the latch and opened the cover. My mother wrote those words when she was a young girl, as alone and invisible as I had been. I opened the first page and began reading. The words pulled me in across time and space and hope and despair. I read as dawn broke over the mountains and merged into day. I read as buttes, woodlands, fen and prairie flew past. I read as I traveled through another world, another time, a world of which Maire often spoke, but I barely comprehended. Finally, I understood. As I closed the book, a brilliant stream of light pierced the horizon. Her final words on the last page seared my brain.

When shall we meet again?
In thunder, lightning or in rain?
When the hurly-burly's done,
When the battle's lost and won.
That will be 'ere set of sun.

I stared into the light. "Gram," I whispered. "I thought I brought you with me to understand your story. Now I know. You brought me with you to understand mine." I placed the journal tenderly back into my bag and studied Ronan. He glanced back at me.

"What?"

"You were always there, always circling, always on guard. You protected Faith just as Sean protected Grace. Ronan, you are the true hero of my mother's story." He rolled his eyes and focused on the road. "You accepted me unconditionally. You are the true hero of my story."

The car slowed as Ronan pulled into the familiar bus station. It felt like a lifetime since I first boarded that bus. "Your car should be over there," Ronan answered. "Let's get breakfast."

He sat facing me in the same booth at Perkins in which my Aunt Maire often sat. His face was serious. "There's more."

"More? What?"

"The Riordens are selling the land."

"Why would Acer go to such lengths to get the land and then sell it? What about the renters?"

"What renters?"

"Acer said he remodeled the farm house for new renters. That's why he took Gram to the farm."

"There are no renters," he answered. "Something happened when they were putting in the carpet. Something about the way the water heater or furnace was vented. The pressure from gas lines may have burst the hot water pipes. No one in the family has gone near that house since."

I watched him drive away as I dialed Maire. As usual, she was in the middle of a thought she had begun days earlier. "Sometimes I wake in the night, tormented with guilt, thinking I should have stayed. I tell myself, that I held them off for so long. I could have held them off longer. But then I tell myself no. God had another plan. It's then that I knew you were right when you told me we had to let this destruction run its course. I didn't think so at the time. I thought surely if God healed anyone, it would have been her. Then I realize that He didn't heal her because He knew she would be captive still and they would continue to hurt her. AA teaches that we are chased by a thousand forms of fear. When you look at life through the eyes of faith, you stop pushing. You stop obsessing. You can sort through the turmoil in your mind. When that happens, all you have to do is wait for the ones that are fear-based to drop their armor. Then you make your move. With faith there's always a victory. God has a plan."

"So does Acer," I said. "Ronan told me he's selling the land. The only problem is that he needs unanimous consent."

"I just received the letter. We should honor our mother by getting top dollar for her land? Her house is a den of robbers!" Maire declared, segueing into scripture. "Will you steal, murder and follow other gods and stand before Me in this house saying you are delivered? No. They have to shake loose of their guilt. Acer locked her up, Crystal Ann strapped her in with Velcro, Bric allowed Blackwater staff to abuse and sedate her. Acer ordered you out of the house. Bric threatened to physically remove you from her side. They barred me from care conferences. They sedated her and paraded her around town on her birthday as the degenerate they portrayed her to be. They made sure she would die alone in anguish. Then they trussed her up in her coffin wrapped like a mummy looking like someone else. They carved up everything she owned now they have the balls to say, 'Honor your mother!' Acer thinks he can absolve his guilt with the word 'honor'?" She laughed with disdain. "Well, you can't be broken and be fixed at the same time. It's a contradiction in terms. No matter what else happens, what's wrong stays wrong. By the way, I got my sign."

"What happened?"

"Loree is apparently facing charges for drug possession and patient abuse. She may be stripped of her license."

"Maybe the Department of Social Services took action after all."

"I doubt it. I think it's Mom. I think she's very busy. What the Son of God sets free is free indeed.

And there's another sign. It's all over the news. A woman disappeared from Blackwater. She apparently walked out through the exit and never came back. There's an all out search, but it's been over a week. The poor thing didn't even take her coat or purse. She apparently just walked away with a pack of cigarettes in her shirt pocket. Blackwater is under a microscope now. Everyone on staff is under scrutiny."

"Was her shirt light blue?"

"Yea, as a matter of fact, it was."

"Maire, I think she was on the bus. Is it possible?"

She laughed. "What the Son of God sets free is free indeed!"

The next day Liam called. The campaign to sell the farm land was in full swing. Liam repeated arguments he had heard from Acer. Mary Caye was getting old, Crystal Ann was ill. Aiden needed the money. Then he repeated Acer's campaign slogan. "We can honor Mom and Dad by getting the best value for the land." Did none of them comprehend the treachery of those words? "How could Scanlon Circle have been sold for a loss?" I asked.

"Well," he answered slowly, "you could delay action on the farm with a lot of questions. But then no one will benefit."

The next day I met with my attorney. Dressed in black turtleneck and creased black pants with a belt of fine leather, he paced the room talking into air, a wireless speaker connected to his ear. He smiled and waved, tapped the gray pod on his face and turned to me. "Acer refuses to release the financials. He says the wards of the trust have no right to any informa-tion. He'll meet with each one and answer questions individually, but he won't release information unilaterally. Looks like he's going to stonewall you."

"What about transparency? What about the IRS? What if I request an investigation?"

He frowned. "The IRS is really a crapshoot. There are so many of these types of inquiries that they usually only pursue the smoking guns. You may not get any response from them."

I felt as if my heart was riding a great wave and it had just crested. I was being sucked under. "So, it's done?"

He stopped pacing and sat back into his leather chair. He looked across his desk, peering at me over stacks of files and a pair of running shoes, waiting patiently for him to finish his work and take them for a jog. "He knows the law. He knows how to use it. You can sue him for the documents, but where does that get you? You would spend a lot of your own money to get...what? You won't know the proceeds of the sale of the farm until it's sold. There's nothing you can do now."

"So Social Services, the legal system and the IRS, for all they purport to offer, actually have nothing to right the wrong done to this woman?"

"It's a family affair, really. Talk to Acer. Try to get him to listen."

I drove away, dialing my phone as I steered through traffic. Maire answered. "That's it," I stated gravely. "We have to accept the cruel fact that Gram gave Acer permission to hurt her. Her love for him blinded her. No wonder he called his mother a pawn. She was incidental to his plan. She was right. The land would be sold over her dead body."

"I don't like the sound of your voice." Maire said cautiously. I heard her voice, but her words were lost in the distant pounding of war drums and the crashing of waves against my brain. I stared across the street at the Federal Building. I knew he was there. Maire was still talking. "Elle? Can you hear me? Are you listening?"

My mind was pulling me deeper and deeper into the vortex. The sound of rushing wind filled my senses. 'What would Sun Tzu do?' I wondered. I reached into my bag. My fingers found the leather journal, then closed around the pink envelope. I held it up against the setting sun. It didn't matter what was inside. It may have been a dollar. It may have been a written gift of the land. No matter. Nothing could ever make me break what my grandmother had sealed. It was Grace's gift. That was the treasure. Then it came to me. *What fury wears the mask of mirth while giving up to lay it's claim?* In an instant I knew both the answer and the reason for Sean's warning. Solving the riddle had taken me to Hell. I slipped the envelope back into my bag. My fingers closed around the cold steel of the gun. Angry words from the argument at Doyle's Bar flew into my head. 'Well, own this, ya dirty bastard!'

"I know what I have to do," I answered, my thoughts racing.

"Listen to me, Elle. Don't do anything out of emotion. Do not take revenge. Leave it to God's wrath. 'It is mine to avenge; I will repay,' says the Lord."

I stared down at the curb, then across the street to the Federal Building. I needed to see him in pain the extent of which my grandmother had been made to suffer. I needed him to die.

"Elle? Pray with me," Maire pleaded. "Behold, I give unto you power to tread on serpents and scorpions, and over all the power of the enemy, and nothing shall by any means hurt you."

"Where are you going, Elle?" Grace called. Sorrow overwhelmed me as I slipped deeper into the void. I took a deep breath. "Where are you going, Elle?" Her voice grew faint as I pushed through the glass doors. Before me stretched a line of characters playing out all kinds of stories ranging from high drama to tedious errands. The line stretched the length of the lobby. Some pushed strollers, some leaned on canes as the line snaked forward. My senses reeled with vertigo. I felt a pull at my elbow.

"So here you are in my world," he drawled.

I scanned the crowded lobby. "I can see that you relish it," I answered. "You have that look in your eye of one who feasts on people."

"I understand that you're grieving and you're angry," he began, leading me by the elbow to a quiet alcove. "You probably don't want to have anything to do with me right now, but I assure you that everything I did..." Yoki's voice came to me. 'Some find their truth in the light; some in the shadows."

"Shut up! Don't patronize me." I recoiled as my voice echoed against the marble. I yanked back from his grip. "And stop giving yourself so much credit. My grief has nothing to do with you and your actions have nothing to do with me! You act on behalf of no one but yourself."

"You shouldn't take this so personally." He modulated his voice to calm me. "Your grandmother's passing was personal, of course, but life is the business of survival and we have to get on with it."

"You are cunning, Acer! You needed to get rid of me to get rid of Gram. You needed to get rid of Gram to get her property into the trust. You needed every one of your little soldiers on your side to get the property out of the trust and into your hands. But I wonder, will you be trapped in your own game?"

"What do you mean?"

"The worst strategy of all is to attack a secure target. I had already landed a job. If it weren't for your cruelty toward Gram, I would have been gone. You're the one who drew me back. And now I have formed a bond with Maire. That is an alliance you may regret." He didn't respond, but his patronizing smirk disappeared. "I reviewed Grandpa's will and the codicil. There are issues."

"You did what?" His face turned crimson, his carefree drawl was a tense snarl. He quickly regained control. "There are certain circumstances when the trustee must act for the betterment of all."

"Are you saying when the trustee takes action, it's not illegal?"

"I'm saying the trustee sometimes has to make decisions which in the strictest sense may be construed as illegal."

"You tell your siblings to honor their mother by getting the best price for her land. Gram's legacy wasn't land. It was love. You portrayed her as a willing victim. She was not. She was, however, willing to find meaning in something greater than herself. Her life embodied that. Respect is a separate currency, Acer. You destroyed everything she stood for by making it about money. If you didn't kill your mother, Acer, you certainly sold her to the people who would."

"What do you want?"

"I want you dead, instead of Gram."

His eyes darted to my hand, still in my bag. "We are all human. We all make mistakes. We all need to forgive."

"Forgiveness isn't mine to give. You considered your mother to be no more than a pawn. She was a pawn, all right. She was God's pawn. I tortured myself with questions, asking, 'Why is this happening? Why did God stand by while she suffered a demeaning, excruciating death?' Then it came to me. God wasn't testing her, Acer. God was testing us. Maire and I were not especially strong or brave or wise. We loved her. Nothing else mattered. You knew Gram's love for you would blind her. You knew she put her complete trust in you. You got rid of her, then you got rid of everything she owned and now you will get rid of her land. And for what? Gram said it best. She said she thought you were smarter than that."

"Why are you here?"

"You have taken this family to an all-time low. You subjected your own mother to torture aimed at breaking her. You stripped her of her identity, declared her incapacitated and restrained her. You endorsed the use of the lift machine, knowing it beat, bruised and terrorized her. You delayed and refused the medical attention she needed for the growth in her jaw then gave orders to physically remove me so that she would be alone when she died. Then you jammed a wig on her head and stuffed into her into her coffin, concealing her arms and the hands she folded in prayer. You took her wedding rings!"

"What do you want?"

"I want you to suffer as Gram suffered. I want you to die a death as gruesome as hers."

His eyes froze again on my hand, still in my bag. "You want me to back off on selling the farm?"

"I had a dream that I was running from you. I hid in a church but you followed and took my wallet. You were after the money and would cross any boundary to get it. A nun gave me a prayer book and sent me back into the street. I asked myself what use are written words when I am trapped in darkness? Then I realized the book was the book of Faith. The prayers were words of truth." He stared at me, speechless. "You are the first-born son of Grace. It is your duty to continue the life of this family. You abused that duty. There is no legacy. There is no honor. There is no beauty. There is only this war you've waged. What makes you think you'll win?" I pulled out the pink envelope, brushing my fingers over Grace's delicate handwriting.

The color drained from his face. "A holographic will?" He grabbed for the envelope. "Whatever is written in that envelope was not written by my mother! I will prove it. You will think you're in Hell by the time I'm done with you!"

"I've been in Hell, Acer. This isn't it. Besides, Maire has an envelope as well."

"Give me that!"

"Whoever wins, wins, Acer."

He softened his tone. "Let's negotiate."

"I have a riddle for you. You may know it. It was Grandpa Jack's favorite. You stand at the edge of a shimmering pool deeper than the deepest well. Fathoms below sits a pot of gold shimmering in the swell. Seven stone steps will lead you but none will appear without solving a clue. When you reach the bottom at the mouth of the cave, the prize will come to you." Acer peered at me. "Do you remember the clues, Acer? I do. What's more blinding than the break of dawn? What is the pleasure that yields only pain? What rights nothing that is wrong? What consumes what it abstains? What measures a man's girth but only on earth? What exalts as often as it shames? What fury wears the mask of mirth while giving up to lay its claim?"

Acer stiffened. "What are you talking about?"

"Maire was right. Solving the puzzle revealed your plan. Sean was right, too. Solving the puzzle took me straight to Hell. The difference between you and me, though, Acer, is that I have a Get Out Of Hell Free Card. You, however, are stuck. You ordered me out. You branded my mother an outcast. You declared your mother incapacitated. Because of that, we hold your fate in our hands." My fingers closed firmly around the cold steel of the revolver. Then I raised my hand.

"You treated your mother like an animal caught in a trap. Now it is you who are caught."

Acer stepped back, pointing frantically. "Stop her! She's got a gun!" To my surprise, no one responded. People filed past in quiet stupor. "I am not a crook!" he screamed.

"Yoo-hoo!" Grace's voice shot through the marbel corrider, reverberating in my brain. I spun around, but I didn't see her. Suddenly there was a flash of light and I was catapulted from the darkness.

When my head finally cleared, I found myself standing at the curb on the busy street, still staring across traffic at the Federal Building. Stunned, I realized I had not taken that step. I had not been in the courthouse. I had only imagined the showdown with Acer. Drained, I turned back to my car. "But, Gram," I sighed, "I want him to suffer as you suffered. I want everyone he loves to turn away from him as he turned away from you." I unlocked the car door and glared at the wide glass doors across the street. Then I obediently slid behind the wheel. There was Grace, smiling patiently from the rear view mirror. "You're here." I blinked and then I blinked again. There was Faith smiling next to her. "Why did you stop me? He knows no consequences! He has no boundaries. He values nothing except winning. I don't understand. Why did you put this information into my hands if I have no power to use it?"

Faith leaned toward me. "The sins that haunt us are to the truth what a blade of grass is to the universe." I stared back, not understanding. "You'll see," she said.

"When we started this journey," Grace explained softly, "you wished that I would find joy."

"Yes," I answered, still not understanding.

"Well," Grace answered. "The journey's not finished. I told you. I'm not done yet."

"Trust faith," my mother added with a mischievous smile. Rely on grace."

"OK." I acquiesced. "OK."

"Then," Faith declared, "I think our work is done here, Elle."

"Yes, let's go," Grace said impatiently. "It's time to get on with life!" She winked at me and settled back in her seat.

"You're a super chick, Gram," I sighed.

"Hey!" my mother quipped. "What about me?"

"Oh, you girls!" Grace giggled. I smiled, amazed that I still could.

The river, like the truth, begins quietly, usually in some obscure place. It is a seeker, determined to find its way. It does not know how to yield to obstacles, which can only deter it for a time but cannot stop it. That may not happen in our lifetime. No one knows how many days we have. The most we can hope for is that each day brings grace, faith, a new dawn and the promise of truth. Like the seasons, like the river, our lives cycle and recycle. Evil will entice good. Fear will seduce faith. Rivers will flow. Spirit and truth will persevere.

I bring the pure flow like water around
The rocks of life won't pull me down
I bring the pure flow, drink so deep
The river of life, my soul at ease

I bring the pure flow like water around
The rocks of life won't pull me down
I bring the pure flow, rising above
The storms of life to live and love
My soul is at ease and i am free
My soul is at ease and i am free

This is my day, my soul is at ease and i am free

The Power Of Grace

We've been down to the bottom, stories we've got 'em
When we hit rock bottom

If you been there put your hands in the air
So let the lost know that someone cares
Cuz we've been down to the bottom, stories we've got em
When we hit rock bottom

If you been there, put your hands in the air
And let somebody know that the Most High cares

Back in the Victorian house in Ronan Doyle's little town where nothing ever changes, I fell asleep each night to echoes of the voices of Grace, Faith, Maire and Liam. Images of tattoo girl, Jerry, Sonja, the researcher, Tiffany, Kevin and Chance, Yoki and Mamori Kami appeared and reappeared throughout each day. Soundbites from scenes replayed in my mind as Mary Caye, Crystal Ann, Acer, Quin, Dierdre, Aiden, Ralph, Ward, Bric, Seth, Riley, Lyssa and Ursula haunted my dreams.

One morning just before dawn I woke, knowing I had dreamed the most bizarre dream of all. The shapes were of nothing I had ever seen or known. It was a world I couldn't imagine or describe. Unsettled, I fell back asleep. Then I woke again to piercing screams. I sat straight up and looked around. The screams stopped, but the echoes of screams lingered. Someone was trapped inside the darkness. Wide awake, I stared into the shadows as dawn crept over the horizon and soft hues drifted across my room. Then morning sun broke brilliantly across the prairie sky. I jumped out of bed and quickly gathered my things. Ronan didn't seem at all surprised to find me standing at his door.

"I have to go," I said simply.

He nodded knowingly. "Yes," was all he said.

"Do you want to come with me?"

"No," he stepped back. "I can never leave this town. What would become of Doyle's Pub?" He smiled. "But remember. You're welcome anytime."

Just as Maire and I led Grace through her wilderness, she led me through mine. I moved to Chicago. Maire moved to Colorado. Grace and Faith move freely between us. My mother's journal is displayed on a shelf in my office. The walls are lined with framed pictures of Grace and Faith and Maire.

Loree was fired, but not stripped of her license, only transferred to another nursing home. Sol remains at Blackwater as does the CEO. Blackwater now advertises a spa environment. Acer sold the farm and along with it the last visible proof of Jack and Grace.

I know now that I began writing Grace's story the moment I stepped onto the bus. I took that first step bogged down by a quicksand of lies. I took the last step freed by truth. From the first step to the last, Grace lead me on a journey to a warm connection with strangers so that I would understand the cold detachment of family. Sometime between the first step and the last, Grace found her voice, articulating her own story through the stories of others. Sometime between the first step and the last I articulated my own.

"The favor of God is the difference between life and death," Maire said. "For those who love Him love life. But those that sin against Him hate Him and love death. The storm of the Lord will burst on the heads of the wicked as a whirling tempest. It is by Grace that we are saved through Faith. It is the gift of God."

I know now that Acer didn't win, because I know now that when we choose between good and evil, we choose between life and death. The only way to be happy is to love. Choosing to love is choosing to live a life with Grace. Life with Grace is a life lived in wonder. Life with Grace is a life lived with Faith.

Across the street there is a park filled with fresh blooms and woodsy pathways. I kick off my sandals and nestle my bare feet into the cushion of soft grass there, and I walk with Grace. A sudden breeze wafts across my face. A single drop of rain lands on my cheek. I smile. I remember. I know. I was there.

Grace by Greyhound

So hold me now Father, human love ain't enough
I've failed and been failed by the people i love
But Your faithful arms, they surround me
And any other soul who has to sail those seas
Of a broken family

We've been down to the bottom, stories we've got em
When we hit rock bottom
If you been there put your hands in the air
So let the lost know that someone cares
Cuz we've been down to the bottom, stories we've got em
When we hit rock bottom
If you been there, put your hands in the air
And let somebody know that the Most High cares